THE BLACK CHAMBER

Black Jamie's coal-black eyes glistered with tiny lights. A shiver shook Calum's body. He could only nod, blood rushing back to his dazed brain. Long, icy fingers swept a lock of damp red hair back from his flushed face.

'You must do everything I say, Calum. You must trust me totally.'

Calum's Adam's apple bobbed convulsively. All he could see was the pale gaunt face, and the eyes which burnt like glowing embers.

'Put yourself in my hands, Pip.'

The desire to correct his guardian's slip of the tongue sprang to his lips. Calum swallowed the words back down. He would be whatever – whoever – James Black wished him to be.

THE BLACK CHAMBER

Jack Gordon

idol

Also by this author:

Dark Rider
HMS Submission

First published in Great Britain in 1999 by
Idol
an imprint of Virgin Publishing Ltd
Thames Wharf Studios,
Rainville Road, London W6 9HT

ISBN 0 352 33373 1

Cover photograph by Colin Clarke Photography

Typeset by SetSystems Ltd, Saffron Walden, Essex
Printed and bound in Great Britain by
Mackays of Chatham PLC

The Terrence Higgins Trust

SAFER SEX GUIDELINES

These books are sexual fantasies – in real life, everyone needs to think about safe sex.

While there have been major advances in the drug treatments for people with HIV and AIDS, there is still no cure for AIDS or a vaccine against HIV. Safe sex is still the only way of being sure of avoiding HIV sexually.

HIV can only be transmitted through blood, come and vaginal fluids (but no other body fluids) passing from one person (with HIV) into another person's bloodstream. It cannot get through healthy, undamaged skin. The only real risk of HIV is through anal sex without a condom – this accounts for almost all HIV transmissions between men.

Being safe

Even if you don't come inside someone, there is still a risk to both partners from blood (tiny cuts in the arse) and pre-come. Using strong condoms and water-based lubricant greatly reduces the risk of HIV. However, condoms can break or slip off, so:

* Make sure that condoms are stored away from hot or damp places.
* Check the expiry date – condoms have a limited life.
* Gently squeeze the air out of the tip.
* Check the condom is put on the right way up and unroll it down the erect cock.
* Use plenty of water-based lubricant (lube), up the arse and on the condom.
* While fucking, check occasionally to see the condom is still in one piece (you could also add more lube).
* When you withdraw, hold the condom tight to your cock as you pull out.

* Never re-use a condom or use the same condom with more than one person.
* If you're not used to condoms you might practise putting them on.
* Sex toys like dildos and plugs are safe. But if you're sharing them use a new condom each time or wash the toys well.

For the safest sex, make sure you use the strongest condoms, such as Durex Ultra Strong, Mates Super Strong, HT Specials and Rubberstuffers packs. Condoms are free in many STD (Sexually Transmitted Disease) clinics (sometimes called GUM clinics) and from many gay bars. It's also essential to use lots of water-based lube such as KY, Wet Stuff, Slik or Liquid Silk. Never use come as a lubricant.

Oral sex

Compared with fucking, sucking someone's cock is far safer. Swallowing come does not necessarily mean that HIV gets absorbed into the bloodstream. While a tiny fraction of cases of HIV infection have been linked to sucking, we know the risk is minimal. But certain factors increase the risk:

* Letting someone come in your mouth
* Throat infections such as gonorrhoea
* If you have cuts, sores or infections in your mouth and throat

So what is safe?

There are so many things you can do which are absolutely safe: wanking each other; rubbing your cocks against one another; kissing, sucking and licking all over the body; rimming – to name but a few.

If you're finding safe sex difficult, call a helpline or speak to someone you feel you can trust for support. The Terrence Higgins Trust Helpline, which is open from noon to 10pm every day, can be reached on 0171 242 1010.

Or, if you're in the United States, you can ring the Center for Disease Control toll free on 1 800 458 5231.

One

The coach creaked.

Dressed in his best jute coat and breeches, Fergie McGregor leant back in his seat. A smile of satisfaction twitched his full lips.

Opposite, two ladies clutched each other as the front wheel of the coach hit another pothole.

Fergie barely felt the motion of the vehicle beneath him. He continued to smile.

'Can't you slow down, fellow?' A man in a clerical collar gripped the window sill and shouted a tentative reprimand in the driver's direction.

'Ye want home tonight or not, minister?' The rhythmic clack of four sets of hooves increased in speed.

Fergie's smile broadened into a grin.

Opposite, one of the ladies shrank back in her seat, then began to whisper to the thin, scholarly-looking gent to her left. Her companion boldly met Fergie's eye and returned his smile. 'I see the roughness of the journey does not bother you, sir. You are a seasoned traveller?'

He bowed his head respectfully. Usually his only companions on such journeys back from Greenock market were the distant hoots of owls and the solid tramp of his boots. Inside his coat, Fergie fingered the heavy money bag, which thumped against his chest each time the coach swerved or dipped. For tonight, at least, he was the equal of any of them. And maybe the deal he'd struck with the tall merchant, for a regular supply of ewes, signalled a change in fortunes for the McGregors. 'This route is bad, but there are worse.' He grinned. 'Are you going all the way to Stirling?'

She opened her mouth to reply then gasped as the crack of a whip from outside urged the horses into a gallop.

Fergie staggered to his feet and stuck a head through the open window. 'Ye want to overturn this coach and kill us all?' A blast of rain hit his face.

'Ye want out, just say so!' The driver chuckled. 'Maybe ye could hitch a ride with the red robber. I hear the Fox is out and about, tonight!'

Fergie frowned, cursing the coachman for his teasing. He drew his head back in, turning to reassure his fellow passengers. It was too late: the driver's cautionary words had travelled better than most of their stomachs.

The two women huddled together.

The minister fingered his prayer book.

The scholar, his pale face blanching further, examined his feet as if they were the pages of some engrossing text.

'The roads are like the natives: they need a thorough levelling!' A military voice boomed across at him.

Everyone tittered nervously.

'And a levelling they will get!'

Fergie stared at the sixth member of their party, who had been sipping steadily from a hip flask ever since they had left Greenock. The man wasn't in uniform, but the puffed-out chest gave him away. As did the accent:

'This Fox character would not dare attack a coach carrying one of his Majesty King George's emissaries. He's a coward and a traitor – all highwaymen are.' The Englishman patted his breast pocket. 'I have a letter here which puts a price of fifty sovereigns on the blackguard's head. We'll see how long he goes undiscovered, once a copy of this is pinned to every tree between Stirling and Greenock.'

One of the women had started to cry.

The minister was now praying silently.

Fergie threw the Englishman a look then refocused on the two ladies and began the same speech he gave his sisters and anyone from Blairhoyle who ventured forth at night. 'Do not upset yourselves. The Fox is an honourable man. He will do you no harm.' It seemed to be true. Whoever he was, the mysterious Fox seemed to have little interest in the fairer sex, concentrating on rich landowners and merchants.

'And how do you know so much?' The voice sneered in drunken suspicion.

The hair on the back of Fergie's neck bristled. He continued to focus reassuringly on his travelling companions. 'If you spent any time in the country you claim to rule, you'd know too.' The retort was out before he could stop it. He smiled at the ladies before turning to face his antagoniser.

The Englishman hastily replaced the hip flask in the folds of his long coat and swayed to his feet. 'You traitorous dog!'

Fergie did likewise. Bracing himself against the swaying motion of the coach, he made his way towards the man.

The puffed-up chest inflated further. 'I am Captain Michael Carmichael, the king's emissary. I will –'

'You'll shut up! Don't you see you are scaring them more than any highwayman could?' Fergie seized Captain Carmichael by his lapels and threw him back into his seat.

'Unhand me, you ruffian!' The man wrenched himself free and bounded up again. 'Fear not, ladies! I will not let the Fox harm you! I will kill him with my bare hands rather than allow such beautiful creatures as yourselves to be –'

A single pistol shot from beyond the window obliterated the end of the boast. Then: 'Stand and deliver!'

The reining in of the horses threw them all to the back of the carriage. Women screamed, the minister began to recite the twenty-third psalm in quavering tones and the scholar fainted. Fergie found himself on top of a flailing, still-blustering Captain Carmichael. One hand grappled for purchase. The other flew instinctively to his hard-earned sovereigns. So much for the family's change in fortune.

Then the coach door was hauled open and they both fell on to the muddy road.

'Apologies for the inconvenience, my good people.'

Brushing mud from his best jute coat, Fergie staggered to his feet.

'And for the weather!'

A moon had emerged from behind a cloud, bathing the scene in a yellow glow. Fergie scowled over to where the bragging Captain Carmichael was now cowering behind the rain-drenched women.

'I will not keep you long.' The sound of hooves on wet ground accompanied the teasing words.

For the first time since his travelling companions had been unceremoniously ordered from the coach, Fergie sneaked a look at the man who had almost become a legend over the past few months.

Dressed in his customary scarlet, and with most of his face hidden by a red eye mask, the Fox loomed down from a fifteen-hand chestnut mare. Holding the reins and a pistol in one hand, the highwayman expertly wove his way between his huddled prisoners. 'Weapons first.' He tapped the minister on the shoulder.

'May God forgive you for this, my son.'

The Fox laughed. 'May he forgive you for all the misery this causes, Reverend.' Deftly, he poked the barrel of his pistol beneath the prayer book and levered it from the minister's shaking hands.

Fergie reluctantly wrenched his skean dhu from inside his sock and tossed it on top of Captain Carmichael's discarded musket.

The scarlet-clad figure guided his horse onward, then paused. 'What's this – more books?'

The scholar shrank back, then turned and tried to run.

'Accept advice from one who knows.' The Fox grabbed the back of the fellow's collar and lifted him off the ground. 'Forget your studies, my friend.' Ignoring the man's air-kicking feet, the highwayman carried him back, dropping the startled scholar beside the woman with whom Fergie had briefly conversed. 'You like her, don't you?'

'No, no –'

'Oh yes, you do!' The Fox released the man, who practically fell on to the ladies.

'Oh, I'm sorry, I did not mean to –'

'Oh yes, you did! I wager you've been thinking about her all the way from Greenock, wondering what it would feel like to –' The highwayman leant forward on his horse, gently seized the scholar's hand and placed it on the lady's nipped-in waist.

Two mouths gaped in horror.

The Fox laughed. 'Come, come – you like him too, don't you?' Releasing the scholar's arm, he plucked a necklace from each of the ladies' throats and thrust them into his pocket. 'Invite me to the wedding, won't you?'

From the roof of the coach, a cackle drifted down. The driver seemed to be enjoying the sport.

'You are an affront to all Godfearing people.' The minister stooped to retrieve his prayer book.

'You are beginning to bore me, parson.' Reining his horse expertly around, one of the Fox's booted feet delivered a resounding kick to the clergyman's arse.

Despite his own apprehension, Fergie found himself smiling as the pious face hit the mud. He also found his attention firmly focused on the masked face.

'Anything in the luggage, coachman?'

'Little of value, Mr Fox. Slim pickings for you tonight, I fear.'

Fergie followed the figure on horseback with his eyes.

The Fox was tall, and broadly built. A wide-brimmed hat hid his hair and most of his face. Although the voice was rich and powerful, it was hard to tell his age. Something about his demeanour and general mischievousness suggested youth, but his bravado and daring would be unusual in one under thirty. He sat well in the saddle, gripping his mount's flanks with muscular thighs.

As the Fox guided his horse left, Fergie suddenly found himself wondering what those same thighs would feel like, tight around his waist. Inside his best breeches, his cock pushed against his underwear.

'Back into the coach, my friends – I'm feeling generous tonight.'

A further vision, of his own legs twined with the highwayman's, shot into Fergie's brain. He shook his head to clear it.

A low laugh brushed his ear. 'Don't you want to go?'

The sudden knowledge that he was going to escape with his hard-earned sovereigns intact sunk in. Fergie pulled himself together. 'No – I, er, I mean yes – I –'

'And here's someone else who evidently wants to remain behind!'

While the ladies, the quivering scholar and a now mud-streaked clergyman were falling over each other to get back into the coach, Captain Carmichael seemed to be trying to hide under it.

With a hoot of amusement, the Fox leapt from his horse. Seconds later, the barrel of his pistol was pressing into Captain Carmichael's neck.

'Don't hurt me – please don't hurt me!' The voice had lost all trace of its previous boastfulness.

Fergie watched the Englishman slowly edge out backward, and laughed out loud.

In a flash, the Fox had darted around him. 'And what amuses you so much, sir?' A different tone had appeared in the highwayman's voice.

Fergie's throat was suddenly dry. Before he could utter any further sound, the Fox had herded His Majesty's emissary and himself away from the coach.

The highwayman's weapon flicked between them. 'You make a handsome pair.' The light, teasing tone was back.

Turning his head slowly, Fergie remembered the captain's drunken arrogance: the man had tempted fate. He regarded the now subdued Englishman with undisguised loathing.

His expression was noted. The Fox feigned solicitation. 'Have you two had a falling-out?'

Fergie bristled. He'd cut off his own bollocks before he'd take an Englishman into his bed.

Then the scarlet-clad figure was moving in between them. Fergie felt a comradely arm around his shoulder and saw the Fox was embracing Captain Carmichael with the other:

'Kiss and make up.'

Chuckles from some distance away told Fergie the coachman was finding this all very amusing. Despite the situation, the proximity of the highwayman's body was having a marked effect on his own. The arm tightened around his shoulders, moving his head closer to the Englishman's flushed, drunken face. Fergie resisted.

The Fox continued to push him forward. 'Come on, do not hold a grudge.'

Fergie pushed back.

'And don't pretend you don't want to.'

The words were whispered, for his ears only. Pulling his gaze from Captain Carmichael's fear-streaked face, Fergie followed a pair of masked eyes down to where his best jute breeches were noticeably tenting. He blushed.

The Fox roared with laughter. 'So it's privacy you require?'

Abruptly, they were released. The highwayman strode to the front of the carriage and delivered a sound slap to equine flanks. 'On your way, coachman! These two have decided to walk.'

Now unsupported by the highwayman's form, Captain Carmichael collapsed in a heap. Fergie watched the carriage disappear into the night. Fear suddenly made itself known to him. But beneath that, a shiver of anticipation flooded his body and as the Fox jumped on to his horse, Fergie thought he saw a ridge of desire shadowed in moonlight along the top of a scarlet-clad thigh.

They walked for miles in darkness, but at least the rain had stopped. Having lost most of his military bearing, Captain Carmichael was ominously silent as they staggered in front of the mounted figure, up off the main road and towards the hills. A jaunty whistle accompanied their progress.

Fergie's eyes were becoming accustomed to the dark. All thoughts of escape had left his brain hours ago, chased by the knowledge he could well end up either dead or caught in a bog.

They had passed a few crofts, some miles back, but despite the fact he knew they had to be somewhere near Blairhoyle, the landscape was alien. He risked a look over his shoulder.

The Fox sat back in the saddle, the reins held casually in one hand. A shard of moonlight glanced off the masked face, and Fergie caught one twinkling eye:

'Your name, sir?'

'Fergus – Fergus McGregor.'

The Fox removed his wide-brimmed hat and swung it low in a gesture of mock respect. 'Glad to make your acquaintance.'

Fergie scowled through his apprehension.

'And your friend?'

Fergie turned away from the grinning face. 'He's no friend of mine.'

The highwayman winked. 'Turn left.' He began whistling again.

While Fergie tried to make sense of the wink, Captain Carmichael veered towards him. 'Don't antagonise him.' The words were a whisper. 'Wait until he dismounts. You jump him and I'll get his pistol.'

'I jump him and you'll be off into the hills, you mean.' Fergie stared sceptically at his unwanted companion.

The night air had sobered the Englishman. 'Better one of us escape and bring help than we both suffer the Lord knows what at this rogue's hands.'

'Ah, the whispered cooing of lovers.' The whistle stopped abruptly. 'Music to my ears.'

Fergie scowled. They were being played with! The knowledge did strange things to his body.

Seconds later, they stood in a clearing, surrounded by tall fir trees. The Fox slipped effortlessly from his horse. 'Now that you're all friends again –' he strode forward, whipping his scarlet cape over one shoulder '– let's see what delights you have for me.' The pistol was once more gripped in the highwayman's fist, aimed at the Englishman.

Fergie's brain was spurred into action. Surreptitiously, he eased one hand inside his coat. If he could slip his bag of sovereigns to the ground and kick it under a tree, perhaps he could come back later and –

'Take it.' Captain Carmichael fished out a large money belt and threw it on to the grass.

'Thank you.' The Fox scooped up the booty and slung it over his horse. 'That's a particularly fine coat you are wearing.'

'Take it too – please.' In a flash, Captain Carmichael had divested himself of the garment and was holding it out.

Fergie's fingers tightened around his hard-earned money. He began to ease his arm from inside his jute coat.

'You are too generous, sir.' The highwayman briskly searched the pockets of the greatcoat, removing a sealed envelop. 'And it goes so well with those elegant breeches.'

'They are yours!' The Englishman struggled out of his trousers.

Even at this distance, Fergie could see the King's distinctive coat of arms in the red wax. The Fox broke the seal, scanned the letter's contents then thrust the envelope into his pocket and returned his attention to the terrified Englishman.

Fergie continued to ease his hand from his jacket.

The Fox leant against a tree, casually enjoying the other man's discomfort.

Now dressed only in shirt and shoes, Captain Carmichael shivered. The thick hair on his pale thighs quivered in the moonlight. Silence descended over the scene, punctuated only by the Englishman's rapid breathing.

Fergie lowered his arm and loosened his fingers. Fearing the sound made by the money pouch hitting the ground, he searched his mind for a diversion.

'You too, Fergus McGregor.' The Fox's voice was low and breathy.

Seizing the opportunity, and unmindful of the cold, Fergie threw the money pouch some distance away and hoped the rustle of his hastily discarded clothing would mask the sound.

He needn't have worried. The scarlet-clad highwayman's attention was totally focused on Fergie's brawny body as it emerged from beneath his Sunday best.

Seconds later, he was down to his shirt.

The Fox chuckled. 'Well, well – who would have guessed that

coach would contain such treasures.' Levering himself from the tree trunk, he wandered over to where Captain Carmichael stood.

Fergie could hear the man's knees knocking. His own body was strangely chill-free.

The scarlet-clad highwayman began to circle the cowering captain. 'Fifty sovereigns – don't you think my head is worth more than that?' The Fox playfully flicked at the hem of the Englishman's shirt with his pistol.

Captain Carmichael yelped. 'Mr Fox, sir – I am merely an emissary. I –'

'Save your excuses.' The Fox laughed. 'If our positions were reversed, you would not hesitate to put a gun to my head and claim that reward.' The highwayman thrust the pistol's barrel beneath the man's shirt once more, raising the garment's hem higher this time.

The sound which escaped Captain Carmichael's lips was half-shriek, half-groan.

Fergie stared at the dark bushiness of the Englishman's crotch.

With a casual grace, the Fox flicked the front tail of the shirt up over the captain's pink face, exposing the Englishman's pale chest and belly. 'That's better!'

Fergie's heart hammered in his ears, obliterating his travelling companion's splutters of fear and indignation. Captain Carmichael's cock was slender and pink, hanging its head in shame. Fergie's own member, much to his surprise, was tracking a sticky trail up over his right hipbone.

'The pride of King George's army!' The Fox tucked his pistol between the Englishman's thin legs and began to move it back and forward. 'The cream of His Majesty's militia.'

Captain Carmichael's sobs of affront were audible over the highwayman's low laughter. Fergie took a step back and debated escape. But something other than enjoyment of the arrogant Englishman's humiliation turned his legs to stone.

Abruptly, the Fox removed the pistol and replaced it with his hand.

Captain Carmichael's legs buckled. The bulk of his shirt still hiding his face, he pitched forward on to his knees.

Fergie winced. His nipples tingled. He was breathing heavily through parted lips, but no longer starting at the subjugated form on its knees.

'Go back to your King George, and tell him he has insulted the Fox with his measly fifty sovereigns.'

Fergie took in the handsome sweep of the Fox's features, at present contorted into a scowl. As the highwayman tightened and untightened his grip on Captain Carmichael's cock and bollocks, Fergie's gaze was held by the shadowed ridge which was now fully engorged along the scarlet-clad thigh.

Unexpectedly, the Fox turned his head and released the Englishman's groin. 'Now what shall I do with you, Mr Fergus McGregor?' The amused, teasing tone had returned to the rich voice.

Fergie flinched under the intense gaze. His mind was blank – even his money pouch was forgotten. Anticipation mixed with dread, drenching his body in a rosy sheen.

The highwayman wandered across to where Fergie stood.

In the background, Captain Carmichael's bare arse was visible as he stumbled away towards the road.

The Fox stopped an inch away.

Fergie could feel the man's breath on his face. He stared into masked eyes and, as a leather-gloved hand placed itself on his shoulder, every sinew trembled. His lips parted further.

The Fox moved his face closer. 'Eh, Fergus McGregor?'

Fergie's bollocks were sweating. He could feel the heat from the man's body, almost taste him. He longed to tell this audacious, handsome rogue he shared his hatred of the English, and show his admiration for the man's dangerous trade. But words would not come.

The Fox's lips brushed his.

Fergie's cock flexed up from his stomach, brushing a scarlet waistband. Just as he raised his arms to embrace the fellow, the Fox leapt on to his horse. 'Find whatever you dropped there and go home, Fergus McGregor. I think I will keep you for another occasion!'

Before he could protest, the highwayman disappeared into the night and Fergie was alone in the clearing, the front of his shirt damp with arousal.

Two

Wind combed his hair and night smells filled his head. Beneath the scarlet, his body tingled as adrenaline flooded his veins. He leant lower on the horse's back, gripping the steed's flanks and urging his mount to greater speed.

The night fled past. His cock pushed against the front of the saddle, swelling further with the motion of the gallop and the tightening of his thighs.

Both he and the horse knew this route by heart. And after a day constrained by their usual pastimes, both looked forward to the night with renewed eagerness.

His steed's coat was sweating beneath him. The scent of his own body mixed with the damp, earthy odours of wet land. On the periphery of his vision, dense pine forests gave way to pastureland. In the distance, crofts and smallholdings appeared.

He rode more furiously, down braes and through more woods, stretching both himself and his mount until the clack of hooves became a blur in his ears and the throb in his groin grew to a tight, heavy pulse.

On the banks of Gonachan Burn he reined in his mount and allowed her a short drink. Straightening up, he slipped one hand inside his coat and tossed tonight's haul into the quietly babbling water. The jewellery sank with a sharp plop.

He watched Captain Carmichael's letter disappear more slowly and smiled to himself while his breathing slowed to normal.

He felt alive. Truly alive. He had come to know the area between Stirling and Greenock very well. He had made the night his friend, and the passengers on board the rickety coaches his sport.

He tossed the confiscated pistol into the burn, where it sank to the bottom quickly. His smile broadened as he thought of the cowering Captain Carmichael. Then his mind moved to Fergie McGregor's strong, pale body. His still-hard cock flexed against the inside of his breeches.

The five-inch skean dhu lay in his palm. He noted its short, razor-sharp blade, which glinted in the moonlight.

Fergie McGregor.

His fingers curled around the dagger's horn handle. He slipped it down the top of his boot.

What a coincidence! What a damned coincidence!

Equine slurping sounds refocused his attention. He patted her neck then tugged gently on the reins. 'Not too much, girl. You can have more when we reach home.'

Reluctantly, his horse raised her head and together they moved along the bank towards the bridge. He dismounted efficiently, tearing off his mask and scarlet garb with practised ease. Withdrawing his clothes from the small cave under the bridge, he quickly dressed then pushed the Fox's garments back into their hiding place.

The Fox. Night hunter. Predator. Wily and wild. He smiled, silently thanking whoever had come up with the title. It was apt for someone who struck quickly and efficiently, then disappeared with the night mists.

Minutes later, he was guiding his horse back up on to the Blairhoyle road, and the Fox was returning to his den.

'You were out late tonight, Calum.'

Boots gripped in one hand, he froze on tiptoe halfway across the Great Hall. He turned, dazzled by the sudden illumination. 'Just taking the air, Uncle Jamie.' He stared at his guardian's tall silhouette, shading his eyes from the oil-lamp. 'I did not want to wake you.'

James Black moved out into the hall, swiftly locking the door of his room behind him. 'I was not asleep.'

Despite his sweaty exhilaration, a chill swept over Calum's still-flushed skin. He feigned a yawn. 'It would seem the night air has worked its usual magic on my insomnia.' He began to move in the direction of his own chamber. 'Good night, uncle –'

'Are you happy, Calum?'

The question took him by surprise. The arm around his shoulder took him further aback: his guardian wasn't one for gestures of affection.

'You must find life at Castle Black a rather dull affair, after the whirl of London court life.'

Calum found himself guided along the corridor. 'Not at all, Uncle Jamie.' The weight of his guardian's arm he hardly noticed: the scrutiny of those dark eyes was something else. 'I am glad of the quiet, to be honest.' He turned his face away from the intense gaze. Calum hated to lie: neither kith nor kin, James Black had taken him into his home, fed and clothed him – a real, blood-related uncle could not have been more kind or generous. But there was no getting away from the fact that the local magistrate and landowner, whose only demand on Calum since coming to live here was that he address him as 'uncle', was hardly the sociable type. 'I am finding plenty to amuse myself with.' That much, at least, was true.

'Do not lie to me, Calum.'

The icy words were low and unemotional. Calum swallowed. A sudden panic took hold of him, tightening the muscles in his throat and rendering him speechless.

'I know I am far from ideal company, for a young, spirited creature as yourself.' His guardian raised the oil-lamp between them.

Calum stared at the sombre, well-chiselled face. In this light, the man's cheekbones shone more prominently than ever:

'The very fact that you find sleep difficult bears testament to your lack of daytime activity. We must remedy that.'

Calum frowned inside, at the thought of more boring visits to farms and markets. He summoned a little of the Fox's courage. 'Since you too have trouble sleeping, perhaps we could ride together, tomorrow night.'

The responding laugh was more chilling than any reprimand. 'Thank you, but no, young Calum.'

He suddenly realised they had reached his chamber, and his back was pressed against the door. 'Well, good night, uncle –'

'However, I was expecting a guest, this evening.' James Black produced a silver Hunter from his waistcoat pocket and studied it. 'Although he is somewhat tardy.' He replaced the watch, then smiled. 'I'm sure Captain Carmichael will be more than happy to accompany you on your nocturnal journeys. And he may even provide some company for you, during the day.'

Calum's fingers trembled as they groped for the doorhandle. 'Captain who?' He twisted then pushed, backing away from the tall, looming form.

'Carmichael – an acquaintance of mine, in Scotland on business. I have offered him our hospitality for the duration of his stay.'

'How pleasant.' Calum continued to edge backward into his chamber. 'I look forward to meeting him.'

His guardian's thin lips were set in what passed for a smile. 'Yes, indeed.' The oil-lamp flickered, mirroring a sudden change in James Black's tone. 'Sleep well, Calum.' The tall man turned abruptly and strode off down the corridor.

'Er, good night, Uncle Jamie.' Calum watched his guardian's angular silhouette disappear round a corner. Heart pounding, he darted into his chamber and silently closed the door.

For once, sleep genuinely eluded him. He was too hot. Then too cold. Then too hot again. Struggling out of his nightshirt, Calum tossed and turned between crisp linen sheets. Soon his slender body was bathed in a fine sheen of sweat.

When Morpheus finally came, he brought dreams of Captain Carmichael staggering around the moors, dressed only in his undershirt and with his white, hairy arse shining in the moonlight.

A smile twitched Calum's slumbering lips. Then the smile faded, replaced by a vision of big Fergie McGregor. Naked.

Calum moaned in his sleep. Flailing arms gripped and twisted the bolster which ran the breadth of the bed. He pulled it on top of himself, wrapping his legs around the long pillow.

Fergie. Bathing in the burn which ran through his land, backlit by the rising sun.

Calum's arms tightened. His knees dug into the padded bolster.

Fergie soaked a rag in the icy water, then raised one arm and began to wash the thick hair in his deeply hollowed pit.

The sheen of sweat became a heavier, muskier film. Calum groaned, rolling over and on to the long pillow.

Dew spangled on the grass beneath Fergie's large feet, caught in the sunlight and transformed into a thousand glittering diamonds.

Calum twined his ankles behind the bolster, moulding it to his body. His hips began to thrust.

Fergie continued his daily ablutions, moving to another, thickly haired armpit before rinsing the wash rag and rubbing it roughly over his heavy pectorals.

Gripping the pillow more tightly, Calum buried his face in its damp surface and thrust more urgently. His mouth was open and following the progress of the wash rag, down through the broad band of black hair on Fergie's stomach into the dense jet forest between the highlander's well-muscled thighs.

Fergie smiled, enjoying the friction on his body. With one hand, he held his heavy cock loosely, pulling back beige-coloured folds of foreskin to wash around the large, pink head.

He could almost smell him! Calum's cry was only partly muffled by the pillow, into which he was now thrusting furiously.

Wiping the velvety skin carefully, Fergie's smile widened to a gasp. Despite the cold water, his cock began to thicken in his hand.

Two damp patches had appeared on Calum's pillow: one where his parted lips frantically gouged at its surface, the other three feet below where the head of his aching prick was trying to burrow into the bolster.

Fergie's attention turned to his bollocks. Bending his knees slightly, he leant down and wiped between his legs.

Calum's dream vision moved back and he found himself staring at the highlander's fine, hard rear. He saw himself, naked and erect, braced behind Fergie, gripping the highlander's jutting hipbones as he pushed his aching length deep between bristling arse-cheeks. Calum gasped, dragging his shaft back violently, longing to feel Fergie's body around his throbbing cock and taste the man's sweet skin as he kissed the side of a straining neck.

The idea was too much for even the Fox to bear. Calum's balls knitted together. He reared up from the bed, legs still wrapped around the bolster. A sharp cry of longing escaped his mouth as his prick flexed against the pillow, drenching starched white linen in a shower of warm spunk.

Through the noise of his gasping breath and the hammer of blood in his ears, he didn't hear the first soft rap at his door. The second pulled him from the delicious dream:

'Calum?'

He moaned, stifling the sound with the bolster as another wave broke in his balls. Shooting a second and a third time, Calum rolled on to his back, still holding tightly to the now soaking pillow.

'Are you all right, my boy?'

Consciousness returned quickly. He manufactured what he hoped was a convincing snore, then lay there blinking rapidly in the warm, sticky darkness.

Eventually, he heard the sound of his guardian's boots retreating from the door. Minutes later sleep reclaimed him, his drained body still clinging to the Fergus McGregor-shaped bolster.

Breaking his fast, Calum devoured the porridge with more gusto than usual: last night had given him an appetite, and he'd leapt from his bed, barely remembering to don his wig.

'This damned Fox had a lucky escape then, I'll be bound.'

Calum ate with concentration, enjoying the exchange

between his guardian and Captain Carmichael, who had evidently finally found his way to his destination.

'He did indeed! Roped and tied me to a tree, stole my clothes then fled like the cowardly scoundrel he is.' Wrapped in a blanket, the King's emissary banged the table for emphasis. 'Had he not caught me unawares, he would be hanging from a scaffold at this very moment!'

Calum almost bit through his spoon.

'Did you get a good look at him, Michael?'

'The ruffian was in disguise, as always, James, but I got the impression of great strength and bulk. Only such a man could have got the better of me.'

Calum remembered the cowering, shivering shape of the previous evening and stifled a smile. He pushed his plate away and raised his head. 'That I can believe, sir.'

A flicker of unease flitted momentarily across Captain Carmichael's ruddy features. Then he gathered himself. 'I could do with a bright youngster such as yourself, to help distribute leaflets detailing the price on this Fox blackguard's head.'

The idea of nailing his own warrant to the trunks of trees was vaguely amusing. 'I would –' His uncle broke in:

'Calum and I have estate business, this morning, I fear – and you look like you could do with a wash, Michael.'

Calum looked at his guardian quizzically.

James Black got up from the table. 'Those damned McGregors – remember, my boy? You expressed an interest in accompanying me?'

Calum masked a frown. He recalled the occasion all too well. But after last night, he wasn't sure he was ready to handle Fergus and his boisterous friend Rab in anything approaching close proximity. He fumbled for an excuse.

But he wasn't quick enough. 'That's settled then, my boy.' James Black turned to his blanket-wrapped friend. 'You will find the water closet at the top of the stairs. Flora, our housekeeper, will draw your bath.' With a curt nod, he stalked towards the door. The talk of washing brought the results of last night's dream back into Calum's mind. Uncle Jamie was very particular about cleanliness and personal hygiene. Bowing briefly to Captain Carmichael, he hurriedly left the room.

Minutes later he was staring at a denuded pillow.

Calum goggled in disbelief. He leapt on to the bed, rummaging between the still-rumpled covers. Where was the damned thing? This wasn't laundry day, so Flora could not have removed it. And anyway, everything else was still here.

Tossing the quilt aside, Calum threw himself over the side of the great bed and peered beneath.

No bolster slip, but the sight of his as-yet-unemptied chamberpot reminded him of something else he had forgotten in his haste to break fast. Grabbing the vessel by its porcelain handle, he dragged it towards himself, scowling in disgust as its contents slapped and splashed against the lipped rim.

Careful not to make matters worse and spill any, Calum gingerly hauled himself upright, still scanning the room for anywhere a pillow cover could have landed, if wrenched off during the course of a vivid dream.

Nothing. His room was its normal, Spartan – if untidy – self.

With a sigh, Calum moved towards one of the leaded glass sections, holding the stinking chamberpot at arm's length. With one hand he undid the window catch, and placed the almost full vessel on the sill. At least he could get rid of this before –

'We shall be late, Calum.'

The voice made him jump. He hastily moved in front of the window, screening the unemptied pot from James Black's eagle eye. 'Sorry, uncle – I was just –'

His guardian regarded him with a steely gaze. 'You were just –?'

Calum cleared his throat. His bed, also, should have been straightened on rising. James was a stickler for attention to detail. He tried to speak, but something about his guardian's gaze always rendered him speechless, and made him feel guilty even when he had nothing to feel guilty about.

It wasn't that he was afraid of the man: James Black had been kindness itself and, anyway, Calum had never seen his guardian raise his hand to as much as a dog. If anything, James had seemed a little wary of Calum, when he'd first arrived at the estate, four months ago. As James Black waited for his ward to answer, the silence lengthened between them and Calum found himself really looking at the man for the first time.

He was almost handsome, in a severe, clerical sort of way. But unlike the clergyman in the coach last night, James Black held himself ramrod straight. Glossy black hair was pulled back from an angular face and tied neatly behind the neck of his high-collared shirt. His clothes were stitched by the finest Savile Row tailors. His boots were of the best quality hide, specially made by a cobbler in London's East End.

And everything was black.

A smile twitched at Calum's lips. He wagered even his guardian's undergarments were of a similarly dark hue.

This smile was noted. 'Something amuses you, my boy?'

The voice drew his gaze back to his uncle's sober face. Calum cleared his throat a second time, and regained the ability to speak. 'No, uncle. Sorry.'

Hands clasped behind his back, his guardian moved further into the room and regarded the coverless bolster and the rumpled bedsheets. 'Have you mislaid something, perhaps?'

The blush took him by surprise. 'Er, no – I was just –' Words were once more beyond his power.

James Black fixed him with a penetrating stare. 'Yes, you said.'

Calum suddenly felt as if the very clothes had been stripped from his body. His uncle's eyes seemed to see into the very heart of him. And beyond – to the chamber pot, perched precariously on the window ledge. Calum edged towards the leaded glass.

'Is this what you are looking for?' Moving his hands from behind his back, his guardian held out a crumpled object.

Beneath his blond wig, the roots of his red hair were tingled with a fiercer blush. Calum hung his head and focused on his guardian's feet.

'I thought as much.' The toes of James' highly polished boots moved a little closer.

Calum's heart pounded against his ribs. Then the soiled pillow slip was thrust directly under his nose. He fumbled for an explanation. 'I, er –' He stared at the stiffened section of fabric.

The smell was stronger, and had changed from a salty tang to a heavier, muskier odour which made his stomach churn. The scent also fired his brain. 'Oh, I am so ashamed, uncle!' Calum fell to his knees, raising his blond head and gazing beseechingly up at his stern-faced guardian. 'I have no idea why my body behaves so.' Ignorance was a lesser crime than wantonness, as far as James was concerned.

His guardian's face softened.

Calum seized the initiative. 'I can control it during the day, but in sleep it has a mind of its own.' He manufactured an expression of wretchedness. 'Please forgive me, uncle. I was about to wash it clean, when –'

'Do not distress yourself, my boy.' James Black placed a slim hand on Calum's wigged head. 'You cannot be held responsible for an occurrence which was neither sought nor desired.'

Calum watched as the fingers of his guardian's other hand tightened over the spunk-stained section of bolster cover:

'I will take care of it for you, this time.' The man gently stroked Calum's head.

Calum flinched.

Abruptly, and with a speed which belied his ramrod form, James Black stepped back and ducked to check under the bed.

'Thank you, uncle.' Calum darted forward, seizing his guardian's arm and preventing him from discovering an omission in another matter of personal fastidiousness.

James Black regarded the fingers on his arm for a moment, then smiled. 'Captain Carmichael is already washed and saddled. He will accompany us as far as Blairhoyle.' He smiled again, and a sudden shiver replaced Calum's previous blush. 'Do not keep us waiting, my boy.'

'I will be with you immediately, Uncle Jamie.'

As the tall, angular figure walked briskly from the room with a curt nod, Calum collapsed with relief against the open window, accidentally closing it with his elbow.

He barely heard the whinny of shock and the cry of horror from below, as the contents of the pisspot met their unintended target.

Three

'You didn't!' Rab gripped the ewe by the loose fleece on the back of her neck and pushed her towards the dip.

'Aye, I did!' Stripped to the waist, Fergie smiled wryly and guided the bleating animal towards the evil-smelling mixture. 'In all his scarlet finery and mounted on the back of a great bay horse!' He wiped his forehead with the back of a brawny forearm.

'I wondered why you got back so late, last night.' Pealing off his own rough cotton shirt, Rab grabbed the struggling sheep around its mid-section. The muscles in his upper arms bulged but he barely broke sweat as he lifted the reluctant animal from the ground and carried it bodily to the dipping trench. 'I thought perhaps you had found yourself some company, on the way home.' His rugged face creased into a frown of concern. He gently lowered the bleating ewe into the foul-smelling liquid.

'And what if I had?' Fergie kept his face expressionless as he followed the sheep's progress. In truth, he had found himself strangely aroused – if confused – by the Fox's actions. And the thought of relating the events of the previous night to a third party, in particular this third party, further stirred his blood.

Rab's response was a wordless grunt. He wiped his calloused hands on the thighs of his ragged breeches.

Fergie couldn't resist teasing further. 'He made me undress.'

Rab's head shot up. 'He stole your clothes?'

Fergie feigned innocence. 'Did I say that?' The sensations which had coursed through his body, standing there so close to the Fox, returned with a vengeance. Not leaving out a single detail, he entertained the rugged-faced man with the events of a mere six hours ago.

By the time he had finished, Rab was staring at him, the sheep-dipping forgotten. His brown eyes widened. 'Were you robbed as well?'

'Of my dignity, maybe.' Fergie grinned, squinting in the early morning sunshine and remembering the vaguely amused eyes of the masked highwayman. 'But Morag's dowry is safe.'

With a splash, the ewe bounded out of the dip-filled ditch and raced to join the rest of the flock. Rab dried his hands on his shirt. He looked away. 'I was not only concerned with Morag's needs.'

Fergie watched the way his herdsman's chest now glistened with sweat. Thick sinew bulged and flexed with each movement. He felt a familiar twitch in his groin.

Herdsman.

His sister's betrothed.

His erstwhile lover.

Fergie busied himself with the breakfast his mother had packed for them. 'Added to your severance pay, Morag's dowry will be more than enough to take both of you across the sea to the Americas.' He withdrew a flagon of ale from a knapsack, turned and walked to where Rab was leaning against a dyke, arms braced in the morning sunshine. He held out the vessel. 'Let us drink to your future.'

Rab ignored it, reaching around to cup the back of Fergie's neck instead.

Fergie smiled, glancing briefly to where the flock were now once more grazing happily. Beyond, the pastureland was devoid of any other human life.

Just he and Rab – as it had been for the past two years. But things were about to change, and it was time to say goodbye to the past. Setting the flagon down on top of the dyke, he turned back to his herdsman.

Rab's craggy face was expressionless.

Fergie's eyes moved lower, over the hard mounds of his friend's chest down to where the man's need was swelling the front of his sheep-dip-stained work breeches. Whether it was their physical proximity, or the somewhat embellished version of last night with the Fox which was responsible for Rab's ardour, Fergie wasn't sure. Neither did he care.

Rab took a step forward, fingers massaging the back of Fergie's sunburnt neck.

One hand rested lightly on his herdsman's shoulder. His other hand slipped between them. Fergie's palm covered the raised outline of Rab's cock. He applied a little pressure.

Rab groaned, his hand moving up into his future brother-in-law's tangled hair.

Fergie's lips parted in a sigh. Then Rab's free hand was on his arse and his mouth opened further.

They kissed hungrily, gnawing at each other's lips. Fergie's tongue explored the inside of his friend's mouth, feeling Rab's cock flex against his palm with each movement of their lips.

Rab ground his body against Fergie's. Chest to chest, thigh to thigh, Fergie could smell the sweat of their shared labour as his own cock bucked and shuddered against the back of his hand. Rab's nipples grazed Fergie's. The sandpapery surface of his chin rasped against his employer and friend's smoother face. Fergie tightened his fist around Rab's shaft and felt more than heard the corresponding gasp. Then his hand was moving lower.

Rab bent his knees, parting his thick thighs and allowing access to his bollocks. The kiss deepened, changing in intensity. Fergie closed his eyes, enjoying the weight and texture of his friend's heavy sac and wanting more.

They had avoided spending time alone with each other, since the announcement of Rab and Morag's betrothal.

Fergie pulled his mouth from Rab's, nuzzling the man's neck and feeling the blood pulse against his lips.

'For auld lang syne?' Rab whispered the words up towards the blue skies overhead.

Fergie smiled: for old time's sake. They had been good times. His cock throbbed against the front of his breeches at the memory of dozens of mornings and afternoons in the pasture-land. But everything had to end, and this seemed a fitting way to say their own, special goodbye. Hauling his hand from between Rab's thighs, Fergie moved back a little, and began to unbutton.

Rab turned away, doing likewise.

Fergie grinned: shy to the last. No doubt Morag was servicing her betrothed's fine cock more than adequately – if the Clan McGregor skills were shared – but he knew there was one part of Rab which would have suffered a certain neglect, over the past weeks. He pulled his shaft free of the roughly woven wool and watched Rab lower his breeches.

The man's arse gleamed sweatily in morning sunshine. Rab moved on to his knees, gripping the two pale mounds and wrenching them apart. 'Put it in me, Fergie! Plough my furrow as I plough your sister's!' The request was low with male desire.

Blood fled from Fergie's brain, swelling his cock further. He stared at the pink, crinkled opening. Need was seeping from his slit. Fergie slicked his thumb with the clear pearl of lust, then ran that thumb over his velvety glans.

'Please, Fergie! Do it!'

He needed no further bidding. Fergie reached into the pocket of his breeches and produced the chunk of hardened lanolin he carried with him at all times. Unwrapped from the cloth, he held the solid block between his fingers and felt the heat from his hand soften the lubricant. The released smell made his cock flex again. The scent of animals and lush grass and Rab's sweat were all part of their clandestine affair.

Now melted into a viscous liquid, the lanolin seeped between his fingers. Fergie dropped to his knees behind Rab and, one hand on the man's right arse-cheek, the greased fingers of the other began to circle the spasming orifice.

Rab moaned.

Fergie watched the crinkled rosette open to receive him. He smiled, kissed the base of Rab's spine then circled again, pointedly avoiding the man's arsehole.

Rab moaned more urgently, pushing back against Fergie's hand.

The smell of the wool grease was stronger now, as the heat from Rab's body and Fergie's fingers warmed it further. It was a sweet-sour odour, mixing with the musk of two men's arousal.

Abruptly, Rab grabbed Fergie's wrist and roughly guided it to where it needed to be.

It was Fergie's turn to moan, as his lanolin-slicked fingers sank into Rab's body.

His friend's low grunt of satisfaction filled his ears and increased his desire for the man. The rest of the greasing was hurriedly perfunctory: the time for teasing was over. Crouching behind Rab, his palm sticky with sex-sweat and lanolin, Fergie leant the head of his prick against the entrance to his friend's body.

A shiver of pleasure erected the hair on the back of Rab's neck.

Fergie lowered his face, leaning over and lightly licking that hair. Then his hips jutted forward. In one smooth, practised movement he thrust past Rab's spasming sphincter and upward.

They both cried out.

Fergie's back arched in arousal as further rings of muscle welcomed his prick, pulling it further into his friend's slick rectum.

Rab released his arse-cheeks and fell forward, hands gripping tufts of lush grass, elbows locked against the impact.

Sweat ran into Fergie's eyes. His bollocks tingled as he pushed on until the entire seven inches of his thick prick was buried in Rab's arse. He rested there, hands slipping beneath his friend's body to grip his hipbones.

The sound of their laboured breathing filled the quiet morning air.

Then Fergie withdrew slowly, teasing himself and his lover. He inhaled sharply, feeling every flex of Rab's arse muscles drag along his shaft and try to keep him there.

Rab was panting, now. The deep, bassy voice was reduced to a hoarse series of grunts.

Fergie hissed through his teeth, then gasped as his cockhead hit Rab's sphincter once more, this time from the other side.

'Fuck me, Fergie! Do it hard, and do it quick!'

Staring down at the five, slick inches of his prick which joined them, a frisson of lust shook Fergie's lean form. Then he was thrusting forward, using Rab's hipbones for leverage and trying to ignore his friend's grunting response as he pistoned in and out of the man's body.

Each slap of his balls against Rab's arse brought him closer to the edge. Every withdrawal brought parting ever closer. Fergie closed his eyes and thought about the great ship which would carry his sister and his best friend to the Americas, in a few weeks' time. As Rab's rings of muscle massaged his prick, Fergie focused on that ship, both wanting release and wanting the fuck never to end. Because this was the last time.

The last time he would crouch naked with the man, in the lush pastureland.

The last time he would smell the sour waves of arousal which rose from his herdsman's body in great, stirring waves.

Rapid movement beneath him told Fergie Rab was jerking himself towards orgasm. The knowledge tipped him over the edge and blasted all thought of the future into a thousand tiny fragments. Thighs tight, bollocks tighter, Fergie bucked forward, feeling his prick flex one last time. His eyes shot open. Then a wet warmth surrounded his shaft and he was falling. Nipples impacted with Rab's spine, knocking the man to the ground.

Fergie howled and released a second volley deep into his friend's arse.

Rab's climax was close behind, his yell of orgasm forcing several squawking pheasant from their nests in the scrub grass.

As his body shuddered and Rab shot thick wads on to the dewy grass, his arse muscles tightened, milking a further sticky load from Fergie's gaping slit.

They collapsed, side by side. Fergie moved his hands to grip Rab's soaking pectorals and felt the viscous spunk slippy beneath his palms. He lay there, drained and exhilarated, holding an exhausted Rab in his arms. When his friend's breathing returned to normal, and his own softening prick slid from Rab's arse, Fergie lightly kissed the man's ear and struggled to his feet.

The last time.

He pulled up his breeches and tucked his sticky cock back inside.

The last time.

Fergie licked a smear of Rab's spunk from his fingers and wandered over to the dyke. Lifting the flagon, he uncorked it and drank deeply, staring around himself.

The last time.

The best time.

'Come with us.' A few minutes later, Rab joined him. The rugged face was flushed, the brown eyes shining.

Fergie smiled. 'I have a farm to run and land to protect.' Shading his gaze, he looked away from Rab's full mouth to the distant outline of Castle Black. 'And, anyway, I would miss our glens and mountains too much.' Strong arms encircled his waist.

'America has glens – I hear there are deep ravines and peaks, the equal of anything around here.'

Lips brushed his bristly neck and he felt Rab's breath on his bare shoulder. His tired cock twitched. Fergie laughed. 'Aye, but does America have heather to turn those peaks purple in autumn?' He inhaled deeply as Rab's rough palms moved upward to grip the solid mounds of his pectorals. 'Does it have the fresh, peaty smell of a summer morn in Stirlingshire? Does it have springy moss, and bramble flowers, burns which run clear and teem with spawning salmon?'

A grouse called overhead, answering its mate in a nest amidst the longer grass.

Fergie leant back against Rab, feeling his friend's mouth move around to his collarbones. 'Does it have birds whose flesh a man can eat and whose plumage he can wear in a cockade?' Rab's laugh rumbled through Fergie's spine, hardening his nipples.

'Does it have rain and cold winters when snow kills the lambs and bitter winds slice through a man's clothes like a knife?' Rab moved his hips.

Fergie laughed. 'Perhaps not.' He returned the languid thrusts, lowering his arms and running his hands down the outside of Rab's thighs. Resting his head on his friend's shoulder, he stared up at the blue sky.

'I will not miss our hard winters, Fergie.'

He felt himself slowly lowered.

'Nor will I be sorry to leave a land now ruled by the English.'

His knees met the wet grass.

'But there is one thing I will miss.'

Fergie's hand moved up further as he leant forward, feeling the strong sinew of Rab's shoulders. He stared at the ground. Then his herdsman's work-callused hands were turning him around. Fergie stared into his friend's eyes.

Rab grinned. 'Your mother's cooking!' He playfully slapped Fergie's cheek then bounded to his feet and grabbed the cloth which wrapped their breakfast. Tearing it open, he began to eat. 'No one makes a potato scone like Mrs McGregor!'

Fergie's responding roar of mirth was deep and genuine. He jumped up and slung an arm around Rab's shoulder. 'There's another thing they don't have in the Americas – potatoes!'

His friend munched. 'Did the potato not come from there, in the first place?'

Fergie snatched the remains of the flat, griddle-fried food from his friend's hand and stuck it in his mouth. 'Did not!' He galloped off towards the flock of ewes, which scattered in surprise.

'Did!' Rab charged after him. 'And give me back my breakfast!'

Fergie spun round, planting his feet apart. 'Come and get it!'

With a whoop, Rab grabbed the cloth of scones and charged towards him.

Fergie laughed, darting left to avoid the bulrush.

Rab caught up with him eventually, seizing his waist and forcing potato scones between Fergie's laughing lips.

Eventually they both fell giggling to the ground. The sun was higher in the sky now, and it was a good day to be alive. As they lay there, happily eating and drinking, the sound of hooves drifted into Fergie's ears. He raised himself on to one elbow, staring towards the bridge path and the two figures approaching on horseback. He groaned.

'What's wrong?' Rab sat up.

Frowning, Fergie continued to stare. 'Black Jamie – again!'

Then he grinned. 'And he's brought that useless article of a ward of his with him.' He turned to Rab, and winked. 'This might be your last chance to have some sport with that flouncing fop.'

Rab winked back. He drained the flagon of ale, then together they scrambled to their feet, making their way stealthily towards the grazing sheep.

Calum maintained his usual unhorsemanlike seat, trotting a little behind. It would not do if people suspected him to be a more than able rider. Staring at a back view of James Black, who sat in a saddle the same way he did most things – that is, both at ease and not at ease – Calum sighed.

He truly regretted the pisspot incident, especially since his guardian had presumed Flora responsible for the carelessly emptied vessel, and had dismissed her on the spot. He promised himself, then and there, that any coinage amongst the spoils of his next nocturnal adventure would go to her family.

Calum gripped the reins one-handed and adjusted his frilled collar. The beginnings of a smile chased the sigh away. It had almost been worth it, to see a spluttering, piss-soaked Captain Carmichael stagger off to draw himself a second bath. And it had taken his guardian's mind off Calum.

'Mr McGregor?'

James Black's commanding voice refocused Calum's attention. He brought his mount to a halt a little away, watching a broad, shirtless shape make its way across the field to where his guardian sat.

'Fine morning for it, Mr Black.' Fergie's lilting voice was tinged, as always, with subtle mockery. He carried a flagon of ale, and was swigging from it in an exaggerated manner.

Calum looked to where Rab McBride was standing, grinning. His heart sank. He eased his horse back, hoping he would not be noticed.

It was too late. 'And young Master Monroe is with you, I see.'

Calum cringed.

Fergie vaulted the four-foot drystone dyke in one effortless bound, then stood in the road in front of them, wiping his lips. 'A drink, sirs.'

Calum's guardian ignored the extended flagon. 'I would like to talk business with you, Mr McGregor.'

Fergie laughed. 'A drink first, though – I never do business without first sharing a flagon with a man.'

Calum knew his guardian had taken a vow of temperance, and never touched alcohol. Fergus was aware of this vow – as was everyone in Blairhoyle. It was another diversionary tactic. Calum sighed.

His guardian talked on. 'Have you thought about my proposition, Mr McGregor?'

'Aye, Mr Black. But I think better when drinking.'

A laugh from the other side of the dyke told him Fergie's herdsman had joined the exchange. Calum moved his gaze to the stocky, also shirtless man, forearms casually resting on the top of the stone wall. There was a closeness between the two men he envied: the closeness of friends – and something else?

A sudden vision of Rab and Fergie naked together turned his mouth to a desert.

'I am offering a good price for your land, Mr McGregor.' James Black continued to ignore all references to alcohol. 'Plus you and your descendants will have jobs for life, as my tenant farmers. The only difference you will notice is two hundred pounds, to do with as you please.

'It is indeed a good price, Mr Black.' Fergie moved forward, taking another exaggerated drink from the flagon and walking towards Calum.

Calum shrank back in his saddle.

'You and your family could use that money to purchase land in another part of the country, Mr McGregor.'

'Aye, that we could.' Unexpectedly, Fergie thrust the flagon up at Calum. 'You'll drink with me, won't you Master Monroe?' The man's tone was even.

The thought of placing his mouth where Fergie's had been, of slicking his lips with liquid which had moistened Fergie's, sent a tremor of longing over his expensively attired body. 'No thank you, Mr McGregor.' He bowed, waving his frill-cuffed hand with a small flourish.

A guffaw from Rab McBride brought a flush of anger to Calum's cheeks.

'Two hundred pounds you say, Mr Black?'

Calum heard the tease in Fergie's voice.

His guardian did not. 'Yes – delivered into your hands, the moment we both sign the transference contract.' James produced a document from his pocket. 'My ward and your herdsman can witness it.'

Fergie continued to hold out the flagon. He moved closer, stroking the nose of Calum's horse. 'Two hundred pounds – that's a great deal of money.'

The sour-smelling sheep dip drifted into Calum's nostrils, mixed with the musky odour of Fergie's sweat. Beneath that, the sharp tang of ale, tinged with the scent of something Calum couldn't quite identify.

'A shared drink would help assure me of your good faith.'

James Black's head snapped around. 'Drink with the fellow, or we shall be here all day!' The request was hissed.

Rab McBride was barely managing to control his amusement. Calum eyed Fergie's beaming countenance suspiciously.

Fergie lowered his head, looking up at him through thick lashes. 'Too good to share a flagon with an honest labourer, Master Monroe?'

Calum bristled. He leant forward, snatched the vessel from the sunburnt hand and took a long, deep draft.

An explosion of laughter from Rab McBride was the first telltale sign.

The second was foul taste in his mouth and a burning in his throat as he swallowed. Calum began to cough. The flagon fell from his grip.

Fergie's grin returned. Then he too was chuckling

Startled by the sudden wriggling and gasping of the man seated on its back, Calum's horse reared up.

'Does the brew disagree with you, Master Monroe?'

Calum's eyes watered. He gasped for breath.

Fergie grabbed the reins. 'Nice drop of sheep piss there,

Master Monroe – from the best flock in Blairhoyle.' He turned to where Calum's guardian was staring. 'I will never sell my land – to you or anyone, Black Jamie. McGregors have worked their own crofts for three centuries, and I will not see the likes of you make tenant farmers out of free men.'

The gorge rose in Calum's throat.

Then Fergie delivered a sound slap to the horse's hind quarters and the beast was bolting, with a retching Calum clinging on for dear life.

The last sound he heard, as the horse threw him into the burn was Fergie McGregor's scornful laugh.

Four

James Black had been solicitation itself, hauling him out of the icy stream and taking him home. Now seated in a tin bath, in front of the fire in his chamber, Calum waited for the freshly boiled water to chase the chill from his bones.

He'd swallowed enough of the burn to finally rid his mouth of that appalling taste, but his stomach muscles still contracted each time he thought of what he'd drunk.

Lowering the wash rag, he turned his face towards the blazing fire.

Why did Fergie hate him so? Ever since he'd arrived to stay with his guardian, Fergie and Rab had gone out of their way to mock and harass him at every available opportunity.

What had he ever done to them?

This morning's indignity was only one of a growing number of incidents.

What was he doing wrong? He'd been polite and respectful from the start: asking the muscular highlander about his farm and enquiring after his health and the health of his herdsman each time they met.

In return he received only jibes and sneers. The pair of them took great delight in laughing at his clothes, his manners – even his very voice seemed to generate uncontrollable mirth.

The water was cooling around him. Stepping out of the bath,

Calum seized a towel and began to dry himself. A sudden frown creased his brow.

The Fox, on the other hand, generated the very response in Fergus McGregor that Calum wished he could. The previous evening, while he'd been more concerned with having fun with Captain Carmichael, Calum had felt admiring eyes on his body. He'd also caught the unmistakable signs of arousal beneath the brawny highlander's shirt.

His cock began to stir against his thigh.

Calum rubbed vigorously at his chest and shoulders. The smile broadened as he recalled the look on Fergus McGregor's countenance when the Fox had brought his face close to his prisoner's. Calum closed his eyes, savouring the memory of Fergie's breath on his skin.

The man's lips were parted.

Calum's own mouth grew slack.

The man's excitement was clearly visible.

Calum's own cock was now steadily thickening.

Less than an inch apart, he'd almost been able to feel the head of Fergie's prick stabbing at the thigh of the Fox's scarlet breeches. Calum moaned, remembering how strong the desire to kiss those parted lips had been –

– to kiss those lips, and thrust his tongue into Fergie McGregor's mouth while slipping a hand beneath the man's tenting shirt.

The towel dropped from Calum's fingers and his hand moved lower. His prick was warm from the bath but increasing in heat and girth with each memory. He held his shaft loosely, feeling the man-flesh swell further against his neatly manicured fingers.

That pale, soft hand became another's rougher skin. Behind him, the fire was reddening his back and arse-cheeks. A flush from a different source stained his chest and belly.

Calum closed his fingers around his hardening manhood. He was back in the clearing, staring into Fergus McGregor's strong features while Fergus McGregor's hand caressed his cock.

His balls clenched and his fist began to move. Eyes closed, knees bending, Calum dragged his hand down to the root of his prick, pulling the foreskin right back until his shaft bucked and shivered with pleasure. Then his fist moved upward again, drawing folds of skin back over the large, pink head.

At the court in London, where he'd received his education in matters other than academic, his unusually long foreskin had been the object of much curiosity. Calum had no idea there was as much variation in members. Frederick – a willowy youth from France – could not stroke himself without the aid of a silk handkerchief, so tight a fit was his cockskin. William of Nottingham had possessed a little more, but still complained of discomfort if his cock was rubbed without ample lubricant. But even when fully hard, Calum Monroe's manhood was draped in a vast sheath of beige-coloured skin.

His cock twitched at the memory of court life. Free from adult interference, he'd had many fine lovers. They had been happy years, from eighteen to nearly twenty-one.

Three months ago, it had ended abruptly, when James Black – who had served in the army with Calum's father – had called him to his Blairhoyle estate.

Three months since his hand had held another's cock.

Three months since he'd run his tongue around the head.

Three months since he'd taken a cock into his arse, or thrust his into a warm, well-muscled tunnel.

Three months of damp Scottish weather and the sight of James Black's dour face each morning at breakfast. Was it any surprise he was driven on to the roads at night?

Calum's hand moved faster, as he recalled one of his last court encounters, and the first time he had experienced the added thrill which danger could bring to lust.

Joshua Levin was a groom at St James Stables, where Calum and his friends kept mounts. A strange-looking youth, with an almost impenetrable accent and an uncanny way with the animals in his care, the lad was the brunt of many of the older ostlers' pranks, including orders to polish the horse's noses and milk a stallion.

Joshua had found an unexpected champion in Calum, who despised bullying in any form and reprimanded the other grooms regularly for their cruelty towards the apprentice ostler. Unfortunately, his interference had only served to increase his elders' resentment of Joshua, as the youth confided to Calum, one evening when they found themselves alone in the stables:

'They make me muck out the stalls morn and night, sir.' Joshua wouldn't look at him. His head of glossy curls remained lowered as he brushed mud from a mare's back.

'That's not too bad, is it?' Prolonged exposure to the youth had enabled Calum to understand his accent quite well.

'They make me do it naked, sir.' Joshua's voice was tinged with shame. 'And they stand and watch me.'

'Ah –' Despite his sympathy for the youth's predicament, Calum's interest was pricked.

'They make me do other things too, sir.' The stable lad's voice was barely audible.

'Are you naked when you do these . . . other things?' Still flushed from his ride, Calum's skin tingled with another heat.

'Always, sir.' Joshua swept the curry comb over the horse's flanks with increasing vigour.

'Why do they do that, do you think?' Calum sidled left to soothe his mount. Standing side-on to the crouching Joshua, he focused on the youth's rosy cheeks.

'Because I am not normal, sir.' The stable lad's arm trembled.

'Stuff and nonsense! You are as normal as the next man!' He could see it was causing Joshua great pain to talk about this, and Calum's sympathy grew to a growing anger at the cruelty of the youth's work companions.

'They call me ugly and deformed, sir.' Joshua inhaled sharply. 'And they are right.'

Calum frowned: the hurt mere words could cause never failed to astound him. 'No, they are wrong. They speak out of envy, because you are so skilled with your charges.'

'You are very kind, good sir, but I know I am . . . different.'

Calum sighed. Different the youth indeed was.

He wore his curly hair long and unfettered, going against current fashion. Every now and again, when he swept it back from his face, gold hooped ear-rings were visible in his neat ears.

His eyes were dark, his lashes thick and almost girlish while beneath the rosy cheeks the skin was swarthy as a Gypsy's. His otherwise pleasant features were marred by a somewhat prominent nose although, if he was honest, Calum had to admit he found the protuberance most attractive. It reminded him of the noble faces of long-dead Romans, depicted in the marble frieze which decorated the wall of the great law courts.

And then there was the thick coating of hair – evident even at this young age – which covered the stable lad's arms and wrists, even sprouting from the knuckles of his exceptionally large hands.

A shiver of curiosity caused Calum's own sparsely haired body to tremble. 'Different is good. What would the world be, if we were all the same, eh?' He tried to inject a note of levity into his voice. 'Everyone is different, when one gets down to basics. Some of us might dress alike, talk alike and look similar, but each of us is a unique person, special in our own way.'

Joshua had fallen silent. As Calum watched, he saw with horror that tears were coursing down the boy's cheeks and dropping on to the horse's coat. The display of emotion took him by surprise. The placing of his hand on the lad's shoulder took him aback further. 'If it bothers you that much, maybe a haircut and some elocution lessons would –'

'A haircut would do little for this, sir!' Joshua dropped the curry comb and hauled at his breeches fastenings.

Seconds later, Calum found himself staring at a stubby, flaccid member. There was indeed something different about the stable lad's rod, although Calum was at a loss to put his finger on exactly what it was.

Joshua held his prick with evident disgust, barely touching the dark cock-flesh, which began to react almost immediately to the warmth of its owner's palm. 'It is the way of my people, sir.' Tentatively, the stable lad pointed to a tiny, nublike scar just below the purplish, uncovered head. 'In order that a man will never be a slave to his bodily desires, the foreskin is cut at birth.'

Calum laughed! That was it – the lad's cock looked hard when it was, in fact, soft.

Joshua misinterpreted the cry of triumph. Great sobs racked his slender body and he turned away.

Calum was immediately at his side, turning him back. 'I was

not laughing at you – or your fine, distinctive prick, Joshua.' It was the first time he had used the apprentice's name, and doing so swept away the barriers between them.

Joshua raised his glossy head, blinking at Calum through teary lashes.

The expression on the lad's face melted his heart. The sight of the youth's hardening prick had a similar effect between Calum's own thighs. He stretched out a hand, curling the stable boy's fingers around the circumcised organ. 'Does it not behave like any other cock?'

Joshua gasped, grabbing Calum's shoulder to steady himself.

Finding a space between the boy's thickly haired fingers, Calum began to stroke. 'Does it not show when you are aroused?'

Joshua's hand tightened on Calum's shoulder, while the fingers of his other slackened.

Gaining more access, Calum cradled the swelling member in his palm, watching the prominent veins fill with desire. 'And is it not capable of giving pleasure, both to you and –' he glanced up at the stable lad '– others?'

Joshua sighed. 'The ladies find me repulsive, sir. One look at my manhood and they are either sniggering or running away.'

'Then they are fools, Joshua.' Calum fell to a crouch, still cradling the now almost erect cock. He removed his fingers, spat into his palm then replaced his hand.

The apprentice shuddered. 'This is wrong –'

Calum raised his head, staring up into eyes which were half-horrified, half-aroused. He formed a ring with his thumb and forefinger, spreading his saliva over the thin cockskin. His other hand gently massaged the base of the lad's spine.

Joshua moaned, gripping Calum's shoulders with both hands. 'You should not be kneeling before such as I.'

A frown tightened Calum's lips. 'We are equals in this, my friend.' He continued to slide the digit ring up and down Joshua's stubby length. While this had all begun as a fraternal exercise in morale boosting, Calum knew the raging between his own thighs was far from brotherly. The stable lad's cock had swollen to a good five, hard inches erect, its girth was not much less. The shaft felt good and heavy in his hand, although the spit-covered, tightly fitting cockskin was already starting to dry out.

Joshua winced at the friction. 'Sir, it hurts – and the other boys may come in at any time. I do not wish to cause you any embarrassment or –'

The stable lad's final word was a groan of pleasure as, moving his hand down to the very root of Joshua, Calum sheathed his teeth and lowered his head. As the pink, engorged cockhead slipped between his lips, Joshua's fingers tightened on Calum's hunched shoulders.

The feel of the lad's cock as it pushed on over his tongue made Calum's own prick throb with desire. The knowledge they could be interrupted at any moment added a strange frisson to their coupling. He rolled his tongue over the unusually rough-feeling glans, flicking the tip into the narrow slit.

Joshua's legs buckled.

Then Calum was gripping the cheeks of the stable lad's arse, hauling Joshua towards him and wanting to take the fellow, balls and all. Joshua's thick pubic hair rasped against his face. His nose buried in its depths, Calum lowered his head a little and widened his lips.

The lad smelled of horses and hay – a good, honest odour.

Calum flicked his tongue again, hearing the corresponding moan from above and tasting the sweet-sour flavour of Joshua's own lubricant.

The youth's bollocks pressed urgently against his sheathed teeth.

Calum's mouth was watering uncontrollably. His fingers spread over the lad's firm arse-cheeks. Beneath his riding breeches, arousal leaked freely from the head of his own prick. As Joshua began to thrust with his hips, Calum's throat muscles spasmed. The head of the stable lad's circumcised prick hit the hard cartilage on the roof of his mouth, eliciting a groan of pleasure from above and a smothered grunt from Calum.

He was choking.

The other grooms were due back any second.

They would be discovered, *in flagrante delicto*.

Would Joshua's tormentors watch? Would they jeer? Or would they join in?

The prospect did strange things to his already inflamed body.

His nipples sprang to attention, rubbing against his tight-fitting hacking jacket. Sweat soaked his pit hair, trailing a warm then cold track down his sides. His gag reflex spasmed more furiously than ever, massaging Joshua's stubby shaft and making the apprentice ram his balls ever more urgently against Calum's sheathed teeth.

Then Calum gasped, moving his lips from their firm O shape. His head was pushed back and sweaty hairiness filled his mouth. Next thing he knew, his shoulders hit the stable floor and Joshua was astride his chest, fucking his face furiously.

Calum's aching prick was rigid against the inside of his riding breeches. He groaned, choking on Joshua's crotch which smashed into his sore lips again and again. He scrabbled for purchase, gripping the lad's arse-cheeks and pressing with his index fingers.

His Gypsy lover arched his back, hissing with pleasure and thrusting more urgently as Calum's fingers sank into his body.

Seconds later, chewing on the youth's bollocks, sucking on Joshua's flexing prick and with two fingers deep in his lover's arse, Calum's spine left the stable floor and the inside of his jodhpurs filled with a sticky warmth.

Almost simultaneously, Joshua's groin covered his face, shooting a salty liquid into Calum's throat.

He couldn't breathe.

He couldn't move.

He couldn't think.

The fear of discovery flooded his body, making his cock flex again and again, long after Joshua's breathing had returned to normal and they were sitting side by side amongst the hay.

Beneath his normally swarthy complexion, a rosy glow stained Joshua's exotic face as he struggled back into his breeches.

Words were not necessary. Leaning over, Calum planted a kiss on the exposed head of the stable lad's cock, just before it disappeared from view.

One with too much foreskin; the other with too little.

One so dark; the other pale and red-haired.

One living at court, with all the accompaniments that fine life brought; the other sleeping in some rough outhouse.

But each had shown the other a fine time.

Standing naked, four months later in front of a roaring log fire, Calum was vaguely aware his fist was still moving. The smile became a grin, then a more urgent expression as he pushed himself towards release, his head still full of Joshua and the edgy fear of discovery.

He came quickly and efficiently, milking his cock while his balls clenched and unclenched. Falling forward on to his knees, head thrown back in pleasure Calum's eyelids shot open –

– and he found himself staring into black pupils.

'I, er – I'm sorry.' A towel now tightly secured around his waist, Calum blushed scarlet: how long had the man been standing there?

Setting a lighted candle on a nearby table, his guardian walked past him, ignoring Calum's blustering words. James Black began to warm his large hands in front of the fire. 'I should apologise.'

Calum grabbed his dressing-gown and struggled into it. The room had grown dark, and the candlelight seemed very bright.

'That was a cruel trick McGregor and his herdsman played on you. If I had not insisted you accompany me, they would not have dared try such a prank.'

Calum sat down in the chair on the other side of the fire, grateful for the change of subject. 'Why do you want his land, Uncle Jamie? You already own every acre for miles around.' It was something to say.

The tall, angular figure gazed into the flames.

Calum waited for an answer, and when none was forthcoming, he eventually stood up. 'Well, I think I will have an early night.'

James Black turned. Light from the fire flickered over his guardian's gaunt face. 'You look so like your mother, sometimes.'

He stiffened. James and his father had been friends, served in the army together many years ago, before Douglas Monroe's untimely death, when Calum was twelve. From then, until the age of sixteen, he had lived with a series of aunts, before being financed to King George's court. He had no memory of his mother, who had died giving birth to Calum, and his guardian had never previously mentioned her. 'I do?'

The heat from the fire lent an unnatural flush to James Black's face, as he raised his head. 'You have her eyes, and her thick red tresses.'

Calum smiled self-consciously. Free of his powdered wig, his auburn hair caught the colour of the flames.

Unexpectedly, his guardian reached out a hand, resting five long fingers on Calum's wrist. 'And you have her spirit.' Something like a smile hovered around the man's thin mouth.

Despite the heat from the fire, Black Jamie's touch was ice. Calum shivered.

The hand was immediately withdrawn. His guardian got to his feet slowly. 'And I know your mother would be proud of the way you are helping me rid this estate of those damned McGregors.'

Calum barely managed a nod.

'Now I will leave you to your rest – I hope your insomnia will not trouble you tonight.' James Black moved towards the open door. 'Captain Carmichael desires my opinion on his strategy to catch this highwayman. We shall no doubt be talking well into the night.'

Calum found his voice. 'Do not work too late, uncle. You need your sleep too.'

James Black paused, just beside the bed. 'Your kindness touches me, but I shall be fine.' The dark eyes moved over his ward's body.

Calum shivered again. His seed was tightening on his stomach, cracking and crystalising beneath his dressing-gown.

'Sleep well, Calum.' With that, the angular, black-clad figure moved swiftly from the room, closing the door behind him.

Calum stood there listening to the receding footsteps, then hauled off his dressing-gown and pulled on underwear.

James Black was a strange one, indeed.

Blowing out the candle, Calum lay on his bed, hearing the tap of branches outside his window.

Should he ride tonight?

Or was it too risky?

Three hours later, with night falling and the castle silent, he was fully dressed and shinning down the tall fir tree and heading for the stables.

Five

'Eat up, son, before other mouths beat you to it.'

Fergie looked up from his broth into Mrs McGregor's smiling eyes. 'I'm not hungry, Ma.' He pushed his plate towards his younger brother, who fell on the soup with relish.

'Not like you to be off your food, Fergus.' His mother dried her hands on an apron, concern creasing her brow.

'I think the Fox has stolen his appetite, Ma.' From across the table, his sister Morag giggled.

Fergie frowned, shooting a look to Rab, who sat at his betrothed's side: the man obviously shared more than his bed with Morag.

Rab looked away, suddenly embarrassed.

'Stop your silly gossiping, girl!' Mrs McGregor's reprimand was swift.

Morag laughed. 'It's true – Rab was late for our meeting with the minister today, because my brother could not concentrate on dipping the sheep.' She playfully kissed her betrothed's lips. 'And you had to do it all on your own, didn't you, my love.'

Rab looked more uncomfortable than ever.

Fergie glowered at his sister. It was on the tip of his tongue to tell her those lips she had just kissed had spent most of the afternoon tight around his future brother-in-law's cock, and that was why Rab had been late for yet another wedding rehearsal.

Then he caught his herdsman's eye, and knew he couldn't ruin two lives, as well as break his mother's heart. 'If you must know, I have been preoccupied with Black Jamie's offer.'

Mrs McGregor patted her son's shoulder. 'Aye, he's tenacious, that one – I'll give him that.'

Fergie placed his hand on top of one almost as calloused as his. Maybe he should sell. Although there was little hope he could purchase land as good elsewhere, the two hundred pounds would buy Mary McGregor a little croft somewhere, so that she could live out her last few years in comfort. He and his siblings could take their chances, as tenant farmers.

'But I know you will never give in to him.' Mrs McGregor's hand was heavy. 'This land was your father's, and his father's before that. McGregors have worked this earth long before Black Jamie bought his estate from the King.' She moved away, beamed at him. 'I named you after the great Fergus, chieftain and warrior, who fought both the Norsemen and the English. Some day soon, you will take a wife, and your children will farm McGregor land too.'

Fergie sighed. His eyes moved around the table, past Rab and Morag, to his three younger brothers: he was doing this for them – for their descendants, not his own. 'Aye, Ma.' Getting up from the table, he made his way morosely towards the door.

'Son, come back and eat something.'

Rab's voice answered for him. 'Leave him, Mrs McGregor. He has a lot on his mind.'

Ignoring the bitter-sweet understanding which tinged his best friend's words, Fergie strode out into the night.

His horse carried him far into the hills. He rode hard, trying to push thoughts of Black Jamie, his ancestors and Morag's approaching wedding from his mind.

Fergie gripped the reins more tightly, lowering his brawny body until he almost merged with the horse.

Wedding – some wedding!

In a land where the wearing of traditional highland dress was proscribed by the King's law, the nuptials would be a sorry affair. Worse still, as head of the family, it was his duty to escort Morag down the aisle, deliver his sister into the arms of a man whose body he knew better than she ever would!

He galloped on into a wood, ignoring the branches which tore at his hair and trying to rid his brain of petty jealousies. Fergie knew, when it came down to it, he would wipe away his mother's tears of joy, kiss his sister and shake his brother-in-law's hand, then wish the couple well on their new life in America.

The tension began to leave his body.

He would advertise for another herdsman: several of the village boys looked able for the job. Perhaps he'd find someone better than Rab, who would be prepared to work the farm with him as an equal, and share his bed the same way.

Reaching the brow of the hill, Fergie reined in his horse and stared into the distance. From this vantage point, Castle Black was an insignificant dot behind him. He was twenty-eight, strong and healthy. A smile broke over his previously strained features as he stared down at the string road which meandered through the valley below. A solitary coach was making its way along the rutted route.

The only sounds were the snorting of his horse, the gradual slowing of his own breath and the nearby babble of Gonachan Burn.

Then the soft clack of hooves on heather seeped into his ears.

Immediately alert, Fergie guided his horse into a copse.

The soft clack increased in speed.

Fergie held his breath, stroking his mount's neck in an attempt to quiet her.

When the approaching horse finally came into view, it was moving very fast –

Fergie stared.

– but not so fast that its rider's distinctive garb wasn't clearly visible. Following the scarlet flash with his eyes, he watched the Fox speed down into the valley towards the Stirling-to-Greenock road. The long red cape fluttered in the wind.

Edging out from his hiding place, Fergie gazed at the now distant form. Curiosity gave way to admiration. The fellow had come from nowhere. But there was no doubt where he was going. The highwayman was bolder than ever, and obviously planning to hold up another carriage even with a fifty-sovereign price on his head.

A sudden tingle in his groin took Fergie by surprise as he remembered the vaguely amused eyes behind the scarlet mask. Admiration was swelling to more physical interest in the daring highway robber.

Taking a more veiled route, he tugged at the reins and began to weave his way down the mountainside.

Fergie could barely stop himself laughing out loud.

The Fox tugged a neatly coiffured wig from the skull of an indignant passenger and placed it carefully between the ears of his own horse. 'Wigs dull the brain, my good sir. How do you hope to plead your next client's case successfully with that heap of horsehair on your head? Better it return to the animal who donated it.'

The lawyer snorted with fury.

The gathered group of female passengers tittered behind their raised hands.

The Fox was ignoring most of the jewellery, and was now engaged in an attempt to gain the pocket watch of a younger man.

'The King himself presented that to me, you rogue!'

The Fox chuckled, snatching the fob from where it dangled against the man's stomach. 'Better he had presented you with a pistol, friend! Then you could have risked your life for a mere trifle.' Throwing the pocket watch in the air and deftly catching it again, the highwayman raised his eyes to the coachman. 'Do you have the time, sir?'

The coachman blinked in surprise. 'I cannot afford a time-piece.'

The Fox quickly scrutinised the inscription on the back of the watch. 'Please accept this as a gift, then.' He tossed the Hunter at the startled man. 'With the good wishes of both the King and Baronet Angus of Dalkeith.'

The coachman looked to the irate young man, then back to the highwayman in some confusion.

The Fox slung an arm around the Baronet's narrow shoulders. 'You want him to have it, don't you?'

In the shelter of a nearby thicket, Fergie dismounted, edging closer for a better view.

Angus of Dalkeith looked about to explode. 'Of course.' The assent was uttered between clenched teeth.

'I thought so!' The Fox slapped the Baronet on the back, then lowered his masked face to the man's ear. 'Because, if I hear you try to get it back, I will come to Dalkeith myself, drag you from your bed and thrash the very devil from you.'

The image was too much to bear. Fergie laughed out loud, then tried to smother the sound with his hand.

Too late. The highwayman's hearing was every bit as acute as that of his namesake. 'I think we have company, my fine people, so I must sadly take my leave of you.' He vaulted back on to his horse, eyes never leaving the thicket in which Fergie was hiding. 'Have a safe journey on to Greenock!' Waving his hat, and with his long red hair flowing in the wind, the Fox galloped off into the night.

Fergie was surprised to see several of his victims waving after him.

He was even more surprised to find himself quickly back in the saddle and following the scarlet-clad figure.

Fergie knew the hills like the back of his hand, but even he was amazed at the Fox's vast knowledge of the land. He made no secret of his pursuit, driving his horse harder and more furiously.

Both riders raced across fields, jumping burns and dykes without thought for their safety.

Flying into deep forests then feeling spray hit his face as they skimmed across bogs, Fergie's blood pounded through his body. He gritted his teeth, urging his mount faster still. He was an excellent horseman, but the Fox still led by a short head.

Few men in Stirlingshire could beat Fergie on dexterity of guidance or speed. The fellow must be an incomer. But how, then, was he so familiar with the bridle paths and byways, even down to each rabbit hole and hidden ditch?

What had started as pursuit now became a race, as Fergie drew level with the scarlet-clad man.

Neither regarded the other. Each only had eyes for the next dyke or twist in the road.

When Gonachan Wood appeared before him, Fergie realised the Fox had led him in a complete circle. A scowl darkened his exhilarated features.

He was being played with – again!

As the realisation reached Fergie's brain, the Fox turned his head and smiled. Then putting on a sudden spurt, he edged a few yards in front and disappeared into the dense forest.

Fergie's scowl deepened. 'I'll get you this time, my crimson friend!' He plunged headlong into the thick wall of trees. Seconds later, emerging from the other side, he saw the Fox was nowhere in sight.

Fergie paused, panting with exhaustion. The highwayman had vanished into thin air. Narrowing his eyes, he peered into the darkness. Then the cold muzzle of a pistol was pressing into the back of his neck:

'Stand and deliver.'

Fergie flinched. The voice was very close.

'Deliver what you have been longing to deliver, my handsome fellow.'

Fergie slipped from his horse. He stumbled in his haste.

The Fox laughed, catching Fergie by his right arm and spinning him around. 'Or maybe I should take it from you myself.'

Pushed back against a great rock, Fergie's body was rigid. The Fox increased his grip, hauling one then both of Fergie's arms above his spinning head and holding them there.

'Is it a kiss you want, Fergus McGregor?'

His name had been remembered! For some reason, the knowledge caused Fergie to go limp in his captor's arms.

'The kiss you failed to secure, last night?' With his free hand, the Fox cast his scarlet cape aside then grabbed the front of Fergie's breeches and pulled. 'Or something more?'

Fergie was trembling. This was a new sensation – as different from what he felt for Rab as that which his herdsman felt for

Morag. His limbs were as weak as one of the kittens which played by his hearth. He felt helpless as a newborn lamb, struggling through the February snow.

While the rest of his body was devoid of all resistance and fight, between his legs his cock was trying to burrow its way into the hand which was now tearing at what remained of his modesty.

Seconds later his breeks were tattered ruins at his ankles. His shirt went the same way, ripped from his body and hanging open to reveal his sweating chest.

Still holding Fergie's wrists against the tree, the Fox quickly divested himself of scarlet shirt and trousers.

Fergie barely registered his captor's increasing nakedness. His gaze was fixed on the man's face – or what he could see of it, behind the crimson mask. 'Take it off.'

The Fox smiled. 'I hardly think you are in a position to make demands, Fergus McGregor.' The highwayman moved closer.

Fergie inhaled deeply, drawing the scent of the man's exertion into his lungs. 'Please – I need to see your face.'

A chuckle brushed his cheek. 'So you can turn me in to the authorities and claim the bounty on my head? I think not, Fergus McGregor.'

'I would never turn you in.' His shoulders slumped. He continued to stare into the masked, vaguely smiling face. Then a moist firmness pressed into his thigh, tearing his eyes lower.

The highwayman's long auburn hair curled over pale shoulders. Like most redheads, the man's torso and arms were smooth and hairless. Between two small but erect nipples, a tiny cluster of freckles marred the flawless skin.

Fergie moaned, wanting to kiss each of those beautiful sun-spots. The fist around his wrists was almost painful. But the discomfort was nothing compared to the raging ache in his heavy bollocks.

Their bodies were separated by two inches of darkness. Fergie's head lolled forward, pupils swelling with desire. Overhead, the moon moved out from behind a bank of cloud. Three feet below Fergie's dilating pupils, his quivering shaft stuck out at a

45-degree angle. He gasped, staring past his own hard cock to his captor's twitching rod, which mirrored his own.

The highwayman's prick flexed, then shuddered as low laughter shook its owner's body. 'Want a bit of fox meat do you, Fergus McGregor?'

The question tore his eyes back to the masked face. Fergie could only moan. He was undulating against the tree trunk, trying to ease the hot itch which was causing his arsehole to spasm uncontrollably.

'Want to taste it?'

Fergie's knees turned to water. His spine was almost raw, dragged bloody against the rough bark.

'Do you want to feel the Fox's cock spurting deep inside you?'

His hips jutted forward. His breath was shallow and uneven. His lower body ground back against the treetrunk while he lunged at his captor's face, mouth yearning to feel another's mouth.

Still holding his captive's wrists in an iron fist, the highwayman ducked away from Fergie's attempt at a kiss, chuckling softly. 'You'll have to earn the Fox's cock, my sweet friend.'

Something cold and hard moved up the inside of his thigh. Fergie cried out, twisting in the grip. 'Please, please –'

His entreaties only increased the highwayman's amusement. 'Words are cheap, Fergus McGregor. Actions are something else.'

The cold hardness playfully stroked the underside of his bollocks. Fergie's back arched in need. He could feel his own arousal dripping from his gaping piss-slit, running down his shaft where it cooled and tightened the delicate skin. His addled brain tried desperately to identify the object. Then the highwayman was pressing the shape against the side of Fergie's cock. His responding howl was half-shock, half-arousal as he made sense of the shape.

'My pistol needs cleaning.'

'Anything – anything!' The words burbled from his dry lips. 'Give me a rag and a rod and I will clean it inside and out with pleasure, sir.' The idea of sitting naked, scouring the man's weapon did strange things to Fergie's already inflamed blood.

His response only served to bring another chuckle from the Fox, who was now standing to one side, playfully running the barrel of his pistol up and down Fergie's shuddering length. 'We don't need a rag –'

The words seemed to condense on the side of Fergie's neck.

'– and we already have two rods.'

He gasped, feeling the Fox's other hand tight around the root of his cock. Seconds later, another length of hard maleness had formed a sandwich around the pistol's seven-inch barrel.

'I think we should see if that mouth of yours is good for anything other than rough, insulting words, Fergus McGregor.'

The change in tone took him by surprise. The playful teasing had gone, replaced by an almost bitter note. Before he had time to think about it further, Fergie's wrists were released and he was falling away from the tree and on to his knees. Hands numb, arms aching, and with his cock jutting up at the night sky, he stared helplessly into the Fox's now cold eyes.

Then the tip of the pistol was stroking his bottom lip and Fergie's mouth was opening.

The muzzle was cold and oily-tasting. Fergie's stomach rebelled as the highwayman roughly pushed the gun past his lips.

The Fox loomed down at him, his pale naked body shining in the moonlight.

Fergie tried to relax, staring at the second rod of iron which pushed through the air in parallel with every thrust of the pistol. His dry mouth was moistening. He could feel but not see the Fox's eyes boring into him with the same intensity as the barrel was now driving between his trembling lips.

He would do it. He would let this fascinating, masked stranger fuck his mouth with the weapon. He would take it willingly.

On top of his clenched thighs, Fergie's bollocks knitted together.

He would do anything the Fox wanted him to, because something about the man was affecting him in a way no other living creature ever had.

Fighting the reflexive clench of his throat and the rising gorge in his gullet, Fergie threw back his head, tightening his lips around the pistol and letting more and more of its seven-inch barrel invade his mouth. His blood turned to ice water, sweat drenched his skin and his prick flexed against his stomach as the Fox's trigger finger impacted with his stubbly chin.

Then the strength returned to his arms, hanging limp and useless at his sides. Fergie's left hand reached up, his shaking fingers curling around the Fox's stiff length. His other hand gripped the pistol butt. Both weapons were cocked. The highwayman's trigger finger trembled.

The knowledge only served to stiffen his cock further. Every hair on his body was erect. His stomach was a tight, twisting knot. Fergie's gag spasmed around seven inches of oily iron. He'd never been so close to death –

Eyes sparkling, heart pounding, he stared up into his executioner's face.

– or felt so alive. Fergie's left hand squeezed, and drew a low moan from the highwayman. His balls clenched painfully, and he pressed down on the Fox's fingers, just as a hot twist deep in his arse sent a volley of release shooting up his prick to splatter his face and neck.

Seconds before a more conventional gunshot shattered the night, the weapon was wrenched from between his lips. The force of the highwayman's push threw Fergie back on to the ground.

Then a hot mouth was on his and he was held tightly in strong, sweating arms.

Six

The sound of pistol fire bounced off Ben Mora and the smaller hills, surrounding two writhing bodies with a thousand echoes.

Calum barely heard it over the rasping breath of the man under him. The acrid stench of gunpowder filled the air. Beneath that, the warm male smell of Fergie's spunk seeped into his nostrils. Muscular legs twisted upward around his back, trying to pull him closer. Calum ground himself against the wetness on the highlander's chest, widening his mouth and sucking Fergie's tongue between his lips.

The taste of his daytime tormentor pushed him over the edge. Gasping into his captive's mouth, Calum's body was suddenly rigid.

Then his cock was shuddering and he was melting into his lover's arms, pumping thick stickiness between his own and Fergie's stomach. Clasped between the highlander's hairy thighs, Calum groaned and shot a second volley. The strength left his body and Fergie's arms tightened.

Calum seized the sides of the highlander's stubbly face and deepened the kiss, thrusting urgently with his tongue while the last dregs of spunk oozed from his slit.

Eventually, their breathing returned to normal.

Sense slowly returned to Calum's spinning brain. Releasing

Fergie's face and bracing his arms each side of the man's head, Calum broke the kiss.

He had done it – he had done what he had promised himself he would never do.

Fergie beamed up at him, an idiotic smile bisecting his flushed face.

The expression only served to increase Calum's regret. Behind the scarlet mask, the skin around his eyes was hot and damp with effort.

Fergie removed one hand from Calum's shoulders and ran his fingers through his lover's thick red hair. 'The colour of a fox's coat, but softer.'

Calum winced at the affection he heard in the words.

Three feet below, their softening cocks lay side by side, their seed mixing.

Abruptly, Calum disentangled himself from the other's sweating limbs. He got to his feet and began to dress.

'Will you take off your mask now?' Fergie's voice was still husky from the sex.

Calum didn't reply. He bent down, grabbed a handful of grass and wiped his cock before struggling into his crumpled red breeches.

'Surely you know you can trust me.' A note of embarrassment entered the highlander's lilting voice. 'I trusted you with my life, when the barrel of your pistol was halfway down my throat.' He laughed self-consciously. Then his voice grew more serious. 'How can you doubt me when I say I would never betray you to the authorities?'

Calum frowned. Captain Carmichael's paltry fifty sovereigns' ransom was the least of his problems. He fumbled for his shirt.

Why hadn't he merely fucked him?

Why hadn't he forced Fergus McGregor to his insolent knees and made the highlander suck the spunk from his cock?

Calum sighed. Why had he kissed him? The memory of their mouths hot and needy against each other caused his curled prick to twitch. And made his chest hurt.

'Please?' The voice was closer.

Hurriedly fastening his shirt, Calum spun round.

Fergie was standing before him, scratching at his balls and with his shaggy head cocked quizzically. Naked, and with his skin still pink from their passion, the highlander suddenly seemed very different. The grinning, brawny farmer with his cruel tricks and hurtful words was a million miles away from this blushing, vulnerable man.

Calum's guts knotted.

Fergie's expression was halfway between fear and apology. 'You know my name – and you know every inch of my body, including part of me no other man has seen.'

Calum watched a further blush drench the worried face.

'But I know nothing about you.' Fergie's head drooped. 'Maybe I am of little consequence, and this is why you chose not to reveal yourself to me. Maybe I am a mere plaything to you. Do you feel only what the fox feels for the vixen, when she is in heat? If that is the case, so be it.' Fergie fell to his knees, grabbing one of Calum's hands. 'Use me any way you wish – tell me when you want me, and I will be there. Tell me what to do, and I will do it.'

Calum's heart raced as Fergie raised the highwayman's still-gloved hand to his lips and kissed it. He knew what it must have cost the man to admit such a thing.

'But give me something to call you, so that he who has stolen my heart can at least have a name.'

Calum's mouth twisted into a frown. He wanted to believe him.

He wanted to believe that if he tore off his mask and announced himself as Calum Monroe, it would make no difference to the feelings of this proud, brawny highlander who knelt before him. His brain told him otherwise.

It also told him to leap on to the horse and race away before he became even more entranced by this man.

Gently, he raised Fergie to his feet, slipping his arms around a sinewy waist. He drew the highlander to him, pushing back a lock of Fergie's tangled hair and nuzzling his neck. 'What need do we have of names, Fergus McGregor?'

Fergie buried his face in Calum's shoulder. 'You felt it too, didn't you?'

Calum stiffened.

'Although we have met barely twice, I feel I have known you all my life.' The highlander's soft lips moved beneath the collar of Calum's shirt. Words vibrated against the back of his neck.

'This is something special, my friend.'

This was foolish – foolish and reckless and defying all logic.

Fergie was stroking his back now, running large rough hands over the silk surface of Calum's crimson shirt. 'And because it is special, I will respect your need for privacy –' a more comradely note entered the lilting voice '– as I respected you as a kindred spirit, when you kicked the English soldier's arse and sent him staggering away over the moors.'

Calum chuckled: that had been most amusing.

Fergie talked on. 'We have more in common than you might think, sir. Perhaps when I prove myself, you will permit me to ride with you some night.'

The laugh died in Calum's throat. 'I work alone, Fergus McGregor. And I'm sure your farm keeps you busy enough.' The words were out before he could stop them.

The highlander raised his head. 'How do you know I am –?'

A sudden whinny from their grazing horses took both men's attention. Moving to the edge of the hilltop in search of what had startled his mare, Calum looked down at the road below.

No carriages. But the approaching band of riders was all too visible. At their head, Calum recognised the greying hair of Captain Carmichael, who was now leading his followers up the steep incline towards them.

'The gunshot must have been reported.' Fergie was immediately at his side.

Calum cursed under his breath. 'Damn Carmichael!'

'Aye, and damn yon Black Jamie who's riding with him!'

A sudden panic drenched Calum's body in a greasy sweat. Turning back from the edge, he pulled on his boots.

Fergie grabbed his arm. 'We can hide until they pass. If we keep quiet they –'

'I must go.' He couldn't risk a double unmasking. Calum pulled away and lunged for his scarlet cape.

But Fergie was too quick. Before Calum could protest, the

highlander was swathing his naked body in the wide scarlet garment and bounding on to his horse:

'Safe home, my Fox!' With a wild cry, Fergie dug his heels into the horse's flanks and both man and mount disappeared down the far side of the hill.

Grabbing his own horse, Calum only just made cover before the pounding hooves of the posse passed within an inch of his nose. When he emerged from the thick copse of trees, he could still hear Fergie's loud whoops, accompanied by the chilling sound of gunfire.

Calum flattened himself on the rocky ground and crawled forward to the cliff edge.

Hundreds of feet below, and heading for Stirling, a scarlet cape was all that remained visible of his courageous stand-in. Calum smiled, removing his mask and tucking it into his pocket. Somehow he knew the pursuing posse would never catch Fergie. He also knew it would take at least an hour for his guardian and Captain Carmichael to realise this, and return home.

Vaulting easily on to his mount, he guided the animal down the far side of the hill and made his way slowly back to Gonachan Bridge.

My Fox.

The unexpected endearment was still circling in Calum's head as he stabled his horse then made his way silently towards the tall fir tree which grew outside his bedroom.

He stopped at its foot, a stupid smile fixed to his face.

There was no need for surreptitious entrances tonight. With a swagger, and once more in his usual clothes, Calum sauntered around to the main door. He walked slowly, staring up at Castle Black's huge stone walls.

Three wings of the building, he knew, were closed off. With only himself, James Black and, until this morning, one housekeeper, there was little point in heating and maintaining chambers no one ever used.

Calum paused, remembering the tiny crofts he'd passed on his way back. As many as eight of his guardian's tenants inhabited two measly rooms, often only one.

Calum sighed. How did they do it? Why did they do it, when others lived in such splendour?

Kicking at a cracked paving stone, Calum wandered on.

For the same reason he could not have gone to court, without James Black's patronage. For the same reason he would be homeless and penniless, if not for James Black's good graces.

Money – or, more precisely, the lack of it. His eyes returned to the steep, dark walls of Castle Black.

And money came from property.

Calum thought about Fergie, one of the few smallholders in the area who actually owned his land. Then those eyes narrowed, and Calum paused a second time. He blinked, then refocused.

Nothing – his eyes were playing tricks on him. He walked on.

There it was again: a flickering on the periphery of his vision. Moving back a little, Calum stopped. And stared.

High up, near the castle's turrets, a tiny flame of light was visible behind a dusty window. Calum's stomach tightened. Had his uncle and Captain Carmichael somehow got back before him? He frowned: no, it wasn't possible – and, anyway, their horses were still missing from the stable.

A worse scenario painted itself in his mind: thieves! Robbers who had watched James Black and the Englishman leave the castle, and were now plundering the place!

He stepped further away from the building, fear sending shivers of adrenaline coursing through his blood. Then he laughed softly to himself. What robber would be so stupid as to leave a candle burning in full view?

Calum straightened his shoulders. Whoever it was, they weren't very bright. That wing of the castle was completely empty – devoid even of the most meagre stick of furniture. His guardian had given him a tour, when he'd first arrived, and Calum knew the few rooms he hadn't seen were locked, their keys lost decades ago.

So what was going on?

Curiosity replaced the fear. Eyes focused on the flickering flame, Calum quickly counted along the windows to the turrets, calculating the approximate location of the lighted room.

Five. On the left side of the building. Then, before he lost his nerve, he strode purposefully towards the main door.

Armed with a candle of his own, he swept another cobweb aside and continued along the dusty corridor.

This was a part of the castle he never knew existed. When conducting him on the guided tour, three months earlier, James Black had waved a dismissive hand towards the rickety staircase which had carried Calum to his floor, claiming it was an architectural folly and led nowhere.

He shivered. His guardian had been wrong – or he'd been lying.

A floorboard creaked underfoot and Calum cried out. Dozens of spiders scuttled away from the sound, their shadows huge and eerie on the pine-panelled walls. Calum's Adam's apple was bobbing convulsively. He tried to steady his hand, hoping his shriek had not reached the ears of whoever was in that room.

The candle gradually stopped shaking, its yellow light illuminating more of his surroundings. Another cobweb wisped across his face. He swallowed down another gasp, then ducked under the corridor-wide web.

Obviously, no one had been here for decades. But if that was so, how had the intruder gained entrance to the room? Had he climbed the sheer wall?

His mind began to race, throwing several unthinkable possibilities into his already confused brain.

On his right, Calum recognised the distinctive bulge of the stairs which led to the turret room. To give himself something solid to concentrate on, he began to count aloud. 'One.' His voice was a quavering whisper as he passed the first, heavy oak door.

'Two.' He cleared his throat, wishing he had retained his pistol, instead of secreting the weapon, as usual, under Gonachan Bridge with the rest of the Fox's equipment.

'Three.' The word was louder than he'd intended. Calum leapt back as a large rat raced over his foot and down to the far end of the corridor.

'Four.' His heart was thumping in his ears. Why hadn't he at least lifted a walking stick from the hall stand downstairs? Why had he come, unarmed, to face God knows what? And what was he going to do, when he confronted whoever – or whatever – lurked in that lighted room? Calum stared at the ancient, pitted surface of the fourth door, reluctant to pass.

He clenched his fists. What was he scared of? What was the worst that could happen? Most likely, James Black had instructed Flora to clean up here, and she'd omitted to extinguish the candle upon leaving. Calum took a deep breath, moving onward. Various factors still made no sense, but he didn't think about them as his trembling hand reached out to seize the door handle.

'Five.' Steeled for the worst, Calum's fist tightened and his fingers began to turn.

Then a hand clutched his shoulder. He screamed, throwing the candlestick into the air and spinning round.

Through the yellow flame of another light, he found himself staring into his guardian's cadaverous features.

'But I did hear something, Uncle Jamie.' Back in his bedchamber, Calum allowed his guardian to help him undress. Despite the shock of being discovered, he had regained enough of his wits to realise mentioning the candlelight would only bring more questions as to what he was doing beyond the walls at this time of night.

'No doubt you thought you did, my boy.' James Black carefully folded his ward's shirt then placed the garment over the back of a chair. 'Dreams can play tricks on the mind.'

'I know the difference between dreams and reality.' Calum sighed, eschewing his nightshirt and jumping into bed. 'And I definitely heard noises.

'You gave me quite a fright, when I found your room empty. I was about to call for assistance, when I heard you counting.'

Calum frowned. 'That's nothing to the fright you gave me, up there.' He raised his eyes to the ceiling, wondering how far above him was the strange, still-lighted room. 'But I did hear something.'

'All right, my boy.' His guardian turned and moved towards him. His gaunt face was creased with concern. 'What sort of something?' James Black sat down on the side of the bed. His dark eyes flicked between Calum's still-flushed face and his ward's hairless chest. 'You know that wing is closed off, and as such unused.'

A cold fist clutched at his bollocks, more unsettling than anything he'd felt in that dusty corridor. 'Just – something.' Calum gripped the edge of the sheet, hauling it up around his neck.

'Can you be more specific?' James Black's gaze intensified. 'Creaking? Banging? Rustlings? Footsteps?' The man leant forward, pushing a stray strand of red hair away from Calum's face.

The cold fist tightened. Calum flinched, edging back on to the bed. Words deserted him.

His guardian began to stroke his hair. 'This is an old building – and old buildings settle at night.'

Calum's naked body was bathed in an icy sweat.

'Maybe I should hire old Jack the rat-catcher, just in case we have an infestation.' The dark eyes were all pupil.

Calum tried to sink into the mattress.

Then the hand moved from his red hair. James Black gently patted his ward's cheek. 'Or maybe you heard the rattling chains of some long-dead warrior, who stalks our ramparts when there is a full moon.'

Calum stiffened, shrinking way from the long, well-manicured fingers.

The movement was noted. And misinterpreted. Abruptly, Calum found himself seized and cradled in sinewy arms.

'Oh, forgive me, Pip! There are no phantoms in Castle Black. I did not mean to frighten you!'

Nearly crushed in the iron embrace, the tone of regret in the man's voice surprised Calum. The use of someone else's name startled him further.

'I would never want you to be afraid, Pip – never, never!'

Pip? Pip? The intensity of the embrace was squeezing the breath from his lungs. Seconds passed, lengthening into minutes. Calum felt dry palms moving down over his bare back, and the man's face buried itself in his hair. Then, as suddenly as he'd been seized, he found himself released.

'Try to get some sleep, Calum.' His guardian's more usual, detached tone was back. James Black stood up, turning away and grabbing the candlestick from the bedside table. 'It was all a bad dream.'

Calum lay there, more shocked by the unexpected affection – and the ferocity of the embrace – than anything else that had occurred that evening. He watched an angular shadow thrown high on the wall.

The shade paused in the doorway. 'But if you do happen to hear anything else, please stay in your room. We don't want you bitten by rats, do we?'

Calum found his voice. 'Er, no, Uncle Jamie. Good night.'

'Sleep well.' His guardian left the room soundlessly.

Calum continued to lie there, barely able to move. When his breathing gradually returned to normal, so did his mind. He frowned.

Old buildings did not need flame to creak by. And neither phantoms nor rats lit candles.

Two questions continued to tug at his still-racing brain while his exhausted body pulled him towards sleep.

Why had James Black come to his bedchamber at all, in the middle of the night?

And who was Pip?

Seven

'Be reasonable, McGregor – at least say you will give some serious thought to my generous offer!'

'The matter preoccupies me day and night, sir.' Fergie hid a grin, savouring the note of exasperation which had crept into the normally patient voice. The previous evening with the Fox filled both his body and mind with a haze of happiness, putting him in an excellent humour – even with Black Jamie. He cocked his head, pretending to think. 'I would dearly love to find a solution to this –'

Black Jamie brightened.

'– but the land is not mine to sell. It belongs to my own and my kinsmen's descendants.'

The soberly dressed man scowled with frustration. 'Your farm is much more south than most McGregor land.'

Fergie stretched his arms above his head, enjoying the tiredness of his muscles while James Black searched for further arguments.

'Don't you miss your more northerly kinsmen?'

'Kin is more than mere name.' The Fox, and their unnerving closeness last night, broadened Fergie's grin. 'It extends to anyone who shows kindness to me and mine.'

'Be that as it may.' Black Jamie frowned impatiently. 'Sell to me, and there will be more than enough for you to transport your entire family – and whomever else you wish – back to the highlands.'

'We are quite content here, thank you.' Fergie's expression became more serious. 'A Royal charter from King James VI grants McGregors the right to farm these acres, in perpetuity.'

Black Jamie smiled. 'No one wants to take that right away from you, sir. Farm until you drop dead, if you wish, but think how much less worry and responsibility you will have, as one of my long-term tenants rather than a landowner.'

'Long term?' The words darkened Fergie's sweet mood. He spat a thick wad of phlegm which fell just short of the toes of the landowner's polished boots. 'Since when was a fifteen-month lease anywhere near any reasonable man's understanding of long term?' Levering himself off the tree, where he had been taking his ease between labours, he took a step forward and squared his broad shoulders. 'As long as I have this land, I have security – and my family have a roof over their heads. No one can take that away from us.' He glowered into the tall man's gaunt face, daring Black Jamie to counter.

They stood there, a few inches apart but separated by ideological miles: one owner of a few mere acres, the other lord of hundreds.

'You are being very foolish, Fergus McGregor.'

Fergie clenched his fists. 'No, you are the foolish one, sir. Would not your energies be better spent trying to capture this wily Fox who robs your coaches, than trying to persuade a man to part with that which signifies his very essence as a Scot?'

'Do not concern yourself with the Fox – he will be caught. But we are all His Majesty King George's loyal British subjects now.' Black Jamie pulled back his own, angular shoulders. 'You are living in the past, McGregor.'

Fergie stiffened. 'And you –' he poked a finger into the middle of Black Jamie's chest '– want me to live in a future where I am little better than your slave.'

'Now, now – do not exaggerate, my friend.' Black Jamie's voice was ice. He gripped Fergie's hand, removing the finger and holding him in a strong grip. 'You highlanders, with your stupid hopes and dreams: I would have thought you would have learnt your lesson, after your own Jacobite father died in futility, at the side of that pretender to the throne, James Stuart!'

Fergie twisted free. 'My father died fighting for the likes of you, you –' his blood was up '– you traitor! It shames me that I must call you a Scot, with your fey lowland ways and your fine English clothes!' He wiped his hand on the front of his shirt, wanting to cleanse himself of the man's very touch.

'Traitor, you call me?' Black Jamie's black eyes narrowed. 'You will regret those words, McGregor. You and your type are disloyal knaves. If I had my way, every Jacobite sympathiser would swing from the gallows, along with this damned Fox character!' The man's face was white with rage.

Fergie's fists clenched into tight balls. He drew back his right arm, then paused. He would not give Black Jamie the satisfaction of seeing him lose his temper – nor the excuse to bring the constables to the door of his mother's house. He manufactured a sigh. 'Very well – you have worn me down, sir.' In a parody of subservience, Fergie tugged an unruly forelock and fell to a crouch. 'I will give you my land.' He raised his eyes, palms spreading on to the muddy ground.

Black Jamie looked started, but pleased. 'I am glad you see sense, McGregor. I will have my lawyers draw up the contract and –'

The first handful of dirt caught Black Jamie squarely in the forehead. Fergie chuckled. 'Take it –' he hurled another muddy missile, which spattered against the retreating man's left cheek '– take it all!' Thoroughly enjoying himself now, Fergie scooped handful after handful of sodden earth, pelting the back of Black Jamie's head as the landowner turned and ran towards his horse. 'What's wrong? Don't you want it any more?' In sheer exhilaration, he squelched the mire between his fingers and smeared it over his own face. 'It's good land, Black Jamie – it's McGregor land! And it will stay so!' His laughter obliterated the sound of galloping hooves as the besmirched rider rode off at speed.

Fergie was still chuckling to himself as he hefted his rucksack over his shoulder and made his way back to his fields.

*

Six hours later, there was little to laugh about.

He looked in horror from the slaughtered ewe on the croft's doorstep into his mother's tear-stained face. 'Tell me again what happened.'

'They came up from behind, when I was lifting the potatoes.' The reply came from Rab, whose head wound was being cleaned by a solicitous Morag. 'I could not tell their number, or who they were, but by the time I came round the field had been churned into mire by many hooves and three full sacks were gone.'

'Someone scared all the cows into the corner of the field, Fergie.' His brother Fraser's barely broken voice was hoarse with anger. 'And when I finally got them into the byre, they would give no milk.'

Fergie's rage was less easily expressed. He swept his frail mother into his arms. 'Do not upset yourself, Ma. I will attend to this matter.' Silently, he leant down and kissed his mother's forehead, then grabbed a sack and threw it over the bloody sheep carcass. 'At least we will eat well tonight.' After calming his brothers and making sure Rab's injury was not serious, Fergie scooped the ewe's still-warm body up into his arms, and went back outside to skin and dress it.

In the falling darkness, and under the shelter of an outhouse, he worked quickly and efficiently, boning the meat while trying to temper his own sense of outrage.

Black Jamie! It had to be!

He raised the cleaver and brought it down on the inert flesh with a satisfying thud.

If he could not buy the McGregors off, the twisted devil was obviously attempting to scare them from their land.

Fergie raised his powerful arm, to bring the cleaver down a second time.

But he had no proof. No one had seen anything and, despite hating him, Fergie knew the other farmers held a certain degree of respect for the laird of Castle Black. He could not count on their support, nor had he any right to expect it.

Black Jamie had influence – he was a local magistrate. No one in his right mind would believe the word of a common farmer over that of such an upstanding member of the community. At best, it would be Fergie's word against his.

At worst? Fergie had a suspicion Black Jamie would bring a libel suit against him, for daring to cast aspersions on his good name. The legal fees necessary to defend such an action would drain what little resources he had at his disposal.

Tossing the mutton haunches into the waiting basket, Fergie wiped his brow on the back of a sweating forearm. His mind returned to more immediate problems.

He could not work in the fields all day, then patrol them with a pistol at night. He couldn't keep his mother and sister indoors, for fear something might happen to them. And he did not possess enough weapons to arm everyone.

Lifting the basket of mutton to carry it back into the croft, Fergie cursed himself for a hot-tempered fool. The mud-throwing had been infantile and stupid, but maybe it had succeeded in revealing Black Jamie's true colours.

Now he knew exactly how desperate the man was to have the land. Not that the knowledge served him well, at the moment. Fixing an expression of carelessness to his handsome features, Fergie returned to the croft, where he made a point of playing the damage down and trying to raise his family's spirits.

By the end of a fine meal of broth and braised mutton, he had almost succeeded. Morag and his mother went to bed early with full stomachs, taking Fergie's younger brothers with them.

In the light of the dying fire, Rab stared at him. 'I'll take the first four hours, if you will do until dawn.'

Fergie smiled with relief. 'I did not wish to ask, my friend.'

'You did not need to.' Rab moved forward, cupping a hand behind Fergie's neck and ruffling the long tangled hair. 'Even if I was not marrying into your family, you know I think of you as a brother.'

A wry grin twitched Fergie's lips, and his hands gripped his herdsman's arse-cheeks. He doubted most brothers knew each other as intimately as he and Rab did.

'McGregor problems are my problems too.' Rab's mouth nuzzled Fergie's neck. 'What are we going to do?'

Fergie sighed, pulling Rab closer and grinding his hips against the swelling in his former lover's breeches. The embrace calmed his mind. 'I am not sure. Perhaps a ride in the hills will clear my brain.' Reluctantly, he eased away, tossing Rab his pistol. 'Guard your betrothed well, my friend.' Fergie rubbed Rab's shoulder and strode out into the night.

At the crossroads, Fergie reined in his horse, looking left towards the dark outline of Castle Black, then right along the path which led down the Stirling Road.

The prospect of another encounter with his wild, masked lover made his cock flex in his work breeches.

But tonight had other purposes. The hour was late, and the roads empty. All Godfearing people were in their beds. Fergie knew Captain Carmichael and his hired constables were again out, on highwayman-catching business. He also knew Black Jamie to be again riding with them.

A frown creased his wind-roughened skin. He looked left then right again.

No proof.

His anger had cooled to a hard, icy ball. The need to strike back in kind twisted his stomach into a vengeful knot. But harming Black Jamie's stock or crops would merely hurt his tenants, and Fergie had no desire to do that.

How could he get back at a man who was above the law? How could Fergie at least let Black Jamie know that he knew?

What – or who – was the man's weak spot? The castle, at present devoid of its stately owner? Fergie sighed. He could hurl rocks at the solid edifice all night and do no discernible damage. A cruel smile curled his large mouth as he remembered the simpering, overdressed fop, fresh from the English court. If Black Jamie could be said to feel anything for anything – or anyone – the protective way he looked at his young ward spoke volumes.

Fergie stared at Castle Black's craggy outline, then urged his horse towards it.

His horse tethered to a nearby tree, he pounded on the great oak door a second time.

Still nothing.

Fergie frowned, sucking his damaged fist. Had the fop decided to join the Fox-hunt? He laughed out loud then hammered on the door's surface with his other hand, remembering Master Calum Monroe's awkward seat and the uneasy way he held the reins.

The fellow rode like a girl – worse than a girl! Like an Englishman!

Leaning back and peering up at the narrow, leaded glass windows which punctured the castle's stony face, Fergie's mind returned to his exhilarating ride towards Stirling the previous evening.

He'd given that fool Carmichael a run for his money, twisting and turning through the glens and up steep braes until pursuit had been called off, the riders exhausted. Fergie smiled to himself. The knowledge was an added bonus on top of the warm glow of satisfaction in his stomach which told him he had been of service to his beloved Fox.

Now there was a rider! There was a man worthy of the title! A bold, reckless fellow who made sport of lawyers, army captains, ministers – the type of people who spent their lives lording it over honest farmers like himself.

The familiar resentment brought back the anger. And the purpose of his visit here. Fergie took a step back and kicked the great door. 'Monroe! Calum Monroe!'

Again nothing.

Fergie continued to kick and shout. The activity increased his rage, but did little to stir the castle's occupant.

He was wasting his time. Scowling with frustration, Fergie walked back towards his horse. Just as he grabbed the tethered reins:

'Go away!' A sleepy voice floated down from an open window.

Fergie peered up through the gloom, focusing on the candlelight. Behind it, a blond head was just visible under the nightcap – the dandy even wore his wig in bed! Chasing the scowl from his face, he cloaked his features in a deferential cast. 'Pray let me in, good sir. I am a traveller, lost my way.' His vowels were as smooth as his expression.

'Go away, Fergus McGregor! You do not fool me!'

Fergie chuckled at the irritated tone. 'Don't you want to share another flagon of sheep piss with me, Monroe? I hear you have developed quite a taste for it.'

The window slammed shut.

'Then come and get a mouthful of man piss, if you prefer.' Fergie hauled down his breeches and pulled out his heavy cock. He jiggled it at the candlelit face, cupping his free hand around his mouth and shouting more loudly. 'I will stay here until you come down and face me like a man, sir. And if necessary, I will wait all night!'

Calum frowned.

What had he done now? After last night's strange encounter, he had kept to his room reading, most of the day, and had intended to give the road a miss tonight. Without his scarlet cape, it wouldn't be the same.

Uncle Jamie was out on patrol with Captain Carmichael, allowing Calum the perfect opportunity to do some exploring. And he had been doing exactly that – clad in nightshirt and nightcap, and ready to feign sleepwalking, should his guardian return unexpectedly – when the racket from below had become impossible to ignore.

Now?

Calum risked a glimpse through the dusty window pane.

Fergus McGregor was still there, now pulling hideous faces at him and gesticulating obscenely with his crotch.

Calum ignored the tightening beneath his nightshirt and ducked back down. He did not doubt Fergie's threat to stay there all night. What was less certain was Uncle Jamie's reaction, should he return and find the man responsible for hurling mud at him waiting half-naked on his very doorstep.

Despite his worry, Calum grinned. How he wished he'd seen that! Then he sobered, making his way along the cobwebby corridor, down the steep stairs and back to his room.

There was nothing else to be done. Minus his cape or not, there was one way to get Fergus McGregor's attention and take his mind off whatever insane purpose had brought him to Castle Black in the middle of the night.

★

There was no need to shin down trees.

Slipping quietly from the side door, Calum crept to the stables. He saddled his horse and rode furiously to Gonachan Bridge, where he exchanged his clothes for the Fox's finery. Fifteen minutes later, dressed in scarlet shirt and breeches, and with his red hair curling around his shoulders, he was trotting back into the castle grounds, coming at the building from the approximate direction of Stirling.

He paused, slowing his mount and moving on to the grass.

Fergie was still standing there. His breeches hung in folds at his ankles. Knees bent, and with his fine arse glinting in the moonlight, the brawny highlander was thrusting his groin towards the castle. 'Puts yours to shame, I'll wager, Monroe! Does an English-lover like you even have a cock?'

Calum stifled a snigger.

Fergie began to parade up and down in front of the castle, bouncing his half-hard cock off one pale hipbone, then the other. 'Calum Monroe walks like a crow!' Elbows bent, the highlander flapped mock wings and began to caw loudly.

Taking advantage of the noise, Calum guided his horse closer, stopping a few feet away. Although intended to mock and insult, the strange dance was rather erotic.

'Big Jamie Black swoops like a bat!' Fergie's gate changed. He craned his head forward in an immediately recognisable imitation of Calum's guardian and walked more stiffly. Elbows locked, he flapped his strong arms. 'Aye, a bat that sucks the very lifeblood from my countrymen!'

The voice took on a less teasing tone, and Calum wondered what Uncle Jamie had said to the man earlier that day, which had caused both the mud-slinging and evidently was still upsetting him.

Then the tone vanished, and Fergie took hold of his now fully hard member. Throwing back a head of tangled hair, he jutted fiercely with his hips, raising one clenched fist. Then he howled.

Calum shivered, half-aroused, half-terrified by the sight. It was told that, centuries ago, Highlanders went into battle naked and erect, so great was their love of their land. Picturing himself facing hundreds of Fergie McGregors, Calum did not wonder why their enemies often fled in sheer fear. Then the howl was replaced by low, lustful words:

'Come and get a bit of McGregor cock, Monroe!'

Calum's bollocks tightened. He stretched out a hand and tapped a rigid shoulder. 'Do not waste that on this Monroe, whoever he is.'

Fergie spun round, face scarlet.

Calum smiled at him from behind the mask. 'I can think of much better uses for that fine staff.' Leaning forward on his horse, he patted the space on the saddle behind him. 'But not here.'

Fergie's face was a study in confusion, then delight. He hauled up his breeches and leapt on to the horse.

Seconds later, with the highlander's arms tight around his waist, Calum was riding like the wind towards the hills.

Eight

High on Ben Mora, they dismounted.

Not a word passed between them. They stood, three feet apart, staring at each other.

Calum's heart retained the thunder of his horse's hooves. An east wind gusted against his face, blowing his thick hair out behind him. He barely felt the icy blast as he stood there in his scarlet finery and watched Fergie undress.

The tall highlander pulled his shirt over his head and tossed it aside.

His lover. His ally. A man who had risked his own life, leading the King's representatives off in another direction so that the Fox could make his escape.

Fergie – not Fergus McGregor, the bane of his life and his constant tormentor, who laughed and sniped at him and tricked him into drinking sheep urine.

Calum took in the lightly tanned muscles on the highlander's shoulders. The thick sinew flexed and rippled as Fergie lowered his hands and began to tug off his work boots.

Calum's gaze moved down over the man's chest.

Stiffened by both lust and the night air, Fergie's nipples stuck out towards him. Large and very pink, they thrust through the light covering of brown hair, inviting the touch of fingers and lips.

Like those of his feral namesake, every muscle in the Fox's slim body tensed for action. Adrenaline pumped through his veins, speeding the blood and sending it rushing ever faster to the thick length which pulsed inside his scarlet breeches.

Fergie was crouching now, hauling at the right, then left boot.

Calum focused on the web of sinew which flexed then unflexed over the man's back.

Then the highlander was upright once more, and Calum could see another muscle pushing against the front of the man's breeches.

Fergie tugged at the fastenings and unceremoniously dragged the coarsely woven fabric down over his thick thighs, kicking his feet free of it. The wind dropped abruptly, its very breath taken away by the sight of the now naked, erect highlander.

Calum reached out a hand, closing the gap between them.

Fergie gasped as fingers curled around his shaft, drawing him forward. His strong legs were suddenly useless again.

Calum moaned. The man's cockskin was damp and sticky against his palm. Freeing his little finger, he gently ran the tip over the surface of the highlander's bollocks. A responding shiver shot up his arm, into his brain then straight down into his groin.

Fergie staggered forward.

The taste of the sheep piss returned to him and Calum took a step back. 'You'll follow me, will you not?' Still gripping his lover's shaft, he retreated further.

Forced to walk bow-legged, his cock bucking like a stallion in the grip of a man who made him feel like no one else did, Fergie could only nod. Sweat drenched his skin, and he knew he was blushing. The knowledge forced a thin, transparent drool from his slit and made his arse muscles clench.

If he was here with Rab, or any of the more flexible village lads, Fergie knew they would be on each other with little ceremony.

Calum continued to smile. And retreat.

Arms hanging loosely by his sides and with his drooling cock pulsing against the Fox's cool palm, Fergie could only follow. The blush intensified, heating his skin then turning his body to a frost-coated automaton by turns. The highwayman was a good few inches smaller than him and, despite the fellow's sinewy strength, Fergie knew he had the advantage of weight and muscle strengthened through years of toil.

The Fox veered right.

Fergie stared at the masked eyes, trying to see the face beneath.

The Fox's smile broadened. He continued to walk slowly backward.

Fergie's bollocks hung heavy with need, swinging between his awkwardly parted thighs. Each time his welcomed captor tightened his fist, the swollen sac clenched higher, squirming for release.

Two very different men moved around the flat plateau atop Ben Mora, the slight scarlet figure in the mask leading the broad, naked highlander by the cock, as if he were a bull being taken to stud.

The idea was too much for him. Fergie lunged forward, mouth open and hungry for the highwayman.

The Fox's free hand impacted with his chest, elbow braced and fingers curling in the soft hair. Trying to ignore the way his own wet need was dampening his scarlet breeches and darkening the bright fabric, he kept the man at arm's length then started to move again.

Fergie's breath speeded up. The Fox's hand became a fist, pushing between his nipples and preventing any closer contact. Fergie scowled with lusty frustration.

He was bigger.

He was stronger.

Staring at what he could see of the Fox's smooth face, he knew he was probably older! Had anyone else treated him with such disdain and obvious amusement, he would have called them a tease, thrown them to the ground and fucked the very devil from them.

Abruptly, the Fox stopped. His fist unclenched against the solid, muscular chest, fingers spreading out. Pinkie and thumb spanned the distance between Fergie's tingling nipples. He began to stroke. Wet with the highlander's clear cock sweat, his other hand moved slowly down to the root of the man's prick. Thick, bristling pubic hair rasped against the side of his hand as he drew the man's foreskin back further.

Fergie grunted. Swollen to a great, rosy bulb, the head of his cock pushed painfully against the narrow band of skin which joined it to the dragging foreskin. His eyes left his tormentor's smiling face and he stared down.

Pulled almost perpendicular to his stomach, his rod was now hard as forged iron. Pulsing veins rippled along its beige-coloured surface, carrying more of his adrenaline-filled blood into the still-expanding member.

He was thicker than he'd ever been – even with Rab. The skin was stretched so tight, Fergie began to wonder if cocks could burst.

Then there was no blood left in his brain to facilitate further thought.

The Fox's grip began to slacken. Fergie sighed, half-relieved, half-disappointed. But the hand was not removed. Instead, it began to lower.

Fergie's eyes watered as his straining shaft was pushed downward, its underside almost contacting the quivering surface of his hairy, spasming bollocks. He stooped forward, trying to lessen the discomfort but unwilling to pull away, even though the grip was loose.

Calum couldn't take his eyes off the man before him. His left hand moving to cup Fergie's left pectoral, he continued to tug the highlander's turgid cock downward. The man meat was throbbing in his fist. He could smell the strong, earthy musk of Fergie's body, which mixed with night scents and made his bollocks tighten unbearably. A sudden spasm of cramp flexed his wrist in a sharp jerk. Calum gasped.

Fergie slumped forward, dragging Calum with him.

Then they both were on their knees. Calum's mouth found Fergie's. The fingers of his left hand sank into the highlander's tangled hair, while Fergie's arms wrapped themselves around Calum's shoulders.

Naked chest pushed against silk-clad skin.

Pale, jutting hipbones thrust themselves into a still-clothed groin.

Thigh to thigh, belly to belly they gouged at each other's lips.

The kiss cast its usual spell. Before he knew what he was doing, Calum was lunging against Fergie's sweating body.

The movement caught the highlander off balance. Pushed on to his back, Fergie's head glanced off a rock. He groaned, arms flailing behind him. Then the Fox was between his thighs, raising Fergie's trembling legs and the pain vanished.

Spine arching up off the ground, knees nearly touching his ears, Fergie moaned with sheer pleasure as sticky palms wrenched the cheeks of his arse apart and something wet and warm began to move up and down his crack.

Calum tried to lap slowly, wanting to tease further but knowing he was now also goading himself beyond the endurance of any mere man. Fergie's crack was moist and fetid. Stubbly arse hair brushed roughly against his face as he increased the speed of his actions. Narrowing his tongue, he eased back a little, then ran the tip down the entire length of the delicate crevice, starting at the base of Fergie's spine and ending at the puckered skin just behind the man's balls.

Fergie howled. 'Fuck me, man! For the Lord's sake, fuck me!'

He couldn't speak. The highlander's musk coated his tongue. Calum swirled the man spice around in his mouth, tasting the sweet-sour fragrance and wanting more. He dragged his mouth back up the furrow, pausing at the spasming pucker.

Then Calum was lapping again, circling around and over Fergie's arsehole. His thumbs pushed, digging into the mounds of hard flesh on each side of the crack.

The star-shaped pucker widened to admit him, and Calum dived in.

Fergie roared. 'Fuck me! For Christ's sake, man!' His exhortation was ignored. His arms flailed as he writhed beneath the passionate highwayman. Hands scrabbling for purchase, his fists curled around the prickly stems of a nearby gorse bush and he gasped in pain.

Calum heard only the hammer of blood in his ears. He knew what he should do. He should pull away, get to his feet and leave the highlander here, writhing in unreleased passion. He should tear off his mask, laugh in Fergus McGregor's face and watch the man's horror.

Calum moaned, aware he could do neither. He burrowed more deeply, exploring the inside of the man's body, thrusting his tongue into and along the pink, fleshy tunnel. Lubricated by his saliva and the highlander's own need, Fergie's rectum was a slick, glistening passage. The texture of the flesh, the smell of male arousal and the way the man was thrusting back against him pushed all thoughts of revenge from Calum's racing mind.

Only one urge remained.

He wanted his cock in there. He wanted to watch Fergie's face as he fucked him. Worst of all, he wanted to tear off the Fox-mask at the moment of Fergie's orgasm and have this wild, wonderful man stare in his naked face.

Hauling his tongue from the aromatic orifice, Calum heaved Fergie's thighs from his shoulders and covered the man's body with his own.

They lay there panting. Calum slowly circled Fergie's dry lips with his tongue, watching the man taste his own body and feeling what that taste was doing to the raging erection which pressed into his still-clothed stomach.

Open-mouthed, the breath squeezed from his body, Fergie stared up at his conqueror. 'I am yours.'

A clever, biting response sprang to Calum's lips, but was halted there by the touch of Fergie's tongue against his. He gasped and stared down, watching the highlander's brown eyes until the man's pupils dilated and all that remained was a thin circle of hazel around the black. 'I have always been yours.' Calum heaved himself upright and hauled off his scarlet clothes. 'And everything I have is yours.' His fingers stumbled in their haste, brushing against the head of his aching cock. Calum groaned and looked down.

Foreskin ruffles were pulled tightly back, stretched by the strength of his need for release. Clenching his teeth against the desire, Calum kicked his clothes away and gripped his shaft. 'Now take what is yours,' he said. He rolled on to his back, one hand behind his head.

Fergie didn't need to be asked twice. As the cheeks of Calum's arse scraped against the rough hilltop, the highlander got to his feet eagerly, if a little unsteadily.

Then their positions were reversed and another hand enclosed Calum's shaft.

Crouching, his dark tangled hair hanging over his broad shoulders, Fergie guided Calum's prick back further, positioning the large head against the entrance to his body. Sweat gathered in his bushy eyebrows, trickling down and stinging his eyes. Fergie ignored it, groaning in anticipation.

The highwayman's glans was huge and unyielding. Fergie's sphincter spasmed in readiness. His arse-lips were wet from the Fox's saliva, and he could still feel the warm intrusion of the man's tongue where it had pushed inside him.

A moan from below rumbled through the highwayman's body.

Fergie felt it in his fist.

Then the Fox bucked upward.

The engorged glans pushed urgently against his arsehole. Fergie fought the need for release, as he had already postponed it numerous times since their arrival on Ben Mora. He wanted to savour every second of this. He needed to savour it – needed to know this was all real, and not some strange dream.

Abruptly, all-too-corporeal hands gripped his waist. Fergie blinked sweat from his lashes and lowered his eyes to his lover's masked face.

Calum stared up at the highlander, mouth twisted into a scowl of longing. His balls churned, knitting together and causing his shaft to pulse painfully. His arse left the ground, hips jutting upward while his fingers gripped Fergie's waist.

He needed to be inside the man.

He needed to feel tight arse muscles draw him deep into the highlander's body.

Three months – three long months since he'd had another man's sphincter tight around his shaft. 'Take it! Take it inside you!' The words were hissed from between clenched teeth. Calum thrust upward again.

The movement made Fergie groan louder. The great glans was pushing urgently. Knees locking, calves cramping, he stared down into masked eyes. His sphincter trembled under the assault. Beyond, other rings of muscle spasmed with longing, while the entrance to his body remained dry and tight.

Irritation mixed with lust. Calum's fingers dug into Fergie's sinewy waist, pulling the man down as he thrust ever upward.

Was it his turn to be teased?

Had Fergie McGregor, now naked and straddling him, known the Fox's identity all along?

Was this one final, cruel taunt which would end in the highlander laughing in Calum's face?

Fergie's breathing was shallow and rapid. What was wrong with him? What was wrong with his body? Why would it not do what he wished it to do? A sudden panic sent anxiety coursing through his veins, knotting the very muscle he most wished to relax. Fergie groaned, annoyance at his own body joining with desire.

He'd pushed his own meat into Rab's eager body dozens of times. Several passing travellers, over the years, had also been more than willing to take his highlander's cock into their arses.

But he, Fergus McGregor, had thought himself above such desires. Although he never held it against any of the men with whom he had lain – truth be told, he admired and loved them all the more for it – at the back of his mind he suspected there was something . . . not quite right about taking a cock into your arse.

Men fucked – they were not on the receiving end.

Men took – they did not give.

Fergie knew there was a long tradition amongst his barbarous ancestors of slaking their lusts with whatever was on hand, be that women – willing or unwilling – beasts in the field or, if the worst came to the worst, each other. He also knew there was a certain loss of status afterward – usually explained by excessive drunkenness – for the party who provided the orifice.

He was not drunk. His head was as clear as it had ever been. He wanted this man's cock.

He wanted to feel another man thrust deep into his muscular body, a body which, at present, was using its own strength to prevent that happening. His grip went slack.

Calum thrust one last time, then howled as, no longer under guidance, the head of his cock flexed away from its intended target. In one smooth movement, his shaft was sliding up past the highlander's balls, brushing the man's own erect cock then slapping back against Calum's stomach.

The friction pushed him over the edge. Arching up off the ground, shoulders scraped raw on the rough mountain top, Calum's bollocks knitted together. His fingers clawed at Fergie's skin and he shot against his own belly.

As viscous ropes of milky spunk pumped from his slit, Calum gazed with unfocused eyes into the other's wide eyes. Eyes from which tears now coursed, tracking silvery trails over the highlander's flushed cheeks.

Before the sight could really register, Fergie was prostrate on top of him and burying that tear-stained face in Calum's thick, red hair.

Calum gasped, the breath rushing from his body along with the last few dregs of release. Calloused hands slipped beneath his arched body and he was being held in trembling arms.

Slowly, the strength returned to his own limbs and Calum twisted his legs up over the prone figure. He gently stroked Fergie's back and shoulders, cradling someone he would wish to call friend as well as lover, and waiting for the sobs to subside.

Sometime later, peeling strands of auburn hair from his scarlet face, Fergie tried to ease out from the embrace.

The Fox's arms refused to release him.

Embarrassment tingled over his skin. He wanted to stay in those arms for ever – and he wanted to grab his clothes and race from the abortive coupling.

A tentative hand stroked his face.

The affection only served to increase Fergie's discomfort. Gathering his strength, he wrenched himself from the embrace and began to dress.

'What's wrong?' There was hurt in the voice now, along with concern.

'I have a lot on my mind, sir.' Fergie's voice was gruff with humiliation. 'I am sure there are others who can better provide . . . that which you desire.'

A hand seized Fergus's wrist. 'I desire you – and your worries are my worries.'

Fergie spun round.

Masked eyes regarded him with obvious solicitude.

Fergie looked down, his gaze roving over the highwayman's handsome body. A restirring in his own crotch only served to increase his unease. The grip on his wrist tightened.

'Tell me.'

Fergie shivered. Bad enough he could not do what he wanted to do – worse still, to be forced to admit it. He pulled away.

Then the Fox was gripping his shoulders, turning him back round. Dry lips brushed his. 'We are not leaving here until you do.'

The events of the past day pushed themselves into his mind. With the highwayman's hands now resting on his waist, Fergie's own arms draped themselves around the Fox's shoulders and he began to talk.

Nine

Calum goggled, unable to believe what he was hearing. 'You are sure?' Fergie's head was heavy on his shoulder.

'The slaughtered ewe was but a warning. I know Black Jamie is desperate, and will stop at nothing to get me and my family off our land. If he cannot buy me out, he will scare me out.'

Calum pushed a lock of tangled brown hair back from the highlander's frowning face and sighed. He knew his guardian desired the McGregor croft. But killing sheep and attacking Fergie's herdsman – much as Calum disliked the fellow – were actions in a different league from mere dogged perseverance. A wind had got up in the course of their conversation, rustling through the gorse and bringing a chill to his skin.

'If he wants a feud, he shall have one.' Fergie talked on. 'He knows I can give as good as I get.'

Calum felt the highlander's brawny body tighten.

'But I have crops to harvest and stock to attend to. And I have the safety of those I care about to consider. I cannot be in two places at once. If I do not pick the potatoes this week, we will have no crop to sell and no money with which to pay our debts. But if I do bring in the harvest, God knows what havoc Black Jamie's men will wreak back at the croft.' He clenched his fists in frustration.

Calum stroked Fergie's hair. This new strategy on his guardian's part was unfair and cowardly. 'Were you waiting at the castle to . . . talk to the man himself?'

Fergie scowled. 'Nothing as rational. I wanted to hurt someone the way Black Jamie hurt me – and mocking that fop of a ward of his seemed a good idea at the time.'

Calum stiffened, then changed the subject. 'Who is guarding your farm, at the moment?'

'Rab!' Fergie pulled away and jumped to his feet. 'I was due to take over from him at least an hour ago!'

'Do not worry. I will get you home in time.' Calum's mind raced. He hauled on his breeches, tucking his sticky cock inside, then grabbing his boots.

Harassment was illegal, as was the killing of the sheep – not to mention the attack on Fergie's herdsman. And James Black a magistrate, too! Calum frowned. Deep down, his guardian was a reasonable man. He would talk to him and make him see sense. If the worst came to the worst, Calum was not above using a little intimidation of his own: it would not go down well in the village should it become known that an upstanding member of the community was using underhand tactics to force another landowner – albeit a small one – to sell.

'You have enough problems avoiding the constables, and there is a bounty on your head, my Fox. Why do you bother with someone like me?' Fergie's voice cracked unexpectedly.

Calum looked up and met a pair of confused, still-uneasy brown eyes.

My Fox. The title turned his stomach to liquid.

Calum smiled. 'Because I have been waiting for someone like you all my life.' His hand moved instinctively to the mask, which still hid his face. Maybe he could conceal his identity from this man, but he could not disguise his feelings. 'Because I –' he hesitated, then fell back on humour '– want you, and if I must take on half of Blairhoyle's landed gentry to get you, I am prepared to do it.' He winked. 'The Fox always gets his prey, Fergus McGregor.'

The first genuine smile in hours bisected the highlander's rugged face. 'Is that right, now?'

Calum laughed, seizing the man's now clothed waist and

pulling him flat against his own scarlet-clad body. He kissed Fergie soundly on his smiling lips, slipping his tongue into the highlander's startled mouth before pulling away. 'Indeed it is, my beauty.' His hands moved lower, gripping Fergie's arse-cheeks and cupping the solid mounds of muscle. 'And when I finally have you –' he ground his hardening prick into the highlander's groin '– I will never let you go.'

Their eyes locked for a second, before Fergie pulled away.

Calum registered the depth of feeling he saw in those eyes, then turned to his horse.

There would be other times and other places. Dozens of opportunities. But for now, he knew they both had different matters on their minds.

Vaulting up into the saddle, he leant forward and made room for the highlander. When Fergie's body was warm behind his, the man's arms tight around his waist and tangled hair tickling the side of his face, Calum gripped the reins and urged the horse back down the side of Ben Mora.

A few yards from the outline of the McGregor farm buildings, where an oil-lamp burnt dimly, warning words brushed his ear. 'Come no further – you have already taken more risks than is wise.'

Reluctantly, Calum slowed the horse and felt Fergie slip from behind. The highlander stared up.

Calum leant down, cupping the man's sandpapery chin and pulling him into one last kiss. 'Do not worry.' His lips moved in whispers over Fergie's. 'I have certain contacts in the gentry. Meet me tomorrow night, on Ben Mora, and I will bring you up to date with my progress.'

Fergie's eyes widened. 'So this is why you wear the mask – and why the Fox rarely steals anything of monetary value from his victims? You already have money and influence, another life away from the highway!'

Calum laughed softly. 'That other life has little consequence, compared to my nights, these days.' He caressed Fergie's cheek, then straightened back up in the saddle. 'Tomorrow night. Ben Mora.' He grabbed the reins and made to turn.

'I cannot – remember? My duty lies with my family and

guarding my croft, as long as Black Jamie's campaign of harassment continues.'

Calum frowned. 'Then I will come here.'

'It is too dangerous.' Fergie's chestnut eyes glowed in the darkness.

Calum quickly scanned the surrounding area, his gaze alighting on a darker building, a little apart from the others. 'Meet me in the byre, tomorrow at midnight. Then we can both see off Black Jamie's men, should they try anything.'

Fergie shook his head in disbelief. 'You take too many risks, my Fox.'

Calum's heart swelled. 'You gave no thought for the risk to yourself last night, when you led Captain Carmichael's posse away from me.' A sudden wind buffeted his arms, blasting through the thin scarlet fabric and reminding him further that his highwayman's garb was still missing one item. 'My scarlet cape – the one you borrowed.' He executed a mock bow. 'May I have it back, good sir?'

'It is no longer in my possession.' Fergie turned away. 'I lost it somewhere around Stirling.'

Calum grinned at the blush which drenched the side of his highlander's rugged face. An image of Fergie, riding home naked brought a flush to his own cheeks. 'No matter.' His voice was low and husky. 'You may have done me a favour and sent a message to that oaf Carmichael that the Fox's den lies east.' He laughed.

'Who is there?' A dark silhouette, holding aloft an oil-lamp, appeared in the doorway of the croft. 'I am armed. If you attempt to damage this property I will –'

'It's me, Rab.' Fergie's voice was once more loud and powerful. 'Hold your fire.' He glanced round briefly, his tone again a whisper. 'Until tomorrow.'

Calum watched Fergie's brawny outline stride towards the lighted form. When both men were inside the croft, and the door closed behind them, he reined the horse left.

As he galloped towards Gonachan Bridge, his heart raced on ahead.

*

Rab grumbled about his lateness, but was pleased to see him.

After thanking his herdsman and sending him off to bed, Fergie sat beside the fire, staring into the dull embers. A warm glow in the pit of his stomach eclipsed the still-burning coals.

The colour of his lover's hair.

The shade of his shirt and breeches –

His hand moved slowly, dipping under the roughly woven rush mat which covered the floor of the croft. Seconds later, his fingers made contact with a slippery silk lining.

– and the hue of the man's cloak.

Fergie buried his face in the soft fabric, inhaling deeply. The Fox's musky male smell filled his lungs, mixing with his own sweat and the scent of the moors. He sat there wondering vaguely about the man's identity. Laird? Lord? Maybe even a well-to-do kinsman.

His cheeks pressed into the silk cloak, Fergie smiled. There was little of the raucous highlander evident in the Fox's demeanour. But the man had more spirit and cunning than most lowlanders.

His handsome, masked lover was indeed a mystery. Fergie sighed and closed his large brown eyes, wishing his body had not let him down, back on Ben Mora. Sitting there, smelling the traces of the man which still lingered on the scarlet cloak, that same body began to respond.

His fingers moved by themselves, one-handedly unfastening the drawstrings of his shirt and pulling the garment over his head. Boots followed, then breeks. Soon he was naked, still holding the now warm cape which rustled and creased against his body like a second, scarlet skin.

In the hearth, the fire was almost out.

Fresh flames of desire licked around Fergie's groin. He removed his face from the cloak and began to rub the soft silk over his chest.

His nipples sprang to attention. Fergie groaned softly, circling each erect nub with silk-clad palms. A shiver shuddered through him. The hair on his chest joined the salute, standing on end and seeming to push back against the luxuriant fabric.

His neck bent, Fergie opened his eyes and stared down at his groin. Slippery folds of silk draped over his jutting shaft. The hem of the garment hung there, its weight pushing down as Fergie's cock flexed up.

He smiled, watching the way the shiny lining caught the light from the oil-lamp and shimmered in orange flickers. Fergie moved handfuls of fabric down further, rubbing the almost liquid garment over his taut belly. A sudden tightening in his bollocks made his fingers go rigid.

The cloak slipped from his grip, but did not fall. Instead, it hung from his thrusting cock, suspended by the thick length of meat and draping in soft folds around his thighs. Fergie bent his knees.

His smile twisted into an expression of longing as the cape brushed sensuously against his balls and sent a hundred tiny shivers of pleasure racing into his swollen prick. Then his right hand dipped behind, catching one end of the cloak and pulling it between his legs. With trembling fingers Fergie seized the other end.

No longer weighed down by the folds of fabric, his prick sprang up towards his belly.

Fergie bent his knees further, staring at the film of clear arousal which slicked the pink head of his cock. Lips frozen in concentration, he tugged gently with his left hand.

A snake of crimson silk moved down the crack of his arse, wriggling past his spasming pucker and slithering over his balls.

Fergie gasped, and pulled the length of silk back.

The reaction of his body was more intense as the fabric tightened. His balls were filling. The hairy skin of his scrotum clenched. Then the almost taut silk was moving over his perineum and up towards where his arsehole gaped in anticipation.

His eyes narrowed. The friction increased. Fergie lowered his torso further, dragging the silk between his parted thighs more furiously.

He could smell himself over the now faint scent of the cloak's owner. Head parallel with groin, he stared at his velvety cock-head. The pink bulb of his glans was mere inches from his mouth.

Fergie dragged the silken length more vigorously, squirming

with a mixture of pain and pleasure as the fabric cut into his arse-crack and rubbed agonisingly.

There was a fierce itch somewhere beyond his spasming sphincter – an itch he needed to scratch or he would go mad with desire. Brow creased with need, his jaw dropped and he gasped.

The blast of his breath tingled over the head of his prick and caused him to again inhale sharply.

Inches from his face, his shaft flexed again, setting up a reaction of cause and effect which intensified the burning sensation between his legs. Muscles cramped in his thighs, tensing into thick bands of hard sinew. His sphincter, which had clamped shut back on Ben Mora, was now flexing rhythmically against each drag of the silk and every breath on his glans.

He wanted the Fox inside him. He wanted to feel stretched and widened. He wanted to know what it was to give his body completely to another man.

And he knew which man he wanted to give his body to.

Fergie's balls twisted in their silken sac, flinching away from another silky prison. He exhaled noisily, then cried out as his prick flexed, inches from his eyes.

The first rays of approaching dawn glinted in through cracks in the croft's stone walls.

Fergie gasped in release and surprise as his own seed splattered wetly on to his face. The spunk clung there for a few seconds, then began to slowly move down his cheek.

He shot a second time, more strongly than the first. A thick, salty-smelling wad hit his upper lip. Fergie's tongue flicked out and he tasted the sour, viscous spunk. His fingers twisted around clammy handfuls of sweat-drenched silk and he slumped forward on to his knees, moving both hands to his flexing prick to coax a last wad from the widening slit.

Finally, his balls sore and his cock still swathed in scarlet silk, Fergie fell asleep in front of the dying fire.

He only just woke in time to scramble into bed, the cloak clutched in his fist, when he heard his mother stirring, an hour later.

*

It was barely worth going to bed at all, but Calum knew he needed his mind fresh and his wits about him if he was to tackle James Black on the matter of the McGregor croft with anything approaching effectiveness.

He slept fitfully, rising a few hours later far from refreshed.

Speed was of the essence. Calum washed and dressed, eschewing breakfast and heading straight for his guardian's study. Outside the door, he heard voices.

One he recognised immediately.

Calum frowned as the second made itself known to him. Captain Carmichael was mid-rant, threatening the Fox with fates worse than death.

The Stirling lawyer whose wig Calum had snatched two nights ago was apparently writing a letter of complaint to the King himself. Carmichael was in for a thorough tongue-drubbing – or worse – if the highwayman continued to insult and humiliate coach passengers much longer.

His guardian's response to this news was inaudible.

Calum drew back his shoulders and knocked.

The door flew open. 'What is it?' James Black's face was creased with irritation.

'I wish to talk to you, concerning a matter of some importance, uncle. May I –?'

'Later, my boy.' James Black made to close the door.

Calum stopped it with his hand. 'It is very urgent, uncle. You know I would not bother you with –'

'I said later!' The door was slammed in his face.

Calum scowled, moving away from the study. He kicked dolefully at the skirtingboard, trying to think of another strategy.

Fergie's worried face floated before him, his blunt highland features pale with concern.

Calum knocked again.

A second time, the door opened.

Before his guardian could say anything, Calum launched into his prepared speech. 'Uncle, I need to speak to you about the McGregors. It has come to my attention that –' He paused, suddenly unsettled.

James Black was staring at him, his expression softening. 'Has that McGregor brute been taunting you, my boy?'

'No, no!' Calum found himself blushing as he remembered his own teasing of a naked, quivering Fergie. 'I need to –'

'Come back in an hour, Calum.' A cool palm placed itself on his shoulder. 'We will talk then.' Closing the door a little, James Black nodded back into the study. 'Captain Carmichael requires my help too, and I fear his need is greater than yours.'

'But –'

'If Fergus McGregor is upsetting you, I will take care of him for you.' His guardian backed away, reopening the door. 'In an hour or so.'

Calum opened his mouth to protest further but the door was already closing. He clenched his fists in frustration, but knew there was nothing to be done.

An hour – it wasn't long. He could be patient. And at least while James Black was closeted with the captain, Fergie and his family would have no harassment problems.

Wandering over to the narrow, leaded glass window, Calum perched on the sill and stared at the tall grandfather clock which sat beside the study door. He was already counting the minutes.

Sixty passed.

He knocked, only to be told to come back in two hours' time.

One hundred and twenty long minutes ticked by. Halfway through, Captain Carmichael opened the study door and galloped up the stairs to his room, only to return a few minutes later with a roll of parchment.

After two hours, Calum knocked a third time.

A drawn-looking James Black apologised, and suggested Calum go and have lunch.

He couldn't eat while this matter remained unresolved.

An appointment was made for three o'clock that afternoon.

Listening to the slow swing of the pendulum, Calum's attention was taken by a group of local constables beyond the window. He watched them dismount, let themselves into Castle Black and troupe unceremoniously into his guardian's study.

Captain Carmichael emerged and asked Calum, in the absence of any housekeeper, to bring wine and a little bread.

Calum obliged: anything to help speed the proceedings along.

The grandfather clock chimed the quarter, half, then three quarters hour.

Calum's mind was filled with Fergus McGregor, and his assignation at the byre later that evening. He wanted to bring good news – or, failing that, he at least had to know he had tried.

Finally, at half past five, the door reopened and, Captain Carmichael at their head, the six constables re-emerged. Calum barely acknowledged their greetings or smiles. He pushed past them into the study, kicking the door shut behind him.

James Black looked up, his face more gaunt than usual. 'My apologies, Calum – that matter took longer than I anticipated. Now, tell me what –'

'Please leave Fergus and his family alone, uncle. I beg you!' Calum gripped the edge of the desk in sheer frustration.

The dark eyes widened. 'Explain yourself, my boy.' The words were low.

'The McGregors have farmed that land for generations. It is only a small piece of land, compared to your extensive estate.' Calum couldn't look into the dark eyes, so he focused at the top of the man's glossy black head. 'Leave them in peace – they are not worth it. If you want more land, expand southward instead.'

'You surprise me, Calum.' There was a sadness in the voice which surprised Calum more and pulled his gaze back to James Black's face. 'Why the sudden concern for a ruffian who has done nothing but pour scorn on you since you arrived here?'

Calum's heart thumped. 'I am not particularly concerned for Fergie himself.' He waved a hand dismissively. 'But his mother and sister are –'

'When did it become Fergie?' The tone of his guardian's voice changed again.

Calum's heart was thumping louder than ever. Words wouldn't come.

'When did Fergus McGregor stop being *that lout and ruffian*, and become *Fergie*?' James Black rephrased his soft question.

Calum's heart was about to explode. He wanted – nay, had to – tell someone. But tell them what? Fergie knew him only as the Fox, and Calum had no idea how his highland lover would react, should he discover the identity of the man with whom he had spent two, passion-filled nights. When he did speak, it was in low, barely audible words. 'He cares nothing for me, I am sure, but I have grown to respect and admire Fergie McGregor and his way of life.' Calum spoke the inadequate words to the toes of his boots. 'I ask you this, as one Scot to another, Uncle Jamie. Turn your attention from the McGregor farm, and leave them to go about their business.' He trembled, meaning every word while leaving out the hundred other things he felt for the brawny highlander.

His guardian didn't speak.

When Calum eventually raised his gaze from the toes of his boots, he was shocked to see tears sparkle on Black Jamie's eyelashes.

The man turned away abruptly. 'I have other matters to think about, my boy. We are mounting a concerted effort to trap this Fox tonight, and our chances are good. Your eloquent plea has spared McGregor for the moment. But we will talk more of this, when the Fox is safely behind bars.' James Black strode stiffly to the door. 'And now, I must ask something of you.'

'Thank you, uncle – oh, thank you!' It was progress, of a kind. 'Anything – anything!'

His guardian turned. 'You will go to your room and stay there until I come for you.'

The lie came easily. 'Certainly, uncle.' Calum almost skipped through the doorway. 'And good luck with trapping the Fox!'

The posse of constables would be away all night! He could slip out easily, and meet Fergie. The idea of both bringing good news and seeing his love's happy face sent a sudden rush of joy through Calum's body.

As he took the steps to his chamber three at a time, he found himself humming softly.

Fergie.

Naked and waiting.

Naked and waiting and hard.

Naked and waiting and hard for his Fox.

So full was his mind of other things, Calum didn't notice the dark eyes as they followed his progress up the long stairway.

Ten

Fergie padded to the byre door and peered out into the darkness for the twentieth time.

Still nothing – and it was well past midnight.

Returning to where the cows were sleeping peacefully in the corner, he sighed. The day had passed uneventfully enough. Rab had attended to work near the croft, while he himself had made a start on the potatoes and let the cattle graze closer to home, for once.

Fergie leant against the rough wall, fingering the butt of the pistol which protruded from the waistband of his work breeks. If Black Jamie or his men did stray on to his land, he was ready for them. The law would be on his side. Trespass was a serious crime.

He rotated his aching shoulders, trying to release a little of the tension which bunched the strong muscle.

Part was anticipation at the thought of seeing his Fox again.

The rest was due to living under these conditions. All day his concentration had been split between his labours and the possibility of another attack. A scowl bisected his sunburnt face.

These lowlanders waged a sophisticated form of warfare, not one he was used to. Highlanders struck hard and fast, in their enemies faces. This was different, and in many ways all the more effective for its inconsistency.

The whole family had been braced from dawn till dusk for an attack which had not come. This war of attrition was unsettling and wearing, and it would not be long before the strains of waiting began to show in other ways. His teenage brothers were already squabbling, picking fights with each other and anyone else who would argue back. Morag and Rab had sat in stony silence all through the evening meal, evidently over some petty disagreement.

The distant clatter of hooves drifted into his ever cocked ears. Fergie's fist tightened around the pistol handle. He blew out the candle and crept to the open door.

Streaked by moonlight, a scarlet-clad figure bounded from his horse.

Fergie smiled. His grip slackened. The tension drained from his shoulders, seeping lower. He gasped. A fleshier weapon made its presence felt, stretching up against the pistol barrel inside his breeches as the highwayman moved towards him. The touch of cold iron against his cock made him flinch. The sight of his lover's long red hair made his balls sweat.

The Fox was glancing around himself, moving stealthily across the cobbled ground.

The moon slipped back behind a cloud. Under cover of darkness, and waiting until the figure was nearly upon him, Fergie reached out and grabbed the man, hauling him into the byre.

'They are more concerned with apprehending me, I think. That will keep Black Jamie busy for quite a while yet –'

The byre door now tightly shut, and the candle relit, Fergie stared at the still-masked face.

'– and give us time to plan strategically.'

Fergie's eyes drifted lower. All thoughts of Black Jamie fled and he was contemplating a different objective.

The crotch of the scarlet breeches was fuller than before. Fergie could see the ridged outline of the man's prick stretching up towards the waistband. His throat was dry.

The Fox talked on. 'Is there anyone in Blairhoyle with whom your family could stay, in order that their safety is ensured?'

Fergie barely heard the question. Despite the intense fantasy in front of the fire earlier that day, he was again pulled in two directions: he wanted to give himself, body and soul – and he didn't. Unable to drag his eyes from the front of the Fox's scarlet breeches, he swallowed the hard lump in his throat. 'Later.' The sound was more gasp than word. Then a hand rested lightly on his shoulder, drawing him closer.

'I think more than a landowner's concerns upset you last night.'

Fergie shivered. His lover's insight was more unsettling than any of Black Jamie's attacks.

'Am I right?' The hand left his shoulder, moving up into his hair.

Fergie groaned. His own arms hung limp and useless at his sides.

'If you do not wish my attentions, you only have to say. What I feel for you goes beyond our bodies, and I will not make you do anything you do not want –'

'I want it.' The admission was husky. The pistol muzzle was digging into his shaft, shooting arrows of pain and pleasure into his balls. 'I want it, but I am . . . fearful.' A blush drenched his entire body. In the side pocket of his breeches, he felt the outline of the tub of lanolin he'd always used with Rab.

The Fox tilted his face upward. 'Tell me your fears.' He removed his hand. Fergie felt its absence and his heart began to pound. 'Tell me, and I will try to allay them.'

The gentle words only increased his discomfort.

They stood there silently. Fergie's erection pushed ever upward, snaking along the barrel of the pistol until the head was grazing the worn, wooden handle. Finally, he began to talk.

The Fox didn't interrupt, but stood quietly, shifting his hand from beneath Fergie's chin and resting it on the small of his back.

'I know it is stupid, but I cannot get it out of my head that it is not . . . right.' Saying the words themselves lifted a huge burden from Fergie's shoulders. 'That it will make me less of a man, in your eyes.' When, at last, he'd finished, and there was no more left to say, he smiled sadly into a masked face which was full of concern.

'Do you trust me, Fergie?'

He nodded.

'Do you trust me enough to let me banish your fears?'

Fergie's sphincter clenched, and he cursed his body for its betrayal.

'Taking another fellow into your arse makes one more – not less – of a man.' The Fox scanned his face. 'Nevertheless, I respect your fears, and I will not lay a finger on you.'

Confusion creased Fergie's rugged face.

'But if you agree to do as I bid you, I promise your apprehensions will vanish with the first ray of dawn.' The Fox picked up the candle from the floor and held it between them. 'What do you say?'

Fergie began to relax slightly. 'What do I have to do?'

The Fox smiled, raising the candle in front of Fergie's quizzical face. 'Nothing you haven't done a hundred times, probably.'

Fergie hesitated. Then his cock spoke for him, flexing against the front of his work breeks. 'Very well.' A shiver of anticipation clutched at his balls.

'Good.' The Fox moved back a little, settling himself against the byre wall. 'First, you must undress.'

This he could do easily enough. In seconds Fergie had wrenched the clothes from his body. The pistol and the lump of lanolin fell out of his pocket as his breeks hit the floor.

The Fox scooped up the wool grease, looked at it then sniffed the solid block.

Fergie stood there, naked and erect in flickering candlelight. The greasy odour drifted into his nostrils.

'Caress yourself.'

Fergie grinned. This was easy too. As his right hand moved to grip his flexing shaft, the Fox's voice took on a harsher tone. 'Not your prick – you can stroke anywhere but there.'

The commanding note in the highwayman's voice made his body hair stand on end. Cocking his head in surprise, Fergie nevertheless obeyed. His right hand moved back up, and he began to stroke his right nipple. As his fingers made contact with the pink nub, a sudden tingle rippled between his arse-cheeks. He inhaled sharply.

'I want to kiss your nipples, Fergie.'

The words caused the tingle to increase.

'I want to take the left then the right between my lips. I want to breathe on each nipple in turn, feeling your body respond to my breath.'

Fergie's knees turned to water. The tingle between his arse-cheeks was stronger than ever, finding a response in his flexing shaft.

'Do you want that, Fergie? Do you want to feel the sharpness of my teeth grazing your flesh?'

The tingle around his hole became an itch. Fergie could only nod.

'Open your legs, my handsome one.'

Already parted, Fergie widened his thighs further. He increased the pressure on his right nipple, feeling it swell and harden. Then it became almost painful to touch, and the itch between the cheeks of his arse intensified.

'Stroke your arse, Fergie.'

Head lowered, knees bent, he reached behind himself and ran rough hands over two hard mounds of muscle. In the middle of the hairy crack, his hole clenched unexpectedly and he found himself pushing against the palms of his own hands. With every backward action, his cock jutted up towards where the Fox stood. Transfixed by the motion of his body, Fergie's fingertips inched closer to the thickly haired crevice.

'You have felt my tongue there.'

He was grunting now, and the itch was becoming almost unbearable. He dug into his own flesh until the knuckles whitened and his spasming pucker gaped pleadingly.

'Now you will feel your own fingers.' The Fox's voice was closer.

Fergie raised his head.

The highwayman was now naked too, his thick, foreskin-heavy cock thrusting out towards Fergie. He extended the chunk of lanolin, which had already softened in his hand.

Fergie shivered, watching the grease ooze over the man's

palm. 'I want your fingers inside me.' His cock flexed at the idea, while between his bristling arse-cheeks his short nails gouged at the ring of muscle.

The Fox smiled. 'Not yet, my highlander. When you are ready, you will take more than my digits.'

Fergie groaned. He'd never touched himself . . . there. His hips jutted forward, then circled back. Every tension was now focused, and all he could think about was scratching the itch deep inside himself. Mouth open, eyes narrowed in a desire tinged with revulsion, Fergie thrust his index finger past the shimmering ring of muscle then gasped as he felt the heat of his own body.

The Fox's voice was very close to his ear. 'My prick is envious, Fergie. It wants to be there.'

Muscle clenched around his first knuckle. Fergie trembled.

'It wants to feel your body's embrace.'

The itch was driving him wild. Fergie pushed on, feeling the rippling walls of his own rectum caress as far as the second knuckle.

'Now two fingers.'

His legs were shaking. Drawing back a little, he aligned his middle finger with the first, then slid both back inside himself.

'It feels good, doesn't it?'

Fergie could only grunt. The itch was still beyond his reach, although the palm of his hand was now flat against his right buttock. He widened the two digits, feeling the walls of his arse pulse wetly back against the pressure.

Then he heard another sound. Turning his head slowly left, Fergie moaned.

The Fox was stroking himself, rubbing the now-liquid lanolin over and up the length of his ruffled prick.

Fergie stifled a sob of need. Withdrawing his own fingers a little, he thrust back inside.

'Now take them out.' The Fox's voice was hoarse.

'No, no!' Fergie continued to fuck himself, increasing the speed and trying in vain to reach the source of the burning itch but failing again and again.

'Now!'

The tone was back – the sharp, commanding tone which demanded obedience.

Fergie was panting now, as he reluctantly wrenched his fingers from his own arse. His hole gaped, empty and swollen by the friction. His nipples ached. His cock felt like it would split its very skin. His balls shimmered within their hair sack, heavy with undisgorged passion.

But his hole hurt most of all. He wanted to be filled. No, he needed to be filled by something larger and stronger than his own fingers. 'Fuck me, my Fox.' The words were whispered.

'We made a deal, Fergie. I will not touch you. If you want my cock inside you, you must put it there yourself.'

He blinked through blurring vision to where his highwayman was now easing himself on to a heap of hay. Barely able to walk, Fergie staggered over to his prostrate lover.

The Fox clasped his hands behind his head, nodding down to where his thick eight inches of engorged manhood lay curved against his stomach. 'Take it. Take it, and use it.'

Fergie's knees gave way. Before he knew what he was doing, he was straddling slender thighs and gripping the man's shaft. He hardly heard the Fox's gasp as he roughly seized the prick, positioning its great head against his spasming hole. Staring into masked eyes, mouth open in longing, Fergie tightened his fist around the root of the Fox and sat down hard.

Two grunts rent the air between them. In the corner of the byre, cattle lowed in concern.

Fergie arched his back as the cheeks of his arse impacted with his own fist and the first four greased inches of Fox-cock slid easily past his sphincter. The large head pulsed against the walls of his arse, widening the tight tunnel of muscle and making his balls shiver. Fergie gasped, clenching his teeth and staring down at what he could see of his lover's pleasure-creased face.

The Fox's head and shoulders raised themselves up. Braced on his forearms and with his long red hair hanging back over his shoulders he lunged with his hips, pushing more urgently into Fergie's fist. 'Take it all.'

Somewhere deep inside him, another set of muscles expanded, then contracted. Fergie groaned and knew he wanted to feel every inch of the Fox. He leant forward a little, placing one hand flat on the man's tensed stomach for support. Slowly he uncurled his other hand from around the last four inches of Fox-cock.

For a second they hovered there. Fergie looked down, staring at the lanolin-slicked, beige-coloured shaft which jutted up from its nest of ginger hair and joined his body to another man's. Then he returned his gaze to his lover's face and the strength left his legs. With a low grunt, Fergie's bollocks impacted with pale thighs and the great, pink cockhead was tearing up into him.

The shaft seemed to stab at his very soul. His mouth gaped. Deep in his arse, muscle tightened, gripping the Fox's length in a shimmering vice. His eyes watered and something in the pit of his stomach turned to a warm mush. Almost before he had time to register the sensation, his prick flexed violently and he was shooting into the air, showering his lover's freckled chest and stomach with thick, milky spunk.

His bollocks clenched a second time. His fists tightened. His legs trembled. Arse crammed with Fox-cock and mind a dizzying blur, Fergie fell forward.

His lover lunged up, gripping his shoulders and pushing him backward.

Then, with his prick still spurting between them, Fergie's spine hit the straw-covered ground. His thighs were raised by other hands, and the back of his knees impacted with strong, bare shoulders. With his legs weak as a lamb's, and his fingers buried in his lover's red hair, Fergie felt the cock in his arse start to retreat.

He moaned, pulling his head and shoulders up from the floor. The strength returned to his legs and he tensed every muscle he could, trying to keep the man there.

A low groan from near his ear told him the Fox wasn't going anywhere. With his lover's glans pushing at the other side of his sphincter, and the man's laboured breath hot on his face, Fergie collapsed on to their bed of straw as his lover thrust back into him.

The Fox fucked hard and fast, pounding up and into Fergie and making him harden all over again. The highlander writhed beneath his energetic lover, his vertebrae scraping along the floor with the force of the fuck.

The masked face was inches from his when the thrusts changed in angle and intensity, and the head of the Fox's cock bumped against the rounded gland which nestled halfway up his rectum.

Fergie howled, suddenly feeling the need to piss.

Then he was gripped by sweating arms. The Fox slid his hands beneath Fergie's shoulders, pulling him up and against his quivering body.

Fergie's hands tightened in the man's sweat-drenched hair as something flexed deep inside his arse.

The Fox slammed into him one final time. Then wet warmth flooded his rectum and Fergie came all over again, locked in an iron embrace and with his lover's lips parted against his.

Sometime later, they eased apart. Shivering, and with his fingers tight around Fergie's, Calum allowed himself to be led from the cold byre into the warm croft.

He huddled in front of the fire, still holding the highlander's hand and smiling into the man's pink face.

Fergie grinned, self-consciously.

Calum moved closer, kissing him gently on the lips. 'Well? Did I not tell you if you trusted me everything would be fine?' His words were a hoarse whisper. The reply was more than he'd dare to hope for.

'I think I love you, my Fox.'

Calum stared into huge pupils. There was no mockery in the voice, only a shy sincerity.

One work-roughened hand stroked his face, a long index finger tracing the outline of the mask.

Calum flinched. He laughed. 'You love my cock, I think.'

Fergie's reply was low and earnest. 'Aye, that's true enough. But I also love other parts of you.'

The finger continued to trace the mask.

'And those parts of you which I do not yet know, I wish to with all my heart.' Lips widened, and the highlander leant forward for a kiss. 'Let me see you.' The finger eased itself beneath the disguise.

Calum seized Fergie's wrist and wrenched the hand away. His heart was pounding. Planting a kiss on Fergie's furrowed forehead, Calum rose to his feet. He grabbed his clothes and began to dress.

'As you wish.'

Calum heard the disappointment in the man's voice. He hated the deceit, but had no idea how else to keep Fergie.

'I love you whoever – or whatever – you are.'

Regret twisted Calum's stomach into a tight knot. He wanted to believe it, but could not take the risk. Pulling on his right boot, he stumbled backward, tripping over an upturned corner of rush matting.

A flash of scarlet from beneath caught his eye and brought a smile to his sober face as he steadied himself.

So his highwayman's cloak was not lost after all. The thought of the garment here, with Fergie – maybe held at night, tight in his lover's arms – brought a flush to Calum's cheeks. He casually nudged the rush matting back in place with the toe of his boot, and turned back.

Fergie was still naked.

Calum stared in awe at the man whose body he had recently explored in the most intimate way – at the man whom he undoubtedly loved, but could not have. Pushing all thoughts of the future from his mind, he pulled Fergie into a kiss and concentrated on the present.

The highlander's mouth was warm and wet against his. Fergie pressed the entire length of his body against his mysterious lover's form, wanting to keep him here, with him, for ever.

Calum eventually broke the kiss, aware that the longer he stayed here, the harder it would be to leave. He nuzzled the skin behind Fergie's ear. 'Tomorrow. Same time, same place.' The response vibrated up through the broad chest into his own:

'Aye, tomorrow, my Fox.'

Dragging himself from the strong embrace, Calum managed a smile before disappearing back into the night.

Eleven

Darkness provided an effective cloak.

Calum rode at speed towards Gonachan Bridges, his body still slick with Fergie's sweat. He felt light-headed and weightless. While his physical self hastened the horse onward, his mind tore itself free and he was back in the McGregors' byre, crouching between the highlander's tensed thighs and pushing himself into the man's arse. Five miles from his destination, the hair on the back of Calum's neck stood on end. He glanced briefly over his shoulder.

Nothing. Just the night and the memory of his prick inside Fergie.

He urged his horse faster, eager to get out of his Fox guise and back into his own clothes. He shivered.

There it was again!

Reining in his mount, Calum paused, ears cocked. He stared around the silent landscape, two senses straining for some explanation of what a sixth was telling him.

Still nothing.

Calum pulled himself together. Captain Carmichael's posse would be miles away: after all, thanks to Fergie's dash two nights ago, they probably believed the Fox to hail from Stirling. Gathering up the reins once more, he rode on.

Reaching the bridge, he dismounted and changed his clothing

quickly. Over the sound of his horse lapping at the burn, the snap of a twig made him jump. Calum's fingers tightened around the handle of his pistol. Flattening himself against the curve of the bridge, he held his breath and listened.

One minute passed.

Two.

Calum peered out from his hiding place. Inches away, two rabbits stared at him with scared eyes, then bounded back into the bracken.

Chuckling, he pushed his scarlet garb deeper into the space between the stones. As he did so, his fingers brushed something metallic. Withdrawing Fergus McGregor's sharp skean dhu, Calum stared at it.

The weapon should be returned to its owner. He would do so tomorrow. Tucking the small dagger back between the stonework, he mounted his horse and galloped off.

Despite the apparently deserted landscape, some feral, vulpine instinct made him follow a convoluted route back to Castle Black, and it was a full hour later that the Fox stole silently into his lair.

He awoke to much clattering and the sound of raised voices beyond the door of his chamber. Throwing himself out of bed, Calum pressed his ear to the keyhole.

'You have the warrant?'

'On its way from Stirling, James, signed by the King's representative himself. It will be in our hands within the hour.

'Excellent! I am looking forward to this!'

Calum frowned. The exchange continued, over the thump of many boot soles.

'A pity the blaggard gave us the slip after Gonachan Bridge, my friend – we could have had him, then and there.'

A cold sweat drenched Calum's body.

'No matter, Michael. We have the items, and I have little doubt when we search that run-down croft of his, we will find all the further proof we need.'

Calum leapt to his feet as the implications of his guardian's words sunk in. He wrenched open the door. 'What has happened?' He stared wide-eyed into James Black's eyes.

'Nothing for you to worry about, my boy.'

The touch of a cold palm on his shoulder reminded Calum he was without his dressing-gown.

A snigger from Captain Carmichael emphasised the fact. 'We are about to apprehend the Fox, young Monroe. Perhaps you would care to join us?'

Calum looked away from his guardian's glowing pupils.

The King's emissary leered. 'But more appropriately clad, I think.'

Calum was past caring. He gripped his guardian's wrist. 'How –? Who –?'

James Black slipped a hand into the pocket of his sombre-hued jacket. Then Calum found himself staring at Fergie's skean dhu.

'We followed McGregor from his croft, late last night. He was spotted two nights ago, without his mask. Led us a merry dance to Stirling, so he did. But this bears his crest and initials –'

Calum blinked at the dagger.

'– and undoubtedly marks him as the Fox.'

Throat dry with panic, Calum turned to Captain Carmichael. The Englishman knew Fergie could not possibly be the Fox: only last week, Calum had held both of them at pistol point. He stared in helpless confusion, aware any such words to that effect would only implicate himself. His mind raced. 'Perhaps the weapon was stolen from McGregor.' He looked back at his guardian.

Black Jamie's black eyes bored into him. 'In that case, he has nothing to fear. A search of his croft will reveal him as an innocent victim.'

Calum nodded vociferously. 'Indeed it will.' Then the words died on his lips as he remembered his scarlet cape, hidden beneath the rush matting in the McGregor croft. Calum stiffened.

'Time will tell, my boy.' His guardian's smile was strange and unsettling. 'But I have a dozen constables waiting to arrest him, if he is the culprit.'

Calum flinched as, almost imperceptibly, a thumb began to stroke the inside of his wrist. He pulled away, covered his genitals and tried to gather his wits about him. 'My apologies for my undressed state, gentlemen. If you will excuse me –' Turning, he darted back into his chamber and began to dress hurriedly.

The warrant was not yet here. He still had a little time.

Minutes later, and now fully clothed, Calum opened the door and peeked out.

James Black and Captain Carmichael had moved into the study.

Silently, and on tip toe, Calum slunk past the door then bolted from the castle. On his way to the stables, he was nearly knocked over by a rider gripping a rolled up section of parchment.

'Give it to me and I will get rid of it!'

When Fergie opened the croft door, Calum ignored the shock on his lover's handsome face and pushed past him.

'I don't remember inviting you in.' The highlander's voice was tinged with amusement.

Calum looked to where an elderly, grey-haired woman was wiping her hands on an apron and moving forward. 'Master Monroe, isn't it?' she said.

Calum nodded respectfully, then turned back to Fergie. 'Give it to me! James Black and his men are on their way here to –'

'Give you what?' Fergie cocked his head. He was sounding less amused.

Calum pushed past him to the hearth where, only hours earlier he had held the man in his arms. Dropping to a crouch, he pulled up a section of matting.

Bare black earth stared up at him.

'What do ye think ye are doing, Monroe?' Fergie's strong hands seized his shoulders.

Calum wrenched himself free. 'Where is it? You've got to get rid of it!' He rushed towards the back of the small croft, opening doors and peering inside.

'Fergus, what is he talking about?' Mrs McGregor's voice trembled.

'Nothing, Ma. He's here to cause trouble, like his damned uncle. And he's not staying.'

Just as Fergie grabbed his neck with one hand and the seat of his breeches with the other, fully intending to eject the unwanted visitor, Calum caught a glimpse of red from beneath a pile of straw. He lunged out of the highlander's grasp, throwing himself on to the crimson fragment and hauling the garment free. 'This! Get rid of it!' He thrust the scarlet cloak into Fergie's bemused face. 'The constables are on their way. I –'

'The constables are already here!'

Calum jumped at the sound of James Black's voice, dropped the cape then spun round.

Armed with a pistol, his guardian regarded him curiously from the doorway. Behind, Captain Carmichael moved swiftly past James Black, spotting the pooling scarlet cape on the floor. 'What's this?'

Constables rushed forward.

Calum froze.

'Fergus McGregor, I arrest you for the crime of robbery on the King's highways. Take him away, men.'

As a struggling Fergie was roughly manhandled past him by five stalwart constables, Calum met the dark eyes.

'Very brave of you to come on ahead, my boy. You took a great risk, but it has paid off,' his guardian complimented him.

In the background, Mrs McGregor was crying softly, pleading with Captain Carmichael to let her son go.

'Brave of him?' A rage-filled voice came from the doorway. 'He is nothing but a cowardly fop!' Calum moved his gaze to where Fergie, his work shirt ripped in the struggle, was staring at him with loathing. 'You will pay for this, Monroe! All of you will pay! I am innocent!'

Black Jamie's laugh was icy. 'I would not be surprised if this place was a hotbed of Jacobite treachery, on top of a den of common thieves. Search it, men! Then impound its contents. They may provide some meagre recompense for what this rogue has stolen from innocent people.'

Attracted by the noise, two younger versions of Fergie tore into the croft and tried to pull the constables off their brother.

Mrs McGregor's sobs grew louder, paralleling Fergie's roars of protest.

Eventually, the entire melee shifted outside.

Alone in the croft, Calum stared at his guardian. James Black's words were low. 'I do not wish to know why you were here, or what you were trying to do.' An unidentifiable expression flickered across the gaunt face.

Then Calum found himself gripped by the arm and propelled out into the yard. In the distance, roped and tied behind Captain Carmichael's horse, Fergie's still-protesting shape was being dragged towards Blairhoyle.

'You have arrested an innocent man!' Two hours later, in the study, Calum paused in his pacing and glowered.

'The proof says otherwise.' Black Jamie barely looked up from his reading matter.

'Proof?' Calum spat the words and recommenced pacing. 'A dagger which may well have been stolen from him, and a cloak he could have found anywhere and taken home?'

'We will see what the judge has to say.' The dark eyes remained fixed on the book.

Calum scratched his head. Fingers tightened in the blond wig and he tore it from his scalp in frustration. 'I heard in the village that Fergie himself was travelling in a coach which was held up by a highwayman! That was probably when his dagger was stolen.' The wig fell from his fingers.

'You know the law, Calum. Ownership of a skean dhu in itself is an offence.' Black Jamie's voice remained irritatingly detached. 'And, if he was robbed, as you say, why did Captain Carmichael's men find a large sum of money in that ramshackle croft?'

Calum groped for a response. 'He has cattle – perhaps he sold a few heads.'

'Perhaps.'

Calum knew when he was being humoured. Striding over to the large desk, he grabbed the book from the man's hands and hurled it across the room. 'Damn it, you know he is innocent!'

He pushed his face closer. 'You merely want him incarcerated long enough to lay claim to his land!'

James Black's icy eyes stared at him. 'And you, Calum – what do you want from Fergus McGregor?'

A cold shiver rippled down his spine. The one certain way of clearing Fergie's name hovered at the back of Calum's throat. He steeled himself, willing to take the consequences, and opened his mouth.

'McGregor's horse was found tied to a tree outside this castle, Calum.' Black Jamie beat him to it. 'What was it doing here?' His guardian stood up, moving out from behind his large desk.

Calum backed away. 'He was with me.' He tore his eyes from tiny, dark pupils. 'And he was with me the night before – and the night before that.' Calum stared at the floor. 'Fergie cannot be the Fox, because each time a coach was robbed, he and I were –' He couldn't say the word.

'You like him, don't you?' There was an unfamiliar, almost tender tone in the voice.

Calum immediately responded to it. 'Oh, Uncle Jamie –' he raised his head '– I have never felt about anyone the way I feel about Fergie.'

James Black's eyes narrowed. His gaunt face was paler than usual. 'Does McGregor reciprocate these . . . feelings?'

Calum's heart threw itself against his ribcage. He looked away.

'From what I have seen, he seems to hate you more than he hates me, my boy. Infatuation moves you to fabricate these tales of you and the highlander together. But McGregor is a bad lot and –' Black Jamie's laugh chilled Calum's cheek '– even if he should ever choose to return your feelings, he is an unfit companion for one such as you.'

Calum sighed, then flinched as his guardian unexpectedly reached out to stroke his bare head. 'You have your mother's hair, Calum – as well as her fierce, albeit misguided loyalty.' Black Jamie's fingers moved slowly, gently combing the auburn locks.

Calum squirmed but couldn't pull away.

Abruptly, the fingers were removed and Black Jamie resumed his cool, detached tone. 'I cannot prevent you saying whatever you wish at McGregor's trial, tomorrow. But I urge you to see sense and forget that troublemaker.' His guardian moved away. 'Now, it has been a long day. I suggest we both get some sleep. Good night.' Black Jamie strode from the room.

Calum remained there, staring beyond the large desk to the window. Somewhere, out there, Fergie languished in a gaol cell.

Calum clenched his fists.

But he wouldn't be there for long. Tomorrow, he would speak up at Fergie McGregor's trial, and take whatever consequences he had to.

'I came as soon as I heard – do not worry, the herd is safely in.'

Fergie flinched as Rab's rough hand snaked between the bars. The man's palm was warm on his arm. 'How is ma? Is she –'

'Your mother and brothers are staying with friends in the village – I thought it better, in the circumstances. The constables are standing guard over your land.'

He frowned. Unoccupied, the croft would be fair game for anyone who wished to lay claim. But Rab was only doing what he thought fit. For the umpteenth time since he'd been thrown into this dank cell, Fergie cursed Black Jamie and that fop of a ward of his!

'People are saying you have taken up Charlie Stuart's cause and are a Jacobite sympathiser, my friend. They say you rob the coaches to get funds for further rebellion. The talk is, you will be charged with treason against the King tomorrow, as well as highway robbery.'

Fergie scowled. 'I never robbed another man in my life, and the Stuart cause was lost decades ago.'

Rab lowered his voice. 'What was the Fox's scarlet cloak doing in your bed, then?'

Fergie stared at Rab's curious face.

'And where were you, two nights ago, while I was guarding the croft alone?' His herdsman's tone was tinged with sudden doubt. 'And the night before that!'

Fergie found himself smiling. 'No, Rab – I am not the Fox. But I carry thoughts of him in my heart.' Talking quietly and quickly, he took his herdsman and former lover into his confidence.

Rab's eyes were wide by the time Fergie had finished. 'Tell me his name and I will go to him! If he is the brave fellow you say, and loves you as you love him, he will not let you dangle from the gallows in his place.'

Fergie sighed. 'I cannot.' For the past eight hours, he had hoped against hope that his Fox had somehow heard of his arrest and would storm the gaol and rescue him. But apart from a sneering Black Jamie, Rab had been his only visitor. 'I know neither his name nor his face.'

'Then listen carefully.' Rab's voice dropped to a whisper. 'Morag will forfeit her dowry. We will get you the best lawyer money can buy.'

Fergie's frown returned. That money was Morag's by right – and Rab's. They should not have to postpone their nuptials to pay some Stirling shyster to prove what he already knew to be true.

'I will bring you a new set of clothes tomorrow morning, so that you can look your best before the court.' Rab talked on, opening his shirt and passing a flagon of ale and two loaves of black bread through the bars. 'Your innocence will be proved, and all will be well again.'

Fergie took the flagon and the food. He had appetite for neither, as his mind pushed forward to the day ahead.

Treason.

Highway robbery.

He'd seen better men than himself sentenced to death on flimsier evidence. With both Black Jamie – an upstanding local landowner as well as magistrate – and Captain Carmichael, the King's emissary himself, speaking against him, no lawyer in the whole of Scotland would stand a chance.

Rab ruffled Fergie's hair. 'Cheer up, man. Soon you will be free.'

Soon he would be kicking his heels in midair, beneath the gallows in the town square, more like, if he didn't act quickly. 'Aye, Rab.' Fergie found a smile and moved back from the bars. 'Remember me to ma and my brothers, Rab. Take good care of

Morag. Now let me eat and drink.' Waving his friend away, and trying to ignore the confusion on Rab's face, Fergie took a bite from the black bread and settled down amidst his gently snoring cell-mates.

The gaoler, Gordon McLeod, came to check on the prisoners every half-hour, during the night. Fergie could hear the large bunch of keys as they rattled against the man's belt. He removed what was left of his shirt, fashioning the ragged garment into something akin to a rope and checking his cell-mates were still asleep.

Everyone knew McLeod had a weakness for cock, despite being the father of twelve children and well into his fifties. Rumour was he would suck the seed from a shaggy highland bull, if there was nothing else available – rumours which usually ended in a black eye for the gossip, should they reach Gordon's ears. Fergie grinned.

Three such visits later, he was ready. The sound of scraping keys signalled the arrival of the gaoler's silhouette on the dark cell wall. Fergie moved closer to the bars. 'Here, my friend.' The words were a low hiss.

Gordon McLeod paused, turned. Rheumy eyes regarded him with irritation.

Fergie stood up, pressing himself against the iron bars and crooking one finger. 'Come and see what I have for you, Gordon.' He moved his hand to rub the crotch of his breeches. Behind his back, he snapped the rope into a loose noose.

The gaoler snorted dismissively. 'Save your cock for your Jacobite friends, McGregor.'

Fergie grinned. 'My prize-winning ram tells a different story, McLeod. Why suck the stock when you could suck the stock's owner!'

The gaoler's bloodshot eyes narrowed.

Fergie stuck out his tongue, waggling it lasciviously. 'I hear sheep spunk has a rather distinctive flavour, McLeod. Your wife says she can smell it on your breath, when you curl up beside her at nights.'

McLeod's face flushed scarlet. 'You filthy dog!'

Fergie chuckled. 'Aye, dogs too – tell me, Gordon, is collie more flavoursome than Irish wolfhound?'

Fists clenched and, speechless with rage, the gaoler rushed towards him, one arm drawn back.

In seconds, Fergie had slipped the coiled shirt through the bars and was pulling it tight around the man's scraggy neck. With his other hand, he wrenched the large bunch of keys from Gordon McLeod's belt. One sharp twist rendered the gaoler instantly unconscious. Fergie lowered the limp but still alive body to the filthy floor, then quickly unlocked the cell door.

In seconds, he was out and running down the corridor.

Minutes after that, he was sprinting over cobblestones and racing towards the shelter of the hills.

Twelve

Outside the Sheriff Court, Calum stared at the newly printed paper. He read notice of the increased bounty on the head of Fergus McGregor aka the Fox and his heart sank further.

'You wanted proof, my boy?' Black Jamie brandished the sheaf victoriously. 'An innocent man would not flee! An innocent man would stay and clear his name.'

Calum looked away, hiding the regret in his eyes. The Sheriff had been sitting all day, while his constables combed the surrounding area and questioned Fergie's family and friends.

The assault on Gordon McLeod had been added to the list of his lover's crimes, one that couldn't be denied.

His guardian's arm placed itself around his shoulders. 'Do you not see the kind of man you wish to protect?' The words were for his ears only. Black Jamie began to steer Calum towards the waiting carriage. 'On foot, and wearing only the clothes he stands up in, McGregor will not get far.'

Calum walked like a somnambulist, barely aware of the increasing pressure of his guardian's hand.

'The treacherous knave will be brought back alive, tried then hanged. Only then will Godfearing people be safe to travel the roads. And you will be free of whatever . . . unnatural influence the fellow seems to exert over you.'

A cold fist clutched at Calum's bowels. He broke away from

the arm and turned back towards the Sheriff Court. 'I wish to put my testimony in writing.' He moved resolutely through the crowd of curious onlookers. 'Fergie is innocent! He is neither highwayman nor traitor! I will –'

'You will come home with me and we will hear no more of this nonsense.'

The strength with which James Black gripped his arm made Calum gasp. Hauled almost off his feet, he found himself bundled into the waiting coach. 'But I –'

'No more, I said!' Black Jamie's words were hissed. He tapped the ceiling of the carriage with the tip of his cane.

Calum slumped back in his seat. Over the sound of hooves and the coachman's exhortations, one thought repeated itself in his head.

Get away, Fergie. Get as far away as you can.

On the top of Ben Mora, shivering with cold and mounting anger, Fergie surveyed the scene hundreds of feet below.

Antlike constables had been combing the fields and woods all day. Safe in the dense foliage of a tall fir tree, he'd watched them, initially with vague amusement.

But his situation was no laughing matter. He couldn't go back to the croft, even to get his pistol. Crouched amidst the branches, his limbs cramped and uncomfortable, Fergie narrowed his eyes. He'd considered waiting until nightfall, then trying to find Rab. He now knew this course of action would only endanger his friend, and his family.

Eyes narrowing further, he followed the progress of what he recognised as Black Jamie's coach along the road which led from Blairhoyle to the castle. There were two throats in that carriage he would, at this moment in time, cheerfully slit from ear to ear.

Reason pushed itself into his fury-filled mind. The light was fading. The search would soon be called off and resumed at dawn.

Black Jamie and his ward could wait. He had better things to do – most of which involved using the hours of darkness to get as far away from Blairhoyle as he could.

East held Stirling, and the semi-anonymity of a bustling city. And the seat of local judiciary, with a large garrison.

Fergie craned his head. North?

Nearly twenty years before, bloody and defeated, his clansmen had made a journey south to look for peace in the lowlands. They had put down their claymores and set aside their warrior ways for a new life –

Fergie scowled.

– a life men like Black Jamie were determined to ruin. Fergie glanced southward, the scowl deepening.

He had no urge to venture further towards the Borders. Turning his head, he stared towards the setting sun. The Gargunnock Hills blazed red, the heather on their rolling sides turned to a vivid purple.

The great glowing globe called to him.

As he stared, anger subsided into apprehension. Then fear. The sun sank lower and the air grew more chilly. The sky flooded as red as the moors of the highlands had been when they were stained scarlet with the blood of his forefathers. That blood still ran through his own veins.

The blood of wandering warriors, who knew how to survive without the comforts of soft, lowland ways.

Proud blood.

Noble blood.

Resourceful blood.

Stretching himself out along a stout bough, Fergie seized a slimmer branch. The muscles in his strong forearms tensed as he broke the length off, hardly feeling the sharp pineneedles as they dug into his hands. Having denuded the staff of its prickly covering, he leant back against the trunk of the fir tree and surveyed the land he had come to call home.

He knew every cave, each hidden hollow for miles around. He knew where deer strolled and rabbits frolicked. There was much food to eat among the berries and the briars which grew wild on the hills and moors. A man could survive admirably – survive and plot his revenge?

Fergie's mind turned to those who still dwelt hundreds of feet below. His family had friends, in the village – friends who would not see his mother or younger brothers go homeless. They would be looked after. His presence in the area was only a continued danger to them.

He seized each end of his newly formed weapon, flexing it into an arc against his broad chest. He thought briefly of his beloved Fox and his own body sweating and naked beneath a masked form. Fergie clenched his teeth, bending the bough until it almost broke.

He was on his own now.

Checking that all was quiet below, he slid down from his hiding place and once more felt solid earth beneath his feet.

The sun had set, leaving the horizon stained with fading pink.

Fergie stared towards it. He would travel west, beyond the hills, to Greenock and the coast. He would travel under cover of darkness, resting during the daylight hours. Less than a week should do it.

His eyes moved to the darkening outline of his croft. A sudden sadness prickled his skin.

And when he got there?

Fergie gripped his staff and turned back to the Gargunnock Hills. The journey itself was more than enough to think about, at the moment. His stomach rumbled and the evening's chills erected the hair on his arms.

He had a weapon. Food and shelter could wait. Bracing himself against the hilltop winds, Fergie began to make his way down the side of Ben Mora.

Between crisp linen sheets, Calum moaned and turned over again.

Beneath his body, the solid mattress became the warm back of his horse. He could feel the animal's coat smoothly against his bare thighs and arse. And beneath that, the pounding of hooves shuddered up into him.

A scarlet cape fluttered behind him, paralleling his red hair as the wind blasted his face and they rode onward. One hand gripping the reins, the other pressed against a hard stomach, Calum held Fergie tightly. His thighs shadowed Fergie's thighs.

His nipples stiffened each side of his lover's spine. His groin pushed against the muscular mounds of Fergie's arse.

The highlander's bare arms snaked backward, wrapping themselves around Calum's waist. A head of brown, sweating tangles leant back against his right shoulder.

Calum moaned again, hauling his face from the clammy bolster and wriggling around on to his back. Between his straining legs, seven hard inches twitched.

They galloped faster, pursued by an army of blue-liveried Captain Carmichaels. Calum twined the reins around the fingers of one hand and leant forward, removing his arms from around his highlander's waist and gripping on to the horse's mane.

The movement pushed Fergie lower until he was almost flat against the animal's sweating back and his arms were tight around the beast's neck.

Calum grabbed fistfuls of linen, twisting the crisp fabric until it was as damp as the rest of his bed.

Their bodies moved in parallel. Calum's nipples tingled, tracking a rough trail each side of the highlander's spine as the motion of the ride dragged his chest down then back up. His balls clenched against hoof vibrations and he could feel each galloping pound deep inside himself.

Face pressed to the animal's neck, and clinging on for dear life, Fergie's thighs tightened. His hips rose up from the horse and his bonnie white arse pushed back against Calum's groin.

Legs spread, back arching against the sweat-soaked mattress, Calum thrust upward, fucking the cold air of his dark bedroom.

His foreskin stretched further, smoothed from its usual ruffles to a taut, membrane-like covering. The large, pink cockhead impacted with the cheeks of Fergie's arse each time the highlander dipped down on to the horse then pivoted up again.

Calum's mouth opened in a deep grunt of longing. Then a hand snatched at his neck, ripping the scarlet cape from his shoulders.

'We have them! We have the Fox and his accomplice, constables!'

Captain Carmichael's triumphant shout rang in his ears. Calum cried out, lips dry against Fergie's spine. Knees digging into the animal's flanks, he urged it faster and harder, twisting away from the clawlike hand which grabbed for his shoulder.

Fergie's arse was buffeting his flexing shaft in short, rhythmic movements. Calum tightened his thighs, manoeuvring left until his aching cock sat between the flexing cheeks of his highlander's fine rear.

They flew through the night, the posse of Captain Carmichaels hot on their tail.

Calum flattened himself on top of Fergie, gasping as his shaft dragged up and down between tensed arse-cheeks and his balls rubbed against the man's thighs. With each upward thrust, he could feel his lover's pucker spasm open against his throbbing rod. Each time Fergie dipped back down, the tight clenching of his arsehole made Calum's eyes water. He pushed upward, ploughing the hairy crevice and feeling the skin on his cock scraped raw by increasing friction. His glans impacted with Fergie's tailbone at the apex of each thrust, his foreskin stretched and thinned.

The pound of his heart synchronised with the hammer of another heart and the steady rhythm of the ride.

Calum felt the throb in the palms of his hands, the pit of his stomach and lower. The veins on his shaft stood out, swollen and pulsing. He hauled himself back down the moist valley, moistening it further as a clear, watery liquid oozed from his gaping slit and coated both cock and crack.

Then the reins were hauled from his fingers and Fergie was gripping them, pulling the lengths of leather down against the horse's neck and using the straps for balance.

Now free, Calum's hands moved to his lover's slick waist. Fingers slipped lower, searching for the man's hipbones. His palms scrabbling for the bony ridges, another bonelike presence made itself known to him. He gasped, Fergie's engorged cock brushing his knuckles. Calum crouched there, every muscle tensed and stretched to breaking point.

Chest braced on the beast's back, elbows locked, Fergie thrust up.

The embrace of his lover's arse-cheeks gone, Calum groaned in disappointment. Then he howled.

Fergie was back and the tight entrance to his body pressed painfully against the head of Calum's prick.

Calum hissed through his teeth. Hands moving from the highlander's hipbones, he spread his palms over two tensed mounds of muscle.

Beneath them, the horse was practically steering itself. The jolting rhythm of the gallop faded. The wind dropped. The cries of Captain Carmichael became a distant, barely audible sound over the thump of their hearts.

They paused there, suspended above time and motion. Fergie was panting, bearing down on him. Calum felt the delicious surface tension shimmer over his aching glans. Pulled in two directions, he wanted the moment to last for ever – and he longed to feel Fergie's sphincter give way as he thrust past the ring of muscle and sank into his highlander's body.

He lunged up from the mattress, eyes tightly shut but every other sense primed.

He could hear his love's rapid breath. He could smell Fergie's arousal. His lips parted, wanting to taste the aromatic fragrance of the man's sweat.

One hand curling around his sticky shaft, Calum reached out with the other, snatching at the cool air. His fingers contacted other flesh.

Warm flesh.

Calum groaned, running his hand over the muscles of an unseen chest. Between his tensed thighs, his other hand moved faster. He dragged his fist over tightly stretched cockskin and felt a familiar clutching in his balls. He lunged forward, moving his palm over Fergie's smooth, hairless skin, wondering vaguely when and why his lover had shaved his pectorals.

Breath brushed his cheek.

His balls knitted together and something deep inside twisted.

Then the same sixth sense he had felt two nights ago kicked in. His eyes shot open and the dream changed into nightmare.

One arm braced against an older, more mature chest, Calum stared into lust-swollen pupils and pumped wad after wad of thick warm spunk between his own fingers. He fell back on the bed, eyes once more shut and mind full of his highlander's brawny form.

Another hand joined his. Alien fingers continued to milk his cock as shudder after shudder racked his writhing body. Through the receding waves of orgasm, words drifted into his ears.

'Oh Pip – oh my dear one!'

His bollocks lay slack and emptied against his thighs. Calum moaned in confusion, feeling his softening prick caressed and massaged.

Then dry lips touched his and he remembered nothing more.

'Did you sleep well?'

Next morning, James Black smiled at him from the top of the long, refectory table.

Calum looked away. Wispy shreds of two very different dreams – one wanted and longed for, the other unsettling and uncalled for – still draped his mind. 'Yes thank you, Uncle Jamie.' Calum poked desultorily at his lumpy porridge. Now that Flora was gone, his guardian was doing the cooking.

'Good, good.' James Black ate with relish. 'With that awkward McGregor business behind us now, I think we should concentrate on getting back to normal. After I have ensured that the croft is secure, I will set about getting us a new housekeeper.' His guardian made a strange sound.

Startled, Calum raised his eyes from the unappetising fare.

James Black was chuckling – at least, Calum presumed from the light which danced in the man's black eyes that the odd noise was a laugh.

The strange sound increased. His guardian beamed at him. 'I am no cook, I fear, and we cannot live on porridge for ever. There must be one amongst the village girls who is able for the job, so with a bit of luck when we break our fast tomorrow there will be something other than this –' James Black scooped a watery spoonful from his bowl and let it drip back with several wet splatters '– to whet your appetite.'

Calum blinked. The man rarely smiled, never mind laughed.

James Black continued to beam, then pushed his chair back

and stood up. 'A fine morning, is it not?' He strolled stiffly down to where Calum sat.

Rain pelted the leaded glass windows. The wind caught the branches of the great pine tree and tapped their tips against the panes.

Calum wasn't sure what to say. The muscles in his throat tightened: a happy James Black was far more disconcerting than the dour man with whom he usually broke his fast, and he wondered vaguely what was responsible for the sudden lightness of mood.

Abruptly, his guardian veered away from the table and over to the far side of the room. Calum followed with his eyes, watching long, elegant fingers grip the catch and haul the windows open.

Wind rushed into the room, flapping the curtains and howling up towards the ceiling.

'A fine morning indeed. Just the weather for one of your long rides over the hills.'

His stomach turned over.

James Black turned towards him, his gaunt face wet and glowing. 'Perhaps I shall accompany you this evening – or maybe you would like to join me tomorrow, on the hunt.'

Calum goggled. There was something new in the tone.

As suddenly as he'd opened them, James Black closed the windows with a loud snap.

Calum jumped. His guardian strode back towards him.

'I think we need to spend some more time with each other.'

Calum shrank back. 'Uncle Jamie, I do not wish to keep you from your other business. I am quite capable of amusing myself.'

'Business can wait.'

The man bore down on him, looming over Calum like a great grinning black crow. 'Do not make excuses for me. I have been neglecting you. But that will be remedied soon.' James Black placed a hand on Calum's shoulder.

A shiver shook his body. Pulling his eyes from the intense gaze, he twisted his head towards the window.

Rain continued to splatter the leaded panes. His guardian talked on, but Calum didn't hear the words.

Somewhere, out there, was Fergie.

Somewhere, beyond where the wind whipped at the branches of the pine tree, the man who meant most to Calum in all the world was fleeing for his life.

His stomach knotted. He opened his mouth, wanting to confess everything and own up as the Fox. Something told him it would do little good, now. The same thought spurred his brain into action, and he knew the reason for his guardian's good mood.

The McGregor farm could now be confiscated.

James Black would, with a little manoeuvring, own all the land for miles around.

Calum sighed. Helplessness flooded his body, tinged with a deep sense of guilt. He should have owned up earlier.

He should have revealed himself to Fergie, that first night. Perhaps he would have lost his love for ever, but it would have been less painful than the heavy sense of regret and shame which now weighed down on him like a huge stone.

'What do you think, eh?' James Black's voice drifted into his mind.

Calum gave himself a shake. 'Yes, uncle – whatever you say, uncle.'

'That's settled, then. We will talk tomorrow, when I have made arrangements.'

Calum nodded wordlessly. Nothing mattered anymore – nothing he did or said could make any difference to anything that had already happened.

'Perhaps the McGregor girl will be grateful for the work. I doubt she and that betrothed of hers will be going anywhere, now that the family is homeless and penniless.' His guardian strode from the room.

Calum's brain began to work. Maybe he couldn't help Fergie directly, but perhaps there was something he could do, to compensate his love's family for the injustice to which he was party.

Thirteen

Dawn brought a change in the weather. The sun rose unseen behind a thick bank of cloud. Rain soaked his exhausted body, drenching his breeches and hair. Fergie coughed.

He'd journeyed all night, trudging through bogs and thick woods, striding over moorland and past dense bracken. He'd fallen many times, tearing his face and arms on thorny briars then stumbling in the thick mud which dragged at his feet and clung to his ankles like earthy fists.

He staggered onward, startling a flock of grazing sheep which bleated and scattered in front of him. Fergie barely saw them. A flash of a red, white-tipped tail disappearing into the undergrowth did register, however. A scowl bisected his face.

Part of him had hoped beyond hope that he might meet his Fox, at some point during the long, lonely hours of darkness. In truth, that hope had kept him going. Fergie shook his head, banishing images of his valiant lover sweeping him up on to his horse and carrying him to safety.

The Fox was probably home in his warm bed. The Fox didn't care what happened to him.

He, Fergus McGregor, had been a brief plaything, an amusement. Nothing more. And now he was on his own.

Fergie paused, coughing again.

It served him right: no good could come of men loving men.

Rab had left him, for Morag. His other lovers had moved on too.

It was the way of the world. Fergie pulled himself together. Grey light filled his vision as he stared to where the fox had vanished back into its den. He too had to find cover. A shiver shook his torso. More importantly, he had to get dry and warm. Wiping water from his face, he scanned the hills. He had been walking parallel to but a little to the left of the road. No one had passed him, and he had spotted nowhere he could seek shelter.

Fergie gripped his pine staff, peering into mist-draped hills. Then he saw it. Blinking rain out of his eyes, he focused on the small, barely visible shape which clung to the side of one of those hills. Rectangular and low-built, it was the type of hide in which shepherds sought shelter during lambing season and, as such, was unused the rest of the year.

The sight brought a last spurt of strength to his tired legs. Gripping his staff firmly, Fergie increased his speed, weaving around rocks and boulders. Then he was running up the sharp incline, scattering the sheep further in his haste. He had eyes only for the roughly erected structure. His feet slipped and stumbled but he rushed on, grabbing now and then at a few, sticklike trees for balance.

Shelter.

Sleep.

Warmth.

Beneath his feet, the hillside steepened abruptly. Fergie stopped briefly, shoving his pine staff into the back of his belt to free his hands. Then he was grabbing at jutting rocks, climbing upward like a monkey. Still mud-covered, his footing was less than firm, but he clung on with his hands and pressed ever upward. Low cloud drifted around his head in grey wisps, obscuring his view of his destination.

His lungs hurt. His legs ached. Sweat cooled on his icy chest, covering him in a greasy film. His palms were bleeding from the sharp rocks and briars. Still he climbed on.

Ahead, he could just see the turfed roof of the shepherd's hide through the banks of low cloud. The peak was almost sheer now. His heart thumped in anticipation and he stretched out a hand.

The footing slipped from beneath him. Fergie yelled, kicking with his feet to find a foothold. His hand located something solid, but it came away in his fist seconds later. Heart thumping, he gripped again, fingers tightening around the base of a slender bush.

Then he was hanging there, loose pebbles tumbling past him and his legs flailing in midair.

His chest was tight, tighter than the muscles in his arms which were taking the weight of his entire body. Gritting his teeth, Fergie tried to haul himself up by hands alone.

The slender bush creaked disturbingly.

He heard the roots tear and felt himself start to fall.

Time suspended itself, along with his dangling body. His life flashed before his eyes – a life of missed opportunities and loves denied. His Fox, Rab and the few other men with whom he had sneaked around and slaked his secret lusts smiled at him. Others, for whom he had felt desire but not acted upon it shook their heads mockingly.

Regret filled his mind and Fergie found himself praying. 'Save me, God. Save me, and I will admit what I am. I will not hide from myself, nor my nature.' His voice resounded in the deep ravine, its echo bouncing back to fill his ears. 'You made me this way and, as one of your creatures, I will rejoice in what I am!' Then just as the roots of the slender bush broke free, a strong hand grabbed his wrist.

'And what is that?'

Fergie gasped, pulling his eyes from where the bush was falling to the ground, hundreds of feet below.

From a yard above, a white-haired, full-bearded face grinned down at him through the mist. 'Eh?' The voice was deep and booming.

His head spun. Relief swept away all rational thought. Had he fallen, and was this his maker? 'I am a man – a man who loves men!' Fergie howled the words into the face of God.

The Almighty's bearded mouth widened into a less-than-celestial leer. 'Are you, indeed!'

'Aye – I love their bodies and the very bones of them!' Fergie watched the white-haired face loom closer as remarkably strong arms hauled him up to safety. Despite the beard, God looked younger than he did in the pictures Fergie had seen in his mother's family bible. And strangely happier. This was no stern-faced Creator but a benign, beaming saviour.

'I am glad to hear it.'

Another arm reached down from the clouds and encircled his waist. The lilting voice rang in his ears – God was a highlander! Fergie grabbed at all-too-corporeal, plaid-clad shoulders.

And he was wearing the outlawed tartan! Maybe this was not God himself, but an angel. Hauled unceremoniously on to a narrow ledge just in front of the shepherd's hide, Fergie searched his rescuer's outline for wings but saw only the long, protruding barrel of a musket poking up from behind his saviour's right shoulder. 'Are you Gabriel? Or perhaps Michael. Do you want me to tell you my sins?'

The angel winked. 'A sinner, eh?'

Lying prostrate on the ledge, Fergie weakly allowed the white-haired figure to scoop him up in his arms and begin to walk. 'Where are you –? What are you –?'

A rich chuckle seeped through the plaid-clad chest into his limp body. 'Let us get you cleaned up, first, then I will answer all your questions and you can tell me more about your desire for men.'

Exhausted from his night's journey, and further drained by his brush with death, Fergie's last sensation before he lost consciousness was of something firm and solid jutting up from the crotch of the angel's breeches and poking against the base of his spine.

He woke up to the smell of wet wool and burning wood.

Opening his eyes, Fergie raised himself up on one elbow from the pile of sheepskins. He peered through wisps of curling smoke, aware he was naked and all the warmer for being freed of his soaking breeches.

On the other side of the small fire, the snow-haired figure was cooking what Fergie could now identify as rabbit. He cleared his throat. 'You saved my life.'

'It was a life worth saving, if you meant what you said out there.' The man looked over at him, the white tails of his moustache twitching upward. 'How are you feeling?'

Fergie pushed himself upright. The smoke brought back panic. Seizing his still-damp breeches, he threw them over the flames. 'We will be seen! I cannot risk –'

'The clouds mask our fire from prying eyes.' A firm hand grabbed his wrist, staying the motion while curious eyes bored into his face. 'You are safe now, friend.'

Fergie felt the man's strength as his wrist was squeezed, forcing him to drop the wet fabric well back from the fire. He slumped against the rough stone wall of the shepherd's hide.

The man chuckled again, releasing Fergie's wrist and gripping his hand instead. 'Rory MacIntosh at your service.'

He winced as his arm was pumped up and down. 'Fergus McGregor thanks you with all his heart, Rory MacIntosh.'

Returning his attention briefly to the cooking flesh, Rory flipped the rabbit over and smiled. 'Save your heart for he who already has it, Fergus.'

Fergie frowned.

Rory grinned. 'You talk in your sleep, my friend. Of someone you have left behind perhaps?' He raised sky-blue eyes from the darting flames. 'A love, of whom you are still thinking?'

Fergie followed the gaze, looking down to where his cock was beginning to stir. For the first time since he'd escaped Blairhoyle Gaol, he laughed. It was a hollow sound. 'He is part of the past, Rory – my sights are set on a new future.' He tried to believe the words as he spoke them, lowering his voice and retelling the tale of the Fox, Black Jamie and his escape from the law.

Halfway through his story, Fergie took the section of rabbit meat offered and continued to talk through periodic munches. By the time he'd finished, his belly was full and his skin had been thoroughly warmed by the fire.

'I am sorry for your troubles, Fergus. But your problems are far from rare, in this occupied land of ours.' Rory sucked on a bone, then tossed it away and wiped his lips on the back of a hairy forearm.

'What brings you this far south?' Fergus asked as, sated and refreshed, he settled back on the sheepskins and really looked at his companion for the first time.

Rory had dispensed with his swathe of MacIntosh tartan and was now sitting, bare-chested, on the other side of the dying embers. Although his beard was full and white, his skin was younger. His silver hair was tied back from his face and hung over one pale shoulder in a snowy tail. His fleshy chest shone in the firelight, sweat glistening around his surprisingly large nipples which glinted pinkly through the dying smoke.

Wondering how he could have mistaken this very male vision for anything as ethereal as an angel, Fergie's cock twitched. 'You do hail from the highlands, I know.'

His question went unanswered. Rory got to his feet and, shoulders lowered beneath the hide's low roof, made his way round to the pile of sheepskins. Beneath his rough wool leggings, the firm muscles in his thighs flexed with every step. Above his low-slung belt, sinew rippled across a stomach hardened by work.

Fergie's eyes registered the swelling bulge some inches below that stomach, and remembered other appetites not yet satisfied. His cock twitched again, its emerging head rubbing wetly against the inside of his right leg.

The crotch of Rory's breeches hung heavily down between his thighs.

Fergie watched the fabric strain, pulled tight in its efforts to contain the sheer weight of the man's cock and bollocks. He studied the way the pouch swayed with every step Rory took. The motion was hypnotic, and he found himself visualising what the man would look like naked. The responding image caused his foreskin to peel back further, the sensitive glans brushing higher on his thigh.

Rory sat down beside him, his long legs stretched out on the sheepskin. 'My troubles are not yours, Fergus.' There was a sadness in the deep, highland lilt. 'And I will not burden you further.' The melancholic quality slowly left Rory's voice as his hand placed itself on Fergie's thigh. 'At least, not now.'

Fergie inhaled sharply. Heat from the man's palm seeped through his skin. His balls tightened. The hair on the back of his neck stood on end.

The touch was light, almost weightless, despite the size of the man's fingers and the breadth of his palm. Rory's hand remained motionless. Neither of them said anything. Then Fergie placed his own palm on top of wind-roughened knuckles and began to move them up his bare thigh.

Rory turned towards him, bracing his other arm behind Fergie's head.

He felt the imprint of each finger as they slid up towards his groin. His cock shuddered, easing up and over his right hipbone. His shaft was lengthening and thickening, filling with desire for this strange, white-haired man. Widening his thighs, he stared into the face of a fellow highlander, lacing his fingers with Rory's larger digits and guiding the man's palm onward.

Two hands made their way towards his quivering bollocks. One edged ahead. A smile twitched Rory's wispy moustache as he cupped Fergie's burgeoning ball sac.

Fergie moaned, leaning further back on the sheepskins. Then soft hair brushed his face and Rory's mouth was on his. He bucked up from the floor, curling one hand around the man's warm shoulder. The other slipped between their bodies, hauling at Rory's breeks.

Unexpectedly, Rory broke the kiss. His moustache dangled down, wisping Fergie's cheek as he moved back a little.

Fergie stared into twinkling blue eyes. His hand lingered on the stout rod of flesh inside his saviour's breeches, fingers curling around the flexing length.

Then Rory's head was moving lower and warm wet facial hair was trailing in the wake of gentle kisses. Fergie arched his back on the bed of sheepskin as Rory's mouth lingered on his left nipple. Both hands flew to the man's head and he pushed his fingers into a luxuriant silver mane.

Sharp teeth nipped playfully.

Fergie yelped, straining up off the floor. Then Rory's tongue was flicking over his sore bud and he was writhing in pleasure, grinding his bare arse down on to the fleecy bed.

Strong hands slipped beneath him, raising his lower body.

Fergie's cock bounced off his stomach.

Rory's lips continued downward, licking the downy fur on

his belly until Fergie's balls clenched and his fingers tightened in thick white hair.

Then the hands were gripping his arse-cheeks. Fergie grunted, thrusting upward with his hips and grinding back into the palms which held him.

Rory chuckled. His breath swept over the now throbbing head of Fergie's cock and he grunted a second time. Then Rory's mouth was moving down the tightly stretched skin on his shaft, pausing to plant a kiss on every inch. 'You have a bonnie prick, Fergus.'

The words shimmered across his balls, which were already shivering under the rasp of the man's beard.

'Little did I think, when I came outside this morning, I would find such a prize on my doorstep.' Rory's hands began to move, massaging the cheeks of Fergie's arse.

Fergie's head and shoulders left the floor. Straining up, he watched his rescuer's head move lower. The sight stimulated him further. He fucked the air with his cock, wanting to bury his length in the man's mouth.

But Rory had other ideas. Spreading his fingers beneath his writhing companion, he curled the tips into the warm, moist crevice and moved his body between Fergie's legs.

Then elbows were casually heaving his thighs on to bare shoulders and Fergie's head hit the floor with a thump. He gasped, feeling himself inverted and held there. His hands slid from Rory's hair and scrabbled amongst curls of sheepskin.

Fingers caressed the crack of his arse.

Fergie's hole spasmed. His cock throbbed against Rory's cheek. Then a rough tongue was laving his balls and Fergie grunted. Staring wide-eyed up at the tiny opening in the hide's ceiling, he clenched his teeth against the pleasure.

Rory's tongue moved expertly, cradling each bollock in turn then flicking down to the puckered skin behind Fergie's swollen sac.

Fergie thrust upward, his aching shaft skimming the top of Rory's head while the man's mouth continued its ministrations. A low chuckle sent jolting shivers across his testicles. 'Patience, Fergus.'

The breathy words made his balls contract. The tongue snaked on, flicking briefly around Fergie's tight pucker.

The muscles in his thighs clenched. Fergie howled, locking his legs either side of Rory's snowy head.

The fingers left his arse. Hairy forearms moved down then up, breaking the stranglehold formed by his thighs.

Fergie's tailbone hit the ground.

Clothed legs shadowed his. Rory's shins impacted with Fergie's, their weight preventing his flailing legs from further movement. One hand flattened itself on his chest, holding him here. The other gripped the root of his shuddering shaft.

Fergie stared up. Fingers loosened from within the sheepskins and he stretched out a hand.

Rory was sitting on his thighs, staring down at him with a smile half-amused, half-frustrated. 'Let me . . .'

Fergie shook his head, lunging upward. His hand found the bulge in the front of Rory's breeches. He grabbed and held on, watching the silver-haired face crease with desire.

Rory's grip tightened around the root of Fergie's cock. 'Knowing the bodies of men works two ways, my friend.' He stroked with his thumb, rubbing the taut skin at the base of Fergie's prick. 'You must allow them to know your body, too.'

Fergie moaned, his own fingers curling around a covered cock.

His hand was knocked away. In one swift movement, Rory seized Fergie's wrists and pinned his arms to his sides. Using the weight of his chest to hold Fergie's legs apart and still, Rory lowered his mouth on to Fergie's cock.

He was panting, straining up from beneath a man who held and kept him there. As sheathed teeth descended slowly over the length of him, Fergie grunted, feeling the delicious envelopment tight around his girth.

He wanted to force himself deeper between the man's lips.

He wanted to feel his glans bump off the hard cartilage on the roof of Rory's mouth.

He wanted to drown the man with his seed.

But, pinned beneath this snowy-haired seducer, he could do nothing. Rory did it all. Using his tongue, and occasionally his sharp teeth, he caressed and massaged Fergie's prick. First he moved slowly, causing that prick's owner to gasp in delight then grunt in annoyance at the deliberate teasing. Each time Rory's mouth descended on to him and pushed down to the root, the man's beard brushed Fergie's tight bollocks and sent spasms of need through his body. Each time the sheathed lips moved back up his shaft and dragged the foreskin over his engorged glans, Fergie growled.

The motion speeded up abruptly. Rory's great fists tightened around Fergie's wrists and he was moving faster. Each drag downward was more firm and, every time Rory's tight lips caressed the swollen cockhead, his tongue flicked around then into Fergie's gaping slit.

The sensation was too much to bear. With a volume that shook the very foundation stones of the shepherd's hide, Fergie roared, bucking upward and shooting into the warm wet vice which gripped his shaft like a third fist. He pushed on deeper, vaguely aware of Rory's chin against his balls and a distant choking sound. Then the warm tightness was rippling around the head of his cock as Rory's gag reflex coaxed wad after wad from Fergie's spasming slit.

Blood drummed in his ears, gradually slowing to a more sedate tattoo.

Then a spunky-tasting mouth was open on his and his wrists were released. Fergie wrapped his arms around Rory's broad form, thrusting with his tongue and drawing his seed back into his own mouth.

A sudden rigidity in Rory's legs told him the man had found release too. Fergie's kiss was as lusty and unending as the shudders which flowed through Rory's body.

Some minutes later, he found himself staring into a sweat-drenched face.

Rory grinned down, licking Fergie's saliva from his lips. 'Are you in the market for some company, on your journey west?'

Fergie smiled back. 'Aye, company like this I can always do with.'

Some minutes after that, and with night falling outside, they were dressed and heading back out on to the steep hillside.

Fourteen

Calum levelled the pistol at the well-dressed man's forehead. 'Your money or your life, sir!' There was no trace of his usual humour in the words.

Shaking, the man tossed his money pouch on to the heap then shrank back between the other passengers.

Calum leant down, scooped up his booty and turned his horse towards the coach driver. 'The luggage!'

The coachman regarded him curiously.

Calum frowned, readjusting the black kerchief which hid the lower half of his face. There was no time for jokes tonight. He brandished the pistol. 'And be quick about it!'

Fear streaking his face, the coachman bounded from his seat and ran to the rear of the carriage, where he began to rifle through bags and suitcases.

Calum sighed, turning back to regard his shivering prisoners. He'd spent the day moping in his room, avoiding James Black. As luck would have it, some business in another part of the shire had taken his guardian off, and Calum had not been forced into spending any more time than he had to with the unsettling, now smiling, man.

All day he'd thought only of Fergie, cursing himself for his own cowardice on two counts: he should have had the courage to take off the mask and declare his identity to Fergie from the very beginning. More importantly, he should have owned up to the robbery, thus clearing his love's name.

It was too late now to do either.

So he did what he could. 'Bring any coins or notes round here.' He stared towards where the coachman was now hurling handfuls of clothes and possessions into the air.

'Ye want the jewellery too, sir?' The coach driver held up a handful of sparkling necklaces.

'Just the money.' Gemstones and the like were too great a risk: money was the only currency to interest him now.

'As ye wish, sir.' The reply was cautiously reverential.

Calum frowned: he had not been called the Fox by any of the unfortunates he'd held up tonight. Even the carriagemen had noted the change in his demeanour. Moving back on his mount, he unbuckled an already half-full saddlebag and pushed this coach's spoils inside.

The driver approached, holding up a sheaf of notes which Calum also seized. Unlike the previous four, the haul from this carriage was good – maybe there would even be enough here to enable Fergie's mother to buy a new piece of land.

'Are you finished with us?'

Calum spun round. He noted the teasing tone in the voice and his prick stirred inside his sombre garb. He stared at the fellow who had spoken.

A slim, behatted youth grinned up at him, thick brown lashes framing wide chestnut eyes.

Calum took in the almost pretty cast of the boy's face. The fellow stood cockily, feet planted wide apart. 'Or is there anything else I can . . . do for you?' The willowy youth's fingers moved almost imperceptibly towards the crotch of his worsted breeches in a lustful challenge.

The rest of the passengers held their breaths. Beneath the dark-coloured kerchief, Calum's lips twitched into a wry smile, noting the ample bulge inside the youth's breeches. He had a reputation to maintain, and one aspect of that reputation, peculiar to only the Fox, would convince all and sundry that the scarlet-haired highwayman was still active in the area.

Without dismounting, he began to circle the forward youth.

'And what could you do for me, pray?' Calum snatched the coachman's whip from its guard.

Beneath his hat, the youth's face paled.

Calum grinned. His uncurling cock began to stretch itself along the inside of his thigh. 'What do you have that could possibly interest me?' Raising his arm above his head, he flicked his wrist.

The fellow's hat spun from his head, revealing shorn, light brown hair. He gasped, backing away with his hands raised in front of him. Quick as lightening, the whip's leather thong had curled around his right wrist.

Calum chuckled, hauling the fellow towards him. 'I do not want your hat, sir.' He deftly uncurled the thong from around the man's arm, then brought the rigid tip of the whip up over the front of the buttoned jerkin.

A popping sound filled the silence, and Calum flicked the garment from the fellow's shoulders. He tutted. 'I have coats enough already.' The long leather thong of the whip hung loose as Calum continued to use the wooden rod to which it was attached. 'And shirts.'

In seconds, the man's chest was bare. He shivered, but held his ground.

Calum laughed. 'Now, this is more like it.' Leaning over on his mount, he traced the outline of the smooth pectorals with the tip of the whip. 'This I like.' Drawing back his arm, Calum extended the whip to its full length. 'And this.'

A sharp crack filled the air and the fellow's breeches dropped to his ankles.

Calum retracted the leather thong, plucking the belt from around its tip and hurling it into nearby bushes. 'Now let's see what else you've got for me.' As the figure stood shivering in his long underwear, Calum began to circle again.

His heart was with Fergie.

His mind was with his fugitive highlander.

His soul would always belong to the broad, tangle-haired crofter.

But there was no denying where his cock wanted to be, right now. This was a welcome diversion, and his gloomy spirits were lifted as the sight of the seminaked figure raised his shaft from its parallel course along his thigh.

Calum tapped the youth's rounded rear with the flat of the whip. 'A fine arse you have there, sir. What's your name?'

The man yelped and looked up at him, suddenly fearful.

'Not a secret, is it?' Calum tapped his behind more forcefully.

'Angus!' The sound was half-word, half-cry as Calum flicked the rod again.

'Angus . . . what?'

The only response was a stifled moan.

Moving a little away, Calum slipped the whip's tip beneath the waistband of the long woollen underwear and lowered the garment a few inches.

The crack of Angus's rounded behind peeked up at him.

Calum chuckled. 'Ah, it's Angus Fine-Arse, is it not?'

The coachman guffawed. A few of the ladies tittered behind their hands while the men shuffled uneasily.

Calum pushed the fabric down further, exposing two well-formed cheeks. 'Would that be the Aberdeen Fine-Arses, or the Dumbartonshire branch of the family?' Guiding his horse closer, he slid the tip of the whip between those exceedingly fine arse-cheeks and drew it up and down the fuzzy-haired crack.

Angus shrieked and tried to get away.

Calum laughed, raising his arm and thrusting the entire rod down the back of the fellow's underwear. Its tip emerged through the back and buried itself in the soft ground.

Angus struggled, flailing like a butterfly pinned to its mount as the garment stretched around him but refused to give.

Releasing his grip on the whip handle, Calum slid from his horse. Arms folded across his chest, he walked slowly round to the front of the whimpering, confused man. His smile broadened into a grin.

In the same way as the whip handle protruded from the back of the underwear, the outline of another stiff rod tented the front.

Calum moved closer, nodding downward. 'And what do you call this, Angus Fine-Arse?' The fellow was sporting at least nine inches.

The man's face was scarlet. 'My prick, Mr Fox.' He mumbled the words to the ground, almost doubled over in an attempt to preserve what little dignity he had left.

'Mr-Fox-sir to you, Fine-Arse!' Calum introduced a sterner note to his voice, noting the way the head of Angus's cock was impacting with the fellow's downy stomach.

'Sorry, Mr Fox sir!' The reply dropped an octave, husky with need.

'Call that a prick, lad?' Calum grabbed the front of the woollen leggings, dragging it up over the swollen head then wrenching the garment down. 'I've seen bigger on a buck rabbit!'

Angus gasped. 'Yes, sir!'

'Yes, Mr Fox sir, you mean!' Calum goggled at the girth of the cock, which would have shamed a stallion. It nestled on its bed of snuggling bollocks, which were pulled tightly up beneath the root. The fellow's pubic hair was lighter than his head hair. The blond tips caught the light from the coach's lantern and shimmered golden in the yellow oil flame.

Calum feigned a further snort of contempt, aware his own prick was now uncomfortably erect along the inside of his thigh. He gripped his shaft through the fabric of his breeches, repositioning the swollen rod so that it stuck straight up from his groin. As he returned his attention to his captive, a pair of lust-engorged pupils met his.

'Please –' the word was a whisper, and for Calum's ears only '– take me, Mr Fox sir.' Angus fell to his knees, gasping as the rod which held him in place pushed back up the crack of his fine arse-cheeks. 'But not here.' His shorn head flicked around the circle of watching coach passengers.

Calum turned his attention back to the fellow's cock, which had engorged further as he spoke the words. A thin film of moisture slicked the swollen glans, seeping slowly over the velvety flesh and gathering just above the rim of Angus's cock-head. He grinned. 'Why not?' He feigned confusion.

Angus blanched, then flushed scarlet. 'I, er I –'

Calum's arm snaked out. 'I see no reason not to.' His fist curled around the root of the fellow's shaft and he hauled Angus to his feet. Looking away from the mortified face, Calum beamed at the gathering crowd. 'You'd like to see some sport, wouldn't you?' He scanned six assorted faces.

Angus' shaft flexed against his palm. Calum tightened his grip, feeling damp cockskin ripple in his fist.

Four pairs of apprehensive, male eyes looked away from his, grateful it was not they who bore the brunt of the humiliation. Calum zeroed in on the remaining two, who held his gaze with a mixture of desire and curiosity.

A tall woman, her blond hair piled up on top of her head.

And an older, balding man with a neat beard.

Calum beamed, beckoning the pair forward with his free hand.

Angus was shaking convulsively, now. Calum could feel each tremor shudder up the man's shaft and only serve to stiffen that rod further. A corresponding clench in his own balls made him gasp as he nodded his volunteers into position and moved back.

His palm was tacky from Angus' cock sweat. Raising his hand to his masked mouth, he slipped his fingers beneath the black kerchief and tasted the man's desire. 'Can I ask your name, my lady?' Calum smiled at the tall woman who was now standing behind a shaking Angus, the broadest part of the whip handle braced between the fellow's arse-cheeks.

'Jinty MacDuff, friend.' She winked.

Calum grinned. 'And you, sir?' He looked to where the older man was now standing, legs planted a yard apart, his groin level with and obscuring Angus' face.

'Donald MacDonald at your service, Fox.'

Calum chuckled. 'Master Angus Fine-Arse here is giving the service this evening, Donald.' He watched the top of Donald's balding head dip slightly, then heard the unmistakable sound of breech-fastenings loosened. 'Isn't that right, Angus?'

The reply was muffled. 'Yes, Mr Fox sir – anything for you, Mr Fox sir.'

Calum stroked his own burgeoning length, moving around for the best view of the proceedings. He stood side on, eyes flicking from Jinty's lust-filled pupils over to where Donald was rubbing the head of his swollen rod around Angus' gasping lips.

He watched the captive's tongue flick out, eager to lick the desire from the older man's glans.

He watched Donald manoeuvre his cockhead neatly just beyond the fellow's grasp. And he watched Angus' own shaft flex at a forty-five-degree angle, fucking the night air in front of himself.

Then a gasp told him Jinty was pushing on the whip. Hot on its heels, a shriek told him the whip handle was sinking into Angus' body, pushing him forward and on to Donald's cock.

Three mouths moaned as one. Donald's bearded mouth curled back in a snarl of satisfaction. Jinty's painted lips parted, and her hand moved somewhere in the folds of her voluminous skirt.

Calum could no longer see Angus' face, but he could hear great nasal breaths and knew the youth's mouth was too full to permit much more. Leaning back against a tree, the Fox's hand began to move more quickly.

As the threefold encounter continued before his eyes, Angus melted away and Calum saw Fergie, pushed to the ground between two strangers, his two holes filled.

Then he saw Fergie slowly fucking another man's arse with the handle of a whip.

Finally, he saw himself on his knees, gripping the highlander's thighs as Angus was now gripping Donald's, and sucking Fergie's proud length deep into his gullet.

Calum's grunt of orgasm took him by surprise. He barely heard the breathy climax from the tableaux inches away as his cock jumped and flexed inside his breeches, damping the sombre fabric a darker shade still.

The muscles in his legs tightened. His cock shuddered again and he felt the warm stickiness against his stomach.

Inches away, Jinty had fallen to a crouch behind Angus, rubbing herself against the fellow's tensed shoulders. Donald was gripping the sides of Angus' head, pumping the last dregs of his seed between the man's lips.

And the centrepiece himself?

Calum looked down, watching the way Angus' cock was flexing against Donald's undone breeches and showering the folds of fabric with hot splatters.

The sight brought a smile to his masked lips, but failed to chase the longing from his stomach. In one bound, Calum was back on his horse and riding off into the night.

Half an hour later, spunk cresting his pubes beneath his breeches, he saw the outline of Castle Black in the distance. The castle was empty. He could have stayed out all night, forcing his attentions on and having sport with the passengers of more coaches.

Calum slowed his horse. His heart wasn't in it. He rubbed the crotch of his trousers. Crystals of dried release itched against his stomach, bringing back memories of other encounters.

With Fergie.

Calum shook his head to clear it, then remembered his full saddlebags. Reining his horse left, he turned away from the gates and raced towards Blairhoyle.

The village was asleep. Dismounting a little beyond his destination, Calum strode quietly to the house where he knew Fergie's family were temporarily lodging.

No lights shone anywhere as he gently eased open the unlocked door and placed the saddlebags inside. Calum lingered a little, longing to wake the herdsman Rab and enquire after news of his highlander.

But he had caused enough trouble already, and this was the least he could do.

Turning away and closing the door, he also knew it was all he could do.

As he approached steep stone walls, guiding his horse through the darkness, a flickering on the periphery of his vision made him flinch.

Calum paused and found himself staring once more at the candle which burnt in one of Castle Black's unused rooms.

The place was empty! He'd seen his guardian leave, over eight hours ago.

Calum reined his mount towards the stables, where a spare stall told him James Black had not yet returned.

He frowned. Was there someone living in the castle he didn't know about? The idea quickened his breath. Who was it? What was it?

Calum shivered, closing the stable door and making his way towards the main door. Despite the tiredness which tugged at his limbs, and the need to wash and eat, he knew he had to find out.

Once inside, he located and lit an oil-lamp.

Minutes later, he was making his way up the great stairway towards the door at the far end of the corridor. Minutes after that, the familiar musty smell of disuse strong in his nostrils, Calum once again crept along the cobwebby hallway. No need to count the doors, this time. He held the lamp low, following his previous footsteps which were still visible on the dusty floor.

Rats scurried away from the oil-light, telling Calum that James Black had done nothing about employing the services of the village vermin-catcher. Heart pounding, he eventually reached his destination. And hesitated.

The large, dust-covered door loomed in front of him. It obviously hadn't been opened in years. Tentatively, Calum reached out a hand towards the handle, checking briefly over his shoulder that his guardian wasn't again about to leap out of the shadows at him.

The hall behind was empty.

Turning back, he released the dusty handle. Something made him curl his hand into a fist and Calum found himself delivering three soft raps to the ancient wooden surface.

The sound echoed around him, but engendered no response.

He knocked again, in case the occupant was sleeping. Wild thoughts careered through his brain. Perhaps the room held some mad relative, hidden away here to avoid disgrace. Perhaps the door would fly open, and he would find himself face to face with some ghastly fiend.

Calum steeled himself, summoning every scrap of courage he could. His fingers moved to the handle. He gripped, closed his eyes, and pushed.

The doorknob turned, but the door itself didn't move.

Calum sighed, half-relieved, half-disappointed. Releasing the handle, he opened his eyes and stared.

Maybe he could force the lock. Placing the oil-lamp at his feet, he leant back against the door and began to rummage through his pockets for some possible tool.

Then he was falling backward, the door yawning open behind him. Calum shrieked, trying to get his balance but failing. Next thing he knew he was face down on a surprisingly dust-free floor. Slowly, he raised his head –

– and found himself staring at a large oil painting of himself, illuminated by a low-burning candle.

No, not himself. Scrambling to his feet, Calum shrank back.

A woman. About his age, with the same long auburn hair and deep green eyes. Bare-shouldered and wearing a long silken gown. But the resemblance was still striking – they could be siblings.

Calum peered into the face of his doppelgänger.

The woman in the painting was smiling, eyes creased in amusement. At the artist? Or at some secret only she knew?

A shiver of unease erected the hair on the back of his neck. He barely noticed the painting's background as he scanned to the bottom of the canvas. Inside the painting's ornate frame, a scrawled signature was just visible:

J.B.

Did his guardian harbour artistic inclinations? If so, why did he choose to hide this more than competent piece of work up here? Calum dragged his gaze away from the portrait, eyes examining the rest of the small room.

It was empty, apart from a few bits of furniture. And, despite the candlelight, it was dark.

Calum moved further in to investigate. His eyes slowly acclimatised to the gloom. The room was bigger than it had at first appeared, and everything was black: a bench, a low bed, a tall cupboard – even the walls were stained black. Opening the doors of the looming tallboy, Calum blinked in surprise.

The crumpled bolster cover.

Two pairs of his long woollen underwear he had presumed Flora the housekeeper had inadvertently lost.

And behind the familiar items, more garments, yellowing with age.

A handkerchief, bearing the initials P. M.

Several lace petticoats, stiff with something which crystallised under Calum's touch.

A gown. An emerald-green gown. Calum reached out, stroking the fine silken fabric. The same dress as worn by the woman in the portrait?

He swiftly withdrew his hand as an odd odour assaulted his nostrils. On the shelf below the garments, something caught his eye.

Two locks of red hair, sealed in a small glass jar. One was faded with age. The other looked more recent.

A cold shiver shook his spine.

Abruptly, his courage left him. Slamming shut the cupboard doors, Calum backed out of the black chamber. The eyes of the woman in the painting seemed to follow him as he closed the door, grabbed the oil-lamp and raced from the strange shrine back to his bed chamber.

Fifteen

A moon rose low in the autumn sky, lighting their progress away from the road and across fields towards the Fintry Hills. It was a fine, clear night and Rory was a pleasant, knowledgeable companion.

'Aye, I miss Kinross, Fergus. But what can a man do when his croft is burnt and his land confiscated to make room for the sheep?' Fergie nodded in sympathy, listening to the lilt in the white-haired man's voice. 'My father fought with Bonnie Dundee, at Kilicrankie, to try and win our freedom from the English.' Fergie pulled the sheepskin more tightly around his shoulders, turning his head to look at his travelling companion. 'I myself kissed James Stuart's hand, back in 1719, when we Jacobites tried one last time to stake a claim for our own land with our own king.'

The strangely youthful face creased with angry resentment. Fergie heard the bitterness in the highlander's voice, and remembered Black Jamie's actions. He himself had no interest in politics: a man had as much to fear from his own countrymen as he did from the English.

Rory fell into a brooding silence.

Fergie sighed, wanting to raise the snowy-haired man's spirits as Rory had raised his, back on the hillside. He slung an arm around the great, plaid-draped shoulders. 'Kissed James Stuart's hand, did ye?' A sly note entered his voice.

'Aye, that I did.' Rory sighed.

Fergie continued. 'And was that all ye kissed, man?'

Rory paused, stared at Fergie, then began to chuckle. 'Aye, sadly it was, my friend. But not for the want of desire, I can tell ye that. A fine figure of a man, he is.' Rory grabbed the folds at the front of his breeches and squeezed. 'The type of man any Scot would be honoured to lie with!'

Fergie grinned. 'Aye, but would James Stuart want to dirty his fine French cock with a stinking great highlander like yourself?' He grabbed Rory's silvery ponytail and gave it a yank.

Rory roared, part pain, part outrage. 'Ye cheeky young pup, ye!' He made a lunge for Fergie, who slipped easily away from the larger man's grasp.

'One look at that vast belly of yours and the Old Pretender would have been on the first ship back to France.' Fergie grinned, dancing in front of Rory, poking at the front of the man's straining plaid swathe. 'In fact, I'll wager it was not the English who chased him from Scotland – he was trying to get away from you!'

Rory charged, snorting with mock fury. 'Was not!'

Fergie roared, darting from side to side and running backward over the dark moors. 'Was!' Tearing the sheepskin from around his shoulders, he sat it on top of his head, where it draped down over his dark tangled locks like some ill-fitting wig. 'Ooh, keep zis uncouth personage away from me, sirs.' He raised the pitch of his voice, assuming what he hoped was a French accent. 'He has designs on my royal body which are less than I expect from one of my loyal highland subjects.'

Rory's snorts were now great heaving chuckles.

'Make him put it away, courtiers! Make him put zat big, smelly highland cock back in his breeks!' Fergie continued the mimicry, as his new friend chased him along the side of a dark, rolling hill. Holding his ersatz wig in place, he danced this way then that, dabbing at his grinning mouth with an imaginary handkerchief and waggling his bushy eyebrows in pretend distaste. Mid-prance, his foot slipped into a rabbit hole and he overbalanced.

Rory seized the opportunity, throwing himself forward and covering Fergie's body with his.

The sheepskin slid down, obscuring Fergie's view. They rolled into a ditch and Rory began to tickle him. 'Take it, James Stuart! Take my cock until it chokes you!' Rory cried.

Fergie howled with laughter, trying to twist away. Then a sound seeped into their ears – a sound which made them both freeze.

Hooves.

At least five horses.

Pulling his face free of the sheepskin, Fergie raised his head tentatively over the brow of the ditch.

Some distance below, on the road, a troupe of riders. Three burning torches illuminated their progress against the star-filled sky.

Rory pushed his own head up beside Fergie's. 'Constables?'

'Militiamen.' Fergie continued to peer. Behind the six mounted men, another was walking, tied to the last horse by a long rope.

Rory tugged at his shoulder, whispering. 'If we continue upward, we will avoid them easily enough.' On his belly, the snowy-haired man began to wriggle out of the ditch and towards the slopes of the Fintry Hills.

Fergie grabbed a leg, eyes still fixed below. The band of men had stopped, and he could see two of them were nailing something to one of the trees which flanked the main road. The remaining four had turned their attention to the roped figure, and were now fashioning a makeshift noose.

'Don't be a fool, Fergus.' Rory's warning was a hiss. 'What can we do against six? And, anyway, this fellow may deserve his punishment.'

Fergie pulled his eyes from the scene below. 'Is this the same man who stood with James Stuart, whose father fought by Bonnie Dundee's side?'

Rory stared back. 'Both those causes were just, my friend.'

Fergie frowned. 'Regardless of his crime, hanging a man in

the middle of the night does not strike me as any sort of justice.' He turned away. 'If you will not help, so be it. But do not try to stop me.' Crawling from the ditch, and flat on his belly, Fergie began to inch down the side of the incline. He had no idea what he was going to do, he only knew he had to do something.

Fifty yards away, the noose was around the bound prisoner's neck, and he was being manhandled on to one of the horses.

As he crept closer, Fergie could see a lifeless Cheviot slung over the back of another of the horses: a sheep stealer – this fellow was about to be hung for the theft of some ewe. Fergie scowled, wriggling closer until he could also make out the wording on the parchment, now nailed to the tree beneath which the noosed prisoner now sat.

Rustling behind and a hand on his shoulder made him flinch. Then Rory's lips were moving quietly against his ear. 'Do you recall how our forefathers went into battle, when weapons were few and the enemy overwhelming?'

A grin spread over Fergie's handsome face as he nodded, listening to further details of Rory's plan.

'Stand and deliver!'

Five minutes later, Fergie charged down the hillside, completely naked and waving Rory's musket. The fingers of his other hand gripped the handle of a powderless weapon.

Startled, one of the militiamen dropped the end of the noose. Another three reached for their side arms.

Fergie leapt into the middle of the road and fired. The blast from the musket nearly knocked him from his bare feet, but had the desired effect on the others. 'Stand and deliver, I say!' He cocked the empty pistol, using the still-warm musket barrel to herd the soldiers away from their prisoner and into a tight group. His flaccid cock swinging between his strong legs, Fergie swaggered towards them, hoping against hope they believed Rory's ancient side arm was similarly primed.

'Don't shoot us, sir.' One of the men risked a plea. 'We are on the King's business.'

'Are you, indeed?' Fergie brandished both weapons with a flourish.

In the background, Rory slipped from the darkness, clasped a broad palm over the mouth of the prisoner and dragged him from the horse.

Fergie strode closer, his eyes alighting on the bundle of printed papers clutched tightly in one of the militiamen's hands. 'I believe those belong to me.' He poked the musket's muzzle beneath the sheaf and flicked upward, scattering the *Wanted* warrants over the potholed road.

Beyond, Rory was dragging the prisoner back up towards the Fintry Hills. Fergie smiled with relief: their object had been achieved.

One of the militiamen eyed him warily. 'You are impeding His Majesty's orders, rogue.'

Ripping the nailed warrant from the tree, Fergie pretended to read it. 'Lies, all lies!' He scrunched the paper up and tossed it away.

A communal gasp rose from the huddle of uniforms. 'The Fox!'

Fergie stuck out his tongue and waved his weapons again. 'This is what I think of His Majesty.' Turning around, he wiggled his hairy arse at the startled men, then bounded off into the darkness. 'And you can tell him so, from me!'

Several pistol shots whizzed past his ear as he zigzagged across the moor, but he kept running. The heather was springy beneath his feet. He could smell the night and the scent of his own body.

Then other footsteps joined his. And a rasping voice. 'Slow down, will ye? They will not venture after us in the dark.'

Adrenaline streaked through his blood and Fergie raced on. Only when Rory grabbed his hair was he forced to stop and collapse breathless into the heather.

On the far side of the Fintry Hills, and with the Campsies just in sight, they found a cave. Soon, Rory was snoring noisily, wrapped in his plaid.

Fergie smiled, still fighting the elation which coursed through his veins. Turning away from the humped, tartan-clad sleeper, he stood at the mouth of the cave and watched the sun slowly rise behind the hills.

The newest member of their wandering band seemed unable to rest either. He had also failed to utter a word, since his rescue.

Fergie watched the shadowed figure, who crouched a little away eating fruit from a nearby blaeberry bush. The man was short – no more than five feet four – with a head of blond curls. Bare-chested, and wearing no shoes, he sat cross-legged, cramming the ripe berries between juice-stained lips.

Fergie's eyes took in the slenderness of the fellow's waist, his gaze moving lower over the swell of tight arse-cheeks then down along taut, well-developed thighs.

The adrenaline which pumped through Fergus' veins gave way to another, equally urgent sensation. Once more covered by ragged breeches, his prick began to uncurl.

Rising higher in the sky, the sun hit the side of the fellow's pointed face, and Fergie got a better look at his sharp features.

The eyes were heavily shadowed. High cheekbones glinted in the growing light. Whereas his neat form gave the impression of relative youth, the face told another story.

Getting to his feet, Fergie moved alongside the still-eating figure. It was getting light, and they should join Rory in the safety of the cave. As he reached out a hand to touch a bare shoulder, Fergie suddenly noticed the deep, red scores which decorated the slender back. Some were old, evidently received many months previously. Others were raw and more recent.

Fergie frowned. His fingers moved up, hovering an inch above a halo of blond curls. Endrick Waters were somewhere nearby – he'd heard a stream as they'd climbed up the hill.

It was risky, but no riskier than allowing those wounds to go uncleaned. Fergie crouched beside the blond-haired fellow, who had eaten all the blaeberries and was now staring westward. 'Who did this to you?' His voice trembled with anger at whoever had beaten the youth with such obvious enthusiasm.

The boy flinched, regarding Fergie with scared-rabbit eyes.

Fergie raised both his palms and moved away a little. 'I mean you no harm, friend.'

The pinched, implike face did not look convinced.

Fergie suddenly wondered if English was the fellow's first language. 'Er –' He tried to remember some of the Gaelic, but his mother had been strict in her attempts to fit in amongst lowlanders.

They sat there, both bare-chested, one trying frantically to communicate to another who had evidently heard only hard words for a very long time.

Fergie tried the little French he'd overheard in a Stirling alehouse. No response.

He attempted sign-language, smiling broadly and trying to reassure the youth. It only served to make the fellow back away further.

Fergie frowned. He was getting nowhere, and time was passing. Soon it would be too late to risk being in the daylight, and those wounds had to be cleaned. He stretched a hand behind his own head, one final time, gesturing to his back then reaching forward to point over the sheep stealer's shoulders.

Lightening-like, a hand darted up, seizing Fergie's wrist and twisting it savagely.

Fergie howled, feeling the bones in his forearm about to snap as the fellow whom he had risked his life to rescue continued to pull back and up. He wrenched himself left.

The youth held on.

Fergie flailed with his other arm, but that too was grabbed and forced behind his back. Staring down at the rapidly lightening ground, Fergie gathered all his strength. And kicked with a well-aimed foot.

The youth gasped, falling backward, his slim fingers flying to cup his bruised groin.

Fergie seized the initiative. There was no time for explanations. He turned, charging forward and scooping the moaning figure up into his arms. He heard breath hiss through clenched teeth as his arm contacted with the raw shoulder wounds. 'Sorry, my friend, but you will have to trust me.' Staggering under the surprising weight, he lurched round the side of the hill, in search of the burn.

Minutes later, he found it.

Seconds after that, he threw the now shrieking sheep stealer into the icy depths and jumped in after him.

After much splashing and flailing, Fergie's intentions evidently became a little clearer. The youth went limp, leaning over a flat rock and allowing Fergie to bathe the deep scores in his flesh.

He dabbed gently, using a handful of sphagnum moss as a sponge.

Still the sheep stealer uttered no word, but Fergie was just as glad. He felt a strong attraction to this wan, thin fellow but did not wish to risk any more intimate involvement. Standing thigh high in the cold water, he shivered and continued to clean the wounds.

The water ran pink with the youth's blood. Slowly the cuts stopped bleeding.

Fergie wiped one final time. 'Are you hurt anywhere else?'

Bent low over the flat rock, the wet blond head shook slowly.

Fergie smiled. 'So you do understand me!'

The sheep stealer raised his head and turned. Gratitude filled his large, pale blue eyes. Behind him, the eastern sky was a sheet of scarlet, reflected down into the babbling water.

Fergie's hand remained on the youth's slender waist. Two pairs of soaking breeches draped soggily over two groins. Fergie glanced down, staring at his own obvious arousal, despite the icy temperature of the burn. He pushed his mind away from the half-naked body beside his.

They couldn't go back to the cave like this. And in the warming air, their clothes would soon dry. Returning his gaze to the pale blue eyes, Fergie nodded and began to undress. He was uncomfortably aware of his desire for the slim youth who was now also hauling wet breeks over goose-fleshed thighs.

But this was neither the time nor the place.

Pulling himself together, Fergie seized the garment, wrapped it around his and squeezed all the water he could from the sodden fabric. He turned to the flat rock and, giving the breeches a shake, spread both pairs out on the sun-warmed surface. As he leant forward to smooth out the creases, a tentative palm placed itself on his waist.

Fergie grinned. Body language had triumphed over mere

words. Reaching around, he lifted the sheep stealer's hand and laced long fingers with his. 'Later, perhaps. For the moment, we need to hide.'

Leading his strangely silent friend by the hand, he made his way back to the cave.

Rory was still sleeping soundly.

Uprooting a couple of heather bushes, Fergie threw them to the other side of the cave and pointed. 'You sleep there.' He hauled at more undergrowth.

The youth still refused to even impart his name, but did as he was bid. Catching sight of the drying water on the fellow's pink face, Fergie smiled to himself: in the absence of something more suitable, he'd call him Endrick, after the burn in which he had washed them both.

By the time he had arranged a wall of bracken and heather in front of the cave, Fergie's body was rosy and warm with exertion. He moved back, glancing to where the silent sheep stealer was stretched out on his stomach. He smiled, noting that the wounds looked much better. Grabbing a length of plaid from where it covered Rory's large feet, Fergie draped it around his shoulders and lay down beside the naked form, covering them both.

Endrick snuffled once, then began to breath more slowly.

Curling on to his side, facing away from the slumbering youth, Fergie closed his eyes and slowly drifted off.

He dreamt of the Fox, in all his scarlet finery.

Fergie scowled in his sleep. That was then – this was now. He pushed the fantasy away, clearing his mind of all such foolishness.

He had a price on his head. He had no money, no home and some vague plans for Greenock. He needed all his wits about him.

Abruptly, he woke up to wet warmth on his brow. Immediately alert, Fergie's eyelids sprang open.

Endrick was kneeling beside him, smiling downward. In the warm, stuffy air of the cave, his hair had dried to a thick blond halo.

Fergie lay motionless as the sheep stealer lowered his lips and kissed him again. He smiled sleepily. 'Later, my friend –'

Then a hand was moving between his legs, gently stroking his uncurling prick. Fergie groaned, eyes glancing over to Rory.

The hand was skilled and subtle. Long, trailing fingers moved up his length, while the youth cupped Fergie's bollocks in the palm of his hand.

Fergie sighed, stifling a moan of pleasure. He reached down, intending to swat the hand away. But another touch from a pair of full lips banished all thoughts in that direction. Fergie leant up into the kiss, curling his hand behind Endrick's neck and pulling him lower. Careful to avoid the wounds, his other fingers sought the small of the sheep stealer's slender back and he began to massage.

The feel of a long, hard length against his thigh brought a gasp to Fergie's lips. Crushing his mouth against Endrick's, he deepened the kiss, pulling the youth down on top of him.

The sheep stealer lay between Fergie's splayed thighs, his hand trapped between their bodies.

Fergie's fingers moved lower, stroking down to the back of Endrick's downy thigh then back up over a clenched buttock.

A long-fingered hand grabbed his wrist, staying his caresses.

Fergie thrust with his tongue, exploring the warm depths of Endrick's mouth while the sheep stealer's stiff cock flexed against his. He groaned and raised his legs, wrapping them around the youth's thighs and allowing Endrick to guide his hand to where he needed it to be.

The crack of the sheep stealer's arse was coated with soft hair.

Fergie arched his back, feeling the tips of his index and middle fingers contact with the entrance to Endrick's body. He drank in the youth's saliva, gnawing the sheep stealer's lips until they bled.

The hand on his wrist pushed forward and Fergie's fingers slipped past the tight ring of muscle. Pulsing warmth enveloped the digits, pulling them further inside until the palm of Fergie's hand was curved around Endrick's left arse-cheek.

Between their bodies, two pricks leaked two drooling streams of need which merged as one. The head of his cock slick with his own and Endrick's precome, Fergie's bollocks clenched.

Endrick began to undulate back, fucking himself on the fingers in his arse.

Fergie groaned. The wordless action spoke volumes in an ancient language. Not breaking the kiss, he bucked with his hips, heaving the youth on to his side and easing himself out from under him.

Endrick read the movement. Avoiding the stones and rocks which littered the floor of the cave, he braced himself on all fours, turning a blond head to glance over his shoulder.

Gripping his sticky shaft with one hand, and bracing the other against the youth's right arse-cheek, Fergie met the gaze and smiled.

The returned look sparkled with a different type of gratitude and an urgent anticipation.

They both wanted this.

And they wanted it now.

To the snuffling accompaniment of Rory's snores, Fergie leant the swollen head of his cock against Endrick's pink sphincter and pushed. His own grunt of pleasure and the corresponding gasp from Endrick all but blocked out Rory.

Endrick's blond curly head hung between his shoulders. He strained to relax, bearing down and back. His slender body moved in small jutting movements, encouraging Fergie onward each time the highlander paused to allow the sheep stealer to become accustomed to the girth in his rectum.

Fergie threw back his head, his body rigid against the delicious tightness which slowly enveloped his entire length. His swollen ball sac impacted with the cheeks of Endrick's arse and he leant forward, kissing the nape of the youth's neck.

Then they were moving, pulling almost apart as Fergie withdrew then slamming back together. Their bodies slapped wetly against each other as the speed increased. Fergie's hands slipped down to hold Endrick's hipbones. A hard length of man meat brushed his knuckles and he grabbed that too, feeling the youth's body respond somewhere deep inside.

Sweat plastered Fergie's dark hair to his face as he thrust harder and faster, his balls shimmering each time Endrick's hard buttocks smashed back against them.

The sheep stealer was less silent now. Low animal sounds escaped his parted lips, alternating with breathy pants. Fergie himself was groaning loudly, trying to temper his audible passion and not wake Rory.

Beyond the mouth of the cave, the sun was high in the sky. Tiny points of light penetrated the wall of heather and dappled Endrick's undulating body in rosy pinpricks.

Fergie felt the sheep stealer's pulsing shaft slip up through his curled fist with every thrust, then recede again with each withdrawal. His own cock was almost rubbed raw by unlubricated friction, and he growled, hammering faster into Endrick's rectum.

Then he no longer felt nor heard nor saw anything. Something hot clutched at his bowels and he was propelled forward. His balls drew up into a tight knot. His prick jerked inside Endrick. Then he was falling on to an ecstatic body, mouth open and panting on a sweating neck as he pumped his release into the sheep stealer's writhing body.

A sudden twist beneath him, then a flood of wetness against his fingers, told Fergie Endrick had found release seconds after him. The strength left his legs. His prick flexed a second, then a third time, filling the slick, pulsing tunnel with his seed.

Endrick collapsed beneath him, twitching and shuddering.

'You really meant what you said, when you were dangling over that precipice, didn't ye?' Gruff, vaguely amused tones made Fergie raise his exhausted head.

Propped up on one elbow, Rory grinned at him.

Fergie's mouth was dry, unable to form a witty reply. He stroked Endrick's hair, moving on to his side and curling his body around the sheep stealer's limp form.

Endrick snuffled contentedly, relaxing back against Fergie's chest.

Rory chuckled. 'Aye, well ye put on a good show, the two of ye.' He winked. 'But perhaps now we can all get some sleep. Goodnight to ye both!' The snowy head ducked back down under the tartan covering.

Fergie laughed softly against Endrick's shoulder, cuddling the youth back against him.

The sheep stealer linked his fingers with Fergie's, pulling the highlander's arms more tightly around his slender chest.

Seconds later, the only sounds in the cave were three, low snores.

Sixteen

'Fine day for it, eh, my boy?'

A hand patted his shoulder, lingering somewhat. 'Yes, Uncle Jamie.' Calum squirmed in his saddle. The bright-red jacket and white jodhpurs which his guardian had presented him with at breakfast fitted well enough. But the object of this morning's ride made him distinctly uncomfortable. As did James Black's continued attentions.

'While Captain Carmichael and his men are tracking down that highwayman McGregor, we will vent our frustration on another type of prey.' His guardian seized a goblet of cordial from a passing serving wench and downed it in one.

'Yes, Uncle Jamie.' Calum refused the proffered drink, repositioning his blond wig beneath his hat. The discovery he'd made last night, in the attic room of Castle Black, twisted and turned in his mind. But the mention of Fergie pulled his thoughts on to more pressing matters. 'How is Captain Carmichael faring, in his search for the Fox?'

James Black's thin lips curled into a sneer. 'McGregor obviously lacks his namesake's wiles, and is stupid enough to remain nearby. He held up another coach only last night.'

Calum lowered his head to hide a smile: if the authorities believed the Fox to be still active in Stirlingshire, they would not look further afield. A hand suddenly slipped beneath his chin, raising his face. Cold, glistering eyes bored into his.

'This amuses you, Calum?'

His stomach tightened but he held the stare. 'McGregor is no highwayman, Uncle Jamie. I –'

A bugled *tally ho* from a few yards away obliterated another attempt at confession. The hounds began to bark uproariously.

James Black released Calum's chin, reining his horse round. 'Tell me later, my boy. Now let us enjoy the chase.'

Scarlet-clad riders trotted past him. Calum frowned into his guardian's wake, watching him join the hunt and move towards the open hills. Maybe he could slip away, ride to the village in search of more accurate news of Fergie.

'Come on, Calum! Stay near me.'

James Black's enthusiastic shout made Calum's stomach tighten a second time. Trailing along at the tail end of the hunters, he reluctantly joined the ramrod-straight horseman and set out across the fields.

The hounds lost the scent at least half a dozen times. Near Gonachan Bridge, a flash of scarlet streaked across the periphery of Calum's vision. Swivelling his head, he watched a fox race off into a thicket. He cupped his hand around his mouth. 'There he goes!' He waved one arm frantically in the opposite direction.

The rest of the hunt, his guardian included, shouted their thanks and galloped off.

Calum sighed, slowing his mount to a trot. His surroundings brought back bitter-sweet memories. Half a mile north lay the clearing in which they'd first kissed. To the south, he could just see the outbuildings of the McGregor croft and the byre where they'd lain together.

Biting back sadness, Calum led his horse down from the bridge and let the beast drink from the flowing waters of the burn. Time passed and he remained there, lost in thoughts of what might have been. His eyes dampened and his chest grew tight. Then movement on the other side of the burn focused his attention.

Over the top of his mount's lowered head, Calum found

himself staring into a pointed, vulpine face. They stared at each other for a few brief seconds. Then the fox turned back into the undergrowth.

Calum's heart thumped as he dismounted. Was that to be Fergie's lot, from now on? Chased from shire to shire, never allowed to rest or find peace? Pursued until he was exhausted and then torn to pieces by Captain Carmichael's men?

Unable to help himself or anyone else, Calum leant against warm, equine flanks, buried his face in his horse's mane and sobbed.

So great was his regret, he did not hear the hooves of an approaching horse nor the sound of another rider dismounting. And when a tentative hand placed itself on his shoulder, Calum didn't care whose it was.

He only knew he wanted to be held. He wanted to be held and told everything was going to be all right.

Spinning round blind, he threw his arms around a ramrod-straight back. 'I'm sorry – it's all my fault!'

Lean, muscular arms hung limply by the sides of a scarlet riding jacket.

Calum continued to sob, face pressed against a solid chest. His hat fell off, taking his wig with it. 'I'm sorry – oh, I am so sorry!' He tightened his grip, pulling himself flat against the startled body.

Then other arms moved, curling around his back and drawing him closer. 'It's not your fault.'

Face still buried in the warm chest, Calum barely heard, never mind recognised, the low tones. 'It is! I was stupid – I started this whole thing! I should have known better.'

'We are both to blame, I think.' The arms tightened, holding him firmly.

He couldn't think straight. All he knew was the warm reassurance which another male body was providing. Calum's sobs slowly subsided. He continued to burrow into the strong embrace.

The voice talked on. 'I tried to fight it, but my feelings are too strong, Pip.'

The words made no sense, but Calum didn't care. Long

fingers tangled themselves into his thick, red hair as Fergie had done. His cock twitched at the memory. He pushed his groin against a bony thigh. Before he knew what he was doing, his body began to undulate.

'I wondered if you felt it also.' The voice was lower now, breathy and hoarse.

A broad palm stroked his back, moving to his lowest vertebra and lingering there. Calum moaned, his own hands now roaming over the rigid web of muscles which spanned a ramrod-straight spine. Mouth open, eyes closed, he raised his face and kissed the side of Fergie's neck.

A shudder ran through the body which was now grinding against his. 'I hoped against hope you would, but did not dare to –'

The rest of the declaration disappeared in a long groan as Calum dragged his half-hard cock up and down his highlander's thigh.

Fergie knew!

Had Fergie always known he, Calum Monroe, was the Fox?

His hands slipped lower, cupping his love's arse-cheeks and pulling the man harder against himself. His mouth moved over the skin on a recently shaven neck, trailing kisses along Fergie's throat and up towards the firm, jutting jawline. 'Do not talk, my love,' Calum whispered. 'There is no need for words – there never was, not between us.' Fergie's cock throbbing against his thigh, his own shaft stiffening further by the minute, Calum opened his eyes and searched for his highlander's face.

Black, glittering irises stared into his. 'Oh, Pip!'

Calum leapt back. James Black's fingers slowly slipped from his hair.

'I have waited for this moment, since I first beheld you fully grown at sixteen.'

Calum's lips fluttered. His mouth opened and shut wordlessly. He backed away further.

'It frightens me too, Pip. And fills my mind with doubts and questions.' James Black smiled. He stroked Calum's ashen face. 'You are right – we two have no need of words.'

Calum's Adam's apple bobbed convulsively. He flinched

under the touch. This was some horrible misunderstanding! How could he ever have mistaken his guardian's angular form for Fergie's well-padded body? And who was Pip? He had to say something – he had to sort this out before it went any further.

James Black's long fingers moved over his face, pausing to trace the outline of his lips.

Calum shivered, horrified to find his prick was still inching along his right thigh. Then a distant *tally ho* call from the master of the hunt refocused his racing mind. He managed to move one foot, then the other. Sidling left, he gripped the reins of his horse. 'We should rejoin the chase, Uncle Jamie. We will have been missed and –'

'I think we have both found the object of another chase, Pip. Let us go home.' His guardian moved away towards his own mount.

At that precise moment, Calum would have chased infinite foxes over infinite moors for an infinite duration: anything was preferable to returning, alone with this man, to the dark gloom of Castle Black.

'Come, Pip.' A note of urgent authority had entered the voice. His guardian urged his horse forward.

Calum's knees turned to water. Doubting his ability to stay on his feet much longer – and not wishing to think of himself, prostrate and helpless here, in the seclusion of Gonachan bridge and at the mercy of this new, strangely unfamiliar man who thought he was someone called Pip – he scrambled on to his mount and followed.

By the time they had reached the castle's ancient stone portals, Calum had recovered a little. A plan of action was forming in his brain.

He had no urge to hurt or offend the man: James Black had, after all, been very kind to the penniless son of his army comrade. And he was not unattractive, in a stern, rigid sort of way. But he knew there was but one fellow for him – wherever Fergie might be, at the moment, and despite Calum's knowledge that his feelings for the tall highlander would never be reciprocated.

So he would pretend his encounter with James Black had

never happened. 'Do you paint, uncle?' Calum stabled his horse and ran to catch up with his guardian, injecting a note of studied casualness into his voice.

The red-jacketed figure paused. 'Why do you ask?'

Grateful his guardian had taken the bait, and regardless of any reprimand he might receive for wandering around the castle's closed wing at night, Calum detailed his discoveries as they walked through the doorway and into the Great Hall.

James Black paused briefly, at the foot of the long staircase, listening.

Calum burbled on, words tripping over themselves in haste. 'And I saw the letters J.B. at the foot of the lady's portrait. So I was wondering if you were the artist, and why the painting does not hang where it can be seen, uncle. It is a most competent piece of work.'

The shadow of a frown creased James Black's gaunt face.

Calum ignored the chill shiver which coursed down his spine and talked on. 'You did paint it, didn't you?' He smiled brightly.

'Yes, I am responsible.' His guardian turned away and slowly walked towards the study.

Calum hesitated. His resemblance to the subject of the portrait tugged at his brain. 'Who is the lady in the painting?'

James Black spun round. 'Did you . . . notice anything else in the chamber?'

Calum gulped under the intensity of the accompanying stare. Should he admit to rummaging through the cupboards? Should he mention his discovery of the spunk-stained bolster cover? 'Your artistic endeavour held my attention completely.' He smiled and reiterated his enquiry. 'Who is the lady?'

'You really have no idea, do you?' His guardian sighed and glanced at the grandfather clock. His long fingers turned the handle of the study door. 'I must be in Stirling, later today.' He paused. 'But I have time to answer at least some of your questions. And you deserve to know. Come.'

Relieved they were not going up to the odd, soberly decorated chamber, and more than a little curious about the painting, Calum joined his uncle in the book-lined room.

In the far corner, James Black removed two volumes from the

third shelf. Calum gasped as a section of the wall slid soundlessly ajar.

His guardian smiled at him, undoing the tight fastenings of his red hunting jacket. 'Pip and I found this passage on one of our first visits here.' He tossed the scarlet jerkin over the back of a chair. Beneath the garment, his chest was bare. 'It became our secret – a secret you will now share'

Calum's heart pounded against his ribs. He found himself staring at his guardian's hard pectorals. He did not want to be part of any secret. He had no wish to know who Pip was, or why he and his guardian kept a shrine to some red-haired woman. His mind told him to run from the room.

Blood fizzing in his ears, and with a dry mouth, Calum followed James Black into the darkness.

A new candle burnt before the oil painting, its flame turning the lady's gown to liquid green. Calum stared at the familiar face. Something was starting to make a horrible kind of sense.

His guardian's voice filled the claustrophobic room. 'You never knew her, did you?'

Calum took in the sweep of an aquiline nose and the vaguely smiling mouth. 'Aunt Marie kept pictures of father, but not –'

'Your mother was a beautiful woman, Calum.' Calum blinked at the portrait, the sadness in his guardian's voice almost eclipsing his own. 'But never a strong one. The struggle of giving you life was already taking its toll on her, even then.'

He found himself moving forward. Calum stretched out a hand to touch the portrait. His fingers hovered less than an inch from the canvas.

'When she died, I thought I should die too.'

Calum could feel James Black's breath on the back of his neck. 'I look so like her.'

The breath became a soft sigh. 'It is more than looks. You have her voice and laugh. You have her bearing, her way of standing. But you also possess something which she lacks.'

Calum withdrew his hand, turning slowly to where James Black stood, staring at him. Eyes dark as night bored into him.

'Life.'

Calum's eyes widened. The shrine suddenly made sense.

'I would never force my attentions on anyone,' his guardian continued as he slipped a hand behind Calum's sweating neck, drawing his head forward. 'Here in this room, I dreamt for twenty years of what could never be, with Pip. Now I have you – we have each other.'

His guardian's lips touched his. Calum's mouth opened in shock.

'Oh, Philippa! I have waited so long for –'

'No!' The use of his mother's name gave Calum the resolve he needed. 'This is not right!' He pulled away, heart pounding.

The candle flickered under the force of his words, its light casting great yellow flickers over James Black's angular face. 'I will give you all the time you need to become accustomed to the idea.'

There was a hint of madness in the calm, measured sentiment. Calum looked away, eyes scanning the dark walls of the chamber for the concealed passageway. 'It is not a matter of time, Uncle Jamie. I –' he searched his mind for an excuse, aware his guardian was now far beyond reason '– I do not think of you that way.'

'So like your mother.' A low chuckle filled his ears. 'Or you will be, my boy. You will be.'

What did the man mean? Backing away further, Calum collided with the strange chair. Panic spurted in his veins, flooding his brain as he stumbled and spurring desperate words to his lips. 'There is something you should know, Uncle Jamie – something which may change your mind.'

His guardian moved towards him, chest glistening with sweat.

Calum clenched his fists. 'I am the Fox! I am a common criminal, a disgrace to the Monroe name and my mother's memory!'

James Black paused.

Calum talked on. 'I have been robbing coaches for the past two months. The scarlet cloak you found in Fergie's croft was mine. The skean dhu you found in the cache beneath Gonachan bridge? I stole that from Fergie, two weeks ago.' He knew he was speaking faster and faster, but could not rein his words in.

'Only last night I stopped another carriage on the Stirling road. I can describe the passengers to you, if you need proof. I can –'

Low laughter forced him to break off.

Calum stared to where his guardian was now smiling coldly. 'This again.'

Calum's fists tightened into balls. 'It is true! Fergie is innocent! I am the Fox!'

The smile left James Black's face. 'Pip had her flights of fancy too, my boy. Like her, you think there is a certain romance in roguish characters.'

Calum tried to think of something else to say.

'But I have seen the way you sit on a horse. You are no natural rider, unlike McGregor.' Calum cursed himself for the convincingness of his performance during the day. Abruptly, his guardian pulled a watch from the pocket of his breeches. 'But there is no time to talk about your overactive imagination, at the moment. We will discuss the matter further, when I return tomorrow.' James Black's voice was once again even and emotionless.

Then his guardian was disappearing into darkness and Calum was alone with the oil painting and the flickering shadows.

Seventeen

Three pairs of very different feet tramped through heather and over the Campsie Hills.

Fergie glanced left to where silver-haired Rory was whistling jauntily, his great length of plaid tucked into his belt. At his right side, slight, blond-haired Endrick's progress was silent but just as resolute.

Straight ahead, he could see the outline of Lennox Forest. It was their agreed plan to circle north, avoiding Glasgow where the constabulary was strong, and cross the river at Clydebank.

And after that?

The bustling port of Greenock lay a mere fifteen miles along the coast, the gateway west to a new life.

In the darkness, a sudden image of the Fox's shining red hair brought a sigh of longing to Fergie's full lips. He pushed the thought away, slinging one arm around Rory's huge shoulders and the other over Endrick's slender back.

What need did he have of gentlemen lovers, especially ones who saved their own skins by allowing others to take the blame for their highway crimes?

Fergie could still feel the heat of the curly-haired blond's arse tight around his cock. He could still smell Rory's sour sweat, taste his own seed on the silver-haired fellow's breath.

Endrick's sheep-stealing skills proved equally adept at entrapping a wild goat. Fergie's belly was full, and he had drunk deeply from a clear burn. His limbs were well rested. His mind reeled with the possibilities of the Americas.

Only his heart still ached a little. Rab would take care of Morag, he was certain. Fergie hoped his mother and brothers had found safety also.

Then a slim arm found its way around his waist and Fergie felt Rory also stoop to embrace him. 'Three free men, Fergus!' The low, lilting voice was full of hope. 'There may be a price on our heads but they will never have our souls.'

'Aye, Rory – it's a fine night to be alive.' Fergie tightened his grip on his companions, and knew his words had a special meaning for blond Endrick, who had narrowly escaped the noose.

The snowy-bearded highlander recommenced his whistling and all three marched in time to the stirring tune.

Although he coughed from time to time, the boy had yet to utter a word. But both Fergie and Rory knew he dreamt the same dreams as they did. He ruffled the fair curls, his mind moving on towards dawn, and thoughts of curling up with two lovers in some warm cave.

Then a sudden movement in the distance took his attention. Fergie paused, motioning with his hand.

Rory's whistling stopped abruptly.

They peered silently into the darkness. Fergie narrowed his eyes.

Less than a hundred yards away, at the fringe of the forest and almost merging with the trees, a horse. And a rider.

Fergie fell to a crouch, dragging the other two with him. He could only see one figure, but that did not mean there might not be others. He glanced from Rory to Endrick then back again. 'Take him round the long way, friend.' He nodded east along the edge of Lennox Forest. 'I will go on alone.'

A hand gripped his arm. Fergie registered Endrick's protest. He turned his head. 'I will meet up with you on the far side. It is foolish for all three of us to risk ambush.'

The sheep stealer stared at him.

'Fergus is right, my lad.' Rory added his whispered assent to the plan. 'We will listen out. If there is a struggle, we will return.'

The grip slackened. Then Endrick raised a hand to stroke Fergie's hair.

Fergie pushed the boy eastward. 'Go – we will all be together again soon.' He remained there, lying in the heather as two shadowed outlines crept away. When Rory and Endrick had reached a point where they were about to become visible to whoever was hiding just beyond the trees, Fergie leapt to his feet and assumed Rory's jaunty whistling. With a slight swagger, and knowing he would draw any eyes towards himself and away from his friends, he strode into the forest.

Whoever lurked there was biding his time.

Fergie marched on, apparently unheeding but in reality taking note of every twig snap and leaf rustle as he plunged deeper into the thicket.

He knew he was being watched: the erect hair on the back of his neck told him that. And he was being followed. Oh, the horseman was adept. But with his ears pricked for every tiny sound, Fergie tracked his tracker as surely as the horseman tracked him.

He wove left, veering away from the rough path. His subtle pursuer did likewise.

Then he changed his mind and strode right, crisscrossing back and forth amongst the trees. Whoever was following him did the same.

Curiosity replaced apprehension: if the horseman was going to rob or kill him, he would surely have done so by now. Fergie slowed his pace to a stroll, almost as if he were taking an afternoon walk rather than making his way through a thick forest in the early hours of the morning. He could see little. From time to time, the moon shone down into a clearing, its brightness no longer obscured by the tightly packed fir trees. Pale luminescence sparkled on the forest floor and its carpet of pineneedles which crunched noisily beneath Fergie's boots.

Four hooves mirrored his measure, following but never overtaking.

Curiosity gave way to impatience.

Fergie heard an occasional low snuffle. He stopped whistling and frowned to himself, wondering if his pursuer's horse was growing equally irked by the length of this strange game. Unsettling though it was, however, it was at least achieving its purpose: his tireless pursuer could not be in two places at once, thus allowing Rory and Endrick to circle Lennox Forest unmolested.

A sudden pressure in his bladder turned the frown into a scowl. Fergie speeded up: why now, of all times? He strode on, ignoring the need to piss.

The pressure grew more urgent. Fergie concentrated on the solid fall of hooves behind, pulling his mind from what his body wanted.

Finally he could bear it no longer. Pausing by a stout fir tree, he wrenched open his tattered breeches one-handed. The other reached inside, fingers curling around the soft length of meat and hauling it free. Fergie planted his feet apart, gripped the root of his shaft and aimed his slit at a section of mossy bark. And waited.

Nothing – just more pressure.

Fergie sighed. Trying to relax the muscles concerned, he changed the angle of his prick and gripped more tightly.

A sudden flex against his fingers made him gasp.

Standing there, thighs apart and holding his cock, he felt the blood leave his brain and pulse downward, thickening and stiffening the flaccid length of flesh. Fergie groaned: he could never piss when someone was watching.

His younger brothers teased him about it. Rab made jokes about it. Fergie smiled wryly. The memory of standing beside his herdsman, their two cocks aimed at a stone dyke only served to send more blood pulsing through the thick veins which wound around his shaft.

Then another need for release reasserted itself. Fergie bent his knees and regripped, applying more pressure with his thumb and fingers. He tried to shake some sense into the recalcitrant length but only succeeded in pushing the ability to piss further away.

Rab's eyes on his prick, as they stood inches apart, brought a flush to his bare chest. Fergie's own gaze narrowed as he stared at the steadily swelling shaft. Two urgencies now vied within him, joined distantly by a third which vaguely told him this was neither the time nor the place for either a wank or a piss.

A soft snuffle close by sent a bolt of lightening through his body. Fergie's cock flexed against his fingers, fighting the grip in its need to be erect. His mind was racing, visualising a yard above those equine nostrils, and the silent rider who was now regarding him with increased scrutiny. The sense of imminent danger only caused his shaft to thicken more steadily.

Fergie stared down at his right hand, watching his foreskin peel back and feeling the delicate ruffles stretch against his fingers. He loosened his grip, allowing arousal to gradually engorge his shaft.

A sharp clenching in his balls was swiftly followed by a burning tightness in his bladder.

Gasping, he winced and tried to will himself soft. His prick had other ideas. The sharp flares of discomfort merely served to push the large, purple glans free of its hood of skin. Fergie was now far past the point where urinating was possible.

Standing in the middle of a wood in the middle of the night, under the scrutiny of someone he didn't know – and with the added betrayal of his own body – brought a sudden anger to his cheeks. Still gripping his now fully erect prick, Fergie spun round and faced his pursuer. 'Happy, now?' He roared into the darkness, his voice husky with need. 'It is a sorry state of affairs, when a man cannot even pish in private!'

No response.

The rider's silence infuriated Fergie further. He took a step towards the outline of a horse. 'What do you want with me, anyway? I have neither money nor anything else worth stealing. Why are you following me?'

Two streams of exhalation condensed in front of two flaring nostrils.

Fergie snorted in parallel, grasping the root of his hard cock and waggling the organ into the darkness. 'Perhaps you like watching men! Perhaps you are ashamed of what arouses you!' He was growing more irate by the moment. His other hand slipped down beneath his full ball sac. 'That is your problem, not mine.'

Still nothing.

Thighs apart, feet clumping over pineneedles, Fergie staggered closer. The intense discomfort in his bladder pushed all rational thought aside. 'Want a bit of man meat, coward?' He thrust with his hips, fucking the air with his prick. 'Why don't you show yourself?' He winced momentarily at a sharp stab of pain somewhere beyond his balls, then scowled. 'Or is it my pish you want?' The words increased his urgent need. Knees bending in towards each other, thigh muscles rigid against the agony, he spat the taunt and threw himself forward.

At the exact moment he stared into startled, equine eyes, a response finally came.

From behind. 'Bessie thanks ye for the kind offer, sir, but she prefers her own species.'

Fergie jumped, glancing up at the empty saddle. His head began to turn slowly.

The cold barrel of a musket stopped its progress. 'What were ye saying, about needing to pish?'

A hand snaked around his hips, pushing his fingers away and replacing them with a chillier grip. Fergie gasped, head flicking abruptly back to the front.

'We'll need to get rid of this first, I think.' An amused snort of breath condensed on his neck. The grip on his shaft tightened.

Fergie's arms hung limply at his sides while his prick raged against unknown fingers. The buttons of a jerkin dug into his spine. He arched away from them, staggering forward.

'Ye want to suffer?' The grip tightened into a fist, holding him there and preventing any escape. 'Maybe ye like the way your balls ache and your pish organ throbs?'

Fergie couldn't speak. Then damp velvet warmth against his swollen sac made him gasp.

A laugh from behind was followed by a whinny of annoyance. 'Get away, Bessie. I know you like the smell of men but this one's mine.' The horse's nose removed itself and the fist began to move. 'Isn't that right, friend?'

Fergie could only nod as the tight embrace made its way

resolutely up his shaft then back down again. He wondered vaguely if fear alone might rid him of the unwanted hard-on. But his erection throbbed with a mind of its own.

The fist moved faster. 'That's it, friend.'

Fergie was almost squatting now. The internal pressure was eclipsed by a more urgent pulse. He thrust forward into the man's fist, moving with the increased rhythm. His breath formed white clouds in the frosty air, mirroring the steam from the nearby horse and the breathy pants on the back of his neck. He was close – very close.

Then the fist paused abruptly and Fergie cried out in frustration. Warm fingers caressed his heavy bollocks.

'That's a fine load you've got there, friend.'

The delicate puckered skin crawled with need. The hair on the back of Fergie's neck stood on end. He hovered there, feeling incipient orgasm recede as he was expertly brought back from the brink.

'I want to feel it spurt from your slit and shower my fingers.'

Fergie gasped. The fist began to move again, faster than ever. He reached behind, wanting to touch his seducer but his hand was knocked away as determinedly as Bessie's inquisitive nose had been. He thrust backward, pressing his arse into the man's groin and feeling the hard ridge of arousal there. The sensation made his balls clench and he was building again.

'Ah, no – not yet.' The fist stopped a second time. A rough thumb and forefinger formed a tight ring around the root of him.

Fergie whimpered. Ripples of release battered against the digits which held them there and prevented the first waves of orgasm going any further. His cock shuddered. The need to piss was the least of his problems. His guts churned. Muscle spasmed deep in his arse and the breath caught in his throat.

The barrel of the musket eased beneath his chin, tilting his lolling head up. Fergie stared at the distant tops of tall pine trees. The forest was silent save for two sets of ragged breathing. Then the pistol fell to the ground. The body behind his moved back a little and the distinctive sound of breeks unbuttoning filled his ears.

'Ye want me in there, friend?'

The words alone were almost enough to force the spunk from his slit. Fergie couldn't speak. The feel of solid man flesh poking between his arse-cheeks brought a louder whimper to his lips.

Then the fist was moving again.

Fergie bent lower, allowing his unseen lover to stroke him harder and faster. The man's own prick had found the hairy crack between Fergie's arse-cheeks and was thrusting in parallel to the jerking motion of his fist. The strength returned to Fergie's arms. He reached behind, grabbing strong thighs to support himself as his cock was roughly caressed by a masterly hand.

Seconds later his legs turned to water and he slumped to his knees. The first wad of spunk hit him squarely between the eyes. The second impacted with his cheeks, sliding wetly down into his open mouth. Fergie howled at the ground, aware of another wetness slick along his arse-crack as his unseen partner continued to milk every last drop from his clenching bollocks.

Immediately he began to soften, a further spurt forced its burning way up through his shaft. Still reeling from the intensity of the first release, Fergie laughed with relief as his piss burst forth, drenching the man's hand and the discarded pistol in a hot, steaming shower.

His senses returned. Fergie scrambled away, seizing the gun and hauling himself upright.

His faceless lover was groaning in orgasm.

Levelling the muzzle at the top of a still-lowered head, Fergie cocked the action and grabbed the reins of the horse which had wandered forward and was now snuffling at smears of spent man seed. 'I think you enjoyed that almost as much as I did, stranger.' He grinned, watching as the lowered head slowly raised itself. 'And, as payment due, I will borrow Bessie here, and your pistol.' A horse and a weapon would enable Rory, Endrick and himself to reach Greenock more speedily and more safely.

'You would rob an honest man, would ye?' The fellow eased himself upright.

Fergie stared at well over six and a half feet of shorn-headed masculinity. He stepped back, overawed by the height of the man. 'I neither rob nor steal, friend – I borrow, and then only because I must. Tell me your name and from whence you hail, and I will return both to you, in due course.' Fergie's eyes moved from the fellow's head to the long length of curling man meat which still drooped from the open crotch of his breeches.

The giant seized his shaft, tucking his cock out of sight. 'They call me Wee Andrew, and I have no home.' He sat down abruptly, rubbing his pale face with huge, work-roughened hands. 'I am heading for Clydebank, where I hope to secure a passage on board a clipper bound for the New World.'

'Fergus McGregor at your service, sir.' Uncocking the weapon, he held it out, butt first. 'And if you do not mind a bit of company, my friends and I would gladly travel with you as far as the river.'

As if on cue, shouts and hurried footsteps heralded the arrival of two who had grown tired of waiting at the far side of the forest. Seconds later, armed with sticks, a broad silver-haired figure and a slight, darting shade burst into the clearing:

'Are you hurt, Fergus?' Rory's voice was low with concern.

Endrick threw himself into Fergie's arms, turning his head to wave his stick at a startled Andrew.

Fergie laughed, embracing the curly-haired boy. 'I am unharmed, as you can see. But, if my new friend here is agreeable, we now have a horse to aid our progress towards the coast.' He kissed the top of Endrick's blond head, his smile broadening as Rory and Wee Andrew exchanged tentative introductions. 'And a weapon.'

The giant of a man shook the pistol. 'If this still works, after having been drenched by your pish, Fergus McGregor.'

Rory's eyes widened with lusty interest. 'Exactly what were you two up to, here? We could hear the yells for at least a mile.'

Gently disentangling himself from Endrick's wordless embrace, Fergie hoisted the youth up and sat him squarely in Bessie's saddle. Wee Andrew took the reins, guiding the horse forward. As the four of them made their way through Lennox Forest and out on to the moors, Fergie satisfied his full-bearded friend's curiosity, mindful not to miss out any detail.

Dawn lightening the sky behind them, four laughing figures – three on foot, one on Bessie – headed for the distant outline of Clydebank.

Eighteen

'Take this and use it.'

In the flickering candlelight, Calum thrust another bag at a startled Rab.

'That money is stolen.' From the other side of the damp outhouse in which the family had sought shelter, Mrs McGregor's words were surprisingly resolute.

Rab hesitated.

Calum tried to inject a note of jaunty bonhomie into his voice. 'Stolen only from those who can well afford to lose it, madam.'

'Stolen, nonetheless.' Mrs McGregor rose slowly and made her way across the room. 'And by someone who is not man enough to reveal himself.'

'I have my reasons, madam.' Beneath the black kerchief which once more hid the lower half of his face, Calum frowned. 'Consider it a gift from those who would have given freely, had they known your circumstances.' Turning his attention back to Fergie's herdsman, he shoved the pouch at Rab's chest. 'Take it – please!'

'Keep your money, highwayman!' Then Mrs McGregor was between them, holding the pouch he had slipped into their dwelling the previous evening. She grabbed tonight's booty from Rab and held both out towards Calum. 'Because of you, my

Fergie is God knows where, with a price on his head.' The strong voice quavered. 'Get out, before I lose my temper.'

Calum felt about six inches high. He could see his beloved highlander in Mrs McGregor's proud bearing, and he knew the truth of her reprimand. Before he had the chance to offer what little comfort he could, Rab had grabbed his arm and was leading him from the low-roofed building.

'She will accept it – eventually. We have lawyers to pay and debts to settle, not to mention mouths to feed.'

Rab's thanks brought little solace to Calum's ears. He leant against the whitewashed building, cursing James Black for not believing his confession, earlier that evening. The moon was rising, and his mind turned once more to his highlander. Calum wondered if Fergie was perhaps staring at that same moon.

'He loved you, you know.' Rab's words had a bitter edge to them. 'He was waiting for you to come and rescue him, the night they threw him in prison.'

Calum pulled his gaze from the night sky.

The herdsman snorted and spat on the ground. 'I tried to convince him his best chance would be before the court with a good lawyer, but he's always been impulsive, has Fergie. He should not have run.'

A note of fondness had entered Rab's voice, tempering his anger at his employer's actions. Calum looked at his other tormentor who, along with Fergie, had mocked and teased him at every opportunity. 'I think you had . . . feelings for him too, my friend.'

Rab blushed. 'Aye, I suppose I did – still do, even though I am betrothed to his sister.' The rough voice grew husky. 'We had some fine times, right enough, Fergie and I. But there is only room in his heart for one man, and I know that man is you, Fox.'

Calum's chest tightened.

'His life is in your hands. Even if that means sacrificing your own to save his.'

His mouth was dry. Unable to face the truth of the words, Calum changed the subject. 'Is there any news of him?'

Rab kicked desultorily at a clod of earth. 'A few nights ago, someone held up a band of the King's soldiers, fifty miles west of here. The fellow was naked as the day he was born and howling like a maniac.' The herdsman suddenly chuckled. 'The tale is that he stole only a young boy, sentenced to death by a court of farmers in Arbroath, then waggled his bare arse at the militiamen and ran off into the hills.'

Despite his heavy heart, Calum smiled. Fergie had the cheek of the devil. 'Where is he bound, do you know?'

Rab shook his shaggy head. 'Far away, I hope. Even if you do find a way of clearing his name, Fox, I fear a certain local landowner around here would be more than happy to disregard any information concerning Fergie's innocence. He will not get a fair trial at any Blairhoyle court.'

Calum frowned. 'If I can get more money, you can afford better lawyers. I will speak to them myself, and perhaps a search party can be made up, to secure his safe return to another, perhaps higher, judiciary.'

Rab looked at him. 'I myself would happily head any such expedition, Fox. If you can get funds, I am not too proud to accept.' He stuck out a hand.

Calum took it between both of his and squeezed warmly. 'Then it is settled. Tomorrow or the day after we will ride westward together. We will find Fergie and we will ensure he has a fair trial.'

Rab's fingers gripped his tightly, and Calum thought about those same fingers tangled in Fergie's thick hair or perhaps encircling his love's stout cock. The image sent a frisson of longing up his spine.

A sudden flush on the herdsman's cheeks told him Rab was entertaining similar thoughts. Almost simultaneously, each pulled away.

Calum smiled with his eyes. 'Until Tuesday eve then, my friend. I will return to this place, just after midnight.'

Rab nodded. 'I will be waiting.'

Calum moved away, untying his horse's reins from around a tree and vaulting into the saddle. 'Wish me luck that tonight's coach from Stirling carries more rich merchants with bulging money belts!'

'Aye, that I will, Fox. Have a productive night's hunting, and safe home!'

With Rab's firm good wishes resounding in his ears, and his heart a little lighter, Calum galloped off towards the main road.

It began to rain – lightly at first, but increasing to a heavy downpour.

Calum drew up his horse in the middle of the muddy road, raised his pistol and fired into the air.

The shot echoed in his head, along with a new sense of purpose.

Horses neighed, reined to a noisy halt. Inside the carriage, someone screamed.

Calum grinned beneath his black kerchief, guiding his horse forward. He bowed to the startled coachman. 'A minute of your time, friend. I am on a mission of mercy.' Continuing on past the front of the carriage, he paused, level with the window. 'I will not force you all to disembark this evening, since the weather is somewhat inclement.' He winked at the huddle of fear-streaked face which gazed out at him. 'But I am sure you will all wish to contribute to the *Fergus McGregor is Innocent* campaign.'

No one moved. No one spoke.

Calum sat back in his saddle. 'In case you are unaware of the situation, Fergus McGregor was unjustly arrested for crimes he did not commit, and is now on the run for his life.' His eyes moved from one frightened face to another, pausing at that of a good-looking woman around whose neck a bejewelled necklace sparkled. 'Along with his friends and family, I am setting up a fund to provide him with the best legal defence money can buy.'

Under the intensity of his stare, the woman's hand instinctively moved to her throat.

Calum beamed. 'Why, thank you, madam! Your generosity is remarkable.' Levelling his pistol, he motioned with the barrel.

Shaking fingers unfastened the neckpiece. Then a white hand draped it over the muzzle.

Calum swiftly pocketed the adornment, then applauded. 'A good start! I know you all to be Godfearing, charitable people, so let's see how generous you can be.' He flicked the pistol at five pairs of startled eyes. The sixth passenger he could not see.

Slowly at first, then with more speed, wallets, money belts and rings were passed out through the open window to him.

'I thank you, good people. Fergus McGregor thanks you.' The booty would fetch enough to finance himself, Rab and maybe a few others on their search for the much wronged highlander. Moving back a little, he removed his wet hat and executed an exaggerated bow. His long red hair flowed down over his shoulders. 'Fergus is no highwayman. There is only one Fox – I am he. When you reach your destinations, remember to tell your friends you had the privilege of encountering the Fox himself, and spread the word that Fergus McGregor is an innocent man.' He gripped the reins, moving to the side of the road. 'Now God speed you on your way!' Firing the pistol a second time, he watched the coach and four bolt off into the night. Around his mouth, the black kerchief was soggy and uncomfortable. Calum wrenched it free, tossing it into the air and staring after the departing carriage.

Tomorrow he would travel to Stirling and employ the services of the best lawyer he could find! The day after that, he and Rab would set out to bring Fergie home!

As he turned away from the wake of the coach, his soaring heart plummeted. A pair of dark, glittering eyes stared out at him from the vehicle's rear window.

James Black was waiting in the Great Hall.

Mouth set in a scowl, Calum made to walk past him.

'So you were not lying.' A clawlike hand shot out, gripping his arm.

'I tried to tell you many times.' Calum spun round, his clothes still soaking. He glowered into black eyes and shook his arm free. 'Fergus McGregor is no criminal. You have seized his lands falsely. Now we can go to the authorities and –'

'You must love him indeed, Calum.' The words were low, colder than February frost.

Calum blinked. 'I told you that also. But I do this because he is innocent, not because of any feelings I have for him. Justice must be served.'

The black eyes bored into him. 'Oh, my boy.' Calum's brow creased at the edge which had entered the voice. 'It grieves me to do this, but as you say, justice must be served.'

In an instant, both Calum's wrists were seized in one iron grip and a bony arm was tight around his neck.

'I have your confession, Calum Monroe. Your own words have doomed you. By order of the King himself, the Fox must hang.'

Calum gasped. His guardian's forearm dug painfully into his windpipe and threatened to cut off his breath. The words sunk in, and his life flashed before his bulging eyes. 'No!' The sound was more cry than word.

'I would be failing in my duty as a magistrate if I did not deliver you this instant to the jail and report the evidence of my own eyes.'

James Black's breath was hot in his ear. His guardian's lean form was pressing into his. Calum felt himself start to lose consciousness. 'I don't want to die.' Now that the moment had come, his cowardly nature reasserted itself.

Somewhere on the edge of his mind, the cold voice continued. 'McGregor is a Jacobite rebel. Even without a highwayman's crimes to his name, he will be tried for treason and found guilty.'

Not only had he failed to secure a pardon for Fergie, he had thrown his own life away. Calum's legs were limp. His knees buckled. A great blackness opened up before him and he wanted to live as he had never wanted anything before.

The grip around his neck slackened slightly.

Calum gasped air into his lungs. 'No, please!'

'You are asking me to lie for you.' James Black's voice froze on the back of his neck. 'I am well-respected around here. And my role as local magistrate insists I tell what I know.'

His guardian's words from earlier that evening reeled back to him. 'Let it be our secret, Uncle Jamie. Do not lie – just . . . don't say anything.'

The grip eased further as James Black seemed to consider the suggestion.

Calum suddenly became aware of a solid hardness digging into the curve of his left arse-cheek. 'I beg you, Uncle Jamie.' He continued to plead. 'I will make reparations to those I robbed. I will do anything you think fit, to atone for my crimes as the Fox.' The vice around his wrists loosened. Calum found himself slowly turned.

'Anything?'

Black Jamie's coal-black eyes glistered with tiny lights. A shiver shook Calum's body. He could only nod, blood rushing back to his dazed brain. Long, icy fingers swept a lock of damp red hair back from his flushed face.

'You must do everything I say, Calum. You must trust me totally.'

Calum's Adam's apple bobbed convulsively. All he could see was the pale gaunt face, and the eyes which burnt like glowing embers.

'Put yourself in my hands, Pip.'

The desire to correct his guardian's slip of the tongue sprang to his lips. Calum swallowed the words back down.

He would be whatever – whoever – James Black wished him to be.

He would do whatever it took to stay alive.

'Come, Pip – come again with me to our room.'

Apprehension erecting every hair on his body, Calum allowed himself to be taken by the hand and led towards the study.

'This will be your chamber, from now on.' Cool fingers eased Calum's arms from the soaking jacket and shirt. 'I saw your face, tonight. We do not know how many others on board that coach now also know your identity.'

The fingers were on his breech fastenings, gently tugging wet fabric down over his goose-fleshed hips.

'Constables may come, to enquire after your whereabouts. I will dispose of all your clothes and tell them you have gone away.'

His shoes and hose were removed. Calum lifted one foot then

the other, allowing his guardian to slip his breeches and underwear over his clenched toes.

'No one knows of the Black Chamber. No one will find you here.' James Black stepped back.

Calum stood there naked, sweating and shivering at the same time. His gaze remained fixed on the large oil painting. He stared at his mother's face, eyes converging on the bright green pupils.

Other eyes surveyed him with quiet interest.

Calum heard his guardian's soft footfall on the pitch floor as the man walked slowly right, then left. His balls clenched under the scrutiny, drawing up tight against his body. Blood pounded in his head, and his windpipe hurt from the earlier pressure.

'Pip, you know I love you more than that rascal to whom you are to be married ever could.' Calum shivered. 'I have hidden my feelings and bitten my lip too often.'

Beyond the words, Calum listened to the soft ruffle of James Black's customary jacket and breeches. Then a hand stroked the back of his neck.

'Do you love me, just a little bit, Pip?'

The pain in the voice tugged at his heart. The fingers moved under his hair, caressing the bristly skin. Despite his horror at the implications of what was happening, Calum felt a stirring between his shivering thighs.

'I know you love me as a friend, but perhaps, during this period of enforced concealment, you will grow to love me in another way.'

The hand made its way down his spine, pausing to stroke each nobbled vertebra. Calum squirmed. With a mind of its own, his thick cock began to swell within its loose covering of beige-coloured skin.

Noticing Calum's arousal, his guardian gave a painful swat to the errant length. Calum gasped.

'This is wrong!' The hand swatted again. 'Pip is a lady – my lady! What is this monstrousness?'

Calum's guts twisted themselves into a knot. His hands flew to his slapped cock.

'Yes, cover yourself, wench – hide it until we can remove that abomination from God's sight!'

He stared up at the portrait of a woman he had never known, but whom he resembled strikingly in so many ways.

'First you betray me with that rogue Monroe. Then you dare to show sympathy for that traitor James Stuart. And now another betrayal lurks between your legs, my Pip.'

His guardian was pacing now. Shielding his groin from further attacks, Calum backed away. He could make no sense of James Black's rantings.

'It is some freak of nature, perhaps.'

Calum was shivering convulsively. Each tremor began at the back of his neck and shuddered down through his entire frame. Despite the slaps, his engorging cock continued to fight against gravity, pulsing against his cupped hands.

'Bind it down, Pip!'

A length of rope hit him in the face. Calum grabbed it, uncertain what he was meant to do. His guardian's voice filled his head. Fergie McGregor was miles away – both literally and figuratively. Calum knew he had his own safety to concern himself with now.

'Do it!'

Calum's spine hit a wall. He cowered there, terrified. The looming shape lurched towards him.

'By God, then I will!'

Then fingers were pulling his hands from his groin, grabbing his shaft and roughly hauling the stiff length downward. Coarse rope followed the fingers, handling and tying in the darkness.

Calum moaned, feeling his balls looped, tugged down and back. The discomfort between his legs gave way to a sharp burning sensation.

'Now get dressed, girl.'

Something cold and slippery hit his face. Calum wrenched the gown away, gripping the garment with fear-trembling fingers.

'Do it quickly, before you catch a chill, my precious.'

The change in tenor was almost more terrifying than the previous explosion of revulsion. Every movement of his legs sent arrows of pain into his tethered cock, but eventually Calum managed it.

'Good, good.'

Attempting to fasten the silk gown, Calum's fingers cramped. Other hands took over, securing the low collar of the dress in place. A mouth nuzzled the side of his sweating neck.

'Now rest, my dear.'

Rigid with fear, Calum stared at the painting of the woman with the long flowing hair and the emerald silk gown. Then an arm encircled his bare shoulders and he found himself guided over to the shadowed outline of a bed.

Nineteen

Another dawn. Another day passed in sleep.

The following evening they took turns in the saddle, before deciding they could travel more quickly with Endrick permanently on the horse. A twelve-hour trek took them past Clydebank, across the Duntocher Bridge and as far as Langbank.

The landscape levelled out, from rolling hills to flat plains. River smells were becoming sea smells and gulls squawked overhead. As the sun rose in the sky behind them, and with the distant, smoking chimneys of Greenock almost in sight, they found a derelict fisherman's cottage and settled down for the day.

Holding Endrick's restless body close to his for warmth, Fergie huddled with his other two companions around the horse's sleeping form. A frown marred his face.

The blond youth had been coughing badly all through the previous night: inhaling the sharp night air was having a detrimental effect on his lungs. Demonstrating an extensive knowledge of herbal remedies, Wee Andrew had gathered several plants from the hedgerows, pounding their leaves into fragrant infusion.

Endrick snuffled, changing his position. The movement served to set off another fit of coughing spasms.

The tall giant's potion had eased the slender sheep stealer's breathing for a short while. But Fergie knew it was only a stop-gap.

As soon as they reached Greenock, a doctor must be found.

Greenock. Tall ships. The ocean.

Freedom.

Fergie hugged Endrick's feverish body more closely.

Rory and Wee Andrew had their own, political reasons for travelling west: all through the previous night they had jabbered on about the Jacobite cause and an imminent visit, from the Continent, by the heir to the Stuart throne, Bonnie Prince Charlie himself.

The horse snuffled, rousing Endrick, whose darkly shadowed eyes suddenly blinked open.

Fergie stared into wide, startled pupils. 'Go back to sleep.' He stroked the halo of blond curls, smiling and murmuring soothing words until the slim sheep stealer drifted off into slumber. As the youth's chest rose and fell more evenly, Fergie's smile slipped into a frown.

Stuart or Tudor, one king was as good as another: neither cared much for the less fortunate amongst their subjects. His and Endrick's need to secure passage from Scotland was more urgent than any doomed rebellion: there was a price on both their heads, and an attempt had been made once already to hang the young sheep stealer.

Fergie tightened the embrace and felt the youth's unconscious trust soothe the anger in him.

When Endrick had recovered from whatever ailed him, they would both start a new life, far from these shores.

Fergie closed his eyes, thinking of distant lands and fresh starts. A sudden image of thick red hair and a masked face thrust itself into his mind. He pushed it away.

The Fox had deserted him, left him to take his chances on the run. Fergie's stomach knotted as he remembered his auburn-haired lover's strong arms tight around him, and the vows they had made to each other.

He had no time for such foolishness now. Shifting his position, he leant back, curling around Endrick's relaxed form.

Foolishness was for those who could afford such things. He had other matters to contend with. Snuggling down between Endrick and the sleeping horse, with Wee Andrew's snores competing with equine snuffles, Fergie eventually drifted into an uneasy sleep.

Nightfall saw the motley band straggle into Greenock.

It also saw a worsening in Endrick's health. Seated behind the limp form on Bessie's back, Fergie felt every cough as it racked the slender frame.

The streets along which they made their way bustled with life, while the man in his arms seemed to be slipping in the opposite direction.

'Is there a physician here? Tell us where we can find a doctor!' Wee Andrew strode on ahead shouting, his giant form cutting through the crowds of beggars.

The few responses he received were heavy with lowland brogue, and disappointingly negative.

Fergie glanced sideways, catching Rory's concerned words. 'Even if we find someone to help him, how will we pay?'

Fergie eyed Rory's pistol. He would find a way. Determinedly guiding Bessie between groups of starving women and children and on past men who pleaded for work, he too called out for a doctor.

Three streets later he was hoarse and losing hope. This was a different Greenock from the one he had seen on his visits to the cattle market. He didn't even recognise these streets, the poverty of which made his meagre croft back in Blairhoyle seem like a palace.

The din was overwhelming.

The stench made his eyes water.

Urging Bessie a little faster and following Wee Andrew's giant form around a corner, Fergie barely registered the whispered sound closer to home.

'Leave me. I am slowing you down.'

He shook his head to clear it, tightening his arm around Endrick's slender waist.

This street was quieter. Tailor. Cobbler. Ostler. Scanning the painted signs which hung outside a row of low-roofed cottages, Fergie failed to find any trace of a physician.

'Leave me, I say!'

The voice was louder, the accent alien. Fergie glanced around. Then the body in his grip turned its head.

The certainty of the message in those pale blue eyes almost made Fergie forget Endrick had not spoken since they had met. 'No! We will find you a doctor! You will be well again soon!'

Bessie stopped. Fergie stared at the blond youth's hollowed cheeks. A faint smile twitched blue-tinged lips.

'You saved my life once. That was more than enough.' Another coughing fit racked the thin frame.

'He can speak?' gasped Rory.

'He can speak English?' Rory and Wee Andrew's expressions mirrored Fergie's. Standing either side of Bessie, the two men peered at the sheep stealer.

The coughing fit subsided. 'I am from Iona. The minister taught me I must forget the Gaelic and learn the King's language.'

Wee Andrew sighed. 'First they take our crown, then they try to steal our tongue. They think they can silence us that way?'

Fergie waved a staying hand: there was no time for political debate. Turning the blond youth around to face him, Fergie smiled. 'You will be well soon. We will find a physician and –'

'Do not waste your time or money. But there is something you can do for me.' A thin arm slowly raised itself over Fergie's shoulder.

'Anything – just name it.'

The voice was now a whisper. Words came between rasping breaths. 'Take me to the top of that tall hill, so I may perhaps lie with my homeland in sight.'

Fergie supported the youth's lolling head, hoping to absorb some of the pain as a final series of shuddering coughs shook the pale form. 'If that is what you wish, my friend, that is what you shall have.' Pressing Endrick's face against his broad chest, he murmured into blond curls. 'But at least tell me your name.'

'Kenneth – Kenneth McAlpine.' The reply was barely audible.

Fergie knew his history. Nearly a thousand years earlier, this wan boy's ancestors had been kings of Scotland. He, Rory and Wee Andrew had been travelling with true royalty.

Kenneth's arms went limp around his neck. A last, husky breath cooled on his shin.

Overwhelmed by the awful unfairness of it all, Fergie embraced the youth and threw back his head. 'A McAlpine is dead! Long live the McAlpines!'

Rory and Wee Andrew stood silently, shocked and uncertain what to do. A light was lit in one of the previously dark cottages. Then more.

Faces appeared at windows. Doors opened and word spread. Slowly, a small crowd gathered. Women pulled shawls around their heads in respect. Men gripped oil-lamps and bent their necks in reverence. Someone held a small cross aloft. Someone else emerged from a ramshackle cottage holding a great length of McGregor plaid.

Fergie's eyes were wet. It wasn't the McAlpine tartan, but the spirit of the gesture made his heart pound. Holding Kenneth's lifeless body tight against his own, he turned his head and looked towards the dark outline of the hill. 'The law cannot harm you now, my silent beauty.' Reining Bessie round, he began the sombre ride to Kenneth McAlpine's final resting place.

More figures joined the slow cortege.

Fergie nodded his thanks as countless hands tucked small sprigs of heather into Bessie's bit and bridle. Both he and Kenneth were now draped in the length of plaid. The wearing of the tartan might be forbidden in life: death was another matter.

Kenneth would have as much of a true Island funeral as they could manage.

The incline steepened and the cold wind blew in from the Clyde's deep waters. Somewhere behind, a wheezing sound gave way to a loud, mournful skirl as a piper joined the procession, playing the traditional dirge which accompanied islanders from this life into the next.

Fergie turned his head briefly and caught sight of the long trail of oil-lamps which formed a lighted tail against the darkening sky and stretched down the side of the hill into distant Greenock. Those who did not hold torches were stooping to pick up stones from the path.

Rory and Wee Andrew walked either side of Bessie's snorting head, escorting the body onward and upward.

Fergie sat straight in his saddle, the wind whistling around him and fanning his long brown hair out from his head. Tears streamed down his face as he thought of Kenneth McAlpine's brief eighteen-odd years on this earth. He knew little of the youth's life before rescuing him from the militiamen's noose, but his heart swelled as he remembered lying naked with the boy and kissing that wan, smiling face.

The wind increased in strength, whipping his hair around his head.

At least, for the last few days of his life, Kenneth had found friendship, warmth and affection. A sudden surge of anger grew in his chest and he cursed the unjust laws which would take a life for the theft of a mere sheep.

Someone began to sing. Quietly at first, a lone female voice intoned ancient Gaelic words of tribute. Others joined in and the sound grew louder, fighting against the wind which howled around the sombre procession.

Wee Andrew's bassy tones underpinned the lament. The giant's voice cracked with emotion, but he sang on.

Soon the rugged hillside rang with a choir of dozens.

Fergie listened to the strange language, not understanding any of it. But words didn't matter. If the song had been sung in French, the sentiment would still be recognisable.

The sadness of the passing of a life – especially one so brief – was a universal cause for regret.

Eventually, Bessie's front hooves hit the summit of the hill. Gathering his charge up in the plaid, Fergie carefully dismounted and continued on foot. At the edge of the flat plateau he paused, raising the arms which held Kenneth's body.

Behind, the singing fell in volume to a soothing murmur, reminding Fergie of the Gaelic lullabies with which his mother still sometimes urged his younger brothers to sleep. The sound of the pipes soared through the night, over the water towards Iona.

One by one, the mourners fell silent, spreading out in a large semicircle around him. Almost all held rocks of varying sizes.

Fergie found his voice. 'Rest in peace, Kenneth McAlpine.' He fell to one knee, arms still outstretched. 'Your spirit will live on in your countrymen.' Other words caught in his throat, words of a love he could have felt for the youth, had there been time. But he kept them to himself, moving back and placing Kenneth's plaid-covered body on the ground. As he tucked the flapping tartan around the slender form, a section tore free from the rest.

The idea came from nowhere. Hauling off his breeks, Fergie hurled the long-enforced garment into the night and deftly secured the spare swathe of tartan around his waist.

The kilt felt strange against his skin. The cool night air seeped up beneath its folds. Bare chested, and wearing the highland dress which was his by birthright, Fergie felt a sudden pride. He stared down at Kenneth's lifeless body. 'I shall wear this in honour of you, McAlpine. And perhaps some day, all our countrymen will have the freedom to do likewise.' Lifting a small rock from nearby, he kissed the stone then placed it on the plaid-wrapped form.

Others did likewise, to the low accompaniment of the pipes.

Soon, a large cairn of rocks covered Kenneth's body. Some mourners murmured prayers. Others patted Fergie's shoulder.

He continued to stand there, shaking hands and accepting condolences from men and women he did not know but who shared the spirit of his grief and his growing discontent with English rule.

Despite the chill of the evening and the sombre occasion, people lingered. Introductions were made. Someone produced whisky and Fergie flinched as a jar of the amber liquid was thrust into his hand. He stared at it in confusion. Then a fraternal palm slapped his shoulder.

'Kenneth would not wish you to be sad, Fergus.' Wee Andrew beamed down at him. 'Now is the time to celebrate life, as well as commemorate death.'

A huge hand tipped the jar upward, and Fergie found himself drinking deeply.

Wee Andrew laughed. 'That's it!'

Abruptly, the piper began to play a different tune.

Fergie took a second drink, wiping his eyes and watching a group of men and women who were now dancing to the jauntier air. Oil-lamps had been placed every few yards, to illuminate the proceedings. Skirts fanned out and heavily booted feet skipped merrily on the high summit.

Rory sauntered past the dancers, his skin flushed beneath the silver beard. One fist beckoned enthusiastically. The other gripped the arm of a smartly dressed man. 'Fergus? Someone wants to meet the first man to wear the kilt in these parts for a hundred years!'

Fergie took another long draft from the jar, feeling the whisky warm his stomach and raise his spirits. He stuck out a hand. 'Fergus McGregor at your service.'

His fingers were gripped in a strong grasp. 'Alexander MacIntosh at yours, friend. Your reputation was not unjustified.'

Fergie stared at the tall, distinguished-looking fellow.

Wigless, and with his sandy hair tied at the nape of his neck, Alexander wore a neat ginger moustache and a small, recently trimmed beard. His face was strong and handsome, a match for his merchant-class clothes. He looked prosperous and well fed, standing out amongst the thinner revellers.

Not having eaten since the previous evening, the whisky went straight to his head. Fergie glowered belligerently. Suspicion prickled up his spine. He wrenched his hand free of the warm grip. 'What brings such a gentleman to the wake of someone he did not know?'

Alexander MacIntosh's small green eyes twinkled. 'I have use for a fine highland lad such as yourself.' Turning his head left then right, to ensure they had privacy, he continued. 'Do you wish to help The Cause?'

Fergie's gaze moved from his interrogator's handsome face down the neatly buttoned waistcoat to the front of the fellow's best linen breeches. A frisson of lust coursed through his body.

Maybe it was the whisky.

Maybe it was the night air.

Maybe it was fond memories of the enthusiastic lover he had found, two days ago, in young McAlpine.

Maybe, as Rory had implied, it was the need to celebrate life and chase away a mortality they all shared.

It most definitely was not due to the vague resemblance between the man who stood before him and the Fox.

Fergie grinned drunkenly, throwing a bare arm around Alexander's shoulders. 'There is another cause which interests me, right now, sir.' With a leer, he slipped his other hand between them and coarsely gripped a swelling handful of best linen. 'And I see you share my concerns.' With Alexander's responding chuckle echoing in his ear, they staggered past the dancers and towards a more secluded area.

The copse of trees had grown at an angle, trunks battered by the cruel sea wind.

Stumbling in his haste, Fergie shoved the redheaded merchant against one of those sloping trunks and held him there with his weight.

Alexander grunted, arching his back from the rough treetrunk and rubbing his body against the bare-chested highlander's.

Fergie buried his face in a recently shaved neck.

A vein pulsed against his cheek, mirroring the throb in the groin which pressed against his and found a violent echo there.

He could feel every twitch of muscle against his open mouth, each quickening of breath as he licked and nibbled the skin of Alexander's throat.

He could smell the man: rich and musky and meaty.

And alive.

Fergie moaned. The head of his desire dragged against coarse plaid, sending shocks of lust through the length of his prick.

Linen-clad legs parted around his. Hands moved over his shoulders, kneading and massaging the taut ropes of muscle.

Fergie groaned, slipping fists clenched with need beneath the small of Alexander's back, forcing the man's body out from the tree further and harder against his own.

Fingers gripped the tuck of fabric at the small of Fergie's back, hauling frantically. The length of plaid unwrapped itself from around his thrusting hips and slid to folds around his ankles.

Pushing himself between Alexander's spread thighs, Fergie cupped the bearded face and searched with his mouth.

Other lips parted, accepting the hurried kiss with an equal urgency.

Grinding his crotch against a linen-covered hardness, and with his bare arse undulating in the night air, Fergie felt Alexander's neat ginger moustache rasp sharply against the side of his mouth. Teeth slid off teeth. Tongues thrust in parallel, slick and hungry. Fergie gasped.

Warm palms clasped his naked buttocks, pulling him closer.

Somewhere in the distance, fiddles had joined the pipes. Shrieking strings soared up into the night sky, carried on the howling wind and transported out to sea.

Fergie barely heard them. Growling with need, he broke the kiss. Shaking fingers raked at the front of an expensive jacket.

A foot below, well-manicured hands reluctantly left Fergie's arse-cheeks and Alexander was tearing at the fastenings of his own breeches.

Buttons popped. Fergie moaned, slipping his hands inside the man's jacket and running warm palms over a surprisingly well-developed chest. Thick hair pushed between fingers which tightened again into fists. A strong length of arousal was flexing hard against his own.

The merchant's prick curved to the left, its bristling root resting against Fergie's heavy balls while the large velvet head slicked the highlander's bare stomach.

Blood rushed from Fergie's brain, pumping lower and stiffening him further. Wet warmth oozed from his slit, cooling on the sensitive glans but only serving to inflame him more.

Then Alexander's hand was wrapping itself around both shafts, gripping them tightly until Fergie could no longer tell where his prick stopped and Alexander's began.

The merchant bent his knees for a better grip, resting his brow on Fergie's shoulder.

Fergie mirrored the movement. One arm around Alexander's back for support, the other digging into strong shoulder-muscle, he stared down between their bodies.

The well-manicured hand slid slowly up, dragging two foreskins in its wake. Fergie's thighs trembled. His balls clenched.

Alexander's fist paused. He inhaled sharply, the fingers of his free hand tangling themselves in Fergie's hair.

The pressure around his glans was unbearable. He could feel the sensitive flesh rub against a warm palm, struggling to flex in the merchant's grip. Fergie continued to focus down beyond Alexander's thick mat of soft chest hair to where the merchant's fingers struggled to meet around their shafts.

The fist retreated slowly.

Fergie watched two purple cockheads sprout from between Alexander's thumb and forefinger. The tight ring continued its unbearable descent, sending shivers of frustration deep into Fergie's bollocks.

He wanted to come. And he wanted to come now!

With a growl, he released Alexander's shoulder and thrust his own fist between them. Half covering the merchant's hand, Fergie increased the speed of the caress. His fingers moved more swiftly, travelling the length of twin shafts with an urgency that brought a cry to Alexander's lips.

In the background, he was vaguely aware that the music had stopped. Loud voices filtered through the howls of the wind. Fergie's brain had no room for such distractions. Alexander's fist slick and sweating beneath his own, he pumped faster, roughly fingering two tight ball sacs with each downward flight of his fist.

The merchant was breathing heavily. His head slipped to rest on Fergie's shoulder.

The highlander's lips were tight amidst thick sandy hair. Cramp spasmed sharply in his wrist. A sudden clench deep inside his body pushed his aching fist to greater, if clumsier speeds. His palm was sticky with Alexander's arousal, which mixed with his own.

Two musket shots flared brightly on the periphery of his vision.

Fergie closed his eyes. His other arm tightened around Alexander's waist and his legs gave way. Falling to his knees, he dragged the merchant down with him.

Then a jerking flex against his fingers made him gasp. A

second shudder parallel to his spurting prick pushed him over the edge.

Mouth open in Alexander's sweaty hair, Fergie shot into his own fist. Wet with warm spunk, another's release joined his own and prompted a second milky wad.

Heads resting on each other's shoulders, they knelt there. Viscous stickiness leaked from between their linked fingers, running down the back of their hands.

The grip loosened a little.

Fergie shot a final time. His wrist was agony. His balls hung slack and depleted, tingling from the force of the orgasm.

Then a further musket report and the sound of footsteps made him flinch. Alexander pushed him to the ground, covering Fergie's body with his own. Voices grew louder.

'This is an unlawful burial. Furthermore, we have received information that, in contravention of his Majesty King George's law, the kilt is being worn by person or persons unknown. Give us his name and you will not be harmed.'

Fergie scowled at the words, snaking out a hand to grab his length of plaid and attempting to rise.

Alexander restrained him. 'They are too many, and you are unarmed.' Close to his, a red head nodded beyond the copse to the steep cliff. 'There is a narrow path, which leads away from the docks. Take it, and go to this address.' Slipping a hand into his pocket, the merchant produced a small printed card. 'I will meet you there.'

Fergie tucked his kilt under one arm and took the card.

Alexander's green eyes sparkled in the darkness. He grabbed Fergie's spunk-slicked fingers, raising them to his bearded mouth and kissing them. 'God speed, highlander. We will meet again soon.' Then he pushed Fergie towards the edge of the steep precipice and leapt to his own feet. 'There he goes!' The merchant ran back to the middle of the plateau, shouting loudly and gesturing in the opposite direction. 'Over there – towards the docks.'

Fergie took advantage of the welcome distraction. Squeezing his eyes shut, he took a deep breath and scrambled down the steep incline, praying that his feet would soon find the path.

Twenty

In the dream he was wearing the green silk gown and staring past the stub of a guttering candle at its original owner. His mother's face shimmered before his eyes, bringing with it a vague memory of a promise made to Rab the herdsman.

Calum shook his head, trying to clear it.

'Oh, Pip – I have waited so long for this.'

The words came from everywhere and nowhere, tearing Calum's gaze from the portrait and disorienting him further. His eyes darted around the dark chamber.

Everything was shadows and outlines.

'Come to me, my dear.'

Fighting down fear, Calum swung his bare legs over the end of the cot, noticing again the biting tightness between his legs. His feet hit the floor. Its cold surface sent shivers through his entire frame.

'Come on, precious.'

Calum tried again to focus on the source of the words. And again failed. Making his way blindly in the dark, each step caused the rough rope around his cock and bollocks to cut in painfully. He moved awkwardly, bumping into the low bench which ran the length of one wall. On its surface, an array of objects wobbled. Calum's throat was dry as he took in the selection of cylindrical articles.

Eight in number, their sizes ranging from a slim four inches to a stout and terrifying near-foot length, with a girth of at least eight. Thicker at the base, tapering to a rounded point.

A blush flared on Calum's cheeks as he remembered Dirk, a Dutchman he'd met at Court, who had owned a similar, if more elegant collection, carved from a variety of materials spanning horn to ebony wood.

'Do not be afraid, my dear.'

Calum coughed, his face scarlet. 'Uncle Jamie, what –?'

'I know you to be a virtuous girl, my precious.' A sigh issued forth from the darkness. 'And inexperienced in the ways of men.'

Calum's fingers trembled. He stretched out a shaking hand towards the slimmest of the objects.

'But we will learn together, Philippa.'

His fist tightened around the slender shaft and the use of his mother's name pushed the last shreds of sleep from his mind. Turning towards the approximate source of the voice, Calum frowned. 'This is wrong, Uncle Jamie.'

'I am not your uncle.' The response was icy.

His balls tightened. He clenched his teeth. 'And I am not Philippa! I am Calum Monroe. We are different people.'

'Yes, we are different in many ways, but similar in others.'

Frustration twisted his frown into a scowl. Why was his guardian deliberately misinterpreting his words? 'That is Philippa!' Calum turned quickly towards the oil painting, pointing with the slender cylindrical object. His eyes fell on the guttering candle. With his free hand he snatched the flickering stub from its position on the table and spun back round, holding the light out at arm's length. 'She is dead! I am –'

The sight which he beheld, mere feet away, froze the breath in his chest and stopped his words in their tracks.

His guardian stood there, wearing a red infantryman's jacket. His well-muscled pectorals gleamed from between the braided revers, slick with sweat. James Black's normally tidy hair was a swirling, curled mass around his angular face. His mouth was a tight, hard line and the glistering eyes burnt wild with madness. 'I am Lieutenant James Black, my lady.'

He barely heard the words. His guardian was naked from the

waist down, and Calum's gaze was rooted by the thick length of engorged man meat which curved up and out at an almost forty-five-degree angle from between the man's thighs.

'Honoured to make your acquaintance, Miss MacFayden.'

Calum backed away, unable to pull his eyes from the great prick. The shaft dwarfed the largest of the cylinders which lined the table, both in length and girth. It was an awesome weapon, almost defying gravity in erection.

'I did not realise your betrothed was so beautiful, Monroe.'

Who was the man talking to now? Calum's stomach twisted into a knot. James Black's cock was at least thirteen inches, with a girth of nearly eight around the thick shaft. The head, however, was even broader, topping the heavily veined stem like a huge, engorged bulb.

'Will you honour me with a dance, my lady?'

Beneath the green silk gown, his knees were water.

James Black moved out of the darkness and closer to the candle's flickering flame. The weighty prick swayed languidly with each step.

Transfixed by the motion of the grossly swollen appendage, Calum watched the web of thick veins pulse blue in the dim light.

'You don't mind, do you, Monroe? As your commanding officer, it is my right, I think.' A low laugh seeped into his ears.

The sound was devoid of all humour. Calum flinched. The slim cylinder slipped from his fingers and clattered to the floor.

'My lady? Shall we?'

Calum finally managed to drag his eyes upward, past a hard stomach and over those glistening pectorals back to his guardian's face. His larynx refused to work.

James Black reached out and seized the candle, extinguishing its guttering flame with a single breath.

The room was plunged into darkness and Calum felt cool hands on his nipped-in waist. Then he was pulled into a boisterous reel.

'You dance like an angel, my dear.'

The force of the movement caused a sudden rasping between

his legs as the rough rope dug into delicate skin. Calum gasped, staggering.

His guardian twirled him this way then that. 'You can do better than that ape Monroe for a husband, Miss MacFayden.'

Calum found his voice just as a soft kiss brushed his bare shoulders. 'I am not –'

'You are not in love with him, I can see that.'

Something wet and solid was poking against the skirts of the green gown. Calum winced, rearing backward. But there was no escape from the strong hands which gripped his waist ever tighter.

'We will be together soon, my lady. Very soon.'

Panic shot through Calum's body. The dance continued. He was dragged around the Black Chamber, tripping over his skirts and now moaning with pain as the coarse ropes around his aching genitals cut in further. Then one hand left his waist and gripped his right arse-cheek.

'You lay with that rogue McGregor. You took his prick into your mouth when you would not take mine. You let his hands rove over your body when you rejected every overture from me.' The accusation was a whisper in his ear.

The thump of his own heart filled Calum's head. Somewhere at the back of his confused brain he realised James Black was confusing past and present, weaving two rejections into one, great, personal slight.

Abruptly, the dance stopped and Calum found himself pushed back against a wall and held there.

'Did you fuck him? Did you push your cock into his traitorous arse?' The questions were hissed.

Calum moaned, fear giving way to sadness then arousal as memories of Fergie's strong body returned to him. Between his sore thighs his tethered prick bucked against its prison of ropes and brought tears to Calum's eyes.

'Did you leave your slimy seed there? Did you taste your own spunk when you ran your tongue around his arsehole afterward?'

'No, no –'

'What was he like, your rebel lover? Was he good? Was he

tighter than a virgin's quim? Did he moan and shudder when you pounded into his hole?'

Despite the acid in the voice, Calum was aroused. They both were. His cock stretched further, the pink head pushing free of the thick ruffles of foreskin and pulsing against coarse rope. 'I love him!' The power of speech returned, banishing any idea of humouring his guardian or going along with whatever insane game the man was playing. 'And I will continue to love him, despite anything you –'

The slap sent him reeling sideways. Calum's knees hit the floor. His hand flew to his injured cheek.

'Love? You do not know the meaning of the word!' Stunned by the blow, Calum's head spun. Spittle hit his stinging cheek. 'By the time I have finished with you, you will rue the day you ever wasted yourself on the traitor McGregor.'

Anger gave him strength. 'He is no traitor!' Fighting the constraints of the green silk gown and the pain between his legs, Calum lunged up into the darkness, fists flailing.

A booted foot caught him in the stomach.

Breath gushed from his lungs. Calum curled into a defensive ball. Despite the fear and anger which coursed through his veins, he was shocked to find his cock was continuing to stretch. 'No, no –' He cringed, braced for another kick and horrified at the whimpering tone which had entered his voice.

'Oh, my Pip!' The change in James Black's tone was more shocking still. 'Do not fight me – it will be worse if you fight me.'

Then Calum was pulled into a tight embrace, words of mumbled regret poured into his sweat-drenched hair. The apologies and soft caresses disoriented him further. His bare arms found his guardian's neck. He clung on, soothed by the warm affection, and only vaguely aware of the stout, impossibly hard length of muscle which pulsed between their entwined bodies.

Slowly, his heart returned to normal. His brain raced less and the tension gradually left his bruised body. The ache between his legs continued to pulsate.

James Black stood up, still cradling his ward in his arms, and walked slowly to the small cot. 'Drink this, Pip.'

Calum gulped thirstily at the strange, bitter-tasting liquid. 'Please untie me. It hurts and I –'

'Soon it will be gone, my love. Soon that offence against nature will be removed and you will be as you should be.' His guardian gently disentangled himself from Calum's embrace.

His head lolled back on the narrow cot. Calum tried to make sense of the words. An unrecognised but not unpleasant numbness filled his sore body, and the last thing he felt before sleep claimed him was the pressure of thin lips on his sweating forehead.

'I thought we might find you here.'

Fergie poked his head up from his hiding place behind the pile of tarred rope and stared in disbelief at the two smartly dressed strangers. There was something oddly familiar about their faces.

On the quayside, his sister Morag smiled, grabbing Rab's arm and hauling her betrothed into her brother's makeshift bedchamber. 'It is good you are safe and well, Fergie.'

Still stunned at the sight of the two most unexpected people in the world standing before him, Fergie found himself pulled into a double embrace.

He hurriedly brought his best friend and his sister up to date with matters, finishing with the illegal funeral last night and his near capture a second time, by militiamen. Worse still, he had lost the merchant MacIntosh's business card and had been forced to seek refuge behind a heap of rigging.

Rab and Morag listened, eyes wide. When Fergie had finished, the herdsman heaved two stout saddlebags from over his shoulder and threw them on to the ground.

'Your problems are over, Fergie.'

He looked down at the bulging satchels, then returned a quizzical gaze to his herdsman and former lover.

Rab grinned. 'Courtesy of your –' he winked '– highwayman friend the Fox, there is enough here to take us all to the Americas.' He unfastened one of the stout leather straps.

Fergie barely registered the great wads of notes and coins which tumbled free. 'You have talked with him?'

Rab nodded. 'Ma McGregor was reluctant to take his money, at first, but –' he circled Morag's slim waist with one arm '– we persuaded her to use a share to journey northward. Your brothers have gone with her.'

Fergie's mind was filled with long red hair and a pair of masked eyes.

'Black Jamie has taken possession of the croft, brother.' Morag's voice was tinged with sadness.

'Tell me about my Fox.' Fergie talked through his sister, eager only for news of the one man who, despite everything which had happened, could still bring an ache to his chest. He listened intently as Rab passed on an account of how the Fox had initially arranged to travel with them, but had failed to turn up.

'He has not been seen since, my friend. Nor have any coaches been robbed since that night, almost a week ago.'

Fergie sighed. Regardless of what he'd endured over the past ten days, he feared for his beloved's safety and would have happily exchanged the contents of those bulging saddlebags for better news.

'That is all in the past, brother.' Morag was talking again, her voice a low whisper beneath the sounds of bustle a few yards away on the quayside. 'We have obtained three passages on board the *Glenmore*. She sails in three hours for Baltimore.' Her eyes shone, flicking from her betrothed to her brother, then pausing to take in the latter's seminaked state. 'But you cannot set foot in the New World like that.' She tugged dismissively at Fergie's ragged kilt, then tapped Rab's arm. 'Give him your coat and hat until we can find a tailor who can work quickly.'

Fergie laughed.

Tailors. Suits of clothes. Great sailing ships.

The Americas! It was almost too much to take in as he hurriedly donned the fine feathered hat and struggled into the heavy brocade coat.

They made a strange trio, laughing and running hand in hand along the quayside: the broad-shouldered fellow in the silk shirt, his lady companion in voluminous skirts, and the tall grinning man with the bare feet and the feathered hat perched rakishly on the back of his tangled locks who still carried a dirty length of plaid.

It was to be his downfall.

As they neared the town centre, an eagle-eyed captain leading a troop of militiamen spotted the outlawed tartan seconds before Fergie spotted him.

His heart missed a beat, then got back on a speedier course. He had two choices: brazen it out, and risk implicating Morag and Rab, or give up all hope of ever seeing the Americas.

The decision was split-second.

Breaking free of his friend and his sister's embrace, Fergie hurled his hat at the advancing line of soldiers and sprinted into the crowd. His legs pumped like pistons. Rough cobbles dug into his feet and made them bleed. Shouts and musket-shots joined the shrieks of seagulls, filling the air around him.

The stench of gunpowder was hot in his nostrils. Head down, pushing through groups of townspeople, he slipped.

A hand grabbed the back of the brocade coat, pulling it from his body.

Fergie pushed his would-be-apprehender away and scrambled to his feet. Lungs bursting, he veered right and doubled back, still clutching the length of plaid.

Dodging past great trunks of luggage and weaving between herds of startled animals, Fergie had no idea where he was going. He tried frantically to recall the address on the card given to him by Alexander, the previous evening, and had almost managed it when a pair of strong hands grabbed his. Fergie struggled, cursing and kicking.

Another two militiamen seized his flailing legs.

Seconds later, he was pinned to the ground, a fifth soldier sitting on his chest. Back arching, Fergie scowled then spat at the face which loomed over him.

The captain wiped a wad of phlegm from his cheek. 'Fergus McGregor, I believe.' The soldier laughed. 'Where's your highwayman's garb now?'

Fergie spat again, and received a hard kick in the kidneys for his trouble.

'Take him to the gaolhouse. Let him cool his filthy highland heels there.'

Writhing and swearing, Fergie could do little as he was dragged up the main street towards a tall building with barred windows.

At least he had a cell to himself, this time. And the gaoler had let him keep the plaid.

Wrapping the length of tartan around his naked shoulders, Fergie scowled at the heavy wooden door then examined his surroundings.

Illuminated only by a tiny window high up in its rough walls, the room was dark and dank.

Fergie's scowl deepened as despair slowly replaced anger.

To have had freedom dangled so tantalisingly in front of him, then see that freedom torn from his grasp was worse than never having escaped in the first place.

It was just a matter of time – it always had been. An armed guard would be dispatched form the garrison in Stirling. He would be escorted back to Blairhoyle, to stand trial.

He had attacked a gaoler. He had accosted militiamen and robbed them of the pleasure of hanging young Kenneth McAlpine. He had worn the kilt, flaunted his heritage.

Even if the Fox did come forward, Fergie knew these offences alone sealed his fate.

Grabbing a handful of filthy straw, he crushed the dull stalks in his fist and considered his future. Low voices from beyond the door seeped through his self-pity.

'I shouldn't let you in. The sheriff said to –'

'I might be able to get the names of his accomplices from him, Archie.'

'Aye, maybe –' the gaoler sounded somewhat uncertain '– but it's more than my job's worth to –'

The unmistakable clink of coins cut through the protestations. 'Just between us, eh, Archie? Buy the bairns a treat, from me.'

'Ah, you're a gentleman, sir.'

Fergie heard the jangle of keys, then a scraping as a heavy lock was turned. The door creaked open, and he peered past Alexander MacIntosh's dapper form to the red-faced gaoler.

'Fifteen minutes, Archie.' The merchant smiled at the ruddy-cheeked man, tipping another three coins into a grimy palm. His voice sank to a confidential whisper. 'And leave the lock free in case I have to exit in a hurry.'

The gaoler's thanks were effusive as he moved back a little then disappeared behind the solid, studded door.

Fergie leapt to his feet. The tartan swathe slipped from his shoulders and he stood there, naked and proud.

Alexander MacIntosh smiled, then walked quickly across the tiny chamber, drawing Fergie into a corner. 'Listen closely, my handsome friend. We do not have much time.'

Fergie raised an eyebrow.

'Do you love your country? Do you want to see Caledonia ruled from home, rather than five hundred miles away in London?'

A mere two weeks before, Fergie would have scoffed at such idealistic questions. Now he nodded slowly.

'I know you have had dealings with a certain landowner, James Black.'

Fergie scowled at the memory of Black Jamie and his simpering ward. 'Aye, there is no love lost between that fellow and myself.'

'I hope I can trust you.' Stroking the soft skin at the back of Fergie's neck, Alexander lowered his voice further. 'Bonnie Prince Charlie will be arriving on the east coast in three days' time, to lead an army of freedom-loving Scotsmen against the English overlords.'

Fergie listened intently, wondering what all this had to do with him.

'We have information that James Black is aware of Charles Stuart's imminent arrival, and plans to turn our rightful king over to the English authorities as soon as he sets foot on Scottish soil.'

'What can I do?' Fergie frowned. 'I am in enough trouble as it is, sir.'

'If you are willing to infiltrate the home of James Black and find out how much he knows, there will be a full pardon in it for you.'

Fergie shook his head. 'It is impossible. I am known to him and his ward.'

'But you also know that part of the country better than any of my other contacts, Fergus. And you are a resourceful man. I have every faith in your abilities.'

The memory of his confiscated land strengthened Fergie's resolve. 'Very well – I am willing to try. But how can I do any of this if I am in custody?'

Alexander chuckled. 'That is a mere detail.' He brought his lips close to Fergie's ear in explanation.

Seconds later, the merchant stood naked.

Fergie couldn't help admiring the man's well-muscled body in the same way as he admired the fellow's cunning. He struggled into Alexander's clothes, pulled the discarded wig on to his head and tucked unruly curls underneath.

'Now hit me.'

Fergie flinched.

Alexander smiled. 'Do not worry – I have a strong jaw, but I also have a reputation to maintain.'

Fergie felt the outline of a pistol as he pulled on the merchant's well-cut coat. The other pocket contained an ample money pouch.

'We are about the same size and build. Keep your face hidden and you will be able to slip out unnoticed, but I cannot risk it becoming known I have helped a rebel.'

Fergie sighed, unwilling to strike this man who had helped him.

'Do it!' Alexander's voice was more urgent now.

Fergie knew it made sense. Gripping Alexander's bare shoulders, he pulled the man against him and kissed the merchant roughly on the mouth.

Neatly moustached lips returned the pressure, before breaking away.

Fergie's right fist silenced Alexander's wish of God speed and good luck as it impacted with the man's right cheekbone.

The merchant slumped into Fergie's arms.

Licking his bruised knuckles, he gently lowered the limp naked body to the floor. Then Fergie was stealthily opening the door, creeping down eight flights of stairs and out into the autumn afternoon.

No one glanced a second time at the tall, prosperous-looking merchant. In fact, except for the wig, he looked very like the Fergie McGregor who had left Greenock a mere three weeks earlier, having sold his sheep for a good price.

Almost smiling at the twists and turns of fate, Fergie set off at a brisk pace towards the Coaching Inn.

Twenty-One

'Deny you have feelings for me now, girl!'

Calum's knees scraped against black stone. Chest supported by the narrow cot, he pressed his face into the hard surface and gasped. Each hoarse exhortation from somewhere above him sent hot shivers rippling through his full balls.

'Deny you want to feel me inside you, in place of that carved substitute.'

Calum moaned into the lumpy mattress. Still tethered, his stiff cock rubbed between his thighs. Slick with sweat, the fingers of his right hand clenched into claws around the broad base and pushed.

The instrument of his instruction slid further into his tight rectum, stretching and widening. Calum's brain reeled with new protests.

His body swept them away in another warm shudder. It was true – he could not deny he wanted this.

He could feel his own knuckles jammed against his arse-cheeks. Beneath the green silk gown his damp skin crawled and a trickle of sweat made its way down his spine. A parallel wetness slicked his perineum as, trapped between his body and the coarse ropes, the head of his swollen prick leaked sticky desire on to both.

'We were meant to be together, Pip.'

The words were directly above him, just audible through the thick veil of auburn hair which was plastered lankly to his flushed face.

'Say it.'

The walls of his arse were gripping the inflexible invader, caressing each lifeless inch and drawing it deeper. Calum bore down and back, impaling himself further on the carved object and urging it to greater depths.

'Say it.'

The exhortation was closer still. Calum ignored the pain in his knees and ground himself on to the carved prick, seeking the dark place in his mind to which he had retreated each time the stern voice had urged a verbal assent over the past, numberless hours.

Then long fingers gripped a hank of his hair and his face was wrenched from the cot. 'Say it, girl!'

Calum winced, staring up into gloom.

Where other senses were overcome by the dark and the fizzing in his ears, one remained true. Calum inhaled a deep breath and drew the musky scent of James Black's arousal into his lungs. He shrank back.

A second, long-fingered hand snaked out, gripping his chin.

The fingers tightened in his hair, hauling his face towards the fearsome, drooling appendage which stuck up from between the man's thighs. His mouth was dry. He closed his eyes to block out the sight, but could not escape from the earthy stench of male lust.

Then the hand released his chin and something solid yet yielding impacted with his upper lip.

The muscles in his face froze. His balls drew up painfully against his body. Calum wanted to cry out. He bit back the urge, unable to move as the head of Black Jamie's great prick moved around the outline of his lips.

Before, he had smelled him. Now Calum could taste the sour need which left a clear trail around his mouth.

His stomach twisted into knots.

Ribs tightened across his heaving lungs.

Two rings of muscle gripped the hard length in his arse.

And his fully erect cock flexed achingly in its rope prison.

'Why will you not admit what your body is screaming from every pore, Pip?'

The great weapon of flesh continued to move, juddering down over Calum's stubbly chin then skimming up past the side of his nose. He felt the tightly stretched cockskin shiver against his face and his mind filled in what his eyes could not see.

Himself, kneeling on the floor for hours clad in the green silk gown, thighs spread and cramping with effort. Arse-cheeks jammed apart by the thick base of the carved object. His own hand holding that object in place.

'Perhaps this will loosen your tongue.'

A sudden current of air signalled movement he could not see. The thick solidity of his guardian's prick slapped wetly against Calum's left cheek. Then he was howling as the carved cock swiftly left his rectum.

A great emptiness overcame his body, mirroring the void in his mind. Only one thought filled his brain. 'No, no – please put it back!' Calum's hips dipped down then rose up as his arse tried to find the soothing hardness and again swallow it up. The muscles in his face relaxed. His mouth lolled in desperation, slack and uncomprehending.

Before he knew what was happening, the first two inches of Black Jamie's drooling prick had pushed past the lip barrier and Calum was moaning again.

His hair was released. A warm palm placed itself on the green silk covering the small of his back. His head supported by a bare thigh, Calum slumped sideways and ran a dry tongue over the velvet glans. Between his quivering arse-cheeks his sphincter gaped open, aching with the memory of the wooden length while another all too real length pushed past his tongue.

James Black was patient, only feeding his ward half an inch at a time.

Calum lay there in his guardian's lap, sucking eagerly on the vast helmet of flesh. The position was awkward but he was past caring. A gentle hand was massaging his back. Soft soothing sounds rained down on his battered body. After the harsh words and the rough treatment, the caresses were sweeter than the sweetest honey, more welcome than any attention he'd ever received.

A strange kind of gratitude filled his chest. Somewhere to his left, heavy hairiness brushed the side of his face.

Calum whimpered, curling his lips over his teeth and accepting another measure of the man's meat. His own cock was somewhere in the darkness, numb and useless and no longer of any concern to him.

All he cared about was the way James Black's thick shaft filled his mouth. All that mattered was ministering and attending to his guardian's prick.

The hand left the small of his back and brushed a lank auburn lock from his pink face.

'A wife's duty, my Pip.' His guardian's voice was low and hoarse.

Moving his head back to nod, Calum gasped as a thick helmet of flesh pushed further into his mouth. The muscles in his throat began to spasm reflexively. Panic gave his limp arms strength. Calum clawed at the hairless chest, trying to push James Black away.

'Be a lady, Philippa – be my wife.' The words were husky and halting. One iron hand seized his wrists, holding them tightly. The other continued to stroke his hair. 'Obey me.' The fleshy invader paused.

Soothed by phrases which had previously unnerved him, Calum tried to relax.

He wanted to please. He wanted to do whatever was necessary. He wanted to carry out a wife's duty to the very letter.

He wanted to obey his husband's every bidding.

Calum opened his mouth wider, lips stretching around the prick's thick girth. He could feel the remainder of the great shaft flexing against his chin while the swollen head brushed the roof of his mouth and threatened to close off the airway.

'Oh, Pip! I have waited decades for this moment.'

Somewhere on the edge of unconsciousness, Calum heard the pleasure in the voice. An immense satisfaction tingled over his flushed skin. His ears were full of pounding blood as the great staff of flesh pushed past his spasming gag reflex, along his soft palate and towards his throat.

Seconds before the sparkling blackness swallowed him completely, a distant warmth splattered the rope which bound his prick. But all Calum knew was the pride of becoming a vessel for another's need.

He travelled through the night, enjoying every pothole and lurch of the carriage as it thundered along the road to Stirling. As Rab had told him, no highwayman attempted to halt the coach.

Fergie's smile of contentment wavered a little. Worry at whatever fate had befallen his Fox dogged his thoughts, joining his concern for Morag and his herdsman. Reason soothed his doubts.

If they had any sense, they would have sailed without him – and he knew his sister was blessed with a logical mind. And as for his Fox . . .

The carriage lurched. A tiny shred of jealousy tugged irrationally at the corners of Fergie's full mouth. He pushed it away, moving his eyes from his dozing travelling companions and focusing his gaze beyond the window to the dawn sky.

He was glad Morag and Rab had each other. He was glad they would have a new start, in the Americas.

He hoped his mother and brothers would find equal happiness, wherever they chose to settle in the North.

Fergie's lips slowly relaxed. His mind moved away from such matters and on to the task in hand.

Before he had boarded the coach, he'd managed to find Wee Andrew and Rory, who had also been contacted by Alexander MacIntosh. Taken into his confidence and now part of the plan, his two friends were travelling to Blairhoyle, on horseback, and would await his signal in the hills above the village.

Fergie shifted in his seat, straightening his fine coat and adjusting the angle of his feathered hat. The disguise had fooled the militiamen at the coaching house, but it would not fool Black Jamie. The frown returned.

Miles slipped by.

His mind drifted occasionally to his brave and strangely absent

Fox: if only he could wear a mask, like a highwayman, or disguise himself in some other way.

The sun was rising. The first dwellings came into view, silhouetted against a clear sky. A fresh wind blew through the carriage window. Fergie's hand flew to secure his wig in place.

It was going to be a fine day.

He watched a crofter's wife as she trudged towards a washing-line and began to secure laundry in place. Half an hour on, the public drying greens flapped with rows of drying, billowing underskirts.

Fergie smiled. One of his last happy memories was of helping his mother and Flora – recently dismissed from her job as housekeeper at Castle Black – carry great baskets of washing to those same drying greens. He wondered vaguely if Black Jamie and that fop of a ward of his were still doing their own laundry, or if they had found anyone desperate enough to replace the sacked Flora.

Slowly, his brain began to work.

Just outside Blairhoyle, he leapt from his seat and rapped urgently on the carriage ceiling.

The coachman reined the horses to a halt and, with a brief bow to his travelling companions, Fergie disembarked. He watched the carriage trundle on down the potholed road, then turned his attention to a nearby croft.

Minutes later, he was undressing hurriedly under cover of a small copse of trees.

Minutes after that, having left a small bundle of notes in exchange for what he took, Fergie was tearing Alexander MacIntosh's powdered wig from his head and cramming his unruly hair beneath another covering.

It was worth a try: he had nothing to lose – and a pardon from the authorities to gain.

'What did you say your name was?'

In the kitchen of Castle Black, Fergie bowed his frilly-capped head and attempted an unsteady curtsey. 'Fiona, sir. Fiona –' he stumbled, swaying slightly '– Fiona Fergusson.'

Black Jamie snorted. 'I hope your domestic skills are better than your deportment, Fiona.'

'Oh, they are, sir!' The strain of having to maintain such a high tone to his voice was starting to hurt. Keeping his eyes respectfully directed towards the dusty floor, Fergie coughed and went into the speech he'd been rehearsing for the past hour. 'I have kept house for Mr Alexander MacIntosh, merchant of Greenock. He will vouch for me – as will Lord Douglas of Balantrae.' He knew the first would do so gladly, and with a bit of luck Balantrae was too far away to contact.

'Hmmm.'

Staring down over his heavy wool skirt and apron, Fergie held his breath.

Black Jamie began to circle silently.

Fergie felt himself under scrutiny. Beneath the purloined clothes a sweat broke out over his tensed body.

'How old are you, Fiona?'

Fergie exhaled noisily. 'Thirty-four, sir.' His voice cracked and dropped an octave. 'I have had a cold, Mister Black. Please excuse my –'

'Are you a virtuous woman?' Black Jamie talked on, seemingly unconcerned by the deepening in the voice of this broad-shouldered would-be housekeeper who stood before him.

The question took Fergie by surprise. He clutched at his shawl, praying his wits would not let him down. 'Sir!' He injected a note of outrage into his voice.

'No sluttish habits, children or some lazy husband who will fill my home with chatter and noise?'

'I am a Godfearing spinster, Mister Black.' Fergie drew himself up to his full six feet. 'No man has laid a finger on Fiona Fergusson's body, and never will.' Having come into being a mere two hours earlier, Fiona, in a manner of speaking, was virginal indeed. And intended to remain that way.

'Good, good – I will have no truck with gentleman visitors.' The circling continued. 'You have a strong back, Fiona –'

Long fingers gripped Fergie's chin, forcing his head upward. Glad he had scraped his face free of growth only half an hour previously, he lowered his lashes and tried to feign what he hoped was a feminine expression.

Black Jamie snorted again. '– and although you are truly one of the ugliest women I have ever seen, your willingness to work for such a small wage and your agreement to live in stand in your favour.'

Fergie bristled: ugly indeed! This from a man who made a corpse look handsome! But he swallowed down an urge to punch Black Jamie in the face and tried another curtsey. 'Thank you, sir. I am a hard worker – just ask Mr MacIntosh and –'

'Yes, yes, you said, Fiona.'

Fergie found his chin released. He watched Black Jamie stride across the kitchen to the huge, filthy range which dominated the far wall.

'You can cook?'

Fergie nodded enthusiastically. 'Cook, clean, sew, wash – I am proficient in all the domestic arts.'

'Your Greenock merchant must have been sorry indeed to see you go.'

Fergie heard the scepticism in the voice. Was he doing too good a job? His wits left him as Black Jamie strolled back towards him. Then he yelped as a long-fingered hand patted his arse.

'Why did you leave the employ of your merchant, Fiona?'

Fergie's brain raced.

Black Jamie answered for him in low leering tones. 'Perhaps there was some scandal?' The hand patted again. 'Perhaps Mister Alexander MacIntosh was not quite the gentleman he seemed?' The words were almost whispered and the hand was moving down the back of Fergie's skirt.

He flinched, wondering how Flora and Castle Black's other, myriad housekeepers had put up with this sort of behaviour.

'Did he perhaps demand other services of you, Fiona?' The hand grabbed a fistful of heavy underskirts and squeezed.

Fergie shrieked and thrust a hand into Black Jamie's chest. 'Sir, you insult me and my previous employer!' He backed away.

Black Jamie's thin lips spread into a grin. 'The strength in your arms matches your back and shoulders, Fiona. No insult was intended, but this is a Christian household and I had to be sure you were of a similar disposition.'

Fergie smoothed down his skirts and manufactured a pious expression. 'You will find me chaste and clean in my habits, sir.' He ran a finger over the grimy range. 'Which is more than I can say for this room, if I may be so bold.'

Black Jamie sighed. 'Yes, we are in need of a woman's touch around Castle Black.'

Fergie picked upon the use of the plural: where was the wigged fop, anyway?

'If you can start immediately, the post is yours, Fiona. My betrothed is staying with me, and is somewhat indisposed, at the moment. We are to be married soon, and there is much to be done.'

Betrothed?

Marriage?

Who would be mad enough to accept a proposal from this monster?

'Thank you, sir.' Fergie hid his surprise and curtseyed, pleased to find he seemed to have mastered the movement. 'Dinner for two, is it?'

Black Jamie's face took on a strange caste. 'Not tonight, Fiona. My precious will eat alone in her room, this evening.' He waved vaguely towards a brace of pheasant which hung from a nearby hook. 'But a nice bit of game for tomorrow might tempt her appetite. And now –'

As his new employer droned on about rooms to be cleaned and washing to be done, Fergie stared at the dead birds. He knew nothing of cooking except what he'd seen his mother do, over the years. Could he replicate the skill? And with all this work to do, when would he have time to search Black Jamie's study for any evidence he was aware of Charles Stuart's plans to head a new uprising?

Then long fingers were pushing money into his hand. 'Buy what you need but always get a receipt, Fiona. I will be tending to my betrothed and do not wish to be disturbed.' With a curt nod, the angular figure turned and walked from the room.

Fergie waited until he heard the sound of a door closing, then hauled off his frilled cap and rubbed his sweating head.

His first objective had been achieved.

But with Charles Stuart due in Scotland the day after tomorrow, Fergie knew he had to act quickly to secure the second.

Twenty-Two

'We have company tonight, Pip.'

Calum stared into the mirror, watching as his long red hair was brushed until it shone. Powdered and lipsticked, an alien face stared back.

'And you must look your best.'

The words circled overhead, their source everywhere and nowhere. Was this real? Or was he still in that dark place in his mind where he seemed to spend most of his time?

His throat still ached, dry and sore despite vast quantities of the soothing liquid he had consumed at his captor's request. Last night, after James Black had removed the final stout hardness from his aching arse, Calum had remained in the dark place. It was there that Fergie came to him.

'Think of this evening as a test, my pet. Once before your loyalty was tested, and was found wanting. Do you remember how that made you feel?' The brushing stopped and a hand gently gripped his elbow.

Dressed in the green silk gown, Calum slowly rose from before the mirror and walked, trancelike, over to the narrow cot.

'You married that rogue Monroe, threw me over for a man of lower rank.'

Calum lay down, damp fingers searching for the ache beneath his silken skirts.

'You regret that, don't you my sweet?'

He heard the pain in the man's voice. Calum moaned, hating the distress he had caused. Tossing and turning on the thin, lumpy mattress, he ran his hands over his thighs and sweaty groin, feeling the solid length of aching flesh. Spunk had dried around his slit and on his auburn pubes. Calum rubbed the salty crystals which turned to dust between his shaking fingers.

'I think you do.'

His ears strained beyond the hoarse words for some glimpse of the voice he'd heard last night, somewhere beyond the walls of the Black Chamber. Beyond the very walls of Castle Black. In the dark place.

'Do you remember the shame of your betrayal, Philippa?'

Calum's eyes were wet with longing. In the dark place, Fergie came to him.

Fergie stroked his hair and murmured soothing words as other hands pushed cold objects into his hot body. Fergie kissed him when the muscles in Calum's arse felt like they might tear at the girth of the intruder. Fergie's mouth moved on his as the other, alien mouth tightened around his right nipple, sucking and then biting into the tender flesh as the cold, solid cylinder pushed on up inside him.

Beneath the smooth fabric of the green silk dress, bands of muscle tightened around his ribcage.

But, sometimes, Fergie left his side, moving back to join the others who watched him from the darkness.

Pip. His father, Sandy Monroe. Lieutenant James Black.

Calum's chest hurt. His stomach knotted. Between his splayed legs, his greased hole spasmed and his lips parted in a silent moan of humiliation.

'Oh, Philippa –'

Long fingers snaked out of the darkness and stroked his hair. Tears rolled down Calum's face. He grabbed a bony wrist, raising the knuckles to his dry lips. Head and shoulders lunging upward from the narrow cot, he fervently kissed the stretched skin. 'Do not go this time, Fergie! Stay – please stay!' The plea was husky.

The fingers wrenched themselves free and seconds later a palm impacted with the side of his powdered face.

Calum fell back on the narrow cot, hands flying to shield himself from another attack.

'Not Fergie!' James Black roared.

Calum rolled into a ball.

'Not Fergie – never Fergie!'

Calum clenched his teeth. With every shout of the name, the stubborn length of desire between his legs throbbed more urgently. Then a sudden shove to his back pushed him off the cot and seconds later Calum was crawling across the floor on his hands and knees.

His head reeled.

He could taste something metallic in his mouth.

The skin on his shins scraped painfully through the silk and along rough stone as he scuttled for cover. And a solid seven inches of aching meat stubbornly poked up from his auburn bush.

His right shoulder hit something heavy and wooden. Then countless cylindrical objects were raining down around him.

Calum shrieked and rolled on to his back, hands clawing at the air in an attempt to fight off the falling objects. Only when he'd blocked the last of the impacts did he realise the only sound left in the room was the harsh rasp of his breathing. He lay there, arms crossed over his face, gulping air into his bursting lungs and trying to listen.

Was he alone?

Had they all left him here, alone and without the comfort of the dark place?

Gradually, the desperate rise and fall of his chest slowed to a more even rhythm. The pounding in his ears ebbed to a low fizzle. Calum stretched out one tentative arm. Then another. His entire body glowed and pulsed, and adrenaline continued to course through his veins.

Trembling fingers inched across the icy floor, then brushed something instantly recognisable.

'Pick it up.'

He flinched. Sweat trickled its way over Calum's already gleaming chest. From the floor, he blinked up into the darkness, searching for the face behind the words.

'Pick it up and stroke it.'

The voice filled the Black Chamber and echoed in Calum's pulsing head. His shaking hands made firmer contact with the cold, greased length and the pulse became a throb between his tensed thighs.

'Kiss it.' The words were low, hoarse with anticipation.

His sweat-drenched skin shimmered. Sandpaper lips trembled against the foot-long length of carved wood.

'Now take it.' His guardian's voice was almost inaudible.

Skull bursting, every sinew stretched to breaking point, Calum's fist tightened. He raised his knees, planting bare feet on the floor and lifting his body from the cold stone.

The curved head pressed against his aching sphincter. His other hand came into play, thrusting itself between the goose-fleshed cheeks of his arse. Using his thumb and forefinger Calum held himself open. And pushed.

Spine and hips left the floor.

Calum gasped. He pushed harder, wanting the dark place.

A ring of muscle shimmered and, despite the grease, held firm.

'Take it, my precious.'

Then other hands slipped beneath his arching back, cupping his arse-cheeks and wrenching the two shivering mounds of muscle wider apart.

On the periphery of awareness, Calum could smell his guardian's crotch. Staring up into the dark, he could just make out the head and shoulders of the man who was now cradling him in long, sinewy arms. He blinked through blurred vision and watched the outline alter and broaden.

Fergie! He shouted the name in his head. His arsehole spasmed. Then Calum was screaming a formless sound and the entire length of the carved cock slid wetly into his gaping, receptive hole.

The strength left his limbs. Tears of effort stung his painted eyes as his body tried to accustom itself to the great girth.

Straining muscles quivered, bowing to the invader and parting to grip the thick shaft in a warm embrace.

Placed gently on the lumpy mattress, new ropes were eased around his thighs then drawn up over his hips and arse. He could feel the brush of fingers as the lengths were secured to something cold and metallic beneath the tightly fitted waistband of the green gown.

A sudden clenching in the depths of his bowels pushed at the solid wooden cock and threatened to expel it from his arse. Calum moaned, feeling something which now ran the length of his crack rub against the base of the ersatz prick, preventing expulsion.

Soothing words condensed on his ear: 'Chastity belts are more normally used to keep cocks out. We will use this one to keep something in, eh, Pip?'

The question focused what was left of his mind.

'We will eat, and we will be a gracious hostess, won't we?' James Black was now easing the sweat and spunk-stained gown back down over Calum's shaking thighs.

'And you will keep this secret, as I keep the secret of the Fox's identity.'

He was back in the present, with his guardian. Calum managed a nod, suddenly aware his neck and shoulders were being washed with a soft flannel and dried with a softer towel. Offering no protest, Calum submitted to a further hair brushing and a reapplication of facepaint.

Sometime later, he swung heavy legs over the side of the narrow cot and staggered to his feet.

The object locked inside his arse seemed to throb with a life of its own. Bound against his stomach by the silken ropes, his cock echoed the tremors. Tight between his legs, his swollen bollocks begged for release.

Each movement towards the door was an effort.

Every stair down the hidden passageway from the Black Chamber to his guardian's study sent jolting pain through his body.

He remained there for a while, dazed and confused. Then, holding on to his guardian's arm, and with his red hair hanging over his powdered shoulders, Calum allowed himself to be led to the dining room.

In the kitchen, Fergie frowned past steaming pans and wiped his sweaty face.

Two days he had been here!

He fell to a crouch, opening the door of the large oven and peering inside.

For two days he had scrubbed and cleaned and washed and cooked, all the time waiting for a chance to get into Black Jamie's study. The opportunity had yet to present itself.

Grabbing a skewer from the range, Fergie poked the brace of pheasant which had been roasting gently all afternoon.

What did the man do in there? He rarely seemed to leave that room, apparently eschewing his bed chamber and even sleeping in the study!

On the countless occasions Fergie had knocked on the door, offering to clean and dust the room, Black Jamie had failed to answer and the door was locked – from the inside.

Where was his mysterious betrothed?

And where was the fop?

While cleaning what he presumed to be Master Monroe's chamber, Fergie had found clothes in the closets but no sign of the dandy himself.

Slamming the oven door shut, Fergie pushed all thoughts of personal vengeance from his mind: there was more at stake here than the injustice done to himself.

He checked the potatoes and neeps. He adjusted his frilled bonnet, wiped his hands on his apron before making sure the broth was thoroughly heated. Jovial voices were audible from the other side of the great hall.

Fergie had escorted Captain Carmichael into the castle an hour ago, taken his coat and curtsied so much he thought his knees might snap.

The balding military man had leered at him, making lewd remarks to Black Jamie while Fergie served whisky and swallowed down the urge to lay out each of the men in turn.

'Fiona? We are ready to eat, now. Pray bring the first course.'

Fergie smiled with relief, patting the pocket in his voluminous skirts and checking that the small phial of sleeping draft he'd bought from the apothecary earlier that day was still there.

He'd already slipped a dose into the whisky, with little effect. The rest he'd save for the main course. The strong gamey flavour of the pheasant would hide any bitter aftertaste and bring on a post-prandial slumber which should allow him an opportunity to gain entrance to the study.

'Fiona! Get a move on, woman!'

The dismissive tone in the voice made him bristle. Moving back to the range, Fergie quickly filled three bowls with hot soup, then paused.

He hated being here. He had slaved and skivvied over two floors of Castle Black and received not one word of praise. Hauling up the front of his underskirts and with the great folds of fabric held out of the way, he gripped his cock and aimed the head at one bowl. 'Enjoy your meal, my friends.'

The first splatters spurted into the nearest dish.

Fergie grinned, directing the steaming stream into the second, then third bowl before shaking the final dribbles into the pot itself. Lowering his skirts, he wiped around the lip of each plate, then lifted the tray.

It wasn't much, but it made him feel a little better. He walked slowly from the kitchen and made his way towards the dining room.

Captain Carmichael made some comment.

Black Jamie tasted his soup, pronounced it a little salty but ate with some relish.

Fergie stared at the third party, seated alone at the far end of the table.

Dressed in an emerald-green gown, a pale girl blankly met his gaze then, as if in a dream, returned her eyes to the plate of soup.

A shiver of recognition rippled over Fergie's spine. He continued to focus on the long, auburn hair which tumbled down over the girl's bare shoulders in a thick luxuriance.

'That will be all, Fiona. You can bring us the main course in ten minutes.'

Fergie dragged his gaze from the stunning, if ill-looking, figure.

Black Jamie stared at him, a frown of irritation creasing his angular face. 'That will be all, I said!'

'Yes, sir.' Grabbing his tray and executing a hurried curtsey, Fergie backed out of the room and made his way quickly to the kitchen.

So that was Black Jamie's intended.

As he rechecked the pheasant and drained the vegetables, adding a liberal dose of the apothecary's powder to the former, Fergie found himself haunted by the wan girl's deeply shadowed eyes.

Where had she come from? If she was staying here, at Castle Black, he had never seen her.

Wiping his hands on his apron, Fergie leant against the preparation table and frowned. Something about Black Jamie's betrothed tugged at his memory. Then he gasped, aware of a tingle of arousal beneath his layers of petticoat. Staring down, he watched movement amongst the thick underskirts. Fergie groaned.

Not now – not now, of all occasions.

He reached down, grabbing his shaft through cotton and cambric and trying to shove it back between his thighs. The touch of his own fingers merely served to stiffen his prick further. The errant appendage rebelled, bucking away from his grasp and curving up and outward.

He thought about those same fingers plunging deep into that thick red hair. He thought about holding that slender, girlish waist and kissing the pale, powdered skin.

Fergie groaned. He'd never felt anything for a woman before, but there was something about this girl which affected him strangely. In the steamy kitchen, his strong masculine body warm beneath the voluminous female garments, Fergie watched through narrowed eyes as the front of his skirts tented further.

Blood was diverted away from his brain, coursing lower and pumping into his throbbing prick. His nipples rubbed against his tight-fitting blouse. His bollocks were sweating, knitting together in their soft hairy sac. Beneath his frilly cap, even the roots of his hair were stiffening.

Raising his head, he looked across the kitchen into the base of a huge metal broiling pan.

A tall, statuesque figure stared back, strong-jawed and frowning.

Fergie stared at his reflection. Ugly? He peered critically and watched Fiona Fergusson do likewise.

No – not ugly. Not quite, at least. But far from feminine, he had to admit.

One hand moving to straighten his frilled cap, the other stroked through the layers of underskirt.

Fergie almost smiled. The reflected image was alien and yet arousing. He closed his eyes, trying to imagine the wan redhead standing where that broiling pan hung, her legs parted beneath the emerald green gown and her slim-fingered hand resting where his rested.

How did women –? A blush drenched his face, and his prick jerked against his curled fingers. He did not know how to phrase the question, even in his mind.

'Fiona? Fiona? Bring us the main course, woman!'

Black Jamie's impatient shout pulled Fergie from his musings. His eyes flew open and he saw his mirrored self was still very noticeably aroused. 'Yes, sir! Coming, sir!' He quickly dished up three servings of the pheasant, groaning at the way the front of his apron reached the table a good few seconds before he did.

He couldn't go through like this.

Scanning the steamy kitchen, his eyes eventually alighted on the length of string which had secured the game birds to an overhead spar. He grabbed the twine, hauled up his skirts and, with a bit of fiddling, managed to bind his throbbing prick into a less obvious erectness between his thighs.

The unnatural position of his tethered length merely served to inflame Fergie further. He pulled his mind away from his desires and grabbed the tray, teeth clenched.

With small, uncomfortable steps, each of which sent arrows of pleasure through his bollocks, Fergie made his way back through to the dining hall.

She had not touched her soup.

Remembering the extra ingredient which had been added, courtesy of his now emptied bladder, Fergie was glad. Having placed the servings in front of the other two diners, he lingered by the wan girl's side. 'Are you not hungry, my lady?'

'Hold your tongue, woman!' Black Jamie's reprimand was sharp. 'Do not be so forward.' Fergie moved back, watching as the gaunt, soberly dressed figure reached across and patted the red-haired lady's hand. 'Try a little, my dear.'

Captain Carmichael's slurred voice joined the exhortations. 'Go on, pet. Eat up.'

Fergie watched the silent figure slowly shake her head.

'Leave her be. She will eat when she is ready.' Captain Carmichael and Black Jamie resumed their conversation, seemingly oblivious to the third member of their party.

Fergie took the chance to resume his place by her side.

She seemed to shrink further in the large, carved chair, her alabaster skin now faintly tinged with a more worrying blue. He lowered his head, pushing the plate a little closer to his slim fingers. 'Try a little pheasant, my lady. Perhaps it will –'

'Help me.'

The words were faint and hoarse, but unmistakable. Startled, Fergie made to take the girl's pale arm.

But James Black was immediately on his feet, saying, 'I will help you back to your room, if that is what you wish, my dear.'

Captain Carmichael rose unsteadily as the sombrely dressed figure eased the pale woman up from her chair and hurried her towards the door.

Fergie followed. 'Perhaps a doctor is in order, sir. The lady does not look well.'

'Attend to your duties, Fiona. I think Captain Carmichael requires more whisky.' The words were harsh.

Fergie flinched, but stopped, watching the unlikely couple make their way out of the room. Before he could give any further thought to what exactly was going on here, a uniformed arm had encircled his waist, pulling him down.

'It's not whisky I require, wench!' Captain Carmichael's leering voice whispered into his ear. Fergie struggled, trying to get up from the militaryman's lap and cursing the apothecary for the ineffectiveness of the potion. Powerful arms held him firm, rough hands straying to the front of his tightly laced blouse.

'Not much tit on you, eh Fiona?' Captain Carmichael cupped Fergie's left pectoral and bit the back of his neck.

'Sir!' With supreme effort, and just as one of the captain's roving hands was fumbling in the direction of his crotch, Fergie leapt to his feet. 'I am a virtuous woman!' He smoothed down his skirts and backed away.

The militaryman leered. 'You are also as ugly as sin.' He patted his lap again. 'But I'm not one for appearances.' He winked and crooked a finger. 'Ever had an army man's cock in your quim, wench?'

Fergie bristled.

'Don't be shy.' Captain Carmichael fondled the front of his serge breeches. 'Come on, girl. I bet you don't get many offers, with a face like that. Come and see what Uncle Mick has for you.'

It was all too much. Before he knew what he was doing, Fergie's right arm flew from where it had been sheltering his nonexistent bosoms and his clenched fist struck Captain Carmichael's left cheek.

The punch knocked the militaryman from the chair and he slumped, face forward, into his plate of pheasant.

Fergie winced and shook his bruised fingers. He had not meant to hit the fellow quite so hard, but perhaps it would speed up the effects of the apothecary's potion. Moving forward, he hauled the unconscious man upright, propping him up against his chair and hoping he looked merely drunk.

Then he quickly added a further liberal dose of the sleeping draught to the remains of Black Jamie's meal, cleared the other dishes from the table and, with his bound prick still snuggling between his legs, scuttled off to the kitchen.

Twenty-Three

An hour later, and with both Black Jamie and his military friend snoring soundly in the dining room, Fergie was in the study, rifling through a second box of papers. In flickering candlelight, his brown eyes widened as he quickly read through another document. He had not yet uncovered any evidence of James Black's involvement in any plan to apprehend Charles Stuart, but there was enough here to thoroughly discredit one of the most influential landowners in the area.

This letter was signed by King George himself, and concerned the clearing of all tenant farmers for two hundred miles around Stirling. Those who owned their land were to be evicted by whatever means necessary.

Fergie rubbed his face. Black Jamie's desire for the McGregor croft fell into place – as did the framing of himself for another's crimes. But he still had no proof.

He quickly read the document underneath, which also bore the royal seal. As the words sank in, excitement coursed through his veins.

Here it was – in the King's own handwriting! The letter congratulated James Black for his ingenuity in both finding a scapegoat for the highway robbery and thus being able, legally, to confiscate and take possession of the McGregor land.

Fergie fingered the document, then kissed it soundly before

thrusting the missive down the front of his bodice for safekeeping. As he loaded the contents of the box back inside, intending to replace them in Black Jamie's desk, an older piece of parchment caught his eye.

Half the page was taken up by a roughly drawn map.

He paused, peering at the seal of a very different king then taking in the archaic legal language. Fergie squinted in the flickering candlelight, moving back to lean against a book-lined wall.

It appeared to be some sort of decree, granting ownership rights to –

Fergie peered closer, angling the parchment.

- Philippa MacFayden and her descendants.

Fergie frowned, one finger tracing the boundary outlines on the rough map. There was the Stirling road and the Gonachan burn dividing his land from Black Jamie's estate. And there was Castle Black!

The design and layout of the delineated section slowly began to make sense.

This land did not belong to James Black at all! It was the heritable property of the descendants of Philippa MacFayden – whoever she might be.

He moved back further, one arm braced against the bookcase and tilting the document upward in order to read more of the tiny print.

Then the very wall behind gave way and he was falling backward into darkness.

By the time he'd picked himself up, the hidden door had swung shut behind him and Fergie was lost in a dusty passageway. Clawing at the wall through which he had fallen, he found the surface seamless.

Panic flaring in his veins, Fergie scrabbled against smooth pine panelling. He had no idea where he was, nor for how long the apothecary's potion would keep his employer and Captain Carmichael asleep. He had to get back to the study.

Calming himself, Fergie moved slowly left. After a few paces, his foot impacted with a step. Then a second. Blinking in the dusty gloom, he followed the stairs upward. If he could not gain exit the way he'd come in maybe there was another way out.

Eventually the surface beneath his fingers gave way and swung noiselessly open. After the gloom of the dusty passageway, even candlelight was dazzling.

Fergie paused, eyes acclimatising to the sudden illumination. This chamber must be directly above the study, in the wing Black Jamie had refused to allow him to clean. Still clutching the title deed to the castle and its lands, he took a tentative step forward and glanced around.

'No – please, no more!'

The hoarse words dragged his eyes from a large portrait of a flaming-haired woman which dominated the claustrophobic room. Fergie moved more quickly now, following the plea to a narrow bed in one corner.

On the cot, her wrists secured to its frame and still wearing her emerald silk gown, the lady from earlier strained weakly away from him. An ashen face paled further with fear.

Fergie knelt by the bed, smoothing the sweat-soaked hair back from the pale face. 'Shhh – it is me, Fiona.'

Confused eyes narrowed in further fear. 'Fiona?'

Fergie managed a smile. 'We met at dinner, my lady. I am here to help, not do you any harm.' He reached for the device which held those finely boned hands in place, then frowned at the locked, iron manacles.

'No – get it out of me! Please just get it out of me!' The pale face turned away, looking back over milk-white shoulders down to the shining green skirts.

Fergie's brow creased in confusion.

The low, hoarse voice was talking rapidly. Bending his head to hear the whispered words, his forehead wrinkled further as the explanation became more clear. In the half-dark, he stared at Black Jamie's betrothed. 'He did this to you?'

Long lashes lowered themselves in shame. 'I beg you – it is tearing me apart.' A sob ended the sentence.

Fergie rose slowly to his feet and walked to the other end of the bed.

On her knees, the rounded swell of the lady's arse pushed itself towards him.

Fergie hesitated. Whatever was going on here was, in reality, none of his business. But the strangely familiar redhead was in such obvious distress he knew he had to do something. 'Keep still.' Moving on to the cot, and kneeling behind the tethered figure, Fergie began to sweep the layers of slippery green silk up and out of the way.

Somewhere beneath the fourth petticoat, his fingers brushed the outline of straps. He pushed the final stiff underskirt aside and heard a stifled moan from the other end of the cot as the palms of his hands met firm flesh. 'Almost there, my lady.' Peering through the half-light, he took in the small, tightly clenched cheeks of the smooth arse and the spreading base of something alien. A sudden blush drenched his face and he was aware of a twitch between his own muscular thighs. He had never gazed upon a lady's nether regions before.

Would the pretty personage on the bed have been so eager to allow him access, had she known Fiona Fergusson was not all she might seem? Fergie paused, clearing his throat. 'I am sorry to render your . . . lower quarters exposed in such a way, but I must in order to –'

'Just do it, damn you!'

The gruffness of the urgent voice took him by surprise, but did little to quash Fergie's reservations or embarrassment. Closing his eyes, and working by touch only, he followed the line of the straps and knots, slowly working out how the device worked. And how to release it.

His fingers shook, tearing at fastenings and untying where he could. Minutes later, the rounded arse beneath his hands was damp and Fergie himself was also sweating profusely. He was getting nowhere fast.

In desperation, he lowered his face to the warm arse-cheeks and began to gnaw at the straps.

A moan from further up the cot made his cock twitch again. Fergie ignored it, biting at the fabric.

Another moan drifted into his ears. Fergie gnawed on, aware the lady seemed to be pushing back against him and moving her arse in smooth circular motions. Somewhere around his chin, he felt pressure. Slipping his hands beneath the undulating body, Fergie gripped surprisingly sharp hipbones and held the lady tightly while he pulled with his teeth, stretching the last strap out and away from the curved mound of flesh.

Suddenly it snapped, one length springing up to hit his face. Then a sharp cry was soon followed by a low groan.

Eyes still closed, Fergie moved back, listening to the long wet sound. His mind filled in the blanks, visualising the great length forced from the tight wet hole. Beneath his own skirts, his prick was rubbing against the first layer of petticoat, staining the stiff fabric. He jumped away, flicking the redhead's silken gown back into place across the glistening rod which now swung free against the lady's pale arse.

'Thank you, Fiona.' The words were breathy with relief.

Opening his eyes, Fergie crawled from the bed on unsteady legs and staggered around to the top.

The redhead was staring at him with great, gratitude-filled irises. 'You are a good woman. Where did my guardian find you?'

Guardian?

Not *my intended*.

Fergie flinched. Something in the eyes was definitely, if still vaguely, familiar. The document in Black Jamie's study began to make sense. 'Are you Philippa MacFayden, by any chance?'

The pale face frowned. 'She was my mother.' The redhead nodded over Fergie's shoulder.

He turned, taking in the woman in the painting for the first time. 'You look very like her.'

'My mother died when I was born – I never knew her, and neither did Uncle Jamie.' The voice was low, almost masculine-sounding. 'At least, not in the sense he wished to.'

Fergie returned his attention to the finely boned face. Most of the lady was still hidden by shadow, but her beguiling eyes shone in the flickering candlelight. His lips twisted in disgust. Uncle and niece? 'Black Jamie is more of a monster than I thought!' His own voice dropped an octave.

Abruptly, slim fingers seized his wrist. 'Fergie?'

He flinched. Was he known to this pretty creature? Narrowing his eyes, he examined the lady's features more closely, feeling an unexpectedly strong grip around his wrist.

'I knew you would come!'

Those eyes.

That voice.

Fergie pulled away, shaking his head to clear it. The dark was playing tricks on him. Gathering his wits, he backed away.

'Listen to me, Fergie.'

'My name is Fiona, mistress.' He turned, grabbing the candle from in front of the portrait and walking quickly to a small, barred window. Raising the flickering stub, he slowly waved the light twice, then paused and drew it a third time across the barred space.

'What are you doing?'

Fergie ignored the question, peering into the dark and waiting for the response. Wee Andrew's returning signal came a few minutes later, indicating that it was safe for Fergie to relay his news in person.

Ducking back down, he replaced the candle and looked one last time at his redheaded companion. 'Tell me your name, lady.'

Full lips parted. Then hesitated and looked away.

Fergie frowned. 'It is no matter. I have business to attend to elsewhere, but I will return, when I can, and we will set you free.'

The only response was a sigh in the darkness.

Fergie echoed the sound, then turned and stumbled towards the doorway in the black wall.

'So we have one of the fairer sex to thank for this?'

'Fair, be damned!' Fergie frowned at the slim, grinning figure who emerged from the cave in the side of Ben Mora, then wrenched off his frilled cap and threw it to the ground as he dismounted. 'Don't talk to me about women!'

Wee Andrew and Rory were immediately by his side. 'Show some respect, Fergus! This is our king!' The latter's words were low and filled with respect.

Fergie stared at Charles Stuart.

The slim man laughed and stuck out a hand. 'This fellow is showing something more valuable than respect. He is risking his life for me.'

Fergie took the extended palm in a firm grip. 'I do what I do for no mere man, sir, but for Scotland.'

'Aye, for Scotland, my friends!' Clasping Fergie's fingers between his, the heir to the Stuart throne thrust their joined fists upward into the sky. 'She will rise again!'

The night rang with a dozen other voices.

Fergie felt his heart soar.

Minutes later, they were all inside the cave and he was recounting his discoveries around a small fire. As he talked, Bonnie Prince Charlie's pale eyes grew darker. Someone gave Fergie whisky when his throat became dry. Others murmured in anger, listening to his tale of a royal decree to evict the tenant farmers.

When he'd finished, the Stuart heir was staring at him. 'The King's Emissary is still at Castle Black?'

Fergie nodded. 'But he is lodging in Blairhoyle, with two dozen men. I heard him tell Black Jamie so, before dinner. I presume the militia are to apprehend the Fox.'

'Highwaymen are the least of his concerns, I fear.' Charlie frowned. 'Will you go back, Fergus McGregor? Will you take further risk for your country, and find out when this clearance of the land is to begin?'

Fergie leant forward, leaning the palms of his hands on his skirt-covered knees and staring into the dying embers. He now had enough evidence to clear his own name and thoroughly discredit Black Jamie. But there were other matters at stake here, not the least of which lay chained to a cot in the dark, secret chamber. Slowly, he nodded.

'Thank you, McGregor. This is what you must do.' Lowering his lips to Fergie's ear, Bonnie Prince Charlie began to talk.

Calum moaned in uneasy sleep, reaching out with tethered arms towards a broad figure while his mind searched once more for the dark place.

Fergie had come to him again. He had stroked his hair and

eased his pain. He had removed the object which now hung wet and unwieldy between Calum's aching thighs.

Then he had gone away, leaving Calum alone again.

'Please – come back. Stay with me.' A whimper escaped his dry lips, echoing in the darkness beyond his tightly shut eyelids.

'I am here, Pip. I will never leave you.'

Abruptly, the black lightened to red and he felt heat on his face. Calum gasped, torn from the dark place and propelled into the here and now. His eyelids shot open and he found himself staring into a gaunt face. A cold finger caressed his cheek, moving over his clammy skin to trace the outline of his rouged, trembling lips.

'You did well, my dear. Your quim should be adequately stretched, by this time.'

The hand left his cheek and moved lower, slipping between his chest and the narrow cot to fondle the front of his tightly laced bodice. Calum flinched. 'No!' The strength of his voice made the hand pause.

James Black stared at him. A leering smile played around the thin lips. 'Ah, you have come to like it, eh my dear?'

Calum cringed. His mind was clearer than it had been for days, and he suddenly realised it was not Fergie who had visited him last night.

A woman. Fiona?

The hand began to move again, slipping past the still-tethered rod of flesh which pulsed against Calum's stomach.

'This is wrong, my precious Pip.'

Fingers curled around his erect prick.

'This is a cruel flaw of nature.'

The fingers tightened and Calum gasped.

'You can never assume your true role as my bride while this –' the voice darkened with distaste '– appurtenance mars your feminine perfection. I have consulted several volumes of surgical technique and –'

'No!' Fear that his guardian should discover the carved wooden cock's removal gave way to a colder, more primal terror. And it gave him strength. For the first time since his imprisonment, Calum began to struggle. 'No! No!' He bucked away from the hand which held his manhood and kicked with his feet, thrashing from side to side amidst his silken skirts.

'Be still, bitch!' Clawlike hands attempted to hold him down.

'Leave me alone!' Gripping the iron bed-head with clenched fists, Calum writhed more violently. His right foot made satisfying impact with soft, yielding flesh.

Black Jamie grunted in pain.

As Calum kicked again, rising up from the cot to almost a crouch, something slipped from underneath his gown and hit the floor with an audible thump. His head whipped round. Peering over his shoulder, he watched the angular figure stoop to retrieve it.

James Black slowly stood up. Silhouetted by candlelight, he held the carved wooden length, turning it slowly in his hands and examining the clearly bitten-through ends of the tether.

Against mounting fear, not only for his own life now, Calum began to babble. 'I freed myself during the night, uncle. It took a while, but I managed to –'

The stinging blow to his face ended the lie in a gasp. Then Black Jamie hurled the carved object at the oil painting, grabbed the candle and stalked furiously from the room.

Twenty-Four

'Witch!'

Fergie dropped the pewter goblet he had been dusting and flinched at the circle of cold iron which pressed into the back of his neck.

'You drugged my dinner guest and myself last night with one of your hellish brews, then interfered with my betrothed!'

Fergie tried to move away from the pistol's muzzle. An arm around his throat prevented any escape. 'Sir, I only sought to help the lady. She was in obvious pain and –'

'How did you come to discover my private chamber, hag?' The arm tightened. 'What were you doing in my study?' A furious voice hissed into Fergie's ear.

Grabbing the arm, Fergie spun round and tried to gain hold of the weapon.

Black Jamie was too quick for him.

Staring down the barrel of the pistol, Fergie scowled. 'Kill me, and I will be missed, sir. Others will come looking for me, and your little secret will be exposed.'

Black Jamie's black eyes bored into him. 'Oh, you will not die, witch! But you may pray for death, by the time I have finished with you.' He motioned with the weapon.

Fergie backed towards the door.

Black Jamie followed. 'But first, you can help me demonstrate to my betrothed the proper behaviour of a wife.' He urged Fergie out into the corridor and towards the study.

Fergie's eyes narrowed. He continued to walk backward, hands raised above his head. His brain could not quite fathom what this madman had in mind, but he was in enough trouble as it was, and he knew his only hope of overpowering Black Jamie was to go along with whatever it was until an opportunity to turn the tables presented itself.

Silently, and with every muscle in his body tensed, Fergie opened the study door and walked at gunpoint towards the hidden doorway and an unknown fate.

Fifteen minutes later, he knew only too well.

Three flickering candelabra now lit the claustrophobic chamber. From her place in the great oil painting on the wall, Philippa MacFayden gazed down unseeingly on the spectacle before her.

On his hands and knees, and with his skirts raised to expose his white hairy arse, Fergie tore his eyes from the portrait and stared at the other, red-haired figure who cowered on the cot.

The pale face was tear-stained, the full mouth set in a frown half-appalled, half-disbelieving.

'An opportunity for your further instruction has unexpectedly presented itself, Pip.'

Fergie shivered. Black Jamie's voice came from behind, its source unseen. But the pressure of all-too-corporeal thighs edging between his was unmistakable. He focused all his attention on the ashen redhead, who was now sliding linked wrists along the metal bed-head towards him.

'Oh, Fiona – I am sorry you have become involved in all this.' The words were a hoarse whisper.

His brown eyes fixed themselves on green irises, and he tried to soothe and reassure with his expression alone. One deception layered itself upon others, as Fergie prayed that his fear-shrivelled cock and balls, at present still hidden within the folds of his underskirts, would continue to go undetected. He inhaled sharply as a cold hand fumbled roughly between the cheeks of his arse:

'Are you watching, my precious?'

Fergie clenched his teeth against unceremonious fingering. He locked eyes with the figure on the bed. Then the digit in his rectum was joined by another and his back arched.

A laugh from behind. 'See how she likes it? See how she longs to feel my full manhood?'

Fergie tried to relax as a third finger joined the duo which widened inside him. Then the digits began to thrust.

'But I will be faithful to you, my sweet one. This ugly wench will be deprived of my prick, but she will serve to demonstrate the accommodating wonders of the human body.'

The figure in the green silk gown edged a little closer. Fergie moaned, the lips of his arse stretching as the three fingers curled into a tight ball and bony joints pressed into the walls of his rectum. Then they thrust back inside him.

'Take my fist, bitch! Take it into your sorry arse and beg me for more!' Black Jamie was raving now, his voice rising to a shout as he detailed every movement and Fergie's supposed response to it.

A husky whisper drifted into his ears, from closer at hand. 'Let your mind lead you away from it, Fiona. Go to the dark place – go to where you feel safe and are with the one you love most in the world.'

He was panting now. Sweat leaked from beneath his frilly cap, trickling over his creased brow. Fergie concentrated on the redhead's voice. The intensifying pressure against the entrance to his body as Black Jamie's smallest finger joined the triumvirate made the words seem impossible.

Then an unexpectedly sharp thrust into his arse propelled him forward. Fergie grunted, gripping the edge of the cot. He broke the gaze, pressing his face to the bed's lumpy surface. A silken-draped leg moved against his forehead and he raised one shaking arm to hold the redhead's slender thigh.

'Breathe through it, Fiona. You must stay conscious. If you do not, I fear for what he might do to you.'

There was sense in the whispered exhortation. Eyes closed, and with a thumb beginning to edge its way into his trembling body, Fergie lengthened each inhalation.

'Talk to me, Fiona. Or let me tell you of the man I love, whom my guardian has grievously wronged.'

The length of four fingers deep in his rectum, Fergie felt the added strain of the approaching knuckles as his arse-lips slowly parted further. He clutched at the redhead's voice more than the words, thinking of other red hair and the way his Fox's cock had felt when the highwayman shot his seed deep inside him.

'My love is a strong, brave highlander, unjustly accused of robbery. I know he is innocent – so does my guardian – and I have done my best to clear his name.'

Something in the voice stirred a memory pushed to the back of his mind. Fergie found himself whispering back. 'My love rides a bay mare and wears a scarlet mask and cloak. He holds me tightly in front of him and we gallop together over the moors at night.'

The pressure was almost unbearable. Somewhere behind him, he could hear laboured grunts as Black Jamie turned his fist, his other arm braced against the base of Fergie's spine.

'And his body is warm and thrusting beneath mine. I can smell his crotch, musky with the scent of the heather. I can taste the sweet clear liquid which leaks from the head of his prick as I run my tongue over it.'

Just as something large burrowed its way into his rectum, Fergie's prick stirred amongst the folds of underskirt and he was miles away, riding with his Fox to somewhere they could both be safe and happy. 'His hair is red – so red it hurts my eyes. I am kissing his nipples, nuzzling his chest with my chin.' Pushed forward by the force of the fist in his arse, Fergie wrapped his arms around silk-clad legs and buried his face between them. 'I do not know who or what he is, but I do not care.' Whispered words drifted down.

'You are with him and nothing can harm you there, Fiona.'

Mouth open in agony, Fergie kissed the silken folds of the dress. Each resolute thrusting inch between his arse-cheeks gave him momentum as he crawled forward in jerking movements. The frilled cap slipped from his head and brown tangles tumbled free. His hands gripped crumpled silk. Slowly, he hauled himself up on to the cot.

A sudden, leering laugh behind drenched Fergie's body in a cold sweat. 'Go to her, you unnatural witch – for all the good it will do you!'

The taunt dragged him back to the present. Fergie could feel the broadening girth of James Black's forearm as it dragged at the bruised and tender flesh around his arsehole. He wanted away from the burning pressure which widened and stretched him until he was sure he would tear. Somewhere inside his body, knuckles rubbed against a sensitive gland. Fergie gasped, piss spurting from his slit and soaking his underskirts.

Lunging forward, a wet warmth seeped through and dampened the hair on his stomach. His arms were around a slender neck, his fingers buried in luxuriant auburn locks and his Fox's face was turned towards his.

The fist in his arse twisted viciously and he gasped.

Then his Fox's lips were pressed to his and Fergie was falling into a black world where men were women, women were men and nothing was quite what it seemed.

'I would give anything to turn the clock back, Fiona.'

He woke up to darkness and the knowledge that his secret was still intact. A dull stinging between his buttocks told him his arse was another matter. Grimacing, Fergie tried to ease his fuzzy head from the silken lap in which it now rested.

'But I must tell someone, and as we are here together, I hope you will let me get this off my chest.'

Fergie slumped back down in confusion, trying to make sense of the red hair, the husky voice and the folds of the gown beneath his face. He knew one thing for sure: this woman – plus the tricks of his own mind – had got him through last night's ordeal. An unexpected knot filled his stomach.

'You have your love, but I will never have mine.' Fergus opened his mouth to protest, but a warm finger pressed itself to his lips. 'No, let me speak.'

Fergie complied, wrapping his arms around a narrow waist and remembering the feel of his Fox's mouth.

'I am not what I seem.'

Yes! His heart soared. It had been no dream! His Fox was

here, somehow captured by Black Jamie and forced, for reasons best known to the man himself, into the green silk gown. Fergie raised his head, staring up at the dark outline of a face which focused away from his and out into the darkness.

'My name is Calum Monroe. I am a penniless orphan, taken in by my dead father's comrade-in-arms, James Black. But others, including the man I love, know me only by my *nom de guerre*, the Fox.'

Fergie's entire body was rigid. The dream was becoming the darkest of nightmares.

'Worse still, the man whose life matters more to me than my own hates and despises me for reasons I do not know.'

Stiff with anger, Fergie clenched his fists in folds of silk.

'Oh, Fiona – there is more. I tried to tell him many times, but I was a coward and feared I would lose him. Then, when I discovered James Black wanted my highlander's land, I went to warn him and get my scarlet cape back, but he would not listen. When he was arrested, I went to the courthouse, ready to turn myself in and exchange my life for his. But he fled justice, and no one would believe I was the Fox.'

Fergie heard the pain in the words.

'My only solace, here in this black chamber, has been thoughts of him. And the knowledge that, with the money I stole to buy his freedom he may be, at this very moment, sailing towards the Americas, with his herdsman and sister.'

Replies and retorts formed on Fergie's cracked lips, only to dissolve in confusion as he struggled with contradictory emotions.

'James Black knows the truth. He knows I alone am responsible for the highway robbery along the Stirling road. We struck a bargain, he and I, although I am now unsure how much of his addled mind is still sound enough to remember.'

Fury vied with gratitude, then hurt, at the deception. As the sorrowful voice talked on, detailing Black Jamie's insane intentions, Fergie thought with something akin to shame of the blond-wigged boy he and Rab had mocked without any real reason, hating Calum Monroe merely because of the way he acted and his English roots.

He remembered the nights with his Fox, high atop Ben Mora.

He remembered the risky playfulness of the beginnings of their love.

He remembered the feelings his Fox had unleashed in him, the satisfaction of lying beneath another man and willingly taking that man's prick into his body.

And he remembered the husky tones which had stayed with him, last night, through every inch of his agonising ordeal at Black Jamie's mad hands.

'He will not hurt you further, Fiona. You must leave Castle Black at the first opportunity. I ask only one thing of you: that you keep my secret. My life depends on it – or what will pass for my life, as James Black's wife. Will you –?'

'I don't care who you are.' Fergie's heart spoke for him, beating a rapid tattoo against his ribs. 'I don't care what you are.' He moved again, tearing at his blouse and skirts with trembling hands. 'All I know is that my Fox now has a name, and if I ever wounded the owner of that name with harsh words or false accusations, I am truly sorry.' On his knees, and with his full skirts in crumples around his ankles, Fergie fumbled in the darkness. He seized a slender wrist, raised a hand to his lips and kissed it.

The response was a low cry. 'Now I know I too am mad, like Black Jamie, for I see my highlander kneeling before me.'

Fergie's laugh was deep and full of joy. 'This is not madness, Fox!' He found the wide neck of the emerald gown, seized two fistfuls of the silken fabric and pulled. A ripping sound rent the dark and then they were both on their feet, swathes of gown hanging from their bodies in torn shreds.

'Fergie?'

A long-fingered hand traced the outline of his face. Fergie smiled, grabbed and kissed it again. 'Aye, Fox. And you are no penniless orphan!' As leanly muscled arms wrapped themselves around him and a pale face buried itself in his neck, Fergie quickly recounted his discoveries in the study. He fingered the thick red hair, stroking and soothing, suddenly aware the mere proximity of Calum Monroe's seminaked body was having its usual effect on his own.

Through layers of petticoat, his prick was determinedly stretching, pushing its robust way between underskirts and straining towards the object of its desire. 'You, not Black Jamie, own this land. You, not he, have the final say what happens on it. The documents are with my friends in the hills. If anything should happen to me, go there.'

Chest to chest, nipple to nipple, they stood there. The body against his flinched.

Calum Monroe raised his face from Fergie's neck. 'I do not care about land. I do not care if I own all of Scotland. All that matters is that you are here and we are both still alive.'

Their bodies separated slightly, and two sets of eyes looked down into the darkness at two tenting shafts which poked resolutely up from the remnants of two skirts.

Somewhere at the back of Fergie's brain, his rational mind told him they had to get out of here. But the hand which had left his neck and was now searching through the folds of his petticoat pushed away all thoughts of anything except the touch of another's fingers.

Mirroring the movement, Fergie reached down and felt a parallel hardness thrust itself into his fist. In seconds he had ripped away the remaining shreds of skirt and Calum had done likewise.

One hand loosely holding his Fox's shaft, the other sinking itself into thick red hair, Fergie drew his highwayman closer. The fist on his own prick tightened. An arm encircled his shoulders and Fergie's knees turned to water. Despite the previous night's invasion, his stinging arsehole spasmed in need as Calum Monroe's full lips parted.

The kiss was tentative and gentle, contradicting the desire which raged between two sets of well-muscled thighs.

Fergie moaned, ginger pubes brushing his knuckles.

His Fox moved closer, deepening the kiss.

Fergie's second moan was through his nose as Calum slipped a warm tongue into his dry mouth. Then he was holding the man with both hands, his prick rubbing against another, thickly ruffled shaft, and the kiss was almost painful in its intensity.

Neither heard the door opening. Nor did they see the flickering candle which slowly illuminated their passion.

The click of a pistol cocking was lost in the wet grind of their urgent bodies.

'McGregor!'

But the roar of outrage was unmistakable.

The blow to the side of his head knocked Fergie to the floor. Somewhere on the edges of consciousness he heard sounds of a further scuffle and Calum's angry voice.

Then everything faded away and he was sinking into a black pit of pain.

Twenty-Five

'Where is he? What have you done with him?' In the candlelit study and wrapped in a blanket, Calum glared at a self-satisfied face.

'Where he belongs.' Seated once more behind his large desk, James Black smiled. 'In the hands of the authorities.'

The smugness of the words only served to increase Calum's rage. 'But he is not guilty of robbery!'

James Black shrugged. 'That matters little now. Sedition will take him to the gallows on its own – plus the theft of documents he stole from this very room.' A chilling grin formed on the gaunt face. 'No one will believe the ravings of a Jacobite traitor, and anything he says to his gaolers will be treated as an attempt to slander my good name.'

Calum's hands clenched into fists. 'You say you loved my mother – what would she think of you now?'

The grin froze. 'She was too headstrong for her own good. Had your rogue of a father not come along when he did, she would have loved me, given time –' his guardian rose slowly '– as you will, Pip.'

Bile rose in his throat. Hawking it into his mouth, Calum spat at the man he most hated in all the world. 'I am not Pip, and I will die rather than continue this charade!'

Calmly, Black Jamie produced a large handkerchief and slowly wiped the spittle from his hollow cheek. 'That is a pity. You have the power to save McGregor's life.' The tall, angular form moved towards the door. 'But if you choose not to use that power, so be it.'

Calum stared. 'What do you mean?'

Fingers gripped the door handle. 'As a magistrate, it is within my jurisdiction to show clemency, in certain cases. McGregor has a strong back. I could recommend his deportation to Virginia rather than allow him to swing at the end of a noose. '

Calum paled. Black Jamie pulled open the door and strode into the corridor.

'Do it, then!' Calum followed. 'Please, uncle – have mercy! Send Fergie away.'

'Why should I?' James Black paused by the grandfather clock, casually checking the time against his own watch.

Calum sprang in front of the gaunt, crowlike figure. 'Because, underneath it all, you know this is wrong.'

James Black smiled, closed the watch and replaced it in his waistcoat pocket. 'Do I?' He walked past his ward, stopping briefly to remove his heavy overcoat from the hall stand. 'I am already sheltering one fugitive from justice, Fox. And you ask me about right and wrong?'

Calum watched his guardian ease long arms into the wool garment. 'I urge you as a fellow human being to use your influence and save a man's life.'

'And again I ask you, why should I?' James Black strode across the Great Hall, the clack of his boot heels echoing up into the vast space.

'Because –' Calum sprinted in front, walking backward towards the door '– because –' His brain raced, attempting to reason with a madman. Placing his body between the heavy door and the man he had once called uncle, Calum lowered his face and summoned every shred of pretence he could. 'Because your Pip asks you too, James.'

Silence greeted his words.

Mouth dry, and not daring to look up, Calum waited.

'My Pip?'

'Yes, James. I have always loved you.'

'What about the highlander, McGregor? What about Sandy Monroe?'

Fighting rising waves of revulsion at the use of his dead father's name, Calum slowly raised his head and dropped to one knee. 'They mean nothing to me, James. It is you I want to be with.'

A black, blistering gaze seared his eyes. 'You do?'

'I am yours, James – I always have been and always will be.' Allowing the blanket to fall from his shoulders, Calum seized his guardian's thighs and pressed his face into the man's groin.

A crowlike hand hesitantly placed itself on the back of his red head. 'You will tell McGregor this?'

Calum winced, feeling the man's groin swell against his cheek. He managed a nod.

'You will come with me to the jail, stand before him and deny you have any feelings for him, to his face?'

The swell against his cheek became a solid, ridged line. Calum shivered. 'I will do anything you want me to, James.' His hands moved round to the front of his guardian's breeches and he fumbled with the fastenings. Other fingers stayed his intentions.

'Later, my dear. There will be all the time in the world, after we have rid ourselves of McGregor.'

Calum felt himself raised to his feet.

James Black's face was almost benign, in the glow of the overhead candelabrum. 'But you cannot accompany me in public, like this. We must find you suitable attire for a lady.'

Calum's stomach was churning: he had no urge to be led back upstairs to the Black Chamber, and he knew time was of the essence. 'Let me wear my son's coat and breeches, James.' He manufactured a wan smile. 'It will be better if McGregor sees me as I was, not as I really am.'

His guardian's face lit up. 'You are right, my precious!'

Cold lips kissed his brow and a shudder of apprehension shook his naked body.

'And I will be there with you, as you tell McGregor everything.'

Fifteen minutes later, clothed and booted, Calum sat in the carriage beside his guardian. His only thoughts were of making this convincing: securing at least some sort of life for his highlander.

'Someone wishes to tell you something, McGregor.'

Fergie lifted his head from his hands.

Black Jamie was standing in the doorway.

Fergie leapt to his feet. 'There is nothing more I wish to hear from –' He fell silent, watching as the gaunt landowner moved back and a slender, familiar figure strode into the stinking cell. His heart stuttered in his chest, then got back on course with a more rapid beat. 'Calum!' He took a step forward, arms outstretched.

'How dare you think to use my first name, you ruffian.' The scornful, sneering words from his Fox's curled lips turned Fergie's blood to ice-water. 'Master Monroe to you, you highland scum!'

Fergie flinched as if struck. His arms fell back by his sides.

The smartly dressed figure in the fine clothes stared at him with undisguised loathing. 'Did you think I loved you, you fool?'

Fergie's stomach tightened into knots. Once more wearing the wig, and with his face powdered, the Calum Monroe at whom he had jeered and laughed sauntered around him.

'I tricked you well, did I not, McGregor?'

Barely able to believe what he was hearing, Fergie glowered at the smiling figure of Black Jamie who stood in the doorway.

'What fun I had at your expense, you traitor.' The fop talked on, walking dismissively back round to stand in front of Fergie. 'James and I were laughing at you, the whole time. After I had fucked your sorry hole, I rode back to Castle Black and we laughed together, did we not, my love?'

'We did that, Pip.'

Black Jamie's low response twisted Fergie's guts. He stared at the jeering man before him. 'But – but –?'

'What's wrong, McGregor? You did not actually believe I could love a ruffian like you?' Calum Monroe flicked a lace-edged handkerchief from his sleeve and stifled a laugh behind it. 'You think I enjoyed pushing my prick into your traitorous body?'

All he had gone through, over the past weeks – all that he had done – he had only been able to do because of thoughts of his Fox. 'But last night – in the Black Chamber? You were held prisoner, and I –'

'You were a joke, McGregor – a joke between James and I. You have been used, fellow. It is a bonus that you were stupid enough to keep a highwayman's scarlet cloak, because it will now deport you to the Americas, and together James and I will have possession of your forfeited land.'

Tears rolled down Fergie's face. Through blurring vision, he stared into icy green eyes and caught a flicker of something he could not quite identify. Then it was gone.

'Let us leave this place, James. The stench of Jacobite traitor is making me feel quite ill.' Calum Monroe sneered one last time, then turned back to his guardian with an extravagant flounce.

Fergie trembled, watching the exquisitely attired man stride haughtily from the cell.

Then Black Jamie moved swiftly forward, grabbing Fergie's chin and wrenching his head up. 'Do not worry, highlander. You will not have long to mourn the loss of your love.'

The taunt was for his ears only, but Fergie barely registered the news. Whatever now happened to the rest of him, something inside him was dying already. He slumped to his knees, fists clenched against the pain of losing a love he now realised had never really been his.

On the periphery of his senses, he heard the creak of a door closing and the jingle of iron keys. Then silence, punctuated only by a heavy thump in his chest and the sound of a heart slowly breaking.

While James Black conferred with the gaoler in low tones, Calum stared at the top of Fergie's lowered head through the tiny barred hatch in the door.

One last look – one last look at his highlander.

Calum's eyes were wet, and he'd despised every manufactured word which had fallen from his lips.

But he'd done it – and, from the steady sobs which racked

Fergie's broad shoulders plus another's icy smile of satisfaction, he'd done it convincingly.

Calum inhaled sharply. Part of him longed for his highlander to look up, so he might somehow signal with his eyes that now, at least, Fergie would live, albeit thousands of miles away on the other side of the world.

Part of him knew it was better this way. As he stood there, fingers curling around the bars and preparing to enter a prison of his own, the conversation between his guardian and the gaoler became more audible.

'Are ye sure, Mister Black? What about his trial?'

'Trial be damned, man! I am magistrate around here, and this order comes directly from King George himself.'

'I don't know, Mister Black. It's all very irregular, and I have no idea where I shall find a carpenter at this late hour.'

'Offer him double – triple – what he is usually paid, if he will work through the night. At dawn tomorrow, in the town square, I will see McGregor's heels kick air and the life drain from his traitor's body if I have to slip the noose around his neck and hang him myself!'

Calum's blood ran cold. He spun round and ran to where bony fingers were now tipping a number of silver coins into the gaoler's grimy palm. 'But Fergie is to be deported!'

James Black's glistering eyes bored into him. 'Not for crimes against the King. Treason carries a mandatory death sentence.' His guardian looked back at the gaoler. 'You will see to it?'

The man's eyes sparkled at the sum of money. 'Certainly, Mister Black! Right away, sir!' He scuttled off.

Calum glowered. 'You gave me your word.'

Black Jamie smiled coldly. 'And you swore McGregor meant nothing to you.' He stared at Calum. 'Why do you care, my precious? We have a new life in front of us, as man and wife.'

Helplessness coursed through his confused brain: his bluff had been called, and he was now powerless to do anything. A wiry arm encircled his shoulders.

'Come, Pip. We shall go home now.'

'No!' Calum wrenched away.

'What other choice do you have?' Black Jamie's smile grew

more menacing by the minute. 'Without my patronage and protection, you are a pauper and a criminal. The very clothes you stand up in were bought and paid for by me. You have no money of your own, and no friends here. Where else can you go?'

Calum's cheeks reddened with fury: it was all too true. Clenching his fists into hard balls of rage, he lashed out, knuckles impacting with a prominent cheekbone. He barely heard his guardian's cry of pain as he turned and charged from the gloomy gaolhouse.

It was raining heavily. His sore fingers fumbled with the wet leather tacking which held the horses in place, ignoring the coachman's gruff words of protest. Minutes later he was vaulting on to the animal's saddleless back and galloping out of the village.

He had no idea what he was doing or where he was going. All he knew was that if he had to spend another minute in the company of the insane man he had once called uncle he would go mad himself.

As Calum urged his mount on to greater speeds, his wig flew off, freeing the long red hair. It fanned out behind him like the cape which had sealed Fergie's fate. Without reins, he gripped handfuls of the horse's thick mane, flattening himself against the steed's back and holding on with his legs.

Black Jamie deserved his nickname: the man's very soul was darker than the blackest pit, his mind twisted and contorted by years alone in that foul castle!

The wind whistled past his lowered head. Pelting rain soon drenched his hair. Calum clenched his jaw and rode faster.

But James Black was right about one thing: Calum had no friends here. The constables would not take his word over that of a magistrate's, and even seeking help from higher powers in Stirling was no guarantee of success.

Somewhere behind him, the church clock struck two, tolling out into the night. The tone struck an echo of a death knell deep in Calum's chest.

Less than four hours until dawn.

Less than four hours of life left for his highlander.

Charging on through the dark pouring night, adrenaline coursed through his veins and rendered rational thought impossible. His horse leapt a drystone wall, pounding off the beaten track and into a wood. Vicious branches tore at his head and arms. Calum felt no pain as man and mount cleared the trees. Then they were ascending the steep slopes of Ben Mora. The wind was stronger here, gusting around them and buffeting against their progress. But it blew the cobwebs from his brain.

Abruptly, his horse stumbled and fell. Tossed from its back, Calum clutched at bushes and managed to haul himself onward.

Amongst the last words his highlander had spoken to him, back in the Black Chamber, one sentence blasted itself into his mind:

If you ever need help, go to the hills. I have friends there.

Where in the hills? What friends?

Clawing his way up the steep incline, Calum eventually slumped on to level, if rocky, ground.

The cloud was low, and covered most of the hill top in a wet shroud. Raising his aching head, Calum began to shout, 'Help – Fergus McGregor needs your help!'

His voice swirled around the neighbouring peaks then echoed back at him.

Only the wind replied. Calum shouted again, louder this time. A particularly icy gust tore the air from his lungs, leaving him breathless and panting.

Still no one came. But at least the rain was easing off.

It had stopped completely and he was just about to give up when something moved in the darkness. Summoning a few final shreds of strength, he called out. 'I come not for my own sake, but for Fergie McGregor's. Please help him.' Calum lay there, watching as the something became man-shaped.

Then two. With flaming torches.

As he blinked through the mist, at least six figures emerged from the darkness. All wore the outlawed kilt, each proclaiming allegiance to a different clan but moving as one band. Yellow and dark blue plaid mixed with the brown and orange hues of other kinship.

The phantoms formed a silent circle around him, ghosts of some battle long fought and lost.

Calum focused on the spectre at their head, who was dressed in the unmistakable red tartan of the Royal Stuarts.

A faintly accented voice boomed forth. 'You are friend to Fergus McGregor?'

'Yes, yes – please help him!'

'And why should we believe you, Englishman?' Sceptical tones to his right greeted his plea.

Calum lurched to his feet. 'Because I love a highlander and would do anything to save his life.'

The ghostly circle fell silent. Calum glanced from pale face to pale face, feeling himself under scrutiny.

'Look at his hair.'

Whispers to his left made him turn.

'Look at the way he rode over those fields.'

The words came from another source. Calum stared at a tall, white-bearded man. 'You are the highwayman called Fox, of whom Fergus spoke?'

Calum was unsure who or what he really was, anymore. But he nodded.

'He is an Englishman! It is a trap!'

Calum shook his head, more in frustration than denial. The motion made him dizzy and he staggered slightly.

Then strong arms broke his fall and a faintly French voice filled his ears. 'Even if he is English, I admire his spirit. Take him to the cave. There are easier ways to entrap Charles Stuart, and I am inclined to believe only a lover would climb this hill on his hands and knees, and in such a night.'

Babbling his thanks, Calum allowed himself to be carried off into the mist.

An hour later, the rest of the rebels had fallen into a light sleep and Calum sat alone with Charlie Stuart by the side of a dying fire.

The heir to the Scottish throne smiled at him over the glowing embers. 'Your mother helped my father when he was in trouble,

Calum. And now her son will be instrumental in another attempt to give the land back to our people.'

He was owner of Castle Black, not Uncle Jamie. On top of every other piece of almost unbelievable information he had received over the past sixty minutes, Calum found this strangely easy to accept. It explained his guardian's bizarre behaviour and the insane plan to marry Calum and thus gain true title to the land.

It also explained the man's need to see Fergie – the only other person, as far as James Black knew, who was aware of this fact – dead.

'You have the look of a MacFayden, Calum. Although Philippa married an Englishman, Island blood also courses through your veins. It colours your hair and gives you the fierce loyalty you show towards your love.' The heir to the Scottish throne stretched out a hand and ran elegant fingers through Calum's still-damp tresses. 'Fergus McGregor is a lucky man.'

Calum looked down at the ancient documents which would support his claim of ownership over the Black estate. But it was the furthest thing from his mind, at the moment. 'He is also a man with a death sentence hanging over his head.'

Charlie Stuart sighed. 'We are but six, here in the hills, and have few weapons. With a strongly armed militia stationed in Blairhoyle, I do not hold out much hope at our chances of lifting that sentence.'

Calum's eyes moved to the fire. It could not end like this. He had to do something!

As the red embers flared scarlet one last time, Calum's brain ground into action.

Twenty-Six

'A little late, but still – you didn't mind the delay, did you, McGregor?'

As the last nail was hammered into place, Fergie pulled his eyes from the tall wooden scaffold. A red glow from the east washed the town square in crimson, staining the faces of the large crowd which was gathering to watch him die.

'Are you ready, you traitorous dog?'

Shoulders hunched, Fergie looked away from the features of many he recognised but whom he knew were powerless to help him. He focused on the source of the icy words.

'What? You no longer deny the crimes of which you are accused?'

The reality of his situation slowly seeped through the early morning frost which tingled on his bare chest. He would not give Black Jamie the satisfaction of hearing him plead for his life. 'If a hatred of injustice and self-serving liars is treason, then I am guilty as charged.'

'Save your brave words, McGregor.' Black Jamie laughed scathingly, his breath condensing in the cold air. 'When the noose tightens around your scrawny neck you will sing a different song.' He nodded to the head of Fergie's military escort.

Someone moved forward, untying his hands.

Someone else pushed him roughly towards the scaffold's first step.

Fergie shook himself free, rubbing his raw wrists. He looked up at the platform, six feet above his head.

The hangman stood there, hooded and waiting.

His mouth was suddenly dry. Beneath the ragged breeches, his strong thighs trembled. Behind, the drum tattoo began, beating the steady beat which would accompany him to his doom.

The crowd was silent apart from the occasionally mewling cry from a hastily shushed babe-in-arms.

Fergie's foot met the second step. He was grateful for the fact his mother was not here to see him hanged. He was glad she and his brothers were far away, oblivious of his ignominious end.

As he took another step, Fergie thought of Rab and Morag, starting their new life in the Americas. They would remain ignorant of his death, and for that he was also grateful.

Pausing on the fourth wooden stair, he glanced over his shoulder. Against his better judgement, Fergie scanned the crowd for Calum Monroe. His heart thumped against his ribs as he remembered the pain of last night's verbal assault.

That had been worse than the feel of any roped noose.

Black Jamie's glistering eyes met his, but there was no sign of the betraying fop.

Fergie turned away and climbed further. His mind turned to Charles Stuart, waiting in the hills with Wee Andrew, Rory and a handful of other rebels. With what was left of his heart, Fergie wished them success for a rebellion in which he had been proud to play some small part.

The drum roll continued, merging with the hum in his ears until it became a long, uninterrupted whine. The sound seemed to Fergie reminiscent of the drone of pipes.

As his bare foot left the final stair and he stepped on to the high platform, Fergie straightened up, raising himself to his full height.

For all their reputation for carousing and fighting, his long-dead ancestors had died as they had lived: with dignity and pride. The drone in his ears lifted his spirits and became a tune.

He was not the first highlander to end his life at the end of a rope. But maybe he might be the last. Head held high and striding forward to where the hangman stood waiting, Fergie smiled to the large crowd. 'As a condemned man, I claim the right to a few last words.' He moved his gaze to where Black Jamie stood. A cruel smile curled the landowner's thin lips.

Some of the soldiers laughed.

Black Jamie silenced them with his hand. 'Make it brief, McGregor.'

His curly brown hair falling loose over his broad shoulders, Fergie took a deep breath. And began to sing.

The tune was as old as Scotland itself, hummed and crooned to babies in their cradles since time immemorial. Originally in Gaelic, Fergie sang the words in English, the language of his kinsmen's oppressors, so that they might know that for every Scotsman who died, a dozen others would take his place.

Soaring up into the cold morning air, his lone baritone told of battles fought and lost, but of a war which would continue as long as there remained one Scottish voice sounding alone in the glens.

But it was not alone.

A quivering tenor accompaniment was audible from amongst the crowd. Then a deep, resounding bass. Slowly, his solo call to arms became a choir. Fergie threw back his bare shoulders and sang louder.

'Shut up! Shut up!' James Black cried.

Behind he was vaguely aware of hurried footsteps mounting the rickety steps. Pulled backward by strong arms, Fergie sang on, barely aware of the rough rope around his neck.

'Make him stop!'

Female voices joined the throng. High sopranos and husky altos swelled the tumult, drowning out the drum beat and the growing sounds of panic in Black Jamie's cries.

Two dozen militiamen to escort a single prisoner was one thing. Subduing a crowd of at least two hundred was quite another.

Fergie watched Black Jamie rush about amongst a now-huddled group of red-coated soldiers, issuing orders no one seemed keen to obey. A tightening around his unshaven neck turned his attention to the hangman, and the one person here who was resolved to carry out an instruction.

Six feet below, the singing was now tinged with anger and discontent. A smile formed on the corners of Fergie's lips as his feet inched towards the neatly cut hole in the middle of the platform.

He was a lost cause. But there were other Causes, more important than any individual life. Closing his eyes, Fergie stared at the image of his Fox's face, branded for ever on his brain. Despite Calum Monroe's fervent denial to the contrary, the shreds of a few wonderful nights together would carry Fergie into the next life.

He had been true to his nature. He had given himself to another man and known the joy of love.

Somewhere in the background, he was vaguely aware the thunder of his heart was taking on the tenor of thundering hooves.

Then gunshots and loud shouts were accompanying the very real approach of horses. Fergie's eyes flew open.

'Stand and deliver!'

Fergie stared.

The crowd was parting to admit a posse of riders who carried flaming torches. At their head, his auburn hair swirling around his shoulders and glinting like fire in the rising sun, Calum Monroe fired his pistol into the air a second time.

The singing stopped. The crowd surged forward.

Wee Andrew snatched firearms from the grips of bemused soldiers. Rory's white hair bristled with anger as he grabbed Black Jamie by the neck and aimed a pistol at his head. Meanwhile, Calum and the slight aristocratic figure of Charles Stuart leapt from their horses and bounded up the scaffold steps.

'Deliver Fergus McGregor to me!' Calum barked.

In a daze, he felt the hangman obey the command. Slumping backward, Fergie staggered to his feet. Then he and his Fox joined Charlie Stuart as the rightful heir to the Scottish throne addressed the assembled villagers.

'There is the one you should hang.' A long finger indicated

Black Jamie's now cowering form. 'Not only has he stolen this land from Lord MacFayden – its rightful owner and Philippa MacFayden of Tiree's son – but he intends to evict all of you, raze your crofts to the ground and graze sheep where you once earned your living!' Charles Stuart held two documents aloft. 'These letters prove it, if my word is not enough.'

Fergie felt his Fox's arms tight around his waist. Whispers caressed his ears. 'I had to say it, my love. I thought it would free you, but Black Jamie lied to me.'

Words didn't matter now – they never really had. Fergie leant his head on Calum's shoulder as Bonnie Prince Charlie talked on.

'James Black is a fraud. He used lies to arrest Fergus McGregor for something he did not do, then seized his property and turned his family off land that is rightfully his.'

Shouts of outrage echoed up from the crowd.

'Are we going to stand for it?'

A resounding *No* rose into the dawn air.

'What are we going to do about it?'

At his side, Fergie felt Calum stiffen. Then his love stepped forward.

'Castle Black has been a symbol of all that is evil in this part of the world, my friends!' Thrusting his torch skyward, Calum took a deep breath. 'It has been my own place of imprisonment too and it is only fitting that it be burnt to the ground as Black Jamie intended to raze your crofts!'

Charles Stuart's voice was low. 'Are you sure, sir?'

Fergie felt his hand seized as Calum thrust both their fists above their heads. 'Raze it to the ground, and dance around the infernal place as it burns to ashes!'

Rage from the body beside his throbbed into Fergie's flesh. Cries of agreement followed a line of villagers who, now armed with torches and led by Wee Andrew, were marching resolutely from the square and out into the streets of Blairhoyle.

Unsteadily, and leaning on his Fox's shoulder, Fergie made his way from the scaffold down to two waiting horses. He looked in gratitude at Charles Stuart's aristocratic face. 'Thank you, sir.'

The heir to the throne bowed. 'Thank you for all your help.'

The blue eyes flicked from his to Calum. 'Black Jamie will be taken to the gaol, to await justice for his crimes. Will you two join us, at the celebrations?' He mounted his horse, reining the animal's head towards the procession of torches.

Fergie found himself looking into sparkling green eyes. 'We have something else to celebrate, my liege. Something overdue.'

Calum broke the gaze and jumped on to his horse.

As Bonnie Prince Charlie's laugh of understanding rang in his ears, Fergie was gripping a saddle and dragging himself on to the mount. 'Aye, something long overdue.' With Calum's arm tight around his waist, Fergie leant back against a well-muscled chest and waved as their horse galloped off in the opposite direction.

On the rocky plateau atop Ben Mora, both east and western skylines flickered red.

Against the backdrop of a burning castle, Calum struggled out of his shirt. His body glowed in the frosty morning light, his skin licked by flames from another fire. His green eyes never left the source of that heat.

Three feet away, Fergie's fingers fumbled at the fastenings of his own breeches.

Calum moved forward, falling to his knees and staying those hands. Wrapping his bare arms around his highlander's slim hips, he pressed his face into Fergie's groin and nuzzled the stretching length of desire he found there. 'I thought I had lost you.' His lips followed the outline of Fergie's prick, feeling its growing contours flex back against his face.

'I feared you had never been mine, in the first place.'

Every word of the response caused the stiffening against Calum's own thigh to intensify. 'I have always been yours, Fergie.' Rough fingers reached down and played with his hair.

'Pip, Fox, Calum – and now Lord MacFayden of Tiree. Which are you, my love? And should it be I who kneels before you?'

Calum moaned, moving his teeth over the fabric-covered outline. 'We are both only men, Fergie.' There had been enough barriers between them in the past: as soon as he could, Calum promised himself he would give the land he owned to those who worked on it. But for now, another impediment to their love must be overcome.

Releasing his highlander's strong thighs, Calum wrenched at the fastenings and hauled the rough fabric down over Fergie's well-muscled legs.

A gasp accompanied the thick length of prick as it sprang free.

Calum took the shaft in his right hand. With his left he cupped Fergie's hairy bollocks, feeling their weight and the corresponding increase in the pressure between his own thighs.

The highlander bent his knees, dipping down and allowing Calum's wrist to slip further between his legs.

Calum kissed his lover's downy belly, running his tongue through whorls of dark hair as the sensitive skin of his inner arm brushed past a tightening ball sac.

Fergie's cock pulsed in his hand. Calum tightened his fist, feeling the meat expand further as if trying to fight its way out of the grip.

Fergie's fingers raked through his Fox's red hair, clenching with desire and a need that had been too long denied. With a shaking fingertip, Calum stroked the puckered skin behind his highlander's balls then moved on.

'Let me see your face.' Fergie's request was hoarse with need.

Calum rubbed his stubbly chin against Fergie's belly one last time then tilted his head upward. At the same time, his questing fingers found the object of their search.

Eclipsed by black pupils, Fergie stared down into the naked face of his lover.

Calum's hair was plastered damply to his pale skin. His mouth was wet with his own saliva and the sweat of another man's body. Long ginger eyelashes framed eyes which shone with contradictory emotions.

Fergie saw his Fox in that face.

He saw the Lady Pip.

Even traces of Master Monroe's haughty expression were still visible.

Looking down at the man who held his cock in a firm grip, Fergie watched all previous identities swept away by a new incarnation. As Castle Black blazed behind them, a phoenix was rising from its ashes.

A man who, like all men, was many things.

A man with different, seemingly contradictory parts.

A man he had sneered at, lain with, kissed, and who had saved his life.

The man with whom Fergie now knew he would spend the rest of that life.

As Calum's index finger circled the delicate skin around his arsehole, Fergie's knees gave way and he fell sprawling on to the damp ground. Pulling his lover on top of him, his hand roved over the semi-dressed body, tearing at Calum's breeks until they both lay naked and entwined, the breath from two breathless mouths searching for one another misting around them.

The kiss was soft to begin with, growing in intensity as two pricks leaked freely against two tensed stomachs. Then Fergie was gripping his lover's hair, gnawing furiously at increasingly bruised lips until Calum's groan of pain echoed against his teeth.

He wanted what he had dreamt of, ever since that night in the byre, so many long weeks ago.

And he wanted it now.

Snarling with need, Fergie tore his lips from Calum's. 'Take me, man! Take me as the Fox takes his mate!'

The surprise in the green shining eyes changed to a parallel glint of lust. The new lord of Blairhoyle faded and Fergie gazed into a more bestial countenance. 'Aye, I'll take you, but you will watch me do so and you will scream the name of the man who shoves his prick into your arse when you come!'

Fergie's head hit the ground just as his heels left it. Gripped roughly, he felt his legs hoisted up over pale shoulders. Then an urgent pressure against his yearning sphincter had him arching up from the damp earth and throwing his arms around his lover's sweating waist.

Calum clenched his teeth against the friction as the swollen head of his aching cock battered against a ring of strong muscle. At the root of his shaft, his bollocks knitted together painfully while a knot of desire twisted in his stomach. He grabbed Fergie's wrists from around his waist, pinning the highlander to the ground. Using his body, he put his full weight behind his throbbing shaft.

Somewhere in the distance, the vague crackle of flames was replaced by shouts of celebration. Then a gasp closer to home and a delicious pressure over his glans made Calum himself cry out. He bucked with his hips, pushing his cock steadily past the circlet of muscle and thrusting deep into his lover's body.

Fergie was grunting now, bearing down on the thick rod of flesh which seemed to swell in girth as it ploughed resolutely up into him. Every muscle in his body strained for release. Every sinew fought the telltale stickiness against his rigid stomach. Each solid thrust against the walls of his rectum drove arrows of lust through his swollen balls.

And he wanted more of the same.

Straining up from the wrists which held him down, Fergie impaled himself further on Calum's prick, drawing the thick staff into his hole inch by solid inch. Only when he felt the hairy rasp of bollocks against the cheeks of his arse did he slump down on to the rocky ground.

Calum rested there, sweating and feeling his prick caressed and held tight by muscles of iron. He lowered his head, running his tongue along the outline of Fergie's jaw, then nibbling and kissing the stubbly skin by turns. Legs slipped from his shoulders, wrapping themselves around his waist while words mumbled in his ears. 'Now make me yours for ever.'

He needed no second bidding. His mouth tracking a trail of kisses over Fergie's throat and down on to the taut muscles of his chest, Calum withdrew slowly and reluctantly. When a sudden jolt of sensation told him his cockhead was once more straining just inside the entrance to his highlander's body, Calum released Fergie's wrists, reared up and plunged back in.

Fergie howled, tightening his legs and pulling Calum closer. Each thrust of his lover's prick resounded throughout his body. With his hands now free, he gripped tensed shoulders, hanging on as the fuck grew more violent.

Their bodies slapped wetly together. Fergie's snort of need was answered by an increase in the speed at which Calum's prick pounded into him. His rectum ached and tingled and burnt with sensation which bypassed pleasure and left lust far behind. His Fox rode him like a highwayman's horse, urging him onward into uncharted territory and unknown experiences.

Sweat dripped from Calum's furrowed brow down on to Fergie's scowling face. Slipping his hands beneath taut shoulders, he raised his lover's upper body off the ground, cradling the man in his arms.

Fergie's head lolled backward. Each jolt tore into him, faster and faster. Calum's balls rubbed against his balls. Their chests ground against each other. Two bodies seemed to merge until Fergie no longer knew which limbs were his and which were not.

But he knew to whom his heart belonged.

Just when he thought his Fox's prick might split him in two, a sudden flex deep inside him tore the breath from his body. 'Calum!' Wet warmth spurted into his arse seconds before a sticky wad of release flew from his own prick.

Somewhere in the distance, a voice was hoarsely calling his name. Fergie clung to his Fox, the racking tremors of two orgasms shaking him to the very bones.

His lover's prick was softening inside him. Fergie clenched his muscles to hold it there. Exhausted, and still pumping warm spunk between their slowly relaxing bodies, Fergie looked up into emerald-green eyes. 'For ever, my love?'

Calum breathlessly kissed his highlander's forehead. 'For ever, Fergie.'

idol

IDOL NEW BOOKS

Also published:

THE KING'S MEN
Christian Fall

Ned Medcombe, spoilt son of an Oxfordshire landowner, has always remembered his first love: the beautiful, golden-haired Lewis. But seventeenth-century England forbids such a love and Ned is content to indulge his domineering passions with the willing members of the local community, including the submissive parish cleric. Until the Civil War changes his world, and he is forced to pursue his desires as a soldier in Cromwell's army – while his long-lost lover fights as one of the King's men.

ISBN 0 352 33207 7

THE VELVET WEB
Christopher Summerisle

The year is 1889. Daniel McGaw arrives at Calverdale, a centre of academic excellence buried deep in the English countryside. But this is like no other college. As Daniel explores, he discovers secret passages in the grounds and forbidden texts in the library. The young male students, isolated from the outside world, share a darkly bizarre brotherhood based on the most extreme forms of erotic expression. It isn't long before Daniel is initiated into the rites that bind together the youths of Calverdale in a web of desire.

ISBN 0 352 33208 5

CHAINS OF DECEIT
Paul C. Alexander

Journalist Nathan Dexter's life is turned around when he meets a young student called Scott – someone who offers him the relationship for which he's been searching. Then Nathan's best friend goes missing, and Nathan uncovers evidence that he has become the victim of a slavery ring which is rumoured to be operating out of London's leather scene. To rescue their friend and expose the perverted slave trade, Nathan and Scott must go undercover, risking detection and betrayal at every turn.

ISBN 0 352 33206 9

DARK RIDER
Jack Gordon

While the rulers of a remote Scottish island play bizarre games of sexual dominance with the Argentinian Angelo, his friend Robert – consumed with jealous longing for his coffee-skinned companion – assuages his desires with the willing locals.

ISBN 0 352 33243 3

CONQUISTADOR
Jeff Hunter

It is the dying days of the Aztec empire. Axaten and Quetzel are members of the Stable, servants of the Sun Prince chosen for their bravery and beauty. But it is not just an honour and a duty to join this society, it is also the ultimate sexual achievement. Until the arrival of Juan, a young Spanish conquistador, sets the men of the Stable on an adventure of bondage, lust and deception.

ISBN 0 352 33244 1

TO SERVE TWO MASTERS
Gordon Neale

In the isolated land of Ilyria men are bought and sold as slaves. Rock, brought up to expect to be treated as mere 'livestock', yearns to be sold to the beautiful youth Dorian. But Dorian's brother is as cruel as he is handsome, and if Rock is bought by one brother he will be owned by both.

ISBN 0 352 33245 X

CUSTOMS OF THE COUNTRY
Rupert Thomas

James Cardell has left school and is looking forward to going to Oxford. That summer of 1924, however, he will spend with his cousins in a tiny village in rural Kent. There he finds he can pursue his love of painting – and begin to explore his obsession with the male physique.

ISBN 0 352 33246 8

DOCTOR REYNARD'S EXPERIMENT
Robert Black

A dark world of secret brothels, dungeons and sexual cabarets exists behind the respectable facade of Victorian London. The degenerate Lord Spearman introduces Dr Richard Reynard, dashing bachelor, to this hidden world. And Walter Starling, the doctor's new footman, finds himself torn between affection for his master and the attractions of London's underworld.

ISBN 0 352 33252 2

CODE OF SUBMISSION
Paul C. Alexander

Having uncovered and defeated a slave ring operating in London's leather scene, journalist Nathan Dexter had hoped to enjoy a peaceful life with his boyfriend Scott. But when it becomes clear that the perverted slave trade has started again, Nathan has no choice but to travel across Europe and America in his bid to stop it.

ISBN 0 352 33272 7

SLAVES OF TARNE
Gordon Neale

Pascal willingly follows the mysterious and alluring Casper to Tarne, a community of men enslaved to men. Tarne is everything that Pascal has ever fantasised about, but he begins to sense a sinister aspect to Casper's magnetism. Pascal has to choose between the pleasures of submission and acting to save the people he loves.

ISBN 0 352 33273 5

ROUGH WITH THE SMOOTH

Dominic Arrow

Amid the crime, violence and unemployment of North London, the young men who attend Jonathan Carey's drop-in centre have few choices. One of the young men, Stewart, finds himself torn between the increasingly intimate horseplay of his fellows and the perverse allure of the criminal underworld. Can Jonathan save Stewart from the bullies on the streets and behind bars?

ISBN 0 352 33292 1

CONVICT CHAINS

Philip Markham

Peter Warren, printer's apprentice in the London of the 1830s, discovers his sexuality and taste for submission at the hands of Richard Barkworth. Thus begins a downward spiral of degradation, of which transportation to the Australian colonies is only the beginning.

ISBN 0 352 33300 6

SHAME

Raydon Pelham

On holiday in West Hollywood, Briton Martyn Townsend meets and falls in love with the daredevil Scott. When Scott is murdered, Martyn's hunt for the truth and for the mysterious Peter, Scott's ex-lover, leads him to the clubs of London and Ibiza.

ISBN 0 352 33302 2

HMS SUBMISSION

Jack Gordon

Under the command of Josiah Rock, a man of cruel passions, HMS *Impregnable* sails to the colonies. Christopher, Viscount Fitzgibbons, is a reluctant officer; Mick Savage part of the wretched cargo. They are on a voyage to a shared destiny.

ISBN 0 352 33301 4

THE FINAL RESTRAINT

Paul C. Alexander

The trilogy that began with *Chains of Deceit* and continued in *Code of Submission* concludes in this powerfully erotic novel. From the dungeons and saunas of London to the deepest jungles of South America, Nathan Dexter is forced to play the ultimate chess game with evil Adrian Delancey – with people as sexual pawns.

ISBN 0 352 33303 0

HARD TIME

Robert Black

HMP Cairncrow prison is a corrupt and cruel institution, but also a sexual minefield. Three new inmates must find their niche in this brutish environment – as sexual victims or lovers, predators or protectors. This is the story of how they find love, sex and redemption behind prison walls.

ISBN 0 352 33304 9

ROMAN GAMES

Tasker Dean

When Sam visits the island of Skate, he is taught how to submit to other men, acting out an elaborate fantasy in which young men become wrestling slaves – just as in ancient Rome. He must learn how to win and how to lose. Indeed, if he is to have his beautiful prize – the wrestler, Robert – he must learn how the Romans played their games.

ISBN 0 352 33322 7

VENETIAN TRADE

Richard Davis

From the deck of the ship that carries him into Venice, Rob Weaver catches his first glimpse of a beautiful but corrupt city where the dark alleys and misty canals hide debauchery and decadence. Here, he must learn to survive among men who would make him a plaything and a slave.

ISBN 0 352 33323 5

THE LOVE OF OLD EGYPT

Philip Markham

It's 1925 and the deluxe cruiser carrying the young gigolo Jeremy Hessling has docked at Luxor. Jeremy dreams of being dominated by the pharaohs of old, but quickly becomes involved with someone more accessible – Khalid, a young man of exceptional beauty.

ISBN 0 352 33354 5

idol

WE NEED YOUR HELP . . .

to plan the future of Idol books –

Yours are the only opinions that matter. Idol is a new and exciting venture: the first British series of books devoted to homoerotic fiction for men.

We're going to do our best to provide the sexiest, best-written books you can buy. And we'd like you to help in these early stages. Tell us what you want to read. There's a freepost address for your filled-in questionnaires, so you won't even need to buy a stamp.

THE IDOL QUESTIONNAIRE

SECTION ONE: ABOUT YOU

1.1 Sex (*we presume you are male, but just in case*)
Are you?

Male	☐		
Female	☐		

1.2 Age

under 21	☐	21–30	☐
31–40	☐	41–50	☐
51–60	☐	over 60	☐

1.3 At what age did you leave full-time education?

still in education	☐	16 or younger	☐
17–19	☐	20 or older	☐

1.4 Occupation ______________________________

1.5 Annual household income ______________________________

1.6 We are perfectly happy for you to remain anonymous; but if you would like us to send you a free booklist of Idol books, please insert your name and address

____

____

____

____

SECTION TWO: ABOUT BUYING IDOL BOOKS

2.1 Where did you get this copy of *The Black Chamber*?

- Bought at chain book shop ☐
- Bought at independent book shop ☐
- Bought at supermarket ☐
- Bought at book exchange or used book shop ☐
- I borrowed it/found it ☐
- My partner bought it ☐

2.2 How did you find out about Idol books?

- I saw them in a shop ☐
- I saw them advertised in a magazine ☐
- I read about them in ______________________
- Other ______________________

2.3 Please tick the following statements you agree with:

- I would be less embarrassed about buying Idol books if the cover pictures were less explicit ☐
- I think that in general the pictures on Idol books are about right ☐
- I think Idol cover pictures should be as explicit as possible ☐

2.4 Would you read an Idol book in a public place – on a train for instance?

Yes ☐ No ☐

SECTION THREE: ABOUT THIS IDOL BOOK

3.1 Do you think the sex content in this book is:

Too much ☐ About right ☐

Not enough ☐

3.2 Do you think the writing style in this book is:

Too unreal/escapist	☐	About right	☐
Too down to earth	☐		

3.3 Do you think the story in this book is:

Too complicated	☐	About right	☐
Too boring/simple	☐		

3.4 Do you think the cover of this book is:

Too explicit	☐	About right	☐
Not explicit enough	☐		

Here's a space for any other comments:

SECTION FOUR: ABOUT OTHER IDOL BOOKS

4.1 How many Idol books have you read?

4.2 If more than one, which one did you prefer?

____

4.3 Why?

SECTION FIVE: ABOUT YOUR IDEAL EROTIC NOVEL

We want to publish the books you want to read – so this is your chance to tell us exactly what your ideal erotic novel would be like.

5.1 Using a scale of 1 to 5 (1 = no interest at all, 5 = your ideal), please rate the following possible settings for an erotic novel:

Roman / Ancient World	☐
Medieval / barbarian / sword 'n' sorcery	☐
Renaissance / Elizabethan / Restoration	☐
Victorian / Edwardian	☐
1920s & 1930s	☐
Present day	☐
Future / Science Fiction	☐

5.2 Using the same scale of 1 to 5, please rate the following themes you may find in an erotic novel:

- Bondage / fetishism ☐
- Romantic love ☐
- SM / corporal punishment ☐
- Bisexuality ☐
- Group sex ☐
- Watersports ☐
- Rent / sex for money ☐

5.3 Using the same scale of 1 to 5, please rate the following styles in which an erotic novel could be written:

- Gritty realism, down to earth ☐
- Set in real life but ignoring its more unpleasant aspects ☐
- Escapist fantasy, but just about believable ☐
- Complete escapism, totally unrealistic ☐

5.4 In a book that features power differentials or sexual initiation, would you prefer the writing to be from the viewpoint of the dominant / experienced or submissive / inexperienced characters:

- Dominant / Experienced ☐
- Submissive / Inexperienced ☐
- Both ☐

5.5 We'd like to include characters close to your ideal lover. What characteristics would your ideal lover have? Tick as many as you want:

Dominant	☐	Caring	☐
Slim	☐	Rugged	☐
Extroverted	☐	Romantic	☐
Bisexual	☐	Old	☐
Working Class	☐	Intellectual	☐
Introverted	☐	Professional	☐
Submissive	☐	Pervy	☐
Cruel	☐	Ordinary	☐
Young	☐	Muscular	☐
Naïve	☐		

Anything else? ______________________________

5.6 Is there one particular setting or subject matter that your ideal erotic novel would contain:

____

5.7 As you'll have seen, we include safe-sex guidelines in every book. However, while our policy is always to show safe sex in stories with contemporary settings, we don't insist on safe-sex practices in stories with historical settings because it would be anachronistic. What, if anything, would you change about this policy?

____

____

SECTION SIX: LAST WORDS

6.1 What do you like best about Idol books?

____

6.2 What do you most dislike about Idol books?

____

6.3 In what way, if any, would you like to change Idol covers?

____

6.4 Here's a space for any other comments:

____

____

____

____

Thanks for completing this questionnaire. Now either tear it out, or photocopy it, then put it in an envelope and send it to:

Idol
FREEPOST
London
W10 5BR

You don't need a stamp if you're in the UK, but you'll need one if you're posting from overseas.